THE GREENWOOD LEGACY

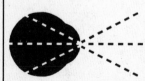

This Large Print Book carries the
Seal of Approval of N.A.V.H.

THE GREENWOOD LEGACY

JACQUELYN COOK

THORNDIKE PRESS

A part of Gale, Cengage Learning

GALE
CENGAGE Learning

Detroit • New York • San Francisco • New Haven, Conn • Waterville, Maine • London

GALE
CENGAGE Learning™

Copyright © 2009 by Jacquelyn Cook.
Permission granted for:
Thomas Jones Family Papers 1819–1878 (MSS # 817)
Courtesy of Hargrett Rare Book and Manuscript Library
University of Georgia Libraries
Thorndike Press, a part of Gale, Cengage Learning.

LIBRARY OF CONGRESS CATALOGING-IN-PUBLICATION DATA

Cook, Jacquelyn.
   The Greenwood legacy / by Jacquelyn Cook. — Large print ed.
      p. cm. — (Thorndike Press large print clean reads)
   Includes bibliographical references.
   ISBN-13: 978-1-4104-2614-7 (alk. paper)
   ISBN-10: 1-4104-2614-9 (alk. paper)
   1. Thomasville (Ga.)—History—Fiction. 2. Georgia—History—Civil War, 1861–1865—Fiction. 3. Large type books. I. Title.
PS3553.O553828G74 2010
813'.54—dc22
                    2010004272

Published in 2010 by arrangement with BelleBooks, Inc.

Printed in the United States of America
1 2 3 4 5 6 7 14 13 12 11 10

Dedication

To the memory of
My husband, J. N. Cook
and
To the honor of our children and
grandchildren
Who are living his legacy of integrity

CAST OF CHARACTERS AT GREENWOOD

Lavinia Young Jones, born 1810
Her husband, Thomas P. Jones, born 1802

Their eleven children:
1. James Young Jones, b. 1827
   (m) Ann Elizabeth Adams (3 children)
   Second wife: Margaret Von Holtzender (4 children)

2. Mary Elizabeth Jones, b. 1830, (m) Furman Chaires
   Children (twins) Born 1849
   Sally Chaires (died as infant,) and Mary Lavinia Chaires — (Livy J.) who married Thomas Price Jones, son of Thomas's brother Mitchell and Eliza Jones

3. Francis Remer Jones
   Born 1831 Died 1833

4. Harriet Lavinia (Livy) (b. 1833), married

Dr. David Smith Brandon (11 children)

5. Mitchell Francis (lived two months born Dec. 1835 died Jan. 31, 1836)

6. Susan Estelle — Born Dec. 1837, Died August 22, 1854

7. Thomas William (m April 9, 1865) Ella Guild Capers (8 children)
   Born 1839 Died July 22, 1894

8. Henry Francis Jones (Frank)
   Born 1841 Died June 13, 1864 (in Civil War battle)

9. Florence (b. 1844 d. 1896), married General John C. Vaughn

10. Martha Tallulah (Mattie) (b. 1846 d. 1934), married Edwin Tralona Davis (2 children)

11. Emma Gertrude (lived 3 weeks and died May 14, 1849)

CHAPTER I

"It feels mysterious!" Lavinia gazed out of the phaeton window at the towering trees whispering in the March wind. "It's as if we're in a secret world hidden in pines."

"Don't be afraid. Look up." Thomas Jones pointed at the treetops one hundred-twenty feet above, where long needles filtered sunlight in shining shafts. "They're like cathedral windows directing light from heaven."

"I will conquer my fear," she promised; but she thought, *How far this is from our cultured homes, how different from the eastern coast of Georgia!*

Thomas dropped the reins of the sporting carriage between his knees and took her in his arms. "I'll keep you safe. Now that Spain has ceded the Florida Territory to the United States and Andrew Jackson has defeated the Creek Confederacy and moved Chief Neamathla and his Fowltown village

9

into Florida, the Indians and outlaws shouldn't . . ."

Lavinia shivered. The imaginary line that proclaimed them protected inside Georgia was a walk away. The nearest help was at the budding village of Thomasville, three miles east. Hostile Seminoles roamed the thirty-six miles to Tallahassee. Savannah floated like a mirage on the gray Atlantic, two hundred miles away.

They had ridden through thousands of acres of Pine Barrens growing on flat ground that bore no other vegetation except stiff clumps of wiregrass. Suddenly agitation seized her. Her leg, pressed against his on the short seat, gave her away with a violent trembling.

Hurt washed over Thomas's face. "I doubt I'll ever make you love this isolated place as I do. You shouldn't have married a fourth son whose entire inheritance is risked on a spot of land and a year's supplies." He gestured behind them at the oxcarts following their carriage through the narrow cut that served as a roadway. "I know you could've had your pick of first-born sons who would inherit a grand plantation."

My pick? Lavinia's soul leaped. She clasped her hands over her cheeks. She had always seen herself as horse-faced. *Doesn't he realize I'm not beautiful enough to be a belle?* She looked at him in awe. She thought his thick black hair and blue eyes made him the handsomest man she had ever seen. His own man at twenty-four, he was so tall that she could stand to her full height and not slouch as she had done with boys her own age.

Misunderstanding her attitude, Thomas flung out. "I know the Pine Barrens seem wasteland to you. Even the Georgia Legislature refuses to build roads here," he mocked sarcastically. " 'We won't spend the state's money to develop a country that God almighty left in an unfinished condition.' "

Lavinia's sudden happiness at his appraisal of her charms overcame her apprehensions. Still shy, she caught her lower lip between her teeth and grinned. "Perhaps the Lord intends for you to help finish it," she said, stroking the bristling brows that dominated his strong features, smoothing his face into a smile.

With the tension broken between them, she felt encouraged to continue. "When our ancestors settled the Georgia Colony nearly a hundred years ago, they faced Indians and wilderness. I believe you — and I — can overcome this."

Thomas kissed her, pouring out relief,

longing, anticipation, making her know she was wanted, loved.

The horse, unfettered, began to run, sensing he was nearing oats, home.

"Keep your eyes closed until we round the bend. I have a surprise."

Lavinia obediently covered her face.

"Whoa, Prince," Thomas commanded the sorrel. As he lifted Lavinia down from the seat, a ball of white fur roused from sleeping on her silk pumps and whimpered.

"Shhh, Hamlet." She scooped the puppy into her arms and turned to look.

"Oh, Thomas!" She sighed in pleasure.

A higher spot, which had been concealed, was suddenly revealed. A tremendous oval space had been cleared of pines. Beauty enclosed it into a sheltered haven with an atmosphere of peace. Gleaming globes of magnolia trees dominated. Cherry laurels and berried yaupon holly created an evergreen backdrop for dogwoods, blooming snowy white. Farther out, various hardwoods, not yet dressed for spring, were robed in swags of purple wisteria. Its heady perfume made her giddy. She had not realized Thomas had such poetry in his soul.

Thomas smiled. "I just moved in some native plants. You can add what you like. I know how much you love live oaks. I intend to line both sides of the road so their spreading arms can form a canopy. Visitors will know they're approaching a plantation of importance." He tilted her chin so that he could gaze into her face. "And when I make enough money, I'll build you a mansion that will endure."

"I adore our home place," she whispered. "I love what you have begun." She breathed the fresh spring air and listened to trilling mockingbirds making soft music drift around them. Suddenly she set down the puppy and ran around the house site, touching each tree and shrub, marveling. The wind snatched her shawl, exposing the slim column of her Empire-waist gown, making the silk cling. She could feel Thomas's eyes upon her.

He loves me, she exhilarated. He created this hidden beauty just for me.

Since their marriage six months ago, Thomas had left her for such long periods that she had feared he didn't love her. He had come ahead with covered wagons loaded with furniture, bringing his people and crates of chickens, ducks, and hogs, preparing a place for her. When they were together, he talked only of their land, and she had even wondered if he planned to hide her from society because she wasn't

13

beautiful. Now she knew. The magnolias told her even more. Hamlet yapped, running behind her, tumbling over his fat stomach. Lavinia laughed, fears gone — at least for the moment.

"Thank you for the flowering trees," she said as she returned to a bemused Thomas. "I'll design a garden in front of them. When the house is built, it will nestle in as if it had always been here and always will."

Husky-voiced, Thomas replied, "For now it will be make-believe."

He kissed her to seal his promise and then led her behind their future home site to a row of notched-log cabins. Men were unloading supplies from the oxcarts that had been driven by shining black twins, Micah and Nahum. She knew Augustus, the giant of a man who had ridden ahead to announce their impending arrival. Thomas introduced a young couple, Samuel and his wife Julie.

It was Julie who spoke up in a sprightly voice. "I done fixed yo' supper."

"Thank you, Julie." Lavinia felt proud of the grown-up graciousness she displayed in greeting them. All the while she struggled to fix her memory so she could call them by name tomorrow.

Thomas showed her the dogtrot cabin that

was to be their temporary home. One shingled roof united two log rooms that were joined by an open-ended porch.

"It's like a dollhouse," exclaimed Lavinia, clapping her hands. "Perfect for two."

She meant what she said, but she envisioned her stepmother, standing in shock, her rope of pearls heaving on her bosom, her fox fur shaking on her shoulders as she compared Lavinia's cabin with her own sprawling mansion. Lavinia's lip protruded. *But this is mine. I like it. It will do fine.*

She glanced at her confident husband. Their servants stood behind him with idle hands, awaiting commands. How would she manage all these new things? Maybe Mama's advice would have helped — occasionally.

Dusk was gathering, and Thomas dismissed the group. He helped her up the step to the porch and opened a door, letting cooking aromas entice her. Beef, turning on a spit over the open fireplace, and biscuits, browning in a Dutch oven placed on the hearth and packed in hot coals, smelled wonderful. She was hungry to her toes. Thomas smiled and stopped her before she could enter. He lifted her in his arms and carried her over the threshold.

He held her aloft as she gazed in delight

15

at her domain. Firelight twinkled over a table laid with damask and set with her heirloom silver in colonial fiddle-thread pattern. Lavinia smiled. Julie had unpacked barrels of their wedding presents. She had placed porcelain treasures about the rough-walled room. *How incongruous, but they make it inviting.*

"Our home," Lavinia whispered.

Thomas kissed her, and she sensed they both felt an excitement that this, rather than their time in her parents' home, was really their wedding night.

All he said was, "We'll mark down today, March 3, 1827."

Thomas Jones stood surveying his acres as dawn streaked a freshly washed sky. Satisfaction overflowed. He had worried about Lavinia's first glimpse of their solitude, but last night a reticent girl had become a wife. He was ready to build her a kingdom, a dynasty. The very air here filled him with vigor.

He had fallen in love with her when she was only fourteen. He had waited, biding his time, knowing she was the one he would give his life to win. The moment Lavinia finished her schooling and was marriage-able age, he had asked for her hand. They had married last September, but he agonized that he had little to offer her because his father, James Jones, had just died, willing him only $730.00 and five workers.

Thomas reflected on how the Jones's fortunes in Georgia had begun when his grandfather, Welshman Francis Jones, had accepted a Royal Grant in Saint George's Parish in 1769 when Georgia was a colony. Others in the clan, including Thomas's father, James, had received additional land grants and had established their homes up the Savannah River toward Augusta. Thomas knew these coastal plantations would never have endured had it not been for the English custom of keeping estates together for first-born sons. Nevertheless, it hurt when the eldest inherited nearly everything.

When I have children, none will feel second best, Thomas vowed. *Everything I do will be different.*

The difference had begun when he looked to the newly available lands in the southwestern corner of Georgia. This area had long been in dispute even after Andrew Jackson broke the Creek Indian power at the Battle of Horseshoe Bend in 1814. The general had to face Neamathla, who had touched off the Seminole War by an "ils ne

17

passerant pas" stand at Fowltown, Georgia. Finally, the United States had paid the Indians for several tracts of land. It was distributed to the citizens by the 1820 land lottery. Many who had won the draw had taken one look and rejected these empty Pine Barrens. Last January, Thomas had bought Land Lot 83 from one of those lottery winners, and then, carefully, had purchased enough surrounding land to make 2500 acres.

People laughed. No one wanted this farm. It was landlocked, they said. How would anyone ever get a crop to market through the wilds of Florida's Indian Territory?

But Thomas had seen it, loved it. He had put his hands in the soil and known it would grow cotton. Excited, he suggested to his younger brother, Mitchell, that he also buy a home place.

Now, exhilarated, he breathed the sharp, clean pine scent. *My land! My air!*

He threw back his shoulders. On rolling red hills, the evergreen trees were spaced six, ten, even twelve feet apart. The Indians had known that long leaf pines would die without sunlight, but they could stand fire and heat as other trees could not. They had managed their woodland by control burning.

So they could maneuver. See game. *Enemies,* Thomas thought. *I'll do that, too.*

Interspersing the open pine stands were dense hardwood hammocks where live oak and hickory grew along creeks that bubbled up from springs, providing constant clear, cool water. He could hear the calling of bobwhites, telling him that his land abounded with the quail. He had seen turkey and deer and knew his family would never go hungry. He owned only one spot that was swamp.

One day, he thought, *my place will stretch all the way to the black waters of the Ochlockonee River.*

Daylight was breaking, and Thomas offered a quick prayer for his good fortune as his workmen appeared, yawning. He strode forward to meet them, ready to do twice what they did.

What first? A proper house for Lavinia and a crop to pay for it.

He directed the twins to the sawpit. He showed Nahum how to climb down into the pit while Micah stood astride the log. Muscles flexed and gleamed as the men drew the saw up and down.

Thomas laughed and joked with Augustus and Samuel as they harnessed the mules. Big Augustus had been on Thomas's father's place as far back as he could remember. The newer hand, Samuel was small and wiry, but he was a willing worker. They set in to plow small fields, some tediously cleared, some merely patches between ever-present pines, which had been girdled to kill them.

Thomas could hardly wait for spring planting.

Lavinia awakened smiling. She could not stop. She hugged the goose-down pillow, hoping Julie wouldn't come in. She wanted to savor her first hours in her own home. She looked pridefully at the canopy of the tester bed. An old English piece, it had been in her family since before she was born. The bed nearly filled the room, and she wondered if Thomas had built the ceiling higher to accommodate the tall, reeded posts.

She adjusted the side curtains and Hamlet, who had slept on a pallet on the floor, struggled up the incline of the cover Thomas had left dragging when he slipped out earlier. Lavinia snuggled him, but she decided she was hungry. In search of food, she ventured across the dogtrot — a chicken trot this morning.

Julie came in bearing buckets of goat's milk. A boy toddled behind her. Seeing Hamlet, he dropped to all fours, nose-to-nose with the puppy.

"Good morning." Lavinia grinned at the child. "Who is this?"

"G'morning." Julie looked at him proudly. "My boy Joe. I be firing up the wash pot, iffen you don't need me. There's meat left for noontime."

"Fine. I — I wanted to cook something special for my husband myself, anyway."

She followed Julie and Joe out on the porch and watched a few moments as Julie dumped dirty clothes in the footed, cast-iron kettle set over a fire. As the clothes boiled in soapy water, Julie agitated them with a strong stick. Next she would transfer them to tubs and scrub them on the corrugated washboard. Rinsing in creek water and hanging them on the line would also be tedious. Lavinia would have plenty of time alone.

She dressed quickly and then searched for the packet of recipes that had been copied from those belonging to her own mother. She was disappointed that she lacked ingredients for some and could not understand the symbols used for others. At last she found a simple dessert.

Caramel Custard

1 C. sugar
1 pt. Rich milk
4 eggs beaten
Any flavoring

Melt the sugar and let brown, stirring constantly. Line a mold with it and allow to cool. Mix the beaten eggs, milk, and flavoring. Put the mixture into mold. Stand in boiling water in the oven for 45 minutes.

The custard was meant to be put in dainty molds, baked, and turned out soft set with a thin, crisp topping. *Perfect. I have milk, a barrel of sugar, and — from the cackling on the porch — I should have eggs.*

Lavinia put the sugar in an iron spider and set the three-legged skillet on the hearth. She had to kneel by the fire to stir, and her cheeks blazed before the sugar browned. It did not melt. It formed rocks. She tried to mash them. Tears slipped down her hot face.

How can I do this by myself? Lavinia mourned.

She gave up on the sugar crystals, deciding they would melt in the oven. Next she tackled the eggs with a whisk. They beat beautifully. *Now the milk. One pt. What's that? A cup? More?* She put more to be sure. She had neither flavoring nor molds. And no oven!

She sat on the floor, sniffling, nuzzling the dog. "Oh, Hammy, how can I learn all these things I've never done before way out here in this wilderness?"

Forlorn, Lavinia let her pent tears flow. She had thought herself an adult, in complete control of her life. Now she realized acutely what it meant that she was only sixteen.

She slumped down, and the rough logs bored into her back. She envisioned the wallpaper in the dining room of the house where she was born. If the ladies of the family tired of the Screven County Plantation, a refreshing ride down the Savannah River took them into the quaint city laid out in lovely squares by English General James Oglethorpe in 1733. In Savannah, entertainment was plentiful, and life was carefree. Thomas had been born in adjoining Bulloch County, and she had assumed they would stay on the coast. Then he had begun talking of western Georgia. At first it had seemed an adventure.

Hamlet licked her face. She straightened her back and tossed her hair. *Oh, Thomas,* she thought, remembering last night. *It is an exciting journey. I'm no longer a child. I'm a woman. A wife.* Suddenly she wanted only to see him.

She poured the custard over the lumpy sugar, placed the pan in the Dutch oven, and packed it in hot coals. She decided it was too hot to stand over the hearth for forty-five minutes.

"Come, Hamlet, let's explore our woods and find Thomas."

The blue skies relaxed her as she followed the wagon track through the clear-floored Pine Barren. Up close, she thought the only vegetation, the two-foot wiregrass, looked like pine needles stuck in the ground. A clump of wiregrass moved. She held her breath and stood immobile. A quail came bobbing out, watching her with bright eyes. Lavinia chuckled. It looked like a fat little old lady in a brown-spotted dress and head-scarf waddling along on tiny feet.

At first the silence had been frightening, but when she listened, she heard sounds all around. A tapping made her look up. A red-cockaded woodpecker was carving its nest in a tall pine. In another spot she saw a large dove, soft gray with a black ring nearly around its neck. It cawed to its mate. A few moments later, from a distance, the answer came.

The ground was not as flat and uninteresting as she had thought. It gently rose and fell, and with each change, the wildflowers lifted faces of different colors and infinite shapes. Fragrance surrounded her when she passed a stand of honeysuckle. The tall, rangy bushes bore spidery blossoms of pinks and yellows. She must take some home to perfume their bedroom.

She crossed a tiny creek and stood in a hammock. Enchanted, she dropped to her knees beneath a live oak. Heart-shaped leaves surrounded tiny violets. She picked a nosegay and kept it close to her cheek. Overhead, rampant vines of yellow jessamine climbed and twined their trumpet-shaped blossoms.

I must move some of these plants to my garden, she mused. *It's so lovely here. I can make it into a wonderful home for Thomas and me — for a family.*

Lavinia listened for a noise of work to indicate where Thomas might be. She called out, but there was no answering cry. All was quiet; and as she descended a sandy path, she realized that silence was stifling here. This place was different. There was no bird-song. She shivered at stands of low-growing

25

saw palmetto. The long fronds made her envision Spanish swords. Wanting to leave this frightening area, she hurried around a bend. She stopped.

A hideous reptile lay completely across the path. Lavinia clapped her hand over her mouth, but a shriek escaped. It brought wandering Hamlet on the run. Bouncing from front feet to back, he emitted sharp threatening barks even though the enemy could eat him in one swallow. She thought the creature must be at least eight feet long. She assumed he would be slow, but when he rose on ridiculous short legs, he waddled toward them at surprising speed. Switching his tail, he opened his long snout, hissing, revealing spiked teeth. He pivoted his head toward Hamlet.

Lavinia inched forward, dared to reach out, grab. Muzzling the feisty pup, she screamed for help.

Eyes on the monster, she backed. She bumped into a warm, wet body. She smelled soap. Resolve forgotten, she began to sob.

Julie exploded with laughter. "That be Mr. Alligator, honey. He won't hurt you none, lessen you provoke him. But that there po' excuse for a dog would make him one gulp."

Lavinia's hysterics continued, bringing the men running. Forgetting the onlookers, she threw herself into Thomas's arms. When she could slow her snuffling, she yelled, "Kill him."

Thomas could not dissuade her.

"Shoot that old 'gator through the eye," said Julie, "and I'll fry his tail." Brown cheeks shining, she smacked her lips. "Tastes just like spring chicken."

Later, Lavinia tried valiantly to eat it, but the alligator meat sprang back from the pressure of her chewing, and her one bite grew ever larger. She wished for Savannah shrimp and rice. Tears filled her eyes as she thought of home, of morning calls, of afternoon teas, of evening musicales. The heaviness of her special pudding made the tears spill over. The sugar had never melted. Like rocks, it threatened to break their teeth.

The following Sunday morning, Thomas decided he had better provide some social life. He hitched Prince to the sporty phaeton, and they drove into Thomasville in search of a church. They found none. A mere outpost, the village was the seat of a county formed only two years before. It consisted of a courthouse of roughly split logs and a few dwellings.

As Thomas walked the sorrel by E. J. Perkins Grocery and a general store run by

James Kirksey, he swallowed a painful lump. *Lavinia will want to go home to her mother.*

As he turned the carriage, they were hailed by a genial, rotund man. "Morning, young folks. I'm Nathaniel Mitchell. May I help you?"

"I'm Thomas P. Jones. My wife, Lavinia Young Jones. We were hoping for a worship service."

"Sorry. There's none here abouts. The Methodist circuit rider has made Thomasville a mission station, but he covers an extensive district on horseback. We're in the South Carolina Conference." Noticing Lavinia's crestfallen appearance, he smiled. "Be here in two weeks, for sure. But get down. Get down and join us for Sunday dinner."

Accepting the hospitality of a cabin only slightly larger than theirs, Thomas was delighted to meet the motherly "Miss Dolly" Mitchell. He thought her fried chicken and milk gravy piled over big fluffy biscuits were the best he had ever tasted. Her cheeks were as round and soft as her biscuits, and they lifted in a perpetual smile.

Thank you, Lord, for someone to help Lavinia, he prayed.

Thomas was eating heartily when he realized the adolescent son was not. John Wil-

liam Henry Mitchell, as he grandly introduced himself, was captivated by Lavinia.

Proud at first, Thomas ignored the boy's
babbling. After a while, he became peevish.
He narrowed his eyes. He knew how enticing Lavinia looked in her stylish gown with
the scooped neckline and puff of sleeves
showing her bare arms. She was giving John
William her full attention, and sometimes
she cocked her beribboned bonnet and
flashed her admirer an impish grin.

*He's never seen a young lady of culture and
charm way out here,* Thomas thought. Too
late, he actually listened to the conversation.

"Have you heard about the Indian mur-
derers?" John William asked in a tone of
high excitement.

"Here?" gasped Lavinia.

"Last fall." John William's head bobbed.
"Phillip and Nathan Paris returned to their
shack to find their gear stolen. They tracked
the Indians and caught them with the
goods."

"What happened?"

"Fightin' and cuttin', but the Paris brothers and their friend, John Chastain, whipped
five Indians and got back their property.
They made peace, left, but the red men
sneaked around and ambushed! Killed both

29

brothers. Shot off John Chastain's right index finger before he escaped in the swamp. His trigger finger!"

"Eat your strawberry shortcake, John William," commanded his mother. Miss Dolly turned to Lavinia, and her cheeks shook as she tried to laugh soothingly. "They were caught. They're in the Tallahassee jail."

John William wiped whipped cream from his chin. "But the trial is here in June!"

"Now don't you worry, young lady," said Mr. Nathaniel. "The United States signed a treaty with the Apalachicola clans in Florida four years ago. The Seminoles were to be reimbursed for cattle and property for a period of twenty years. They agreed to be relocated."

"Nobody's budged them yet," said John William.

All the way home Lavinia peered behind the trees.

Thomas anguished. *This land has such special promise, but is Lavinia strong enough for the challenge?*

With springtime the pace of life accelerated. Lavinia believed Thomas when he joked that farmers worked from "can to can't," but she was busy, too, laying out a garden at what would be the entrance to her home some future day. She hadn't known that the hammocks would yield such a diversity of lovely plants; consequently, she had brought Cape jasmine and roses from Savannah as well as an assortment of bulbs and seeds.

Lavinia and Julie — and Samuel when Thomas could spare him — cleared weeds and swept the yard with brooms of dogwood branches, leaving it clean and bare. The magnolias Thomas had moved in were flourishing, framing the house site with their leathery green leaves. Before she laid out her design in front of them, Lavinia consulted an old book, *English Gardens*. She considered different patterns, drawing with a stick. Since she didn't have English boxwood to outline geometric parterres, she decided on six circular beds to accent the walkway.

Samuel watched her silently for a while. Then he began to grumble as he dug. "Best let me grub out them yaupon holly."

"No. My husband moved them in from the woods," Lavinia protested. "Besides, they're evergreen and make a pretty background."

Samuel shook his head. "Them leaves be what them red men parch to make the Black Drink. They have ceremonies and vomit it up to clean theyselves to go on the warpath."

Lavinia could feel the blood drain from her cheeks. But she stamped her foot. "No! I won't be scared off. We paid money for this land. We've put our hands in this good red dirt to plant. It's ours."

Lavinia insisted they must declare the fourteenth of May a holiday. Thomas would be twenty-five; coincidently, it was Lavinia's birthday, too. She'd be seventeen. The garden was to be the scene of a special celebration. Two beds of poppies and lark-spurs in pinks and purples swayed in the breeze. Two circles filled with lemon daylil-ies blazed in the sun. At the right moment, Julie was to spread a quilt by the glossy-leaved Cape jasmine bushes where their white blossoms could shed fragrance over a picnic lunch.

Lavinia could hardly wait for noon when she planned to bestow the cake and her surprise. She smiled as she sniffed the pound cake, Thomas's favorite. She had gone into town for Miss Dolly to help her. She had carried the pound of butter, pound of sugar, and pound of flour, but the moth-erly woman had insisted all twelve eggs must come from her special flock of guinea hens. Miss Dolly had shown her how to squeeze the butter in her fingers and fold the batter with her hands. Then Lavinia had whisked the egg whites until her arm was about to drop off. It was worth the effort as the aroma drifted from Miss Dolly's oven, which was built into a brick wall. Lavinia could not have resisted tasting it if it had not been an occasion.

At last, the moment arrived. First, they rode over their land, she on loping Prince, Thomas on prancing Zeus, his new black stallion. Savoring the feeling of ownership, they examined the fields lying ready for cottonseeds. They stopped to walk in knee-high corn, holding hands, as proud of the plants as parents.

When the sun was directly overhead, they headed for the garden. Her mouth had been watering for the deviled eggs; now, emotion filled her and she could not swallow.

"Do you think you can stay happy here?" Thomas asked, munching a ham biscuit. "It will be years before a house can be built in your garden."

Lavinia hunched on her knees and scooted against him. A mockingbird's melody trembled to a high note and held. Then everything stilled. She whispered, "I want only one thing: to make a home for you. No, two. I shall help others discover and respect the worth I see in you. I'll work with you to make this land that people laughed at into a special place."

Thomas caught his breath, clasped his big hands over hers. "I want to establish characteristics of lasting value." He ducked his head, reddened. "I admit it, I need to prove myself the equal of any first-born son."

"You will. Some of your brothers — Mitchell for one — have more blind ambition, but you will set the benchmark."

Thomas beamed. "We must provide inheritance to honor *all* our children."

Lavinia sat back, disconcerted. "Our children?" She might have figured he'd guess her secret. He was so perceptive. "You know?"

"Is it true? I'd watched you. Hoped. Prayed."

She snuggled into his arms. "Isn't it wonderful? We should have a child by New Year's Day."

They held each other for a long while, savoring their joy, but when Thomas spoke, there was trouble in his tone.

"Would you want to go to your mother or could you have our baby here? We don't know what danger . . . I can't imagine how I'd bear for you to go — but the isolation . . ."

Lavinia was serene. "I'll be fine. I've been

reading the eighth chapter of Romans. Nothing can separate us from the love of Christ. We are more than conquerors through Him that loved us." *Can I convince him with a show of faith?* Lavinia wondered.

Thomas sighed. "You're right. Life can never defeat us, but can we stick this out? Can we lick these Pine Barrens?"

He shook off his worried tone and lifted her to her feet, smiling. "Now, come see *my* surprise."

CHAPTER II

Lavinia wanted to keep the fragrance of their morning. Plucking a creamy Cape jasmine blossom, she tucked it into her hair before she followed an excited Thomas behind the row of cabins.

"My surprise isn't much compared to yours. It's been a spare-time job, but since you've told me your news, we'll have to work in earnest."

He showed her five racks of lumber in readiness. "Yellow pines are hard to saw, but since they're tall and straight and free from small branches, they make good lumber," he explained.

Next, he pointed out forms filled with clay and sand, drying in the sun. "This is the way we start making bricks for the foundation and chimneys."

"What in the world is that?" Lavinia stopped beside a beehive-shaped object with smoke curling from the top.

Thomas laughed. "A kiln. Pine branches are burning inside it to bake the dry clay into lasting bricks."

"What a wonderful surprise!" Lavinia exclaimed. "Are we building a real house already?"

"Wait, now. A temporary one. You must understand. But bigger, better for you and our baby." He smiled. "Family will want to visit. I know my mother will come."

Lavinia's face stiffened. She tried to hold her expression of delight, but this last thought filled her with panic. *My mother-in-law . . . so soon?*

Oblivious, Thomas drew in the dirt. "See. Like this. A plantation plain structure. Two rooms upstairs, two down, and a lean-to at back. Still a dogtrot, but we'll close the ends. Folks around here leave them open because they think the fresh air prevents disease, but I can't let our baby get cold and wet."

Lavinia kissed him, feeling as if she would burst with happiness. "Can we have a porch where we can rock him?"

A month later, Lavinia sat in the log kitchen, picking at her breakfast, restless, longing for a woman to talk with of babies and events. *I need some excitement,* she thought. Her eyes flashed as she remembered that today, June twenty-seventh, was time for the Indian trial.

"I think I'll drive into town to visit Miss Dolly," she told Thomas. "The wildflowers are at their prettiest now, and as Keats said, 'a thing of beauty is a joy forever.' I'll take her an armload of cinnamon fern and some yellow hibiscus . . ." She paused, realizing the tone of voice she was using had always caused her brother Remer to tease and call her "fakey."

Thomas is so honest and innocent that he doesn't even suspect, she thought. Squirming guiltily, she added, "I may even find orchids in the bogs."

"Good. Today would be a fine time to press flowers for the book you're making. But you should stay at home."

Lavinia frowned. She had found a delightful occupation in collecting the array of plants that grew on Greenwood and identifying them. Fortunately, a book on wildflowers and one with blank pages had been among her treasured — if meager — library. She considered the idea, but her mind was made up. She shook her head.

Thomas put down his coffee. "Court is today. I have to be available in case they call me for the jury, but you shouldn't be there.

38

Feeling is high against the Indians. It wouldn't be good for you to be around such ugly doings in your condition."

Julie, who had been unabashedly eavesdropping from the dogtrot, stuck her head in the kitchen. "Don't go. You'll mark that baby!" she cried, voice adamant.

Lavinia laughed. They all argued, but she would not be dissuaded. "I promise to stay on the Mitchell's porch. I've bought flannel for receiving blankets and muslin for day gowns, and Miss Dolly can show me how to cut the cloth."

At last the matter was settled, and they drove into town. Lavinia hummed, but Thomas kept his lips pursed. He left her with Miss Dolly, sitting on the porch.

Even with the happy task busying her hands, Lavinia's curiosity burned. The village — normally deserted — was throbbing like a carnival. She could hear peddlers hawking their wares. She leaned out from the dogtrot and saw women in sunbonnets, evidently the wives of yeoman farmers.

"Can't we join those women clustered on the corner?" Lavinia begged

Miss Dolly shook her head. "No, young lady, I promised your husband to keep you protected."

As she crocheted edging, she kept eyeing

the street, hoping to see John William. At last he appeared.

With one foot on the step as if he were ready to run, the open-faced boy reported that the trial had ended. He spoke in high-pitched excitement. "The crowd's moving to the gallows for the hanging."

John William scurried away, but he soon came running back. He wiped his high forehead with his handkerchief and caught his breath. "The two older Indians were hanged all right, but the young one is so stout that he broke the rope! He begged not to be hung again — said he'd been taught it was all right to kill white men. He repented and asked to be made a slave."

"Oh, surely since he said that, they will free him," cried Lavinia. "I wish I could go and see what's happening."

"I'll let you know." He ran, puffing in the heat.

When at last John William returned to say the Indian boy had been hung, Lavinia wept at the ways of the wilderness.

As soon as the house was roughed in, providing sleeping space for a visitor, Thomas sent a messenger to his younger brother, who had bought land south of Thomasville. Mitchell Jones came to spend a

40

weekend.

Lavinia enjoyed presiding over supper in the cabin kitchen for their first guest as if it were a banquet. She was pleased that the men sat long at the table, relishing Julie's "cooter" stew. The striped turtle reminded her too much of alligator, and she ate little, preferring to listen to the lively brothers laugh and joke.

She smiled from one to the other, admiring their sensual Welsh manliness. Thomas's black hair grew thick and straight, adding to his serious expression, while Mitchell's fell over his forehead with a rakish curl, increasing his devil-may-care appearance. *Yet they are so much alike.* She thought they looked equally dashing when they were attired in the frock coats and slim trousers that were the style of the day.

They began to tell her stories of their adolescent mischief. "One of the funniest times was jump boarding." Thomas gave a warm chuckle deep in his throat.

"It wasn't funny," Mitchell growled.

Thomas ignored his brother. "Papa had built a new pole barn. We stuck a short scrap of pole in the ground — about four inches high — and laid a board across it."

With good humor, Mitchell took up the story. "Our big sister, the one who's also named Lavinia, was a champion jump boarder. She could keep her footing on the board no matter how hard we jumped, but she'd give us a few licks, and we'd and fall off. This particular time she really pounced and sent me sailing. I came down on another board that was lying in the grass. It had nails sticking straight up, and I sat on a nail that felt as big as a spike."

"Ohhh." Lavinia shuddered. She could feel goose bumps run down her thighs.

"I grabbed his legs and Sister took his arms and we *pulled* him off," Thomas interjected. "We were scared to tell Papa, but Sister said we'd better. That evening the doctor came and filled a chamber pot with wool rags. He lighted the fire and set Mitchell over the smoldering." Thomas filled the room with his deep laughter.

"They smoked me all night," said Mitchell, making a face. "It wasn't funny."

Lavinia giggled until she had to fan and hold her side.

"Honey, we've tired you out. You'd better get to bed." Thomas helped her from the bench.

"Why don't you and I go fox hunting?" suggested Mitchell.

"This late?" she asked, clinging onto Thomas's hand, wanting him near her.

"Midnight foxhunts are the best kind."
Thomas grinned.

As they went off in high spirits, Lavinia
climbed into bed, loosening the curtains
from the bedposts to hang around her, making it cozier. She lay listening to the deep
throated baying of the rag-tag pack of
foxhounds Mitchell had brought with him.

It set her thinking. Thomas needs a dog.
Not a scraggly hound, a fine dog. That's
what I'll get him for Christmas.

As she considered breeds, she decided on
one to hunt quail. *That's a bit selfish,* she
admitted. She had discovered to her dismay
that the beef she enjoyed on her first night
here had been a rarity. Thomas had sent
Augustus ahead to have the special meal
prepared. Now they lived on venison, turkey,
or terrapin stew. Of it all, the game she
really liked was the tender white meat of
quail.

*I'll need Mr. Nathaniel's help to get a pure-
bred dog,* she realized. She could hardly wait
for an excuse to go into Thomasville.

Nathaniel Mitchell jingled the watch chain
that spread across the broad expanse of his
vest. "Now let me think . . . I know the very
thing! I heard about it the last time I was in
Savannah. There's a new breed. It's not a

43

flushing dog. When it smells a bird, it stops, quietly alerting the hunter."

"I want something fine, now," Lavinia reminded him. "I've money set aside." She was proud that she had been stingy spending her inheritance. She had bought only what they needed most for housekeeping. The rest she had saved toward babies and presents for Thomas.

"The dog I'm thinking of is exactly right." The old man had become as excited as she. "We'll have to import one from England where it's bred from Spanish lineage."

Lavinia's eyes sparkled as he talked.

"On the royal game preserves in Spain, they developed dogs that are longer of body, Spanish Pointers that set game. In England, they were bred to curly-haired retrieving dogs. The offspring are called Setters."

"Get one!"

Work on the house progressed with frantic haste during the July laying-by time for the crops, when the rows could no longer be plowed, and Thomas could do nothing more than to pray for rain and few insects. Lavinia, gaining weight and miserable with summer's heat and humidity, watched the carpentering hopefully. Surely the upstairs bedroom would capture breezes.

She wrote her news to her stepmother and was bombarded with advice, the works of Shakespeare and Virgil to read during her confinement, and the promise of sending Tossie, her childhood nurse to aid her when the time came. The kind mammy had cared for her and her sister Sarah when their mother, Mary Henderson Young, had died on Lavinia's birthday when she was a year old. After the proper year of mourning, Papa had married again, but Tossie had stayed.

She's an old woman now and will want to boss me, Lavinia thought, regretting the loss of her newfound independence. *I wish I hadn't written.*

Soon after the letters an oddly shaped package arrived atop the stagecoach. Thomas brought it from Thomasville. He untied the ropes and stood back smiling as Lavinia unwrapped layer after layer of quilts. The top ones were ragged, meant only for packing; but the inner three were fresh and bright and intended for use. They brought memories of everyone in the family seated around the quilting frame, telling stories as they made dainty stitches.

Ceremoniously, Lavinia removed the last piece. When she saw the shining wood, she began to cry. The cradle had been in the attic of her home as long as she could remember. On rainy days she had played there and rocked her doll. She smoothed her fingers over the mahogany hood of the small bed and set it swinging between the carved posts. How it had comforted her when she was five and Papa had died! Her oldest brother, James Young, who coincidentally married Thomas's sister named Lavinia, had inherited the plantation, as first-born sons always did. Kindly, he let his stepmother and younger siblings remain.

"I can't believe they sent this treasure to me, the youngest of the nine children," Lavinia said, wonderingly. "It belonged to my maternal grandmother, who married in London and brought the cradle to the colonies."

"Maybe it's your family's seal of approval on the line we're starting."

Lavinia stroked the cradle. "I can hardly wait to rock our child. It's a lovely link of past and future."

By August, Thomas could not let himself think about how hot and tired he was. Somehow he managed to finish the house just as the cotton bolls began to open. He had a sick feeling that had come with knowing all of his money was gone.

All efforts turned to harvesting the white gold. Everyone — except Lavinia, who could no longer see her feet — was equipped with shoulder-slung burlap bags that were dragged down the rows as the cotton was picked. Fat sacks were emptied on osnaburg sheets at the edge of the field. Bundles mounted up in readiness for transporting to market, but Thomas fretted that he could not afford a gin. The oily seeds had to be pulled from the lint by hand. Before the laborious process was completed, winter arrived.

Finally, on a crisp December morning, Thomas saddled Zeus for the fifty-mile trip through Tallahassee to Saint Marks on the Gulf of Mexico. It was a new port of entry for the United States and did not even have a lighthouse yet, but it was his only access to the ocean. Thomas tried to quell the churning in his stomach as his excitement over selling his first crop vied with his nervousness at the possibility of encountering Indians. He motioned Micah and Nahum to pull out with the loaded carts while he went back one last time to kiss Lavinia good-bye.

"I wish you could sell the cotton at Savannah," she said.

Thomas smoothed the tense lines of her

face with a tender finger. "Honey, you know I can't haul it two hundred miles. And I'd never forgive myself if I wasn't back by the time the baby came."

"But I'll worry so with you traveling through Indian Territory. I keep thinking of the Paris brothers."

"Don't. That was just an incident. They happen occasionally. I promise I won't provoke anyone." He frowned, noticing she was cupping the weight of the baby with her hand. He threw out his chest, exhibiting more confidence than he felt.

"I'm sure Territorial Governor Du Val is keeping peace. Besides, the Indians must be accustomed to farmers taking cotton to the sea." As Thomas bent down from the saddle for a last embrace, he was careful to hide his musket beneath his greatcoat. Surprise attacks were common. He hoped Lavinia had not noticed how heavily they were armed.

Thomas tensed the moment they crossed the boundary into the Florida Territory. The scenery changed, and so did the mood. No longer were they in open Pine Barrens where they could see a friend — or foe. Ancient live oaks meshed their spreading arms over the road, casting it into shadow.

Spanish moss draped the gnarled and twisted limbs, hanging in long gray beards that shivered in the wind, revealing, then concealing the tunnel-like way before them.

Looking back, Thomas saw Micah and Nahum jerking their heads, darting rounded eyes, trying to penetrate dense hardwood hammocks. Silence seemed an entity. Hair stood on the back of his neck. *Are we really being watched?* Thomas wondered. *I wish Lavinia hadn't mentioned the Paris brothers' murder.*

As the terrain became higher, they passed a large lake. Oak and pine were mixed with hickory and persimmon. *We must be near the old Mikasuki villages,* he thought. Fields showed evidence of rich soil, black loam mixed with the clay and sand. Obviously it could have been easily worked with light hoes by the Indian women. Here they had raised corn, rice, potatoes, beans, peas, and groundnuts. *No wonder General Jackson found it impossible to remove the tribes from here to the sand and swamps of southern Florida.*

Thomas knew that after Andrew Jackson humbled the Indians in Fowltown, Georgia, the old chief, Neamathla, had set up several fowl towns in the Florida Territory. Gover-

nor Du Val took one of them, Tallahassa Ta-
loofa, for the territorial capital and renamed
it Tallahassee. The Indians were commanded
to stay on a small reservation along the
Apalachicola River, but Neamathla and the
other chiefs he advised, wandered. Thomas
understood why they felt no affection for
the white man.

The cold darkness settling around him
made him wonder. *Am I still on the road?* He
had not realized he was holding his breath
until at last he saw lights on a hill. He must
have made the thirty-six miles to Tallahassee.

Thomas chuckled when he entered the
town, remembering a newspaper account of
a grand celebration held here that "marked
the infant metropolis as a place of urbanity
and style". Actually, it looked like a little
woods village with the few houses almost
concealed by ancient live oaks still holding
their small green leaves in winter. Lavinia
would be disappointed. She had poured
over details of a ball attended by people
from half of the twenty-four states to welcome Prince Achille Murat, Napoleon's
nephew, who had moved to Tallahassee to
seek his fortune.

None of this mattered to Thomas now as
he made his way through dark streets. His

50

wagon train passed a brick capitol building that looked new. At last he found what he was searching for. A swinging board proclaimed: "Wyatt's Hotel."

The next morning dawned bright and warm, and the remaining twenty miles to Saint Marks was an easy descent across flat sands. The tropical growth along the road abounded with turtles. He had never seen so many alligators. Frequently they lay in the middle of the road and his team was forced to stop until they lumbered out of the way.

A growing sense of urgency made Thomas crack the whip over his animals when the road cleared. *What if all of the ships have sailed for New York?*

At last the heavy vegetation thinned around scattered houses. Glad as he was to reach the dock, Thomas was disappointed that the Saint Marks River was narrow and dark and wound through marsh before it emptied into the sea. He had expected to see the Gulf of Mexico, which was said to sparkle a clear blue-green

No matter, he laughed at himself, as long as the ships sail out with my crop.

Negotiations with the cotton factor took time. Thomas felt glorious when he again had the freedom of money in his pocket.

In Saint Marks, Thomas bought oranges, coconuts, and Brazil nuts, the tastes of Christmas. He wished he could take home some of the grouper and oysters that everyone here was feasting upon. He completed his shopping in Tallahassee, where a jewelers shop yielded the aquamarine ring he had imagined as a reminder of the Gulf, their gateway to the world. He could hardly wait to see Lavinia.

Before day the next morning, they started for home.

Thomas rode carelessly. Micah and Nahum sang an old carol. In the first cart, Micah sang a phrase; then Nahum echoed the next line from the cart behind. The song stopped suddenly. A party of Indians burst from a concealing hammock.

The leader wore a red coat from a British uniform. He sported a Spanish-style mustache and a drape of silk scarves. His eyes showed intelligence, fire, and hostility. Thomas reined Zeus and bowed low in deference, guessing he was merely parading his preeminence. He recognized this powerful man and his unique apparel from a picture. As the entourage crossed, Thomas let out his breath, knowing he had seen — and survived — the implacable chieftain,

Neamathla.

Foggy darkness was penetrated primarily by the animals' sense that they were nearing home. It was Christmas Eve.

Thomas rapped impatiently on the door of the dark house. A candle flickered down the staircase; then the bolt slid back. He sprang to enfold Lavinia in his arms.

A strange black face, on a level with his six feet two, startled him.

"Bout time you got here," the woman who must be Tossie said grumpily. "The pains be startin'."

Thomas ignored the rude greeting and bounded up the stairs.

Lavinia lay with the bed curtains pushed back and perspiration shining on her face. She held out her arms.

Thomas kissed her. He was too filled with emotion to speak. *I thought she had until New Year's Day.*

"Darling! I'm so glad you're here. I may have a second present for you by tomorrow so I'd better give you your first gift now." She took a heavy breath. "Look in that box in the corner."

Thomas knelt and gazed into the widely spaced eyes of a large puppy. Amazed, realizing the good breeding, he cupped the white, domed head and fingered the long ear leather, feathered with bluish black. He lifted the dog to cradle in his arms. "Where did you get him?"

Lavinia laughed. "Mr. Nathaniel helped me import him from England. The spots and ticking are called Belton blue. He's a fine dog. One for hunting. Just wait 'til I tell you his pedigree-ee."

She ended in a screech that made Thomas set down the dog and rush to her bedside.

"How could you think about me in your condition?"

"Because I love you," she replied, panting. "Better call Tossie. You got home just in time."

CHAPTER III

Thomas paced the hallway. Tossie had banished him from Lavinia's bedside, and even though he knew she needed the midwife, he resented this strange woman who was in command of his whole world. Lavinia's moans became screams, making him cringe. He dropped to the top step, head in hands. The puppy nudged under his arm and licked his face.

"You little rascal. You sense I'm hurting, don't you?" Thomas gathered the long-boned bundle onto his lap and stroked the feathered fur on his ears. "Rascal. That's a good name for you. We'll be buddies."

He buried his face against the dog, fearing for Lavinia. He paid no attention to Julie, who kept hurrying in and out. Day had broken before he heard a cry.

Julie stuck her head out of the door, beaming. "It be a boy!"

"Lavinia?"

"She be fine."

With Rascal trotting at his heels, Thomas tiptoed to her bedside.

Lavinia pulled the crocheted corner of a receiving blanket from a tiny, red face. "Meet James Young Jones," she said.

Pleased that she verified the honor to his father and to her ancestry, Thomas clasped his family in his arms. Sun shone through the draperies. Only then did he realize it was Christmas Day.

Contentment blanketed Lavinia as she lay in the tester bed, smiling down at James who was nestled in the curve of her arm. She flashed her aquamarine ring in a sunray. *One day I must see the Gulf of Mexico and the strange Indians that Thomas described.* Soon she would set some goals for herself. For now, she had everything she desired.

She reflected that Christmas had been wonderful, even if dinner was late. Samuel had shot and roasted a twenty-pound turkey, and Julie had fixed cornbread dressing that was good even without oysters. The oranges and coconut made juicy, sweet ambrosia. James had slept in his cradle while Rascal received turkey tidbits under the table at Thomas's feet. She was pleased at how much he loved the dog.

What bliss it had been with Thomas staying in the house! Of course, no one worked until the Yule log burned up after New Years. Burly Augustus had brought in the largest log he could carry. Lavinia suspected he had soaked one end in water to slow the burning, but that was fine with her.

Now, though, everyone had gone back to jobs. Lavinia lay against the pillows, fidgeting. Full of energy, she wanted to straighten up her house and wash her sweaty, matted hair. *I'm fine,* she thought. But Tossie decreed she must stay in bed and not even lift the baby for six weeks.

Suddenly she heard many feet stomping up the stairs. Thomas had sent the news to everyone, but she was not ready to receive guests.

Her excited husband peered in. "Mama and the children have come to see James," he said.

Lavinia frowned. Elizabeth Mills Jones was a lovely lady, but she did not need her mother-in-law now. *Where was she when I was lonely?*

She watched with narrowed eyes and barely managed a smile as the small woman, who was ramrod straight, bustled in with a rustling of black taffeta. Behind her trooped

57

the three youngest of the handsome Jones clan. John, eighteen, and Elizabeth, fifteen, stood back, looking bored. The baby of the family, Harriet, who was only eleven, rushed forward, eager to see James.

Looking at Harriet, Lavinia cringed at her own dishevelment. *She's more beautiful than any child has a right to be.* Dark hair clung in ringlets around her perfect oval face. *It's her eyes that arrest attention,* Lavinia thought. Large, quiet, they held a depth of wisdom far beyond her years.

Lavinia gritted her teeth as they passed James around. She remained separated by silence as chatter reverberated in the bedroom. Then Thomas's mother tucked the baby in his cradle, and Harriet swung the little wooden ark, rocking him too high.

"Don't do that! You'll turn him over," Lavinia snapped, lashing out at Harriet even though she knew the trestle feet were steady. *My mother-in-law is taking my son away from me,* she thought bitterly.

Elizabeth Jones realized her agitation. "You youngsters shoo out of the room. We're making the new mother nervous." She turned to Lavinia with a smile. "I brought a copy of Sir Walter Scott's *Waverley.* Perhaps it will soothe you if I read to you," she said as she sat down beside the cradle.

Thomas felt he had all he wanted out of life as he rode over his land. Rascal ran ahead of Zeus. *I can hardly wait to train him to hunt quail,* he thought, *but I have a great deal of work with 1828 before me.*

He had plans to improve and enlarge the plantation now that he had a son. Most planters grew only cotton, but as he looked at his fields, he decided to diversify. Like the Indians he had observed, he would grow corn and peas and start a herd of cattle.

His mother's arrival solved the anxiety that had plagued him about her since his father's death. *I'll build her a house right here close to mine,* he thought. *Then I can take care of everyone.*

Loneliness was no longer Lavinia's problem. As her mother-in-law's house rose during the warm days of February's false spring, she exhausted her frustration by digging in her flowerbeds. She planted roses to bloom in April and crape myrtles for color during the sultry heat of July and August. She leaned on her mattock, looked up at the sky, and wondered, *Will the home Thomas dreamed for me ever exist in the midst of this garden?*

At least she could be glad that Thomas's brother John and sister Elizabeth were intent on making their own lives. Elizabeth was already being courted by Joseph Neely. It was Harriet who troubled her. The child followed behind her as she worked like a worshipful puppy.

I don't know why, Lavinia thought, looking into the solemn eyes that watched as she dropped to her knees, weeding. *I feel terrible that I'm always yelling at her.* She sighed, reflecting that when her mother-in-law irritated her, she managed to smile and hold in her anger; then, at the least of Harriet's infractions, she exploded. Harriet's lip might tremble, but she never replied.

The quiet child surprised her with a question. "Why do you always have your hair dressed on top of your head and your clothes so clean and neat even out here?"

Lavinia turned to her. Harriet seemed to grow taller and prettier every day. *I must be perfectly groomed because I'm not beautiful like you,* she thought. She sat back on her heels and considered.

"I guess it's because I'm Thomas Jones's wife."

"Why? He's not special. He's just a

farmer."

"One day you'll see that your brother is a man of great worth."

At last Thomas's family moved into their own house. It was quite close by, but Lavinia felt that she could breathe freely again.

When Miss Elizabeth unpacked mahogany furniture, English Chippendale that gleamed darkly against a pastel Chinese rug, Lavinia tried to repress the green of her envy as she compared her own sparse parlor. *One day I'll have something beautiful besides my bed to polish with beeswax.*

Lavinia surprised herself at how often she visited. Miss Elizabeth set a delightful afternoon tea. With James on a quilt pallet to protect the carpeting, Lavinia sewed while Miss Elizabeth read aloud. Between them, they owned some favorite books; however, for current events, they had to rely on old newspapers, which had come by slow stagecoach from Savannah. After Andrew Jackson became President in 1829, they combed the pages for word of what the old Indian fighter might do.

One afternoon, Miss Elizabeth looked over her cup of tea with anxiety puckering her face. "I fear Jackson's hatred of Indians will cause more trouble with our neighbors in the Florida Territory."

Lavinia tried to reassure her. "We're guarded by the local militia," she said, but she knew they afforded mighty little protection.

As news of Indian raids grew worse, Lavinia thought she felt ill from Miss Elizabeth's contagious nervousness. By summer, she realized her queasiness was because she was carrying a second child. She had to admit it was nice to have another pair of loving arms to care for toddling, talkative James.

On the coldest night in January of 1830, she bore a daughter. A delighted Thomas named her Mary Elizabeth. Busy days tumbled one after the other, and another son was born September 12, 1831. They christened him Francis Remer Jones, ancestral names, but especially honoring Lavinia's brother, Remer Young, who had moved into the area and bought a large acreage.

The Pine Barrens no longer seem such a wilderness, Lavinia thought. *How good it is to have family settling here, even if the plantations are miles apart.*

Lavinia felt that nothing could mar their happiness. Then rumblings of actual war spread over the plantations of Thomas County.

"Listen to this!" Elizabeth Jones read from the newspaper: " 'President Jackson has determined that the Five Civilized Tribes, the Cherokees, Creeks, Choctaws, Chickasaws, and Seminoles, must be removed to the west side of the Mississippi River immediately!' "

Eyes fearful, she looked at Lavinia. "The article goes on to say that the government had believed that the treaty signed in 1823 meant the clans would be relocated at their earliest convenience; however, the Seminoles have insisted they could stay for the twenty years the reimbursement was to be paid. Nevertheless, Jackson is standing firm that they must move now."

As the afternoon shadows were lengthening, Thomas joined them with startling word of impending danger. "Neamathla has led the Lower Creeks to revolt. In the Florida Territory, red war poles are up. The black drink is passing around."

The threat of war in Florida receded in importance for Lavinia when she received an invitation to a high tea celebrating the completion of the Hardy Bryan's new home. The first two-story house in Thomasville, it boasted white columns and a second-story balcony. Lavinia could hardly wait to see the inside. She was excited that a real social life was beginning here.

"Do come with me, Miss Elizabeth," she urged. "Tossie can keep the children."

Her mother-in-law shook her head. "March has roared in, and the wind just cuts through me. I'd rather stay by the fire. Besides, Francis seems a little droopy."

Lavinia looked at her eighteen-month-old who was sucking his thumb as he snuggled in his grandmother's lap.

She's just spoiling him, she thought. *They're fine for me to go and enjoy myself.*

James, sturdy and all boy at six, was playing fetch with Hamlet while three-year-old Mary Elizabeth fed her doll.

Lavinia dressed excitedly. She had a new-styled hat Thomas had brought from Tallahassee. The wide, flat brim was piled high with bows. As she preened, trying to see the ribbon streamers down her back, she glimpsed Thomas's face watching her in the mirror.

"You'll have to take the carriage and Augustus to drive you. The Indians are making daring raids on the army along the coast. They haven't crossed into Georgia yet, but these times are too dangerous for you to go alone."

■ ■ ■ ■

As she rode along, Lavinia's anticipation at seeing the Bryan's house was dimmed. Would she ever have the home Thomas had promised? The plantation was prospering, but he spent the cotton money on things like this family carriage. Of course, he never wanted to go anywhere without the children.

And land, she thought. *I wonder if he will ever have enough?* She knew she should be proud that he always sat down with her to explain how buying at a sheriff's sale would be a bargain or selling one parcel for profit and buying another was good business.

She sighed, realizing suddenly that she had not considered the worst. *What if the Indians burn us out? The war is a walk away.*

The carriage rolled into the village. A number of residents had moved to town, and it was always fun to meet interesting new people. Natural exuberance lifted her spirits, and she straightened her hat.

Lavinia knew she had lingered too long. Augustus snapped a whip over the horse's heads, urging speed because gathering darkness obscured the trees along their roadway. She hurried to the rough door of her temporary home, displeased with it since she had seen the Bryan's new house. The moment she stepped inside, she sensed something was wrong. She paused, wondering. Francis's wail drew her upstairs.

Miss Elizabeth was walking the floor with him. She cast a frantic glance at Lavinia. "He can't retain any food. I've even let Tossie try some of her herb remedies. Nothing works."

Lavinia took her son, kissing and crooning. He fell limp in her arms, and each whimper seemed weaker. "Tossie, bring me a cup of very sweet tea."

The big woman went out, shaking her head.

"I wish Harriet wasn't away at school," said Miss Elizabeth in a far-away voice. "She always seemed to amuse him and make him eat."

Thomas came striding into the room. With confidence, he held Francis high, but the baby did not respond.

As the child worsened, Lavinia began to sob. "He must get well. Oh, surely God won't punish me for leaving my children."

CHAPTER **IV**

As dawn broke on the morning of March 3, 1833, Lavinia gripped Thomas's hand. She felt cold, numb. Francis Remer had quieted, and they had laid him on their bed. Slowly, uncomprehending at first, she realized their son had taken his last breath.

Thomas's face was wet with tears as he tried to embrace her, but she felt she could not bare his touch. She shook him off.

Did I cause this grief? Lavinia wondered as hysteria swept through her, making her tremble. She began to scream. "If God is good, how can He let this happen?" She sank to the floor, hiding her face in the bedclothes, sobbing.

Miss Elizabeth moved quietly to her side and stroked her hair. "Bless your heart honey. God is loving. He understands our grief, but death is a part of life. Many babies can't survive this world. Remember when King David lost his child? He prophesied that he would see him in heaven."

David lost that son because of his sin, Lavinia thought.

She cried in great shaking sobs, unable to stop, refusing to be comforted, even when Julie whispered in her ear. "Miss Vinnie, you'll mark that baby you be carrying."

Thomas knew he must swallow his heartache and watch over the children when he saw James and Joe, Julie's nine-year old son, with bamboo fishing poles over their shoulders. He caught them before they left the yard and asked, "Would you like for me to take you fishing?"

"Yes, sir!" they chorused.

"First we must go to the woodshed." He laughed as their faces fell. They thought he meant a spanking. "It's the best place to dig worms," he explained.

Mary Elizabeth toddled after them as they trooped to the woodshed. They dug in the loose black dirt accumulated from rotted pine bark. Each forkful turned up several large worms.

The three-year-old squealed as the worms wiggled, but after watching the boys, Mary Elizabeth picked up a long one and put it in their cloth sack, making Thomas realize he should take her along.

Because of the baby, he hitched up the wagon. Thomas swung her up to the seat beside him. The foursome sang as they rode through the pines to the largest creek on the place. It wound through the dense forest of a hardwood hammock. He carried his daughter piggyback the rest of the way. The sweet feeling of her plump arms around his neck made him wish Lavinia could come out of her depression and appreciate her.

"Watch out for snakes," Thomas instructed the boys. "And listen. Rattlesnakes will warn you away with a sound like a baby rattle."

James and Joe, inseparable friends, were soon pulling in four-inch fish, whispering soft exclamations, "Got 'im." They stayed quiet as if they did not want to disturb the serenity of their surroundings.

Just as Mary Elizabeth was tiring of the game, a tug on her line elicited a loud shriek, "I caught one!" Her pole was bending, and Thomas helped her land a large catfish, which had swum up the creek from the Ochlockonee.

Suddenly everyone was hungry. As they sat on a sand beach to eat their lunches, Thomas directed their attention to the gold-green beauty of the April day shining through the different shades of the trees around them. Mary Elizabeth fell asleep. When they headed home, James and Joe were well pleased, except for the fact that a girl had caught the biggest fish.

Thomas had thought Lavinia would recover; however, even as summer's heat filled her garden with blossoms — and weeds — she continued to move about as though she could not see them.

He pleaded with her. "Remember how you told me we can be more than conquerors through Christ who loves us?"

"I'm the one who's conquered," Lavinia said in a limp voice. "Where was God when my son died?"

"Right here beside us ready to share our grief. The only thing that limits God is when we shut him out. Please, Lavinia . . ."

She turned her back, and he knew he could not reach her.

Thomas went out to tramp the woods with Rascal, praying that when the circuit rider came to Thomasville, he would be able to comfort her. She had always liked Rev. John Talley and extended the hospitality of her table and guestroom.

A few weeks later when the minister came to visit her, she remained cold. She refused to attend mission services.

Thomas's hopes were raised again when formal beginnings were made for a constituted church. Lavinia had often wished for a real church sanctuary, and at last the population had increased in the Pine Barrens so that a Georgia Conference was formed. With the promise of a preacher on the field more regularly, the Church Stewards purchased land. Thomas was proud to be one of the trustees to whom the deed was conveyed. Surely when they had a building, Lavinia would relent.

However, as summer plodded through the scorching days of August, she made no change. Thomas's heart ached when he took his mother and the children to mission services and Lavinia stayed home.

He knew she was using her growing bulk as an excuse. *Surely if she has another son, she'll be happy again.*

The baby born on November 10, 1833, was a girl. Thomas rocked his new daughter in the hooded cradle, singing softly. He glanced at his wife who was sunk in her pillow. "What shall we name her?"

Lavinia's face was glum. "I don't care. You decide."

He frowned, swallowed a protest. With forced cheerfulness, he said, "What about Harriet Lavinia for my baby sister and for you? We can call her Livy."

Lavinia shrugged.

Thomas hoped Lavinia was herself again during the festivities when his sister Elizabeth married Joseph Neely and moved to adjoining Pleasant Hill Plantation; however, he discovered his wife had only resumed the motions of life. He had noticed that new baby Livy's clothes were faded and worn, old garments that had belonged to James and Mary Elizabeth instead of the ones she had made for Francis Remer. He wondered why.

On a crisp December morning, he decided he needed a jacket and started back into the bedroom. He saw Lavinia kneel by the bed, move aside the bed skirt, and surreptitiously take a box from its hiding place. He drew back into the shadows of the hall, knowing he was intruding on a private moment, yearning to find the cause of her continuing melancholy.

One by one Lavinia lifted tiny garments from their secret spot. She held them to her cheek and wet them with her tears. Watching the sad tableau, Thomas felt the hair prickling on the back of his neck. They were little dead Francis Remer's clothes.

Choking on his own tears, Thomas tiptoed

down the stairs. He grabbed his shotgun and hurried outside. Dazzled by the sunlight, he hesitated. *I have to walk or I'll explode,* he thought. He needed the comfort of Rascal, who usually appeared instantly. Not seeing him, Thomas turned toward the cookhouse.

Nahum was scraping a pan. A regular part of his job was cooking for the plantation's dogs. He baked big skillets of cornbread and cooked greens to mix in, to prevent black tongue. Table scraps made the mix tasty.

The hounds were pushing and shoving and grabbing each other's place. Set apart, Rascal looked up from his dish as he scented his master. Noting the gun, the Setter left his food and loped to Thomas, ready to hunt.

Thomas grinned. *I'll feed him extra later,* he thought. He had noticed a large covey of bobwhites gathering in the field where he had harvested corn. As he started in that direction, Rascal ran ahead, enjoying the cool breeze that ruffled his long hair. Thomas followed with the shotgun cradled in his arms, ready.

Suddenly the dog stopped before plumes of grass. He stood poised, nose pointing, feathered tail flagging high. His raised foreleg indicated to Thomas that the birds were unsettled and he wanted to get closer, but he waited for his master to flush the birds.

He's a picture etched against the lowering winter sky, Thomas thought.

A covey of seventeen or eighteen flew up with a whirr of wings. Thomas shot, hitting one. "Dead bird," he said quietly. Rascal obeyed the command, retrieving the prey, carrying it softly in his mouth.

Since it was early in the season, Thomas knew the quail would drift down close together. He squinted to spot their landing place across the field as he took black powder and ramrod to reload. Then the process began again.

When his game bag was filled with all they would need for a meal, Thomas breeched his gun. Without hunting to concentrate upon, his mind seethed with worry. He walked without noticing where he was going.

Rascal, freed from duty, explored. Suddenly, he bounded toward a hammock and disappeared.

Thomas looked around, realizing that he had never visited this particular clump of woods, even though it was quite unusual because bamboo vines intertwined the dense growth of scrub oak to such an extent that they made an impenetrable barrier.

Rascal popped out of a concealed opening. Chin wet, eyes bright, he looked so refreshed that Thomas laughed. He knelt to stroke the silky ears.

"Found a spring did you? I'm thirsty, too. Show me."

Obediently, Rascal led him to a clear, cold, spring-fed stream that flowed from the undergrowth.

Thomas drank. Then, curious, he waded the stream into the jungle-like forest and stopped, amazed. Inside the thick edging, the hammock was as clear-floored as a park.

The area, perhaps a mile long and a half-mile wide, held only two spreading live oaks, one magnolia, a sprinkling of pines, and one hickory. Blazing as gold as a sunset, the hickory drew him to sit down.

He hugged Rascal. "This place is like a secret cathedral," he whispered as peace filled him. He knew they would come again and again. He praised God for the beauty, and then he began to pray for Lavinia. He asked God to forgive her for blaming Him. "Please, Lord, strengthen her faith. Help her to accept the tragedy and become her happy self again."

By 1835, Thomas had prospered enough to

buy land all the way to the Ochlockonee River. As he inspected his property, he stood looking at the black water swollen with January rains. Rushing over sandbars, it splashed up the white banks. *I must haul some of this good sand home. It's time again to make bricks and dry lumber.*

When he told Lavinia their prospects for starting a permanent home, she lifted her shoulders, and her eyes took on the sparkle and interest that had always made her so attractive.

They sat at the supper table, pushing back the dishes that had held leftovers from dinner. Thomas spread paper and drew the candles closer so that he could make notes and sketches.

"What do you want?" he asked.

"I'd like an elegant entrance hall for receiving guests," Lavinia replied dreamily.

Thomas laughed in delight. "What about the outside?" he teased.

"Oh, a big, deep porch. And could we have a balcony over the front door?"

"I'd better start inquiring about an expert architect . . . Preparing will take a long time, you know. We must make lots of bricks — for the outside, of course — but even for the interior walls to prevent the spread of fire. I want our house to last forever."

Lavinia came around the table to hug him. With a thankful heart, he lifted his face for her kiss.

"What shall we name our home?" He pulled her into his lap.

Lavinia considered only a moment. "The first day I got here and saw the evergreens you planted to encircle the house site, I thought how beautiful and green it was and that it always would be. What about Green-wood?"

"Greenwood Plantation. I like it." He did not risk asking her to pray with him, but he nestled his face against her neck and silently asked God's blessing that their home would be a place of happiness and peace. *Please, Lord, hold us in the hollow of your hand.*

On a warm February morning a few weeks later, Lavinia sat in her parlor with her rose-wood rocker keeping time to the tune she was humming as she mended. *I'd begun to wonder if there would be a home here,* she thought. *I feel more alive than I have in the two years since Francis Remer left us. It's time I make more effort for Thomas's sake.* She began singing a nursery rhyme to seven-year-old James, Mary Elizabeth, and Livy, who at fifteen months was walking and trying to talk.

A knock interrupted. The front door opened, and Harriet called in a lilting voice as she came into the hall. Since she had returned from finishing school, Thomas's youngest sister had tried again to be her friend. Lavinia sighed, knowing she must accept the overture.

After all, I'm twenty-five and secure in my husband's love. I must stop being jealous of her. I should do something for her in March when she turns eighteen. She took a deep breath.

"I'm in the parlor, Harriet. Do come in."

Harriet appeared framed in the doorway. She had remained petite, but she had matured into a young lady of startling beauty. Over-large eyes still dominated her perfect oval face like quiet pools of wisdom. She paused for a moment, serene.

Lavinia bit off her thread. "I'm glad you've come. Plan to stay for dinner. Thomas has a guest you must meet."

Harriet showed surprise at the warmth in Lavinia's voice. She stammered, "Well, I-I just came for a minute to play with the children . . ." She looked at Lavinia accusingly, "You have a matchmaking gleam in your eye!"

"You caught me," said Lavinia, laughing. "Who?"

"James Joseph Blackshear. He's from an illustrious family. It was his uncle, General David Blackshear, who made such a name for himself in the Seminole War, and I understand James has been in Florida helping to quiet this latest uprising."

Harriet pursed her lips. "I've seen him. He has such a bland face. Besides, he's never noticed me. He's probably ten years older than I."

Lavinia laughed. "He'll notice you now. You've blossomed into a belle. Anyway, aren't you too particular? He's one of the largest planters in our area. After all, you . . ."

"Don't say it. Mama tells me often enough that I'm passing marriageable age." Harriet bent to pick up Livy.

Lavinia clenched her teeth. Harriet came often to play with her namesake, proclaiming her adorable even though she was plain-faced and would never be pretty. Lavinia knew Harriet's reason for the attention went deeper. *She thinks I don't care about Livy, but I do. It's just that I was numb with grief when she was born so soon after Francis Remer . . .* Emotion threatened to choke her, and she tightened her resolve to do better.

The clomping of work boots on the porch saved Lavinia from having to speak. She

79

regained her composure and smiled as she watched Harriet smoothing her black curls and straightening the white, tiered collar on her print dress.

Thomas ushered a tall man into the room ahead of him. "Mr. Blackshear, you know my wife, but may I present my baby sister, Harriet?"

Harriet wrinkled her nose at Thomas before she shifted Livy to her hip and turned to extend her hand to James Blackshear.

A slow smile appeared over Blackshear's neat, regular features and became a look of delight. Their eyes met, held. "A great pleasure, Miss Jones."

"Mr. Blackshear," she murmured, blushing as he bent low to kiss her hand.

Unaware of the intrigue crackling in the room, Thomas announced that he was hungry. Lavinia chuckled to herself, thinking the hunger evident on Mr. Blackshear's face was not for food. She left a flustered Harriet to entertain the men while she checked on dinner.

Noon was always the largest meal of the day when the stove was fired and enough was cooked to satisfy hard-working appetites, with some left over for supper. However, Lavinia had prepared a special menu today. She smiled proudly as they gathered around the table for the first course: quail with grits, gravy, and biscuits. This time instead of deep-frying the birds whole, she had split them lengthwise, wrapped the halves in bacon, and grilled them in the cast-iron frying pan. Next came collards, fresh from her garden, served with the best ham from the smokehouse. She noticed that Harriet picked at the salty-peppery fried ham while she stole glances at James Blackshear.

Lavinia was annoyed that Thomas kept him discussing cotton gins. As the dried-peach half-moon pies were served, she decided she must seize the conversation. In the end it became unnecessary, and Lavinia felt triumphant.

James Blackshear cleared his throat and fixed his eyes on Thomas. "Sir, may I have your permission to call upon your sister?"

By mid-March, Mr. Blackshear had come courting only twice, and Lavinia decided that the party for Harriet's eighteenth birthday would be the perfect time to move things along.

When she mentioned it to Thomas, he objected. "No, not a party. You know Rev. Talley preaches that dancing is a sin."

Lavinia poked out her lower lip. Suddenly, her eyes twinkled. "A social then — with games."

"Fine."

She considered the problem of food. In Savannah, all manner of seafood was available for special fare, but here — what? And the house . . . Rough-hewn, it would not take to polish and shine.

Oh well, Lavinia thought, no one around here has better — except Hardy Bryan. I'll do the best I can.

When the young couples began arriving on the evening of March 26, 1835, Lavinia was pleased with her preparations. The parlor looked special with arrangements of snowy dogwood and fragrant honeysuckle.

The games began with dumbo crambo, and laughter broke the tension as couples tried to act out titles of books and songs. Lavinia was surprised that the young men seemed to stand back in awe of Harriet. *Perhaps there is a problem in being too beautiful, after all.*

After awhile, the games lagged, and Lavinia sprang her surprise. "How many know how to play twistification?"

John William Mitchell was the only one who nodded. "I'll teach you," said Lavinia as she ushered the group into the wide hall. Micah, Nahum, and a new hand named Moses waited with guitar, fiddle, and banjo.

Lavinia stood on the third step and pointed directions. "Ladies line here. Gentlemen, there. Partners facing. Harriet and Mr. Blackshear, bow, clasp hands." She signaled for the trio to strike up a lively tune, and toes began tapping. "Now, swing each other around."

Still swirling, Harriet and James Blackshear grasped the hands of the next couple and continued to swing each person until they reached the end.

As the lines twisted and undulated again and again, Lavinia watched Harriet. She had an inner glow and charm besides her surface beauty. It was obvious that she had made a conquest because Blackshear brightened each time they were partnered again.

Satisfied, Lavinia reached for Thomas's hand. "Let's join the fun."

Thomas gave her a stern look.

Registering innocence, she replied, "Twistification is considered a game allowed for people whose churches might turn them out for dancing."

Thomas grinned, defeated, and swung her into the confusion.

When everyone was thoroughly exhausted,

Lavinia invited her guests to the table covered with delightful fare. Medallions of wild boar, sautéed, and served with thyme and sage sauce from Lavinia's herb garden were accompanied by tiny, beaten biscuits. The mushrooms alongside had been gathered by Julie who knew how to test them on white paper to see if they were safe to eat.

There was rabbit pâté made by mixing the roasted meat with rosemary and cheese, chicken salad with plenty of egg, and ham biscuits. For dessert, Miss Dolly had helped make fancy cakes, but everyone gravitated to Miss Elizabeth's biscuit shortcake overflowing with whipped cream and strawberries fresh from the woods. The young folks left stuffed full but singing as the buggies pulled away.

The genial mood warmed the widely spaced community long after the occasion, but in mid-June Harriet burst into Lavinia's house without knocking, calling out in a way that alerted Lavinia that something was wrong.

Harriet flung herself down on the floor beside Lavinia's rocker. "They say in Thomasville that hostilities have started again in the Florida Territory — an incident at a settlement called Hog Town."

"Isn't that nearly mid-Florida? That won't

bother us." Lavinia's voice was soothing, but she could not help asking, "What happened?"

"Seven Seminoles left the reservation to hunt and were encountered by a party of white settlers who commenced flogging them. Shooting began. One Seminole was killed, and there were several wounded on both sides."

Lavinia knew the Indians would seek revenge, but she pressed her lips together.

"James Blackshear has joined the militia," Harriet wailed.

"All our men have to give some time. Thomas served." She spoke brightly, but her thoughts were dark. *His ten days were the longest I've ever endured.*

"But not way down in the Florida Territory!"

"You're in love with him, aren't you?"

"Yes." Harriet began to cry.

Lavinia put her arm around Harriet's shoulder. "Has he proposed?"

"No." She snuffed. "But I think he will — if he doesn't get himself killed first. He's so serious about everything he does . . . With his uncle a general and his father a colonel, he thinks he must uphold the family name."

Harriet picked up Livy and cuddled her for solace, burying her face in the child's brown hair.

Watching her distraught sister-in-law hug the baby, Lavinia fully expected this visit to be repeated.

It was. Throughout June and July, the lovesick girl came. On a sultry August day, Harriet burst in animated again. "He's back!" She exclaimed, throwing her arms wide and then hugging herself.

"You look as if he's proposed."

"No . . . but he said he missed me. Oh, sister, he told me he loves me!"

Lavinia laughed. "Maybe he's working himself up slowly. Do you want me to have Thomas speak . . ."

Harriet shook her head. "Not now. He's disturbed about the report he brought. Six Indians grabbed the army mail carrier on the road from Tampa Bay to Fort King, near the center of the territory. Mr. Blackshear says they shot him, mutilated his body, and stole the mail."

"Why would they want the mail? Oh! They must have been the six who were shamed at Hogtown. Maybe things will quiet down now. They didn't just take revenge, they took exact retribution."

Suddenly Lavinia gasped, forgetting Indians as the baby she was carrying gave her a hard kick.

■ ■ ■ ■

Thomas watched Lavinia carefully as her pregnancy became difficult. At last in late November, she bore a son. She insisted upon carrying on family traditions by naming him Mitchell Francis.

Thomas feared the unnatural glitter in her eyes and the nearly frantic sort of happiness that seized her. He put off taking the cotton to Saint Marks as long as possible. But with the year ending, Thomas knew he could wait no longer. He must sell his money crop.

Before he made the trip south, he rode to Thomasville to explain to the storekeepers why he was late paying his bills. He was surprised to find men converging on the courthouse steps. He joined the group gathering around Daniel McIntyre, who had come from his plantation near the Florida line.

McIntyre shocked them as he said, "The scattered Indian incidents have exploded into what has now been declared the Second Seminole War."

McIntyre moved up to the courthouse porch where all could hear him before he related the sequence of events. "On December 28, General Clinch evacuated Fort King because of lack of supplies. He marched the garrison toward his own plantation, leaving only General Wiley Thompson and eight others at the fort. Osceola and his band attacked, killing Thompson with the same silver-plated rifle he had given Osceola for his help in keeping peace."

McIntyre waited as the men exclaimed over the treachery. Then he continued his grim recital. "Meanwhile, Clinch had sent a messenger to Fort Brooke on Tampa Bay, requesting help. Clinch meant food; however, Brevet Major Francis Langhorne Dade, expecting the worst, marched a column toward Fort King. Near Wahoo Swamp, Seminoles ambushed them, killing Dade and most of his command. The massacre was one of the worst defeats ever suffered by the United States Army at the hands of native people."

The news devastated Thomas. "What am I to do if I can't get to Saint Marks? I haven't sold my cotton."

McIntyre offered him some hope. "The west coast seems to be safe. Refugees are gathering at my plantation. You're welcome to leave your family at my place."

Thomas thanked him and hurried home to break the news to Lavinia. At first she surprised him by saying that being with new people would be fun, but when the time came for Thomas to leave her with the crowd at McIntyre's, Lavinia clung to him. He kissed her. They said nothing, but their eyes spoke. Each was more frightened for the other.

As Thomas escorted his wagons down the long road to Tallahassee and Saint Marks, he feared every moving bush. All the while he was conducting his business, he felt as if he were holding his breath. When he returned, he was relieved to see the McIntyre house intact, but he relaxed only when they were safely back at Greenwood.

January of 1836 came in with a freak ice storm. Everyone in the household had colds. Their new little son, Mitchell Francis, became croupy. Lavinia worried because Miss Elizabeth, at 72, insisted on helping with him. On January 31, the infant died.

As they buried the baby in the rain, Lavinia tried not to break down, tried to take hope from the resurrection fern growing on the brick wall surrounding the family graveyard.

In the days following, Lavinia had to hold back her heartache as she waited upon Miss Elizabeth. Already frail, she struggled to breathe as congestion settled in her chest.

Tossie tore an old sheet into pieces that she spread with a paste of dry mustard. The hot moist plasters placed on Miss Elizabeth's chest seemed to help. For a time, she sat up in bed and took a little broth.

Then she worsened. Thomas stayed by his mother's bedside as pneumonia threatened her life. Lavinia, Harriet, and Elizabeth, who had been summoned from Pleasant Hill, looked at one another and had to go out in the hall.

As they wept on each other's shoulders, Tossie put her arms around them. "Best now to pray for God's mercy," the big woman said.

During the cold night of February 27, 1836, Elizabeth Mills Jones died.

When they buried her in the Greenwood cemetery next to the babies, they placed a headstone quoting Revelation: "And I heard a voice from Heaven saying, Blessed are the dead which die in the Lord . . . that they may have rest from their labors; and their works do follow them."

Standing at the graveside with grief piled upon grief, Lavinia realized how much she had come to value her mother-in-law.

Astride Zeus, Thomas rode over his fields on a bright March day, sorrowful, worrying.

For eight months now, the war in the Florida Territory had escalated, and he wondered how to plan for the new year.

News traveled slowly, and they seldom knew how much threat they were living under.

I'm letting myself get too tense, Thomas thought as he felt hackles rise on the back of his neck. His hand slid toward his gun as he glanced back.

Someone is following.

Rascal gave a soft woof and wagged his tail, making Thomas pause. He laughed at himself as James Blackshear hailed him. They exchanged pleasantries, and then he asked his friend about the war.

Blackshear's face became more serious than usual. "The Seminole force has grown to over a thousand. More troops than the army, but that's not the problem. They keep crisscrossing the territory. Surprise attacks come, first from thick hammocks, next from open Pine Barrens where they conceal themselves behind fans of palmetto. They forced our men back into a swamp."

Thomas grunted.

"Florida has no roads. We have few maps. I'll tell you, Jones, I wonder if we'll ever end such a war."

"Will you go back, then?"

91

"No. The regular army has pretty nearly taken over. Our militia doesn't mix in well." Blackshear took off his hat and wiped his high forehead.

Thomas wondered why his friend seemed so nervous.

"It's — It's time I got on with my life . . . You know my prospects are good. I'm headed toward being the largest slave owner and the biggest planter around here. Rains have seasoned my land this winter, and I plan to plant every field in cotton . . ."

Thomas waited.

"My condolences on the loss of your mother. I know a wedding is not proper with your family in mourning, but Miss Harriet needs looking after. She can't live alone in such dangerous times . . . May I ask you for your sister's hand in marriage?"

CHAPTER V

Lavinia sang as she sewed, pushing the Seminole War out of her mind in her joy. She and Harriet had poured over the fashion plates in *Godey's Lady's Book* from the moment the magazine arrived. Now she was making tiny dresses for Mary Elizabeth, a serious six, and Livy, three, in the same pale blue silk as the bride's gown.

Lavinia looked at her daughters through different eyes now, thinking how exciting it would be when their marriages came. *I'm in my element planning social events,* she thought. *By then we'll have a proper house. We must have a grand staircase for brides to descend . . . Girls can be such fun!*

Her hands fell idle as she considered that she had set too much store in giving Thomas sons to perpetuate his name. *I must stop grieving. He seems quite satisfied with having only James. S*he smiled as she pictured the boy who resembled her with auburn glinting in his hair and freckles dancing on his nose. Like Rascal, James dogged Thomas's every step.

Sewing, cleaning, gardening, cooking filled every moment until April 21, 1836: the wedding day. It dawned without rain to keep guests from traveling the poor roads or to spoil the reception.

The flower girls fairly danced across the polished parlor of Miss Elizabeth's house, scattering rose petals ahead of the bride. How proud Lavinia was as Harriet entered looking perfect with huge puff sleeves and a boat neck emphasizing her tiny waist. *What beautiful creatures these Joneses are,* she thought when Thomas placed his sister's hand in James Blackshear's. Thomas stepped back, rocking Harriet's wide, ankle-length skirt, showing off her blue pumps with tiny heels. Lavinia held her breath. Livy thought the shoes were the cutest she had ever seen, and Lavinia feared her piping voice might announce this to everyone.

Without mishap, Harriet lifted her face for her new husband's kiss.

I wish Miss Elizabeth could see them. Maybe she can, Lavinia thought. She stirred out of her reverie. She must hurry. The reception was set up in her garden, which was a mass of roses.

■ ■ ■ ■

Thomas strolled through the grounds enjoying the feast the ladies had prepared. The ham, cooked in the Virginia manner, was especially to his liking. Lavinia had outdone herself.

I'm so glad she and Harriet have settled into a warm and compatible friendship. He had never figured out his wife's early resentment of his baby sister. He beamed across the crowd of family and friends at the happy bride. *I hadn't realized how pretty she is. With her hair up and roses and ribbons intertwining, she's a picture. I hope Blackshear makes her happy . . .*

At that moment Blackshear lifted a slender glass of creamy syllabub.

"A toast to my new wife," he said. "I promise to build you a grand mansion as soon as the threat of Indian burning is over."

The guests gasped, and Thomas frowned. Their expressions told him it was not the house that evoked surprise. They had chosen to forget the attacks raging south of them.

As the bride and groom rode away in a buggy dragging old shoes, the crowd threw rice; but worried whispers dampened their enthusiasm.

Thomas regretted that Blackshear had reminded them of war.

War remained in the forefront of everyone's thoughts as June's perfect days turned into July's heat and thunderstorms. In spite of the weather, the Seminoles waged a heavy campaign against the army. The Indians were far more able to move about the Florida Territory than the soldiers, and they could better withstand the summer diseases. At last the United States had to abandon some of its forts.

Thomas was too busy to worry. He had never seen such an abundant cotton crop. It looked as if every seed had come up. The big-leaved plants were flourishing. White blossoms, which turned pink as they faded the next day, covered each stalk with promise. When he laid-by his crop in July, having done all he could do but wait, he was eager for Blackshear to visit. For once, Thomas intended to brag.

However, when the bride and groom came from their home in Duncanville, twelve miles away, and Thomas showed his new brother-in-law his fields, Blackshear laughed.

"My crop is this good — or better," he

said, "Everybody's is. Best season we've ever had."

The two men continued to talk cotton, and they were planning harvest time when they returned to the house and sat down to the dinner Lavinia had waiting.

"Have you heard about the railroad?" asked Blackshear.

Everyone looked at him in surprise.

"From Savannah?" Lavinia asked, putting down her fork.

"No, no. From Tallahassee down to the harbor at Saint Marks. With all of the plantations in the area making banner yields, promising prosperity, a man names Chaires and a couple of others are backing it."

"A real locomotive like the 'Best Friend of Charleston' they built in South Carolina six years ago?" Harriet leaned up, glowing.

"Well, no . . . they tried that, but the weight sank the rails in the deep sand. This is more like the ones they've been using in English coal mines. Six mules pull cars on rails down the grade. They plan to have it ready by late fall. That will make it quicker and easier to get our cotton to market."

Lavinia turned to Thomas, and he could see that her eyes were frightened.

"Surely you can't go through Florida this

year with the Indians making constant surprise attacks!"

Thomas patted her hand, but before he could think of something soothing to say, Blackshear interrupted.

"We can get in and out quickly. Besides, the fighting is away from Tallahassee — along the Withlacoochee River — even over on the east coast at Saint Augustine and down at the southern tip near Key Biscayne."

Thomas spoke up quickly. "We'll make more profit this year. Before this, our cotton has gone to New York. Now a new merchant, R.H. Berry, is going to ship directly to Liverpool, England. I hear that money is flowing at Tallahassee and Saint Marks because of the war . . ."

Thomas broke off, wishing he could bite his tongue for speaking that word. "Uh, Lavinia, could I have another helping of that peach cobbler?"

Behind her back, he motioned to Blackshear who took the cue. The conversation was changed, and, Thomas hoped, forgotten.

However, that night when he and Lavinia were settled into the coziness of the tester bed, she brought up the subject again.

"Darling, I don't want you to leave home

with next fall's harvest."

He pulled her into his arms and kissed her. "Don't start worrying about something that's months away. By then things might be different. I hate to be gone from you a minute, but the only attacks on the Georgia side have been remote homesteads. The militia is doing a good job of guarding. You should be in no danger."

"But you . . ."

He silenced her with a kiss.

A few days later, Thomas felt himself choking on his words. On the hottest day in July, citizen soldiers of Thomas County met the Seminoles in a spirited skirmish near home at the battle of Brushy Creek. Then in neighboring Alabama, Neamathla led the Lower Creeks in a revolt that took 10,000 soldiers to suppress.

Concerned, Thomas met with a group of sixteen prominent planters. They signed a petition to Governor Schley, requesting protection, citing that the county was frontier on both its northern and southern boundaries. Georgia's governor, in turn, appealed for Federal troops to guard them.

When the news reached Greenwood that Neamathla had been arrested, Thomas thought Lavinia would feel safer. Instead, she cried when they heard that sixteen hundred Indian men, women, and children had been handcuffed, chained together, and forced to march ninety miles in the July heat to Montgomery, Alabama. From there, they were removed to the Oklahoma Territory.

"They say the ninety-four-year-old chieftain walked to Montgomery without a complaint," said Thomas.

"In spite of my fears," Lavinia replied, "I weep for such treatment of human beings."

Cotton harvest for the fall of 1836, progressed under the protection of two companies of the United States Army. By mid-December, all seemed peaceful, and Thomas felt he could leave his family without worrying.

As he prepared for the journey, Lavinia insisted he take Samuel and Augustus and some of the bigger men along for protection. At last her tears made him agree, but he could not leave his family unguarded. He told a few men to stay with the women and children in the quarters. Micah and Nahum were to guard the big house.

Rascal had already stationed himself beside Zeus. Just as Thomas swung into the saddle, James ran to his father's side.

"Please, Papa, let me go. I'll be nine at

Christmas, and I'm a good rider. I can fight Indians."

Thomas leaned down and ruffled the boy's hair. "You *are* growing up, James, but for that reason, I need you to be the man of the family *here*. Look after the ladies, son — you, too, Rascal. Stay."

The white head snapped up. The widely spaced eyes showed uneasiness. The big dog edged closer to his master's horse.

"I mean it, Rascal," Thomas said firmly. "Stay. Take care of Lavinia."

Rascal waved his plumed tail in understanding. Feet dragging with disappointment, he moved beside his mistress and lay with his head between his paws.

"We'll be fine," said Lavinia, blowing Thomas a kiss. "Just — hurry!"

The exhilaration of his bountiful harvest, and the excitement of the railroad carried Thomas to Saint Marks. The thrill of extra money swept him back north. Miles went swiftly as he dreamed of the home he could now afford to build for Lavinia.

Back at Tallahassee, war news set him worrying. Miles inched; Thomas fretted.

At last they passed the Georgia boundary. He took a deep breath. This was undisputed land because payments had been made to the Indians. They should be free from attack here.

Thomas looked back at his caravan of mules and wagons. The animals needed water.

"We'd better swing by the Purifoy place," he called to Samuel.

As they neared the plantation, smoke drifted toward them. The stench of burned flesh stung their nostrils. Thomas raised his hand to halt his crew. He eased ahead stealthily.

Charred remains of the house and outbuildings still smoldered. Thomas drew back as a horse nickered. Then he glimpsed the blue of cavalry uniforms. Young men stood about looking as horrified as he felt.

"Captain John Wilson, sir," the leader said, saluting him. "We arrived too late. Rev. Purifoy must have been gone on his circuit. They tomahawked Mrs. Purifoy and left her for dead." He pointed to the woman laid on a horse blanket under a tree. A man was working over her.

Thomas nearly gagged at her wounds as he knelt beside her. Mrs. Purifoy stared at him wild-eyed.

"They burned my children," she screamed. "The little ones would run out of the house and those fiends would throw them back into the fire." She fainted.

Thomas counted the mutilated bodies. "The whole family. Dead . . . No, there's another daughter — somewhere." He looked questioningly at Wilson. "Have you been by Greenwood?"

"No, sir."

Shouting to his men to follow, Thomas motioned to Augustus and Samuel. "Let's make haste."

Thomas flapped the reigns across Zeus's shoulders and clucked to him. The horse surged forward, sensing his master's urgency, ready to break his own heart for him.

Praying for his family, Thomas moaned, "Lord, oh Lord, how could I live without Lavinia?"

A cloud of black smoke boiled above the treetops of Greenwood. Thomas kneed Zeus. He gave a last burst of speed. Thomas cried out when he saw the cabins. Flames still leaped, engulfing everything in the quarters. The few men he had left lay about, dead. There was no sign of women or children.

Shuddering, he moved toward the big house, which, miraculously, was not afire. There he found Micah, shot, scalped. Nahum was a few steps from his twin, impaled with a three-foot arrow.

Thomas searched all the hiding places in the looted house and the grounds. He screamed until he was hoarse, "Lavinia! Lavinia!"

CHAPTER VI

Swirling smoke obscured Lavinia as she stumbled along with Mary Elizabeth clinging to her shoulder and Livy bouncing on her hip. Through streaming eyes, she tried to make out James, who seemed to be following Rascal.

Behind them, war whoops pierced the air. *I've always heard the word bloodcurdling,* Lavinia thought. *Now I know what it means.*

A sob escaped her, and she fell to her knees. Her back twisted as she protected her daughters from hitting the ground. Pain seared her, and she could not get up. She must. She had lost sight of James. *Do our lives depend on a little boy and a dog?*

"Oh, God! Help us. Save us. We can't do this alone," she cried out.

James stood over her. Solemnly he hefted Livy, whose feet dangled below his knees.

Mary Elizabeth stood tall. "I can run!"

Rascal nudged Lavinia. He ran ahead,

whirled, came back, and went forward as if beckoning them.

"He seems to know where he's going," said Lavinia. "We don't. We'll have to trust God and follow Rascal."

As they ran across an open Pine Barren, Lavinia prayed in snatches. *Be merciful to me, a sinner. Forgive my hardness of heart. Forgive my shutting you out when I needed you most. Help us, please.*

Throat burning, mouth parched, Lavinia scrubbed tears from her eyes, blinked. Rascal had disappeared.

Exhausted, Thomas sat down with his head in his hands. It was evident this had just happened. *Have the Indians kidnapped my family? Is there any hope they escaped?*

"My Julie, she'd run for the swamp," said Samuel as if he had read Thomas's mind.

"Not Miss Lavinia," replied Thomas. "She's afraid of alligators. James and Rascal — Rascal! Is it possible?"

Suddenly energized, he remounted Zeus. "Y'all search the swamp. I'll try over yonder."

Lavinia and the children had run beyond the smoke and the sound of screaming. She could see now. Before them was a dense hammock.

"A hiding place, James," she gasped, but when they reached it, encircling vines made it impenetrable.

Rascal reappeared at her side, nuzzling her hand with his wet face.

"Water! Show me, Rascal, show me water!"

They followed the dog and quickly realized he was leading them through an opening. Inside the hammock, Lavinia stood in amazement, staring at the open space that was as beautiful as a garden.

James tugged at her. "Com'on, Mama. That magnolia. It's like a tent. It'll hide us."

"And keep us warm."

They scrambled between the ground-sweeping branches and settled against the thick trunk. The stiff, evergreen leaves were lapped like shingles against the wind. Huddled close, with the girls between them and Rascal's heat warming their feet, Lavinia and James grinned at each other.

They had sunk into weary sleep when Rascal started bristling, emitting a grumbling deep in his throat. He inched forward on his stomach, peered between the branches, burst out.

Lavinia took in a breath and held it. It seemed she could not let it go as the magnolia parted.

Suddenly they were in the comforting circle of Thomas's arms. Kisses and tears and licks from Rascal mingled with babbled explanations.

With Lavinia and the girls on Zeus and James and Rascal proudly walking beside Thomas, they headed home.

Joyful cries greeted the family as they reached the homeplace. Their workers stood around the smoldering cabins, shivering as cold night air settled over them. Julie and the others had indeed been hidden in the swamp.

"Honey, can you manage?" Thomas asked quietly. At her nod, he called out reassuringly to his people. "We'll start rebuilding your homes tomorrow. For now, follow me to my mother's old house. Everyone can bed down there."

Lavinia went into her dark, cold home with a prayer of thanksgiving that it was still standing.

James built a fire in the bedroom. Mary Elizabeth declared she could dress herself and Livy in flannel gowns while Lavinia searched to see what food the scavengers had left. The Indians had stolen a wagon and carted out barrels of flour, sugar, and other supplies, but she found milk, eggs, and butter. The always-saved biscuits were gone from the pierced-tin-fronted pie safe. Her wooden dough bowl still held just enough flour.

Lavinia put the waffle iron in the bedroom fireplace to heat while she mixed the batter. By the time Thomas came in, delicious smells steamed out. The children gathered around the hearth and ate waffles, sitting on the floor. All declared it a feast.

Bed warmers prepared the children's sheets, and they were immediately asleep.

"I'm so glad our beautiful bed wasn't burned," Lavinia said as she let her hair down. She smiled at Thomas who had settled under the quilts. Rascal lay on his feet, but she did not mind. She scooted across from the fire and jumped into the space Thomas made for her.

Thomas snuggled her close. "My darling, you know I thought the army was protecting you," he said, burying his face in her hair. "Even so, I don't know how I could have left you alone."

"You didn't. I had James and your amazing Rascal and . . ."

"I couldn't live without you. I was praying so hard . . ."

As he broke off, Lavinia knew he was

unsure of her reaction, and she hurried to tell him. "And I had God. He was reaching down, forgiving me — even before I asked."

Thomas leaned up on his elbow, trying to see her face in the moonlight.

"Yes," she continued, "I opened my heart. I turned back to the Lord. He hid us with the smoke, strengthened us. I know now. No one can live real life alone without God."

As he bent over her, kissing her, she felt his tears wetting her cheeks. She responded to his warmth, murmuring, "I love you."

"I love you so much," Thomas said over and over as he smothered her with kisses.

They lay long in after-talk, unwilling to say goodnight. Thomas told her of the day Rascal had shown him the entrance to the hammock and how he returned often to this special place to pray.

"We must send to England for a royal mate for Rascal," he said. "Such intelligent breeding as his must be continued."

Lavinia dozed for a moment. She shook her head, trying to clear it. "Tell me about the cotton sale."

"A wonderful profit! We can afford to build — but . . ." his excitement dropped. "Should we? Must we give up our dream? What if we built our home and the Indians burned it — or — worse? Maybe we ought to move away."

"Nonsense!" Lavinia exclaimed, fully awake. She started laughing. "I couldn't leave my garden. Greenwood is home. This war won't last forever. Besides, the Bible says we are more than conquerors. The Indians can't defeat us."

"You goose. That's not what the Scripture means. It's a noble way of conquest by faith and patience rather than by fire and sword. As Christians, we are told we will have troubles, but they cannot separate us from the love of Christ Jesus."

"With patience and faith, we'll stay," Lavinia said firmly. She settled close against him. Then she murmured a last sleepy word. "Darling, in the morning, see about getting Rev. Talley to hold a service for Micah and Nahum and the rest."

The happiness that settled over Greenwood as 1837 moved forward made Thomas forget about the worries of the outside world.

Yet another general took command of the war. This one, Thomas Sidney Jesup, realized massed armies had no effect chasing small bands of Indians. He divided his men into groups that engaged the enemy, containing them in the Florida Territory. Georgia remained unmolested.

Thomas County, hidden in the pines, untouched by the new craze for railroads, remote from news, hardly noticed the panic that shook the nation. Over one thousand miles of railroad were built across the United States, necessitating borrowing by state governments and excessive extension of credit by banks. This caused panic, then depression. Banks closed, businesses failed.

However, on Greenwood, Thomas ignored it all, and his planting progressed peacefully. Spring rains turned his world into beauty as wildflowers sprang up and birds filled the air with song. In the lushness of May, the family's joy spilled over when a messenger arrived from Cedar Grove. They were invited to visit Harriet's first child.

Thomas listened in amusement as his excited brood rode along arguing if the baby would be a boy or girl and guessing what its name would be.

When they entered Harriet's bedroom, Thomas stood back, smiling. His children gathered beside the canopied bed as the beaming mother pulled back a receiving blanket. The room stilled as with one held breath.

"His name," said Harriet, lengthening the suspense, "is Thomas Blackshear. For you, dear brother."

Thomas swallowed emotion, unable to respond.

Lavinia enjoyed Harriet's company even more now that she was a mother. Her only regret was the long time it took to drive the twelve miles between their houses. They had to content themselves with chatting by letter.

The letters increased the next month when an eighteen-year-old girl named Victoria became Queen of Great Britain and Ireland on June 20, 1837. The sisters-in-law devoured and shared every tidbit.

Suddenly it was December, and the Blackshear family visited Greenwood for the birth of Susan Estelle Jones.

The men discussed their farming for next year, and the women planned their hoped-for houses. Happy as she cuddled her new baby girl, Lavinia felt her home was nearing reality. The brick pile was immense. Timber waited for foundation and rafters. The Seminole dangers were lessening because their strongest leader, Osceola, had contracted malaria in prison and died. It seemed safe now to begin building; however, there was still no available architect.

Then, in mid-1838, a letter came from

Harriet:

. . . Our neighbor, Jackson Jones Mash, has been on a trip to New York.

There he learned of an Englishman working as a joiner in Boston, I think he is only about twenty-three, but he is qualified as an architect, and he is willing to come south. I am thrilled to report his diploma from Queen's College is said to bear the signature of Queen Victoria! . . .

Lavinia could hardly wait for Thomas to be able to take a day off to drive to Duncanville. As they rode along Thomas voiced misgivings.

"I want something American — not English."

"Silly," Lavinia said, catching her lip in her teeth and grinning. "We don't have any stones. But I don't want New England either. I want something southern. Special."

When they met John Wind, Lavinia liked the look of him immediately. He had a broad forehead and straight, serious brows, but there was something about his hair combed neatly over his ears and his little bow tie that made her think he might be amenable to her wishes.

"He's mighty young," Thomas whispered in her ear.

"Yes, but give him a chance," she pleaded.

They looked at plans for the Mash house, brick with a balcony and round white columns. Thomas raised a quizzical eyebrow at her. She nodded enthusiastically.

"Mr. Wind," Thomas said, "we'd like you to visit us to discuss building Greenwood."

Lavinia knew her quiet husband was as excited as she because oxcarts loaded with lime and cement arrived from Saint Marks even before John Wind came to draw the plans.

When at last the Englishman was seated at their table, he looked from one to the other and asked what they had in mind.

"A house built to endure," said Thomas.

"I'd like a wide, deep porch," said Lavinia, her old shyness suddenly returning. "Those fat columns in Mr. Mash's plans looked lovely."

His deep-set eyes suddenly shined, and his face transformed as he smiled for the first time. "That's my favorite style, too. It's called Greek Revival. Your President Thomas Jefferson started it in the South. When he was in France, the first-century Roman temple at Nimes inspired him, and he drew the design for the Virginia state capitol. It was revolutionary — the first break with traditional Georgian style. He was the first architect anywhere in the world to design a modern functional building in the form of an ancient temple. Later, he created the awe-inspiring academic village for the University of Virginia."

Wind paused for breath and beamed at Lavinia. "I predict this is the beginning of a new fashion in architecture." He turned toward Thomas. "Don't worry. Greek Revival is so classically elegant it will never go out of favor."

Lavinia met Thomas's eyes, and they clasped hands. He squeezed her fingers and told the architect, "You may begin."

"Good. Then I suggest Ionic columns. I believe Corinthian would be too ornate for this lovely, simple setting." Wind made a quick sketch and turned to Thomas. "I follow some of Jefferson's ideas, but one thing about my work is unique."

He showed the drawing. "My columns are free standing. I place them on foundations directly on the ground."

"Instead of on the porch?"

"Right. You said you wanted the house to endure. In this humid climate, porticos rot and have to be replaced. If the columns are forward of the porch, they remain solid."

Lavinia listened as the men discussed interior brick walls for fire protection. Mr. Wind's clipped English accent amused her. After only four generations in Georgia, their families' voices had gentled. They elongated syllables in an effort to communicate with the patois of their servants.

When she had a chance for a word, Lavinia mentioned her desire for a grand staircase.

Mr. Wind outlined a broad central hall. Near the rear, a flattened arch supported by simple columns framed a winding staircase that rose on one side, curved upward, and turned from view on the opposite wall.

"Pretty," said Thomas. "But it looks mighty delicate. Is it substantial?"

"Quite. I agree about building to last."

When John Wind left with a promise of returning with completed drawings, Lavinia felt she would soon have the home of her dreams. She found out that such a building would take years to complete.

On February 9, 1839, when Lavinia bore a fat, robust son, she knew the time had come. "Dear," she said, stroking her husband's arm as he bent over the cradle, "Now that you are to be laird of a great manor, you should have a son named for you. I propose Thomas William Jones."

Thomas started to shake his head. Then he grinned.

Daily Lavinia grew more proud of her husband. He was beginning to make a mark in the development of the area. He constructed the first bridge across the Ochlockonee River, after which the route was known as Jones Bridge Road. With Thomas's support and ideas, the first sanctuary built in Thomasville, the Methodist Church, was completed in 1840.

Lavinia felt that she was maturing also. When Harriet's second child, Mitchell Jones Blackshear, died in infancy, she left her own children in the care of Julie to spend several days consoling her bereaved sister-in-law. She went again at the happy birth of Anne Elizabeth Blackshear.

The two women devoured newspaper accounts of Queen Victoria's marriage to Prince Albert Saxe-Coburg on February 10, 1840.

"Wouldn't you have loved to have seen her white satin wedding gown?" asked Harriet.

"Yes. I'm certain she's set a new tradition for weddings just as she has in government and morals and everyday clothing."

Harriet laughed. "Now that she's decreed that limbs won't be seen, we look like discarded fashion plates with our dresses above our ankles. We need to get some patterns and start sewing."

Lavinia sighed, "I s'pose so, but I don't know how I'll ever get my work done in tight-fitting sleeves and ground sweeping skirts. Besides that, the house is taking shape, and all I want to do is watch."

Lavinia found that she was not the only one wanting to watch the construction. She had difficulty keeping the children away from the temptation of brick mason Samuel Austin's mortar boxes; however, James, at thirteen, was a willing worker. He was fascinated by John Wind.

It amused Lavinia how the youthful architect set himself apart from the carpenters he had brought from New York. He directed the work dressed in a black dress coat and silk top hat. Soon two itinerant German carpenters were added to the crew. They worked in white shirts and bow ties to proclaim themselves master craftsmen.

Wind patiently taught James simple things like using a spirit level. When he had proved himself adept, he was allowed to sit on the wood-boring machine and turn the crank.

It fascinated James that the auger could bore holes at any angle, and he proudly showed Lavinia when he learned to insert a flaring tenon into a mortise to perfectly dovetail a joint.

At first she was pleased, but as summer's heat intensified, Lavinia worried that James was overtiring himself. One July morning when she went to visit the site, she was alarmed to see him sitting on a pile of lumber with his hands pressed to his temples.

"What's wrong, son?" she asked, restraining herself from throwing her arms around him.

"Just a headache, Mama."

By the time Lavinia had gotten him into the cool of the house, James's headache was intense. His fever was rising. Then he began vomiting.

"Mary Elizabeth," Lavinia called. "Find Daddy. Then take all of the children on the porch and play school."

Thomas rushed in and examined James, discovering his neck was stiffening.

"Herbs and home remedies won't do this time," said Lavinia. "We must have a doctor — but how? Tallahassee is too far."

"Don't you remember? I saw Doctor Edward Bradley's shingle at the entrance to his Pine Hill Plantation. It's only about twenty miles."

"Twenty?" Lavinia clutched her throat in fear.

"Zeus can cover ten in an hour."

A gurgle made them turn. James was struggling for breath.

"Julie . . ." Thomas said.

She ran from the room as he lifted his tall son. He staggered with the first step, then steadied. By the time they reached the yard, Zeus stood waiting.

Thomas had no need to command the stallion. He responded to the sense of urgency. They reached the Georgia line quickly, and then settled into a slower pace because the jolting had started James breathing normally.

At dusk they came upon a creek at a halfway point. Thomas reined the lathered horse and let him drink. He laid James on the ground and knelt over him, bathing his face and wrists. He heard no sound, but hackles began to rise on the back of his neck. He looked up. He felt like a rabbit trapped by wolves.

Around them towered a circle of Indians.

CHAPTER VII

Thomas kept his hands upon James with what he hoped was a reassuring squeeze. His own skin was prickling, and he was afraid to stand up lest the Indians circling them react too quickly with violence.

"My son very sick," Thomas said in a voice that carried more bravery than he felt. "I'm taking him to see doctor."

The Indians remained unmoving, but their eyes communicated one with another.

Thomas knew that after the battle at Tea Table Key, hostilities had temporarily ceased in hopes that the Indians would agree to leave the Territory.

These men probably don't know that, he thought, staying as still as he could. It was hard because the leader was rubbing a cloth over Zeus.

"You take fresh horse," the chief said, nodding. "Son very sick."

"I-I thank you," Thomas faltered, knowing he would never see his beloved Zeus again.

Stoic as they were, the group could not hide their admiration for his smooth English saddle and the finely embroidered quilt Julie had added in front to pad James's ride. With obvious reluctance, they put it on the Indian pony they had selected for Thomas to use. Then they carefully lifted James into Thomas's arms.

"I thank you," Thomas repeated, bowing his head toward each in turn.

The lively horse sped over the remaining miles to the Bradford land. Thomas's chest hurt, and he realized he had not been breathing normally until he saw a gateway with a swinging sign: *Dr. Edward Bradford, Pine Hill Plantation.*

James had fainted miles back, but as Thomas rode up the lane toward a large house, he felt renewed hope. Several people rushed out to help carry James into the doctor's office. When they laid him on a table, he began choking again.

"I don't like the looks of this," said Dr. Bradford, without preliminaries. "I must perform a tracheotomy."

"What?" gasped Thomas.

"Don't worry. It's been done for a century. I cut an opening into the trachea to let air into the tube to his lungs. It will look bad. You'd best wait outside, Mr. Jones."

Reluctantly, Thomas went into the waiting room and sank into a chair. Mrs. Bradford brought him tea and a plate of scones, but his hands were shaking so violently that he barely got the food to his mouth.

It seemed an eternity before Dr. Bradford admitted him. James was breathing quietly, but when Thomas touched him, new fear leaped. His body was rigid.

"His neck is stiff and his spine is sensitive," said Bradford in an undertone.

Suddenly James was wracked by convulsions. As they worked over him, James talked wildly of animals running across the ceiling. He did not know Thomas, and he cried for his mother. Exhausted, Thomas longed for Lavinia, too. By nightfall, the thrashing and vomiting stopped and James was completely paralyzed. He cried out if he was touched, so Dr. Bradford drugged him with laudanum.

Only then did the doctor turn to Thomas. "You must get some rest, Mr. Jones, or you will be a patient. My wife has prepared a room for you."

Thomas protested, "I want to remain at James's bedside."

Mrs. Bradford took him by the arm. "You

must get some sleep. Someone else will watch your son."

The next day, it was obvious that James could not be moved. Thomas wrote Lavinia what had transpired. Hospitality was gracious, but she must not to come. Travel through the Indian Territory was too dangerous for a woman.

After two weeks, James's pain lessened enough for Dr. Bradford to begin treatments with warm, wet cloths.

"If this eases him, you may begin exercising his arms and legs and think about moving him home," said Dr. Bradford.

"What about the other children?"

"Isolate James . . . just in case. Keep the others well fed and don't let them get overtired, but I doubt they will catch it."

"What is it?"

Dr. Bradford frowned. "I've consulted with the doctors in Tallahassee. Dr. W. W. Waddell, who is a noted physician from Pennsylvania, said that the disease has just been recognized this year. Epidemics have appeared both in Europe and America."

"Epidemics? Then the others . . ."

"No. It doesn't spread like smallpox. Often there will be a single case in a family or city apartment building." He sighed deeply. "The poison in the patient's system affects the spinal column and causes paralysis of the muscles. We just don't know the cause."

"Does it have no name?"

"It's been called 'a pestilence that walketh in darkness.' "

The mule team plodded slowly beneath the canopy of live oaks. Thomas drove the covered wagon he had bought in Tallahassee as carefully as he could. He knew that even though James lay on as soft a bed as he could fashion, each jolt must cause pain. Not once did he cry out. Tears stung Thomas's eyes as he thought of the courage with which his son had faced the ordeal.

The sun was shining, but Thomas shivered when they reached the place where they had met the Indians. He stopped, called out. All was silent, but he had expected no reply. As he released the Indians' pony, he knew that he was taking a chance that they might not find the animal; however, he had placed a pack of foodstuffs on his back.

When at last the wagon neared Greenwood, Thomas's relief was tinged with the dread of Lavinia's seeing how the muscles in James's left leg had shriveled into nothingness.

I don't know how I can tell her that the

doctor said he will never walk again.

Rascal's yelping pricked Lavinia's ears. His new mate, Queen Victoria, joined him in making noise, but Lavinia could still discern Rascal's voice seemingly speaking. The key word was joy.

"Thomas," Lavinia gasped. Only he could inspire that sound. She ran down the stairs and into the yard. Thomas was driving a covered wagon. As he stepped down, she flung herself into his arms.

"James?"

"Inside."

Beholding her son, Lavinia could not keep from weeping. As she smothered him with kisses the brave thirteen-year-old could no longer hold back his tears.

Thomas explained the treatments Dr. Bradford had prescribed. Lavinia began them the next morning. Trying to keep up a pleasant conversation, she wrung cloths from hot water until her hands were red, and she exercised James's limbs until her own shoulders and back ached. Pausing, she saw movement in the gloom of the hall. *I was sure the children understood they must stay away from James,* she thought, making a surprise jump into the hall.

Dark-skinned Joe tried to hide in the

shadow of the tall case clock. It struck ten, making the husky boy cry out. Hunched into a ball of misery, Joe was obviously hurting for his playmate. When he saw he was discovered, he pleaded, "Can't I help?"

Lavinia smiled at him. "Yes. Go and get more hot water."

When Lavinia began the treatments the next day, she kept seeing Joe out of the corner of her eye. At first he was sitting in the hall, but inch-by-inch, he moved inside the room just as James grimaced.

Lavinia had an idea. "James, Joe and I are going to take on your pain until the clock chimes the quarter hour. Joe, clench your teeth and hurt for his right side." She sat down. "I will hurt for his left. James you concentrate on letting the pain float off the bed into us."

They remained quiet until the old cherry clock tolled. Then they all had a relaxing laugh.

On other days, nothing gave James relief. Then Lavinia wished for Tossie.

The old woman had slipped away quietly in her sleep; however, she evidently had a premonition of her death because she had taught Julie her skills of midwifery and plants. The remembrance made Lavinia send Julie into the meadow to search for what the Indians had named "toothache plant." When the stem was peeled back and the stalk chewed, it gave relief for aching teeth for hours. To some extent, it eased James's pain.

Heat continued to blaze through October, but Lavinia felt it did not equal the searing in her heart as she watched James suffering. He lay stiff against the sweaty sheet. Only when the days melted into November did he make the slightest movements on his own.

One morning when Lavinia went into James's room to begin the treatments, she found the bed empty. He lay face down on the floor.

"Thomas!" Lavinia screamed, throwing herself over her son. He lifted a grinning face.

"Since I've regained the use of my arms, I'm teaching myself to crawl," James said. "If the house caught on fire, I'd need to be able to get out."

Thomas had bounded up the stairs from his office, and Lavinia was thankful that he could make a reply, even though his voice was gruff.

"That's a smart move, son. The right spirit."

"I think you've become one of the Jones

men," Lavinia managed to say, trying not to look at the leg that was merely one round bone.

Thomas cleared his throat. "I have a surprise, too. Rascal's a proud father. Victoria had a litter last night."

"Can I pick out one for my very own?"

"Of course. Do you feel like my carrying you outside?"

"Yes!"

As Thomas lifted James in his arms he said, "My, how you've grown!"

Lavinia looked into Thomas's eyes, and they passed the pain. Only James's right leg had grown. The left remained as short as it had been.

Her smile returned as she gazed at the picture her family made crowding around the dog's bed. James sat on a stool with the other children dancing about. Ignoring his deformity, James looked as happy as Rascal, who was nuzzling Victoria's head. She was intent upon the pups, squirming blindly, trying to nurse.

Lavinia put her arms around Thomas's waist and whispered, "James looks like himself again."

Early on a December morning, Thomas went into the yard and found Zeus standing there. He threw his arms around the stallion's neck, hugging him and stroking his velvet nose. Zeus's eyes looked tired, and he was thin; otherwise, he seemed fine. Full of happiness, Thomas talked softly, welcoming him home.

Suddenly a chill trickled down the back of Thomas's neck. It had been five months since the Indians took Zeus. He had not run away and found the trail this far. The Indians brought him . . . *How unnerving it is to realize they know where I live!* He drew a deep breath. *I must let the family see only my pleasure.* He turned Zeus over to Augustus and went to tell James.

He entered the bedroom to find the boy sitting up.

"That's wonderful news, Papa. It makes me feel so good that I want to see the new house."

"Certainly, son."

When they reached the building site, John Wind tipped his stovepipe hat and said, "Good morning, James. It's about time you showed up for work again."

"You've done so much without me," James exclaimed. "It's so tall. So beautiful."

Thomas looked at the structure through his son's eyes. The house now rose two stories. Four towering columns lifted the

131

spreading gable on high. Inside of that, the porch and balcony reached across the entire width.

I've been so worried, I had hardly noticed, Thomas realized. Suddenly he saw that James's color had risen, and he feared he was tired. Instead, it was because Mr. Wind had handed him a penknife and a piece of yellow pine, which was soft when freshly cut.

Wind had a knife and large piece of wood in his hand. "Don't tell about this. It's a surprise for your mum. I'm carving a cartouche for the tympanum."

Thomas wondered what he meant, but it did not matter. As he walked away, all he could think of was that his son was participating in life again.

I'll make James a little pony cart so he can come every day, he vowed.

John Wind brought his new wife, Beverly Donaldson, with him to the Jones's Christmas open house. Suddenly shy, Wind told Lavinia he had a surprise for her.

Mystified, Lavinia invited the guests to follow to the new house.

There, on a long table made of boards resting on sawhorses, something was concealed with canvas.

"It's a cartouche. If you like it I'll put it on the tympanum," Wind said, ceremoniously throwing back the covering.

Lavinia caught her breath. "How beautiful!" She ran her fingers over a large magnolia blossom. Eight smaller flowers surrounded it, and two more connected with spreading garlands. "You carved this lovely thing?"

"I helped on a little flower," James piped up.

"It's magnificent! Of course I want it on the front gable as the first thing guests will see. You know how I love magnolias. Thank you — both."

As the new year, 1841, progressed, Lavinia felt that John Wind had set out to keep her enchanted. Every detail of Greenwood was carefully crafted. Even though they had brought in new artisans, Wind insisted upon carving out the paneling for the parlor himself.

Lavinia was pleased that James continued to supervise whenever the wet spring weather let him feel well enough. He had established a bond with John Wind, but Lavinia realized by the sly looks that passed between them that something else was afoot.

On May fourteenth when she and Thomas

strolled in the garden, celebrating their birthdays and remembering their happiness here the day she had announced James's impending birth, John Wind called to them.

Expecting to see some new facet of the house, they turned and gasped. Tears sprang to their eyes, and they held to each other in disbelief.

James was standing. Aided by a crutch and splints strapped around his leg, no doubt whittled by John, the boy took two faltering steps and fell into his parents' arms.

A month later, on June 19, 1841, Lavinia bore her eighth child, a son they christened Henry Francis Jones. The children declared his round face and tuft of red hair too cute for the formal name. They called him Frank.

When the Blackshears visited for the grand occasion, Harriet exclaimed in delight at the looks of Greenwood.

"Oh, Thomas, it's the most beautiful house I've ever seen! Mr. Blackshear, can we hire John Wind to design ours, too?"

"Yes," replied Blackshear hesitantly, "but I don't want to build until the war is settled."

"Oh, it will never be over," Harriet replied with petulance.

Thomas winked at his sister. "I think the war is winding down. I heard that quite a few Indians have turned themselves in for removal to the West."

"Is this true?" asked Blackshear.

"Oh, yes. It seems Chief Coacoochee presented himself at Fort Cummings costumed as Hamlet. His entourage was dressed as Horatio and Richard III."

"How could they do that? They're uncivilized," said Harriet.

Thomas chuckled. "They robbed a baggage train of an actor troupe that was performing in the territory."

Everyone laughed at the picture that conjured, but Blackshear persisted.

"Do you really think all of the Indians are being removed?"

"Yes, some are surrendering, and the ones who've escaped have followed Billy Bowlegs into the Everglades. They are so deep in the swamps that nobody will ever find them."

"Then maybe it is time to hire Mr. Wind and start our house."

Harriet threw her arms around him. "I'm going to plant sunflowers everywhere. Their happy faces can help me celebrate!"

Just as Lavinia began to feel safe, they discovered the war was not over as they had thought. It dragged on, and in January 1842, Tiger Tail escaped and encouraged other Indians to resist to the last man. In April a band of warriors was cornered in a hammock. The army fired, but the Indians disappeared. It was considered the last battle. Throughout the summer, Colonel William Worth parlayed with the Indians and finally granted them homesteads. He declared the Second Seminole War over on August 14, 1842. However, Billy Bowlegs' band remained in the Everglades; consequently, the Seminole War never really ended.

Even as Lavinia felt relief from the fear of attack, she agonized as she saw her son try to walk. As James grew, the leg affected by paralysis did not. The small round bone, unbound by muscle, was eight inches shorter than its mate, lowering his hip, making his gait slow, rocking

On a hot September afternoon as she lolled on the back steps watching the children play, Lavinia felt consumed by fatigue that she realized was part depression because James remained so helpless after two years. He lay on his back on the cleanly swept yard with the puppy he had chosen sleeping on his chest. Rascal stayed beside them for a while. Then the aging dog began to prowl around, nervously snorting and rolling his eyes. Rascal could no longer run after Zeus or jump up on a wagon. The faithful Setter was terribly upset when Thomas left him, as he had now to go into town. Lavinia observed boy and dog with sorrow.

The young ones were unaware of any problems. Livy, domineering for a nine-year-old, bossed her little sister Susan and three-year-old Tommy as they romped with the rest of Victoria's litter. Twelve-year-old Mary Elizabeth dutifully followed Frank as he toddled after them, spending more time sitting down hard than walking.

James saw his mother looking at him and rubbing her furrowed brow. "Stop worrying, Mama. You're always saying we are more than conquerors. I won't give in. This thing won't lick me."

She tried to smile confidently at him, but she was glad when she saw Thomas returning with the mail. He was waving a letter high above his head and smiling so wide he looked as if he were about to burst out laughing.

CHAPTER VIII

Lavinia wiped the perspiration that beaded her upper lip, wondering why Thomas was so amused. *He's moving too fast for this heat,* she thought as he hurried across the yard waving the letter.

"You'll never guess." He gulped for a breath of the humid September air. "My little brother Mitch is finally engaged."

"Really? To whom?"

"Doesn't say. He's keeping that for a surprise."

"I wonder why?"

"We'll soon know. He's bringing her for a visit." He scooped up Frank, whose little round face glowed as he bounced about the yard on Thomas's back.

"Me, me!" cried Susan, a plump load at five. "Piggyback."

Lavinia pitched her voice above the din. "Well, it's time Mitchell married. He's thirty-eight, and he's made quite a fortune . . . Maybe that was wise before he was saddled with — as the servants say — 'a passel of chillun'."

Winded, Thomas dropped to the step beside her and nuzzled her neck. "When I saw you, I fell in love so hard that I couldn't have waited another minute. *And* — I wanted every one of these 'chillun'." He squeezed Susan, who was snuggled in his lap.

Thomas dropped his bantering tone and looked at her seriously. "Honey, I know I've put you through some terrible times here, but I couldn't have stuck it out without you."

"I wouldn't have missed one single day we've had together." Lavinia leaned over Susan and met Thomas's kiss. She felt her depression lifting from her shoulders as she hugged them both. With renewed hope, she smiled at James.

A few weeks later, October cleared the skies to such a brilliant blue that Lavinia kept bursting into song as she prepared for the betrothed couple's visit. Curiosity consumed her, and she ran to the door the minute she heard an approaching carriage.

Mitchell Jones, looking more handsome than ever, alighted from an elegant coach-

and-four. As he turned and held out his hand, he blocked her view of the young lady's face. Lavinia glimpsed her attire. She wore the latest fashion from her feathered bonnet to her ground-sweeping skirt, trimmed with elaborate braiding and held wide by crinoline.

The girl deliberately concealed her face with her parasol and did not lift it until she stepped onto the porch. Then she tossed it aside, and with an impish grin, she said, "Hello, Aunt Lavinia."

Convulsed with laughter at the surprise, Lavinia opened her arms to her sister Sarah's twenty-year-old daughter. "Eliza Ann Price! You scamps! Why didn't you tell us?"

Lavinia cuffed Mitchell on the chin. Thomas came around the corner of the house, and the brothers greeted each other with their usual high spirits. Eliza had the look of Lavinia's side of the family with dark auburn hair, but animation kept her features from being plain as the excited couple shared their plans to be married the following March.

In the ensuing merriment, Lavinia ushered them to the tea table. She basked in Eliza's appreciation that her scones were flaky and the clotted cream was cool. The dainty open-faced sandwiches and the tiny cakes were too small for Mitchell's appetite, but Lavinia had intended to impress an unknown lady.

She could not help a smug thought. I've laid out enough delights to have made Miss Elizabeth proud. But the men aren't even noticing. They were engrossed in conversation.

"The Central Railroad is nearing completion from Savannah to Macon," Mitchell said. "We let them get ahead of us."

"Yes," Thomas agreed. "It's taken years to build since the state legislature passed the bill allowing it. We need to get started on public meetings to promote a railroad here."

When Eliza could get in a word, she said, "May I see the magnificent house Mitchell has been telling me about?"

Thomas chuckled mischievously. "You passed it on the road."

Mitchell's eyes twinkled. "She never sees anything except me."

Lavinia motioned to Thomas to remind him they had agreed to show their guests the full vista.

As they approached through the alleé of live oaks, Eliza protested that she could not have missed it. Understanding dawned when they entered a gap where the gates would one day stand. The driveway curved through thick evergreens, and then it straightened to reveal the perfect view.

Eliza gasped. "Breathtaking," she said. Her eyes traveled up the white-sand walkway bordered by circular beds ablaze with chrysanthemums and blue asters. Next, magnolia trees created a frame for the towering house. The expanse of red brick was broken by a trellis. A Cherokee Rose on one side of the house and a Lady Banksia on the other seemed in a race to twine their evergreen leaves across to the balcony. Fresh white paint sparkled on the columns lifting the portico. Eliza's lips parted in a sigh.

"Magnificent! Oh, that magnolia blossom on the gable looks like a bride's cake. Please, Aunt 'Vinia, may we have our wedding here in Greenwood?"

"But-but . . . It's not completed," Lavinia gulped. She stood open mouthed. *I love Eliza,* she thought, *but I want Mary Elizabeth to be the first bride to descend the staircase.*

Thomas filled the awkward pause. "It only looks finished because of Lavinia's garden. We won't be living in the house in time for a spring wedding. Come inside. We're still working on the interior."

Eliza was not deterred by signs of workmen. The wainscoting and doorframes, all hand-carved by John Wind, were already painted. "It can't get any prettier," she declared.

"But the stairs . . . the stairs aren't . . ." Lavinia flung her hand toward the ladder-like steps that went to the upper story. "Mr. Wind doesn't want to build the cantilevered staircase as long as workmen are tramping up and down. They're still walling the bedrooms."

She cleared her throat and finished with finality, "The staircase will be the last thing built."

Eliza ran about. "The house is perfect without it," she said, fingering the carved arch that delineated the front hall from the back. "Those rough stairs wouldn't be seen if we filled this arch with an altar of greenery. I can just see it! Since so many Jones and Young families have settled in this area, Greenwood would be the perfect place."

Lavinia looked at her niece's sparkling eyes and threw up her hands. "How can I refuse?"

Lavinia felt guilty as she instructed John Wind not to build the circular staircase that was to be his pièce de résistance. To make up for the lack, she promised herself she would do everything else she could think of to make Greenwood perfect for next spring's wedding.

When November cooled the weather, Thomas let her use some of the field hands to add more shrubbery around the house. They responded to her warmth and did their best to please her. As Lavinia moved back and forth, making sure the plants were even, she heard a heavy sigh behind her.

Rascal, his back legs stiff, was trying to stay close to her. She took his beautiful head between her hands and looked into his rheumy eyes.

"Do you feel so bad, fellow? I wish I could make you better." She knew he was spending his time with her for comfort since he could no longer work with Thomas. "I tell you what," she said. "It might turn cold tonight. I'll fix you a quilt by the fireplace in our bedroom."

That evening as she and Thomas were making Rascal comfortable, she said, "It seems like yesterday when James was born and you got Rascal."

Thomas nodded. "Care has extended his lifespan. I can't believe it's been nearly sixteen years."

A few weeks later, the beloved dog did not wake up. The family wept as if Rascal had been a person. Lavinia worried about Thomas. Long after the others had dried their tears, he was still seized by a restlessness that would not let him relax. Even though many dogs had been bred from Rascal's lineage, he refused to claim one for his own.

When harvest was completed and Thomas and Rascal normally would have enjoyed hunting, he let some of his men bag game for the table.

Thomas was still wandering about when December came. Lavinia was not surprised when he burst into the log kitchen, where she and Julie were elbow deep in fruitcake batter, but his words astonished her. "Let's pack up the family and go to Tallahassee. Shopping!"

Lavinia was no less excited than the children as the family — including Julie — crowded into the carriage. She has long wanted to see Florida, the fabled "Feast of Flowers," and she peered from the window as, ten miles from home, they crossed the boundary and were out of the United States.

The Florida Territory looked little different from their part of Georgia except that she noticed more live oaks. As they neared Tallahassee, the ancient trees formed a magnificent canopy over the road. Long gray beards of Spanish moss, hanging from the spreading branches made her think of the armored explorers.

"Quiet down, children, and I'll tell you the exciting tale of the Spaniards who blazed this trail. They landed on the Gulf coast in 1539. It's thought they wintered at the site of the main town of the Apalachee Indians, which is now Tallahassee. That means they probably celebrated Christmas here like we are. On March 3, 1540, they headed into Georgia. They had two hundred horses, barking bloodhounds, squealing pigs . . ." Lavinia paused, and as she lowered her voice, the children's eyes widened. ". . . and silent Indian burden bearers chained together by iron neck collars. Missionary priests carried crosses . . ."

Lavinia spun out her tale until the children's sudden exclamations interrupted her. They had entered the territory capital.

"I've never seen so many stores!" exclaimed Mary Elizabeth. "I love it."

"Or so many people scurrying about like squirrels," James replied. "I like plantation life better."

Lavinia bit her lip, trying to hide her disappointment. *Tallahassee is just a little cotton market town,* she thought. "Oh, honey," she said turning to Thomas, "I expected it to be large and artistically laid out like Savannah."

Thomas laughed. "You forget it was just an outpost in Indian Territory. But I think you'll be pleased. The harbor at Saint Marks gives it access to the world. You'll find plenty of shopping — but first, the hotel and food."

"Food! Yea!" the children chorused.

They settled in quickly, ate, and put the babies down for naps under Julie's watchful care. Then Thomas dispensed coins to the older ones to purchase Christmas gifts for each other. Together they strolled down in the street. With eyes wide and mouths agape, they peered in shop windows. When the children found one they agreed upon, they went in and roamed the aisles with such deliberations that James could keep up in spite of his leg straps and crutch.

Thomas grinned at Lavinia. "This is going to take a long time. I'll supervise. You go have your fun."

Moving quickly, Lavinia concentrated on furnishings for Greenwood's wide center hall where Mitchell and Eliza's wedding would be performed. She ordered French wallpaper and Chinese rugs. She found two gilt mirrors, a velvet sofa, paintings . . . Exhilarated but exhausted, she realized that she would have to leave the dining room selections for another day.

When she returned to the hotel suite and sat with her feet up, considering her plunder, she felt Thomas gazing at her with his eyes crinkled with tenderness.

Thomas held out both hands to draw her near. "You're so happy and excited, you look as young as Mary Elizabeth."

On the ninth of March 1843, Lavinia stood at the double doors of her half-finished home, greeting guests. She had draped the archway with smilax vine and formed an altar beneath it with magnolia leaves.

As Eliza entered from the parlor and moved toward the altar with a soft swish of cream-colored silk, everyone sighed. The minister's words were stern, but Mitchell's eyes were twinkling. When he turned Eliza's veil back across her bonnet, he kissed her so soundly that the assembled Jones and Young families laughed.

Lavinia stepped into the dining room to check the reception delicacies. Surprised that no one was coming for food, she saw that guests had gravitated to John Wind. She realized that only Mitchell's charm and Eliza's vivacity were going to keep their wedding from being overshadowed by

Greenwood.

Thomas's sister Elizabeth, widowed by Joseph Neely and married again, was the first to claim the quiet little architect's attention. "I really like what you've created for Thomas and my sister Harriet," she said. "My husband Thomas Bratton Winn has already built a large house with a shed-roof porch, but you must add a columned portico in front of that as soon as you've finished Harriet's Cedar Grove."

Mitchell broke off from receiving congratulations to move beside her. "Look here, Wind, I've bought a new place for Eliza. You must build a grand house for Oak Lawn."

Lavinia heard Thomas's quiet chuckle from behind her. She leaned against him as others gathered around Mr. Wind. Several families from surrounding plantations spoke up. They had prospered and outgrown their first houses, and all wanted John Wind's designs for permanent homes.

Lavinia sighed contentedly. I won't be lonely or hungry for social life any longer. By the time the children are ready, there will be house parties galore.

Thomas's pleasure that his siblings wanted to follow his lead in settling the area and doing so with style and grace continued to spur him as summer rushed by in a blur of days when work lasted from sunup to sundown.

When he finally slowed at laying-by time during the thunderstorms of July, he realized that Zeus was having difficulty keeping up his pace. His black coat was salted with gray. It was time for him to retire and stay close to home. Feeling that he was betraying an old friend, but knowing he must if he were to sustain the best breeding stock, he purchased a new young stallion for the exorbitant price for five hundred dollars.

While horse-trading, Thomas decided the time had come to buy mounts for everyone. On a hot July morning, he and Lavinia went out to teach the children horsemanship. Mary Elizabeth had been riding astride in her tomboy days, but now that she was a young lady of thirteen, Thomas had bought her a sidesaddle and a small horse of her own. He had known that Livy, precocious at ten, would demand the same. Lavinia demonstrated the difficult art of riding with ladylike grace.

The little ones, Susan, Tommy, and Frank had been following alongside with James in his pony cart. They begged to ride horseback so Thomas placed all three on the broad back of faithful Zeus and walked them about the yard. James laughed and called out encouragements to the youngsters, but his eyes betrayed his deep sadness.

Thomas ached for him and wrote Dr. Bradford, seeking a ray of hope. The good man's reply gave none.

The disease has now been named Infantile Paralysis, but neither cause nor cure has been found. What walking your son can do will always be with a pronounced limp. There is nothing I can do to help him have a normal life.

He did not tell James about the letter, but he watched him with heaviness in his heart during the daily riding lessons.

One afternoon, James suddenly burst out. "Papa! I can't sit for the rest of my life." He called out to Joe, who always hovered near him, more friend than servant, "Help me. Lift me to a horse's back. I *will* ride!"

"No!" Lavinia shrieked. "It's too dangerous."

James laughed harshly. "More dangerous than you ladies riding sidesaddle, Mama?"

"More painful," she whimpered.

Fear rose like bile in Thomas's throat, but

he raised his hand to stop Lavinia's protest. *We must let go,* he thought. *He must have a chance to be a man.*

Thomas chose the gentlest mare. He and tall, strapping Joe hoisted the frail sixteen-year-old to her back, positioning his splinted leg as gently as possible.

Pain and emotion contorted James's face as he strove for courage to stay on the high perch. He spoke through clenched teeth. "I'm not steady enough, Papa. You'd better strap me on."

As James walked the mare about the yard, Thomas put his arm around Lavinia's shoulders to sustain himself as well as her. After a few turns, it was obvious that James was aching in every joint, and he suggested stopping and riding longer next time. When he lifted James down, Thomas's hands shook as he felt his son's clothing. It was soaked with sweat. Even though James insisted he would try again tomorrow, Thomas wondered if his body would ever be able to stand the punishment so that he could ride without overtiring.

Thomas was gratified that Lavinia enjoyed riding over their acres as much as he did. One day when they slipped off alone to check the crops, he said, "We need more land."

"Why?" asked Lavinia.

Even though they usually shared their thoughts, he could not tell her it was to bolster his hopes that James would one day ride and do the work of a man.

"I want to enlarge our herd of cattle," was all he could say. "There's a sheriff's sale coming up — a good time to get land at a bargain. I'll take you with me and show you how to bid."

In October of 1843, when the deeds were duly signed, Thomas and Lavinia rode over their newly acquired land. He watched her reaction to gauge her opinion. He was pleased that her dark eyes snapped with approval when they stopped at the Ochlockonee River to water the horses.

"This is such a lovely place," Lavinia exclaimed, gazing at the tea-colored water of the sluggish stream. It was nearly dry from lack of rain, and she pointed to the sandbar exposed in the middle.

"While the water is so low, we could wade out to that island. Let's get the children and have a picnic."

Lavinia awoke on the morning of November

5, 1843, to depressing gray skies. *Today is supposed to be a celebration,* she chided herself. Somehow the clouds gave her a sense of foreboding.

Mitchell and Eliza, still acting like newly-weds, had spent last night so they all could get an early start for the twelve-mile drive to Duncanville. Cedar Grove Plantation had a new screw press. James Blackshear had been bragging that the cotton press would turn out tightly compressed bales that would arrive in England still top grade.

During the entire trip, the brothers discussed the new equipment. Lavinia thought that she and Eliza might as well be in the next carriage with the children.

As their entourage approached Cedar Grove, a crowd was converging toward the gin on foot. Harriet's house-servants promenaded in their Sunday best hoop skirts and parasols. Field hands sang spirituals as they came to join the fun. As their deep voices rolled, their feet kept time to the rhythm. Cedar Grove's people were ready to applaud the first square bale. They knew that cotton made all, black or white, live well.

As Lavinia alighted from the carriage into the mélange of men and mules and machinery, she was caught up in the music, but she felt Eliza shrinking behind her.

"I've been spending harvest time in Savannah," Eliza confided, clenching her fists over her heart. "This equipment is so . . . so . . . frightening."

Lavinia laughed. "I'll show you how it works."

Taking Eliza's elbow to guide her through the crowd, Lavinia led her toward the two-story gin house. One end of the structure was open, a roof supported by posts. In this space, two sweating mules shackled to a shrieking wheel circled endlessly.

Lavinia shouted close to Eliza's ear, "Their force moves that belt slanting up through the ceiling. It's attached to a small wheel mounted on the gin. Would you like to go up and see the actual gin?"

"Yes," Eliza grinned. "I ought to know what Eli Whitney's marvelous inventions looks like, since it crowned cotton king."

Lavinia smiled in agreement as they climbed the skeleton stairway. "You're right. As long as the seeds had to be pulled from the lint by hand, the South could not have out-distanced the North in millionaires like we have. Neither could we have supplied the looms at Lancashire that have under girded Queen Victoria's English economy."

As they entered the dim room, Lavinia pointed to a wooden box about as wide and deep as she could spread her hands. "That's the actual gin."

Eliza gaped. "That little nothing?"

The ginner laughed at her as he emptied another basket of cotton over the top. "But this took an inventor's brain. See how the saw pulls the fibers through the ribs? The seeds fall out the front and the lint goes down the chute to the room below. From there, the lint is toted to the press."

They looked out the window and saw Harriet standing below with two-year-old James Mitchell Blackshear in her arms. He was trying to catch one of the luminous puffs of cotton drifting from the chute room.

Lavinia marveled at Harriet's serenity in spite of the ear-splitting noise. Her lace shawl, held by a cameo, almost concealed the fact that she was expecting another baby. Every hair was in place, and as she lifted her eyes, Lavinia thought they were tranquil pools.

Harriet motioned. "Come down," she called. "It's time for the press to begin its mysterious task."

They followed men carrying split-oak baskets of cotton lint to an open structure. From a pagoda-like extension above the roof, a shaft made from a heavy beam extended outside its perimeter. Two mules were harnessed to it, waiting.

Poised in the center, a tremendous log, which was carved out to form a giant screw, hung over a three-by-five foot box fitted with metal bands and white bagging.

The box was big enough to conceal a child, and Eliza's fear suddenly infected Lavinia. She counted her little ones. Thomas was too interested to pay attention to Tommy, but he was tagging along after his father as usual. Frank perched on Julie's hip while Susan shrank against her skirts. Mary Elizabeth pulled Livy back from the mules.

Not fully relieved, Lavinia looked at the workers' faces and realized that everyone felt the tension as men threw cotton into the opening. They closed the door. Lavinia held her breath as James Blackshear motioned everyone back and gave the command for the new screw press to start.

Lavinia stood transfixed as the mules circled, turning the massive shaft. The screw turned, tightening, compressing the cotton in the box. A shout. Something wrong. Mules backed. The ram lifted. Blackshear opened the door and smoothed out the cotton of the half-finished bale. He signaled to begin again.

The screw tightened. Someone screamed,

"The shaft is breaking!"

The shaft snapped in two. Freed from the mules, the long end spun backwards, unwinding the screw. Whipping around, the shaft struck James Blackshear on his temple, flinging him through the crowd. Men stared dumbly as he fell on the ground, landing like a rag doll.

Lavinia whirled toward her sisters-in-law. A shocked Eliza clutched the Blackshear's two-year-old. Harriet lay sprawled, her face as white as her husband's.

CHAPTER IX

Lavinia sat beside Harriet's canopied bed, feeling numb from shock. Harriet's unconscious form looked as if it had been carved of Carrara marble. The case clock in the hall ticked the minutes so slowly it seemed it would stop. When the chimes struck the hour, Lavinia jumped. Harriet did not move.

Lavinia wet the cloth and wiped her pale face again. Harriet's dark lashes fluttered. Her limp form stiffened; she sat bolt upright.

"James! I must go to him!"

"Rest dear," Lavinia whispered, easing her back. "It's all right. Mr. Blackshear isn't suffering. He . . ." She drew a shuddering breath. "Darling, he did not wake up. He never knew he was hit."

A sob tore from Harriet, and she sank into the pillows. Tears seeped beneath her closed lids. "Oh, it can't be." She wept softly for a while and then whispered, "What shall I do with no one to love me? How can I live without him?"

Lavinia had seen James Blackshear as cold and unfeeling. *I never realized how deeply Harriet loved him.* She searched for something comforting to say.

"You have your children. Thomas and I love you. You know we'll help you."

"But-but Mama's gone, too. There's no one to care day by day — how I feel — what I think. I've no one to cherish me."

Lavinia wiped the tears running down her own cheeks. "It's so hard, but remember what a proud man he was. He would not have wanted to be bedridden. He'd have preferred . . ."

She reached for Harriet's hand and laid her head against the bed, realizing her presence meant more than words.

It's so tragic, but I know now that God makes no mistakes, Lavinia thought. The image of her son James, struggling to ride a horse, swam before her eyes. We don't know why things happen. He, as well as Harriet, is destined for a sad and lonely life, but what character he has developed from having to depend on God!

Harriet's hand felt icy in hers. Lavinia knew she must control her own emotions. She stood up, chafing Harriet's cold fingers, looking at her lovely face contorted with pain.

Harriet is as bright as she is beautiful. She doesn't think she can handle this, but I know she can. She cast her eyes upward. How can I help her to find the strength, Lord?

Suddenly, Harriet spoke with calmness born of shock. "I must see to the children." She started to rise, clutched her side and cried out. Her writhing had the unmistakable mark of labor.

Lavinia ran into the hall, shouting, "Someone fetch the midwife."

Thomas rushed up the stairs, looking ashen from making funeral arrangements.

Lavinia threw herself against him, and even when his arms closed around her, she could not stop shaking.

"Her baby is coming too early," she said against his chest. "I'm afraid she won't fight. She doesn't have much will to live."

Harriet screamed.

Thomas thrust Lavinia aside. "I'll try to encourage her. You get some help. Quick!"

By the time she reached the first floor, Harriet's maid and midwife were coming at a run. They did all they knew to relax her, but Harriet's labor was far too brief. Emily was born tiny and frail.

Lavinia remained at Cedar Grove until Harriet could stand a trip, then they moved her to Miss Elizabeth's old house so that she and Thomas could look after her and the children.

Lavinia managed to make Christmas as happy as possible for them, but on January 3, 1844, she was forced to stop waiting on everyone when she, too, gave birth to a baby girl. Her ninth child, Florence was long boned and robust.

Lavinia lay with Florence in the curve of her arm, looking at the red glinting in her hair and listening to her smacking as she nursed.

What have I done, she thought. *She's going to be as horse-faced and gangling as her mother. How can I keep her from being jealous of dainty Emily?*

Six weeks later, after days of cold, gray rain, the sun came out at last. Lavinia stood at the bedroom window, blinking at the brilliance, smiling at quince that dared the cold. In front of the scarlet bushes, daffodils stood stiff and stately as if trumpeting that spring was here.

Thomas came in. He dropped a kiss on Florence in the cradle before stepping up behind Lavinia He enveloped her in his arms and kissed her ear.

"I feel the urge to plant," he said, looking out at the sunshine, "but I know winter will make another appearance."

"February always does its best to fool us," she replied. "Spring fever is upon me, too. I need to do something."

Thomas's familiar chuckle made her turn to face him and search his twinkling eyes. She asked, "What are you up to?"

"I've had the men carry in the rest of the new furniture. John Wind says the last touch is done. The staircase is complete. When you're strong enough, we can move into Greenwood."

Happy tears filled her eyes. "I can hardly believe our dream has come true! I'm ready now. We must all put on our Sunday clothes and walk in like first-time guests, through the front garden."

As the family climbed the steps to Greenwood, even the little ones remained in awed silence. Thomas carried Florence in the crook of his elbow. He made as if to open the double doors and then stepped back and bowed to Lavinia.

"You are the mistress of the manor house. You do the honors."

Lavinia tried, but they were locked. Her

puzzlement was short-lived because she detected a chuckle deep in Thomas's throat. He reached in the skirt of his coat and drew a package from his pocket.

Opening it, Lavinia took out a mother-of-pearl broach set with hanging gold key chains. "This is the prettiest chatelaine I've ever seen," she said. There was room for all of her household keys, but for now it held one. She unlocked the door and fastened the broach to her waist. Quietly, the family stepped inside.

"God bless our home," Thomas prayed. "Help us to make it a place of peace and joy with thee always at the center. Amen."

Then three cheers erupted, and the children scattered. Frank ran up and down the hall, talking so fast that no one could understand him.

Lavinia let him go. She drank in the magnificence of the winding staircase. Framed by the pillared arch, it hung suspended from the ceiling on the left of the hall as if by John Wind's magic; then it curved across the back and down the opposite wall.

Suddenly, feet appeared at the top of the stairs. Five-year-old Tommy came whizzing down the banister.

"Catch him, James," Lavinia shrieked

before she thought. Livy and Susan ran back from the parlor and clutched her skirts.

James laughed as he braced with his crutch and grabbed Tommy. "I wish I could do that."

Heaving a sigh, Lavinia turned to Mary Elizabeth, who had just celebrated her fourteenth birthday and was blossoming into the Jones beauty.

"You must practice gliding down the stairs gracefully," Lavinia told her. "I've dreamed of you coming down as a bride. You'll be breath-taking."

Mary Elizabeth giggled. "Just who have you picked for my groom?" Suddenly her face clouded. "Oh, Mama, I'm liable to be a spinster way out here in the middle of nowhere."

Lavinia lifted Mary Elizabeth's chin with a firm hand. "Your prince charming will find someone as special as you — when the time comes. For now you must learn to become a gracious lady. I'd best send to Savannah for a tutor."

Six weeks after they had moved in, Anna Eliza Knight arrived. Small, slim, with skin two shades lighter than Julie's, Anna moved with aristocratic bearing. Her neat hair was not turbaned like the other servants.

Lavinia liked the soft, sweet tones she used for instructing the girls. She peeped in occasionally as Anna coached Mary Elizabeth, Livy, and even little Susan in the art of walking with books balanced on proud heads. She taught them to sit with ankles crossed and one hand placed gently on the palm of the other.

Satisfied that the lessons were progressing well, Lavinia placed trusted Julie in charge of the rest of the household retinue and turned her own attention to hanging draperies and placing Wedgwood and porcelain treasures.

By April the last picture was hung and the new growth of the garden was a glow of yellow green. Iris added blues and whites against a watercolor sky. Roses were budding.

One morning at daybreak, as Lavinia awakened to mockingbirds singing in the pine trees filling the air with intricate melodies, she said, "Now is the perfect time."

"For anything, yes, but what in particular?" Thomas replied, pulling her close for those tender moments before they had to get up.

"To have an open house and invite everyone from the surrounding plantations."

■ ■ ■ ■

Lavinia was pleased to have Harriet nearby to help with fixing refreshments and flower arrangements, but as they stood putting the last touches on the bowls of roses, her joy in the party was suddenly dimmed at the sight of her sister-in-law. Garbed in black crepe, Harriet looked small and forlorn. She was only twenty-seven, but her vibrancy had vanished.

Lavinia stopped with a rose in mid-air. For weeks Harriet had talked of moving back home, but she lacked the energy to start. Now an idea came to Lavinia.

"Sister, why don't you stay in Miss Elizabeth's house permanently? After all, it was your childhood home, and you know we love having you."

Harriet looked at her dumbly, and she fumbled with the flowers.

"You could sell Cedar Grove," Lavinia continued. "It's the largest plantation in the county and could surely bring enough proceeds for you to live without lifting a finger."

Harriet sighed. "Cedar Grove also has the most people. What if someone uprooted them — or split up families? Oh, I'm so torn. I want my children to be brought up in gracious living like your lovely Greenwood . . ." She sniffed. ". . . But I told Mr. Wind to stop work at Cedar Grove. Our new house is the skeleton it was when the accident . . . when my James . . ."

Lavinia opened her arms and held Harriet close. "I can finish this. Go lie down. Wet a cloth with lavender water and put it on your forehead. Rest so you can enjoy the guests when they arrive."

Carriages rolled down the approach beneath the live-oak canopy before the appointed time. Guests spilled across the porch and into the hall where they stopped in amazement. Lavinia's secret smile threatened to give away her duplicity as friends gasped at the addition of the magnificent staircase.

Lavinia drifted through the parlors greeting guests. In the dining room, she was smug because, of all the food on the bountiful table, her caramel cake was disappearing first. They did not need to know that she had thrown away many batches of hard lumps before she had mastered the art of browning white sugar in an iron skillet. Lavinia intended for her caramel cake to become known as best in the county.

People are eating it and coming back for

seconds, but do they even taste it? Lavinia wondered. They are all so engrossed in conversation about Florida's petition for statehood.

After an hour, Lavinia slipped into the nook behind the stairs to rest her feet. Eliza followed her.

"Aunt 'Vinia? I don't understand all this fuss about the Florida Territory. Only Indians can live in the middle with the fevers that come from the miasmas rising from the swamps. The coast is good-for-nothing sand. Why should it be a state?"

Lavinia laughed. "You've heard right about the peninsula, but you've never been to Tallahassee. The fertile red hills surrounding it are covered with plantations of rich and famous, even royalty. Prince Murat, the son of the King of Naples and Napoleon's sister Caroline, built a mansion called Lipona for his wife Catherine Willis. She is a great-grandniece of George Washington."

"Imagine that!"

"The area has settlers from Charleston and the Old Dominion."

Eliza giggled, "And those Virginians think they're royalty, too."

Lavinia nodded. "Thomas has met many fine families while down there selling his cotton — the Gadsdens, the Gambles, the Whites. His special friend was the late Benjamin Chaires. Major Chaires is said to have been Florida's first millionaire."

She slid her feet into her shoes. "We'd best be getting back . . . By the way, have you seen Harriet?

"Not at all."

"I'd better check on her. Will you hostess for me a little while?"

"Certainly"

Lavinia found Harriet still in bed. She bent over to kiss her cheek and felt the tear-soaked pillow.

Harriet sighed. "I just couldn't face the gaiety. When it's people I haven't seen, they give me too much sympathy or want to know all of the details of the accident. Then I can't talk without breaking down."

"I thought the party would cheer you up. I should have understood," said Lavinia with a reassuring hug.

"I've been lying here thinking that you're right. I'll move back in Mama's house so I won't have to face the world." She looked completely hopeless.

Oh, dear, Lavinia thought. *How can I undo that mistake?* She picked up the Bible from the bedside table and held it, praying for guidance.

"I was wrong. I was selfish, wanting you here. You have your children to think about — and your people. You're young. Smart. A good horsewoman. You can ride and advise the overseer. You won't grieve as much if you're busy. Thomas will help you get started planting the cotton. Prove you have brains as well as beauty. Prove a woman can run a plantation."

Harriet's fingers pressed her temples. "I don't know."

"You love sunflowers . . ." said Lavinia, riffling the pages of the Bible. ". . . because they lift their blossoms to the heavens and turn all day, keeping their faces to the sun. Take hold of Philippians 4:13." She read, " 'I can do all things through Christ who strengtheneth me.' " She put down the Bible and squeezed Harriet's hands. "Keep your eyes upon the Son of God."

Throughout the spring and summer, Lavinia and Thomas visited Cedar Grove. They often found Harriet riding over the plantation, directing the field hands with baby Emily in front of her in the saddle.

Thomas complimented how well she was following his advice on handling the labor and planting the crop.

Lavinia rejoiced that Harriet was facing the world. She still looked sad, and Lavinia saw that grief occasionally did overwhelm her, but for the most part, she seemed to be winning her struggle to rise above it.

In the fall, John Wind and the artisans who had worked on Greenwood started back to work, creating a similar Greek Revival mansion; yet, Cedar Grove had distinctive details such as a small balcony suspended over the front door. Already the gable end was boasting a sunflower.

Lavinia loved Christmas. Celebrating in their new house made this year special. She began preparations in late November soon after the sweet potato crop was dug. Eager to try out the oven built into the brick wall of their new kitchen house, she filled it full of potato pies.

The scent of cinnamon drifted into the yard, enticing Thomas and the children into the building. Thomas looked in the oven.

"You're making so many pies there won't be a sweet potato left on the place," Thomas teased.

"We'll eat them," said James as he settled at the big table. The little ones clustered around him to wait because this was their favorite pie.

172

Mary Elizabeth said, "Isn't it time for a family shopping trip to Tallahassee? I think that should become an annual affair."

Everyone agreed.

"We'll go as soon as I get some fruit cakes made so they can be mellowing," Lavinia promised.

Early in December — too early for safety's sake — came the quest for the perfect tree. The family piled into the wagon and rode along a creek where red cedars grew. The children insisted upon examining every tree. Each child had his say.

Lavinia smiled, knowing this was part of the fun, certain that Thomas would subtly direct their choice to the perfect size for the parlor.

The tree half-filled the wagon, but holly, magnolia and pine boughs were piled around the children, too. They stopped to gather a basket of sweetgum burrs. As evening fell, clumps of mistletoe in the top of a pecan tree were silhouetted against the sunset. Thomas shot down two large pieces. They rode back singing, "Joy to the World."

At home, they carried their treasures into the kitchen. Lavinia made hot chocolate while James perched on a stool and shook the long handled popcorn popper over the fire. Mary Elizabeth and Livy made ready to string the fluffy corn. Florence, who would soon have her first birthday, had gone to sleep during the singing. Thomas bedded her in a drawer. Then he helped Susan and Tommy dip the prickly sweetgum burrs in paint to make star-like ornaments.

Lavinia suddenly realized that she had not seen Frank since he drank his chocolate. She found the roly-poly toddler under the table on the brick floor sound asleep.

"Bedtime," she called to the rest of the children. "Finish your work and lay it out to dry. Tomorrow night we'll trim the tree."

The next day, Lavinia and Mary Elizabeth made swags of pine to outline the curve of the banister. They placed sprigs of holly on every picture in the hall.

When Thomas came in from work, the family gathered ceremoniously around the tree. The hand-made decorations went on first. Lastly, Thomas fastened small candles to the tips of the branches.

On Christmas Eve the candles were lit. Thomas remained close to buckets of water and sand just in case of fire. After the children hung their stockings, Lavnina read Clement Moore's poem, "An Account of a Visit from St. Nicholas." She changed her voice and made gestures to the delight of her little ones. Before bed, Thomas read the Christmas story from Matthew and Luke.

The next morning the halls rang with, "Christmas give!" soon after daylight. Feet scampered down the stairs.

Thomas stretched and said, "Christmas give." Lavinia laughed as he claimed his kiss.

Putting on dressing gowns, they pocketed coins, knowing that servants would be popping out to surprise them with, "Christmas give. I seed you first." They must pretend to be caught and dispense the silver. Hand in hand they went down to see what Santa Claus had brought.

Later, around the dinner table laden with baked ham as well as turkey and dressing, Lavinia felt especially thankful. They joined hands for the blessing, and then she said, "Now that we've celebrated Christmas here, I feel that Greenwood is truly home."

CHAPTER X

Moonlight played over Lavinia's happy face as she sat in the garden of Verdura, the late Benjamin Chaires' nearly ten-thousand-acre plantation east of Tallahassee. The March night was mild, and as she waited for Thomas to bring her a cup of punch, she reflected that it was pure pleasure to be among flowers she did not have to weed and guests she did not have to feed.

Especially a place as lavish as this, she thought. How delightful that the signing of the bill that admitted Florida to the Union on March 3, 1845, had touched off celebrations!

This house party was being hosted by Benjamin's widow, Sarah. The Chaires sons and daughters, some of whom had established their own plantations forming Chaires Community, were all in attendance. Lavinia knew that in Benjamin's lifetime, he had established the Central Bank of Florida, constructed the railroad to Saint Marks, and financed the first vessel built to ship cotton directly from Saint Marks to Liverpool and short-circuit the Yankee middleman. *There is no telling what his children are accomplishing.*

Lavinia looked up at Verdura in wonderment. Ten columns on both east and west towered three stories high, supporting balconies on the second and third floor. Over the south-facing front porch, a white banner with letters formed of greenery proclaimed "State of Florida." The Greek Revival mansion was ablaze with light from each of the fifteen rooms. In the formal garden where Lavinia sat, lanterns hung in the shrubbery. Even the live oak grove surrounding the house was bright from bonfires.

Lavinia reveled in being part of this. She had a fashionable new wardrobe, and she felt that, at thirty-five, she looked better than she had in her life. Her hair had darkened and her face and figure had filled out to pleasant proportions. Her green moiré ball gown bared good shoulders above three-quarter-length sleeves of fluttering lace. She smiled coquettishly as Thomas approached.

"Whew!" he said. "It's good to get out in

the cool."

"I'm glad we came," she said, taking the cup he brought. "Even if I did have to drag you away from the plowing."

Thomas frowned, but as she reached up and smoothed the furrows between his bristling brows, he relented. "I guess it's mostly that I hated to come to Benjamin Chaires' house now that he has passed away. I suppose we do need to celebrate free access to the ocean through a real state — but I should be working."

Lavinia pinched him. "Here we are breathing the heady perfume of tea olive and you're thinking of work."

Thomas chuckled. He nibbled at her shoulder and bent her backwards for a passionate kiss.

"Thomas!" she exclaimed when she could catch her breath. "Someone will see." She patted her curls, not really displeased.

"I thought you came here wanting romance."

"Well, I did — but really for Mary Elizabeth."

"What? She's just a child!"

"She turned fifteen in January. Have you looked at her tonight? She's in love with love, and it behooves us to make certain she has suitors from acceptable families."

"Now you've spoiled the party for me. I was already displeased about the dancing."

"Oh, now. This is not the 'kicking up the heels' type that was scandalous when we were young. It's an elegant cotillion with many couples interacting in formal patterns . . . We've cooled off, and I hear the orchestra tuning up again. If you'll feel better, let's go watch."

They climbed twenty-five steps to the entrance and stood in the doorway. Verdura was one hundred feet wide across the front. Two downstairs parlors and the hallway had been cleared of furniture to make the ballroom eighty feet long. Thomas frowned, trying to spot Mary Elizabeth amid the swirling of spreading skirts.

Women's fashions are so silly nowadays, he thought. Since they started putting steel hoops in their petticoats, they move about like so many bells trying to ring.

Suddenly he realized that his own daughter had passed him twice as the group formed changing figures. He suddenly glimpsed her glowing face as couples ducked out from under arched arms.

He swallowed hard, feeling sick. *Lavinia's right. Mary Elizabeth's a young lady.* He had not seen her in her ball gown. It bared her graceful neck and arms except for tiny sleeves and short gloves. Her black hair bobbed about her face in long ringlets. He was glad that she was beautiful, but the fact that silk flowers cascading from her shoulders to her waist emphasized her blossoming figure made him uncomfortable.

I'm not ready to give her up.

The music assaulted his ears as he watched. He relaxed a bit when he saw that partners changed constantly.

When the music ended, boys clustered around Mary Elizabeth. She unfolded a lace fan and wafted it expertly, revealing and concealing her smiles. She dispatched one boy for punch and another for cake. Then she covered her face except for her eyes. She batted her dark lashes at the remaining young man.

The fellow was looking at her cow-eyed.

Thomas grimaced. *If he comes calling, I'd best be cleaning my gun.*

The other two boys returned, and Thomas was about to turn away to check on James when he noticed the group around Mary Elizabeth falling back.

A suave young man, in elegant evening clothes of the latest cut, bent over her hand and then swept her away in a waltz. Thomas recognized him as one of Benjamin's sons,

Furman Chaires.

Verdura stood on a five-hundred-acre hill encircled by a picturesque stream. The next day's lunch was a picnic by the water. Sitting down beside a waterfall, Lavinia smoothed her new plaid day dress made fashionable by Queen Victoria. She tried to hide her smug smile.

I must chat with the other ladies without showing my elation that my daughter has captured the attention of the most eligible bachelor here, she thought, but she could not stop glancing surreptiously at her. Mary Elizabeth sparkled as Furman Chaires selected a spot for them to lunch together.

What a handsome son-in-law he would make, thought Lavinia. His French ancestry shows in his dark hair and the intriguing curl of his lip.

Sighing happily, Lavinia turned so that her bonnet concealed her face from the ladies and whispered to Thomas who sat beside her on a quilt, "Our little girl has made a conquest."

Thomas shook a chicken drumstick at her. "She needs finishing school," he growled.

Lavinia tossed her head at him. Oh, well, she thought, they should have some time to enjoy courtship. But not too much. He's already twenty-nine.

The laughter of the group flowed around her as she nibbled a fried peach pie. It's all very well for Thomas to make his mark starting churches and schools, but if we're to have a community of culture and wealth, proper matches might be up to me.

As the Jones's carriage recrossed the Florida state line and headed toward Greenwood, Mary Elizabeth burst into tears.

"Oh, Papa, must we go back to — to the wilderness? If we miss the other celebrations, I'll never meet — anybody!"

Lavinia had already realized that Mary Elizabeth needed to be seen at the round of house parties in Southwest Georgia, which had been touched off by Florida's statehood. Thomas had insisted on returning home, but Lavinia decided to try again.

"Must we miss them, Thomas? Everyone's wanting to proclaim peace and prosperity."

"If we're to be part of the prosperity, I must get the land prepared to plant," Thomas said firmly.

"Colonel Mitchell will be offended if we don't accept his invitation to Fair Oaks." She tried to make him smile. "You know he holds grudges. He's never forgiven the British for the War of 1812. He even plans to be buried so he won't look toward the rising sun like everybody else, just so he won't face England."

"Ha! He's been coveting one of Rascal's offspring. He'll forgive me anything if I give him a puppy."

James leaned forward and interjected, "I'm ready to go back to work, Papa."

His bitter tone silenced Lavinia. Remorse pierced her. She had been so focused on her oldest daughter that she had barely noticed that James could participate only when there was riding.

An hour went by with Mary Elizabeth's sniffling the only sound. Then they passed a long avenue bordered by clipped boxwood and saw other carriages that had been at the Chaires' plantation turning in to Fair Oaks.

Thomas thrust his fingers through his thick hair and groaned. He called to the coachman to turn around.

"All right, Lavinia. I'll drop you and the girls at the party. We men must go home."

Thomas and James continued their journey in pregnant silence. Thomas fiddled with his pocket watch, waiting.

Finally James burst out, "Papa, do you think any girl will ever look at me — except with pity?" He hid his red face in his hands.

Thomas caressed the bowed head; he was glad that his son could not see the tears welling in his own eyes. He cleared his throat.

"Of course! All Jones men charm the ladies." He laughed. "You're only eighteen. You'll get the hang of flirtation."

James raised a tear-streaked face. It was the first time he had revealed his despair.

"But — I'm . . ." he flung out the hated word, "a cripple."

"No you're not! You have a game leg, but you also have a spirit that soars with the eagles. In God's strength, you can do anything." The clopping of the horses' hooves seemed loud in Thomas's ears. He remembered being this age, knowing his older brother would receive his father's inheritance. He recalled when he first saw the land at Greenwood and his vow that all of his children would share his wealth.

"James, I'm planning to buy you a plantation of your own. You are perfectly capable of running it on horseback now that you've conditioned yourself to ride."

James wiped his face and grasped his father's hand. " 'Til then, I'll work hard to learn and to make your crop pay."

They talked of land preparations and

planting schedules and then lapsed into their own thoughts.

James sighed. "A plantation would be incomplete without a wife."

"You'll find the right girl. It will take time because she must be special. You must endure more parties. Sit in on silly games. Watch the dancing as if you're enjoying the music. Show 'em all it doesn't matter if you can't walk smoothly. Intelligence counts. With the ladies, show your charm and wit."

Thomas looked out of the carriage window and saw that they had entered the avenue of live oaks that approached Greenwood. He rubbed his hands together.

"I can hardly wait to get back to work."

Lavinia liked Colonel Richard Mitchell and his wife Sophronia because they were known for philanthropy. The tall, distinguished gentleman was the son of one of Thomas County's original settlers.

Sophronia greeted them warmly. She assured them she was glad they decided to come after all because she had arranged a musicale.

That evening the guests sat in rows of chairs that filled both the music room and parlor. The three musicians played a violin, an English concertina, and a hammered dulcimer. Lavinia noticed Mary Elizabeth looking alert, as if she were listening intently.

That's odd, she thought. *She's always hated the somber sounds of Beethoven.* Then she saw Furman Chaires walk into the room. *Aha! Mary Elizabeth must have known he was coming.*

The violin soared, and Lavinia wished for Harriet. *I know she has to observe the rituals of mourning, but she must be so lonely.* As the melody resounded through the rooms filled with congenial people, she decided she must write and beg Harriet to come to the next social.

Since it will be a quiet one at her sister-in-law's home, surely no one would think it improper.

Three weeks later as Lavinia prepared to leave for the Coalson-Wyche Place, she was standing at the hall mirror pinning her hat when she saw James's reflection. He was dressed in his Sunday clothes.

Surprised because he had suffered such pain at the Chaires' celebration, she wondered why he was subjecting himself to it again. He had been silent since their return, burying himself in the books in Greenwood's library.

She lifted questioning eyebrows toward

Thomas.

"I told James that I could spare him," he said with a secretive smile. He kissed her cheek and whispered, "He'll be fine."

"He can escort Mary Elizabeth," she whispered back. "She hasn't heard from Furman."

When they settled in the carriage, James pulled out a book of Shakespeare's Sonnets. Mary Elizabeth stared out the window on the brink of tears.

What is about to happen with my children? Lavinia wondered. And why haven't I heard from Harriet?

She did not quite know what to expect herself. They were heading to one of the oldest plantations in the county, settled by Paul Coalson. He had married James Blackshear's sister Elizabeth. After Coalson's death, she had remained unwed for the prescribed five years of widowhood before marrying Henry Wyche. Lavinia had not met him, but she had heard that he added to Elizabeth's land and increased production. They could well afford this hospitality; therefore, Lavinia was surprised to see the house had remained unpretentious. One story clapboard, it was built with a central hall and symmetrical wings after the pattern of the old dogtrot cabins.

Mary Elizabeth and James left her immediately to join the young folks, and Lavinia settled on the front porch shaded by pungent climbing roses. Glad that she had left the younger children with Thomas, she sighed pleasurably at the moment to relax. Soon, however, she began fretting because Harriet had not arrived. She left her friends and strolled toward the stables.

James was showing off his horsemanship to the prettiest girl in the group.

So, this was the reason for Thomas's smile. He's been coaching him on courting, Lavinia thought. *I fear he will be hurt.* She knew this girl to be so self-centered that she would have no patience when she saw James without the horse.

There's Furman after all. Oh my! He was escorting a girl nearer his age.

Where is Mary Elizabeth?

Lavinia turned back toward the house and recognized the Cedar Grove carriage. The moment Harriet alighted, she was surrounded by a group of men.

Why not? She's young and beautiful even in black crepe, and she owns one of the richest plantations from here to Tallahassee.

When she neared, Lavinia heard the talk was of rice production. She stood back until the discussion ended.

"They certainly were giving your opinions respect," she greeted Harriet.

"And well they should. The county records show my yields topping theirs." Harriet laughed a good warm sound. "I've read everything I could find about growing rice, and I've worked hard. I've decided I can survive, and I intend to do it splendidly."

Lavinia gave her a hug as she said, "We've got a lot of catching up to do."

By mid-April, the celebrating ended but the pattern was set to have house parties. Everyone agreed they must continue the visiting during the winter season when little work could be done on the land.

Lavinia was satisfied to be at home again for the summer, but in the fall it seemed that life was rushing by too fast.

Thomas sent Mary Elizabeth to finishing school. Lavinia worried that she heard little from her daughter through the winter. Her heart ached for James. He had attempted to court several girls, but no one seemed to respond to him. She half-listened when Thomas talked of buying him land. She knew he would never be able to live on his own.

Her mind was soon occupied elsewhere. The next spring, on May 25, 1846, Martha

Tallulah was born. Thomas stood rocking the mahogany cradle and gazing at her curly black hair and clear blue eyes.

He grinned crookedly at Lavinia. "I guess I'm feeling my forty-four years, but I'm thinking that our older children are leaving the nest, and how quickly this one will, too. She's the prettiest one yet. Mattie will be a stunning beauty!"

CHAPTER XI

"Children — children! Don't all speak at once. I can't hear myself think!" Lavinia looked down the dining table at her own eight and tried to remember the names of the latest visitors. Livy, at fourteen, always had houseguests, and this one had brought a little sister to play with Susan.

"Let's have a little polite conversation," Thomas said in a voice that reinforced Lavinia's words. "This is supposed to be your parents' birthday dinner."

Lavinia could hardly believe that it was May 14, 1847, and she was thirty-seven; Thomas was forty-five. *Our lives are rushing by too fast.*

Quiet talk lasted five minutes. Then James claimed his father's attention with the suggestion that they plant rice like Harriet Blackshear was doing.

Thomas regarded the serious-faced young man and replied, "Perhaps you're right, son." He considered for a moment. "But with this hungry horde to feed, I'm thankful the cotton and cattle are prospering. I'm not sure we should take a risk."

Mary Elizabeth plucked at Lavinia's sleeve. "Mama," she wailed, "you promised we'd discuss my trousseau."

"Really, dear, it's a year until your wedding. We'll talk after dinner." She smiled at her emotional daughter who was newly engaged. Unattainable to Furman Chaires when she was away at finishing school, she became the desire of his heart. Correspondence had culminated in engagement. Lavinia had been disappointed that she was shut out from the courtship; however, the couple had made plans for a big wedding. Lavinia was looking forward to it as much as Mary Elizabeth.

At that moment, Frank turned over his milk. He looked up at her with tears spilling over his freckled cheeks. His hair was cropped off because of a gash where he had hit his head, and his front teeth had fallen out. He was so pathetic he was cute, and Lavinia laughed and kissed him.

"That's all right, honey," she said as she mopped up the mess. "Mama spills things, too."

Livy tapped her spoon against her glass.

"Attention, everyone! I have an announcement to make. I'm going to Wesleyan Female College in Macon, Georgia." She faltered at the shocked silence and amended meekly. "May I, Papa? I don't want mere finishing school."

Livy turned up her nose and wrinkled it at Mary Elizabeth. "Wesleyan is the first college in the world to give degrees to women like universities do to men."

"You, a woman?" Tommy sneered.

"I have a brain. I'll prove it. And I don't intend to marry a farmer!"

Thomas spoke in a quiet voice. "Livy, do you realize Macon is nearly two hundred miles and a hard trip?"

Mary Elizabeth interrupted. "Mama's got to be fixing clothes for me. She won't have time to make college clothes, too."

"Miss Smarty! That's all you know. I talked with Reverend Adams when he came 'round on his circuit. Wesleyan has strict rules. They require simplicity of dress and allow no jewelry."

Livy turned back to Thomas. "Papa, the trip would be part of my education."

"If you are serious about it, we'll see," said Thomas. "Wesleyan is a fine Methodist school that will also teach you morals and how to be a lady. I'll speak to Reverend Adams when he comes back."

Livy jumped up and hugged him.

"You must be patient," Thomas warned. "You know his circuit takes him to Tallahassee and Tampa before he'll be here preaching again."

"Ma-ma!" Florence squirmed in her highchair and began to cry. Frank, recovered from his accident, was picking on her. He seemed to relate to her because they both had red hair.

Lavinia shook her head, wondering, *who are all these people?* In the last year, every one of them had changed into strangers. *To think, I've been in a hurry for Mattie to start talking.*

Suddenly a hush fell. The new cook, Cherry, entered the room with a three-tiered birthday cake. As Lavinia met Thomas's eyes at the other end of the table, the bedlam did not matter. They were alone and young again.

A rainbow of silks and satins spilled over the upstairs rooms of Greenwood during the ensuing months as the dressmaker worked on Mary Elizabeth's trousseau.

Lavinia was relieved that Livy needed little for Wesleyan because Mary Elizabeth's life in the Chaires Community would require morning dresses, skirts, waists, afternoon frocks, riding habits, traveling costumes, ballgowns, shoes, gloves, handkerchiefs, and of course, daintily embroidered muslin lingerie.

One afternoon, Mary Elizabeth's chums from Thomasville came bearing scraps of silk from their favorite dresses. Laughing and chattering, the girls pieced the remnants together to make a crazy quilt as a remembrance of their friendship when Mary Elizabeth moved to Tallahassee. Lavinia featherstitched the joinings and made a lovely souvenir to grace the fainting couch in her daughter's future boudoir.

Getting ready for a wedding is such fun, Lavinia thought as she listened to the lively group. She felt that she and her daughters had never been so close.

All too soon, June 15, 1848, was upon them. As Lavinia and Thomas stood at Greenwood's double doors and greeted guests, she took note of the elaborately ornamented crinolined skirts. Some of the Tallahassee ladies' outfits bore the mark of New York City.

We might still be hidden from the eyes of the world by the Pine Barrens, Lavinia thought, but King Cotton brings the best to us.

Music began. A hush fell over the crowd as time came for the ceremony. The bridesmaids descended the staircase. Tears filled Lavinia's eyes as the long-anticipated moment came. Pure white tiers of Mary Elizabeth's bell shaped skirt showed at the top of the stairs. Thomas, stalwart as always, provided his steadying arm as slowly, gracefully, she executed the turn with her veil floating out behind. She paused for a moment in full view before she stepped down to an awestruck Furman.

Reverend Adams began the vows. Everything blurred.

Lavinia moved about the reception speaking to friends, checking food. In a daze, she hardly knew what was happening until she noticed the bridal couple had changed clothes.

She rushed onto the porch to hug Mary Elizabeth before she threw the rose that had adorned the prayer book she had carried. She seemed to be aiming at James.

A willowy blonde beside him caught it.

Who is she? Oh, yes. Ann Adams, the preacher's granddaughter. She dismissed her until she saw that Ann remained at James's side when the young people ran out to throw rice.

Too tired to wonder about them, Lavinia

sagged against the column. She saw Thomas standing by the carriage bedecked with "Just Married" signs and burdened with old shoes. His face desolate, he kissed Mary Elizabeth good-bye and pressed something into her hand.

Lavinia realized how close they had always been. During those awful days when I let my grief over Francis Remer's death consume me, he was father and mother.

She wiped tears. Getting ready for the wedding had been such fun that she had not understood what a loss she and Thomas would feel.

I can write to her and visit, and there will be grandchildren, she consoled herself, but darling Thomas looks as if it is breaking his heart to give his daughter to another man.

Lavinia felt better when Mary Elizabeth wrote that she was enjoying the company of Furman's family, in-laws, and cousins.

It has taken me a while to get this large family straight, but they seem to like me.

Tallahassee society is such fun! Furman tells me the city has a big May Party with a throne for the queen. Her court dances around the Maypole. Then everyone goes to the City Hotel ballroom, where grown-ups mingle with the small fry for the dancing. Maybe we will have a daughter who will grow up to be the May Queen.

Everyone here is reading Sir Walter Scott's stories, especially Ivanhoe. Well, you'd never guess what they are planning. A ring tournament! The newspaper calls it "a touch of Ashby de la Zouche." Knights will gallop across the valley to capture an ivory ring on their lances. Don't you just love knights and chivalry?

Thomas took the whole family to Tallahassee Christmas shopping, and they visited the Chaires' plantation.

Lavinia discovered that both she and her daughter were expecting babies the following May. Furman had insisted Mary Elizabeth see a doctor, and he discovered she was having twins.

Lavinia lay on the bed with Julie washing her splotched face. The baby was coming too soon. It was still April of 1849.

"Oh, Julie," she gasped, "this is the eleventh child I've borne, and I've never been in such pain."

"Just you rest easy, Miss 'Vinia. Mr. Thomas be back soon with that new doctor what done moved to Thomasville."

"This makes me glad Mary Elizabeth will have a doctor. I never thought I'd need one."

Thomas knocked and entered with a man who was so young and handsome that Lavinia found herself blushing. He introduced Dr. David Brandon.

I'm glad Livy is at college, she thought. *She'd be embarrassed with her old mother having a baby anyway and especially with him around.*

Dr. Brandon determined that it was a breech birth. Hours passed before the ordeal was over and tiny Emma Gertrude was born.

Lavinia was still exhausted, and Emma was almost too weak to nurse when a letter arrived that the twins, Sally and Lavinia, had been born on May 2, 1849.

Emma struggled for three weeks and five days and died on her parents' birthdays.

Lavinia felt numb as she stood in the cemetery with Thomas supporting her.

"Honey," he said when the brief service was over, "you know I love children as much as you do, but today I'm forty-seven and you are thirty-nine. I believe that Emma should be our last baby."

Lavinia buried her face against his shoulder, and he stoked her hair.

"Get your strength back, and I'll take you

to Florida to enjoy our grandchildren."

Lavinia's recovery was slow, and Sally Chaires died before they could make the trip. She forced herself to get out of bed and go to console her daughter. Holding her namesake, Mary Lavinia Jones Chaires, eased the ache of her own empty arms.

At laying-by time in July, Lavinia realized the wisdom of Thomas's decision to conclude their family. The seven still at home kept her in a tizzy, and on the day they drove with the two eldest to a social at the Thomas Jefferson Johnson plantation, she glimpsed a future whirlwind.

Thomas began grumbling as soon as the carriage was out of sight of Greenwood. "I don't know why I let you talk me into going. Why should I?"

Lavinia laughed. "Because we need to visit Tom Johnson's widow, Martha, and we should also congratulate John William Henry Mitchell on his recent marriage to their daughter Julia Ann."

Thomas grunted. "Your young admirer will have a hard time filling his father-in-law's shoes. Did you know, Johnson was the state legislator who introduced the bill creating Thomas County just before we moved here?"

Lavinia merely smiled. She was glad her devotee from their early days had married so well. Not only did John William and Julia Ann stand to inherit three thousand acres of one of the first plantations in the county, but also an immense fortune due to the fact that her father had extended loans at interest.

"John William is the reason I didn't want to come," Thomas complained. "He's a Democrat! Why isn't he a Whig like the rest of the planters?"

Livy spoke up. "Don't think about turning around, Papa," she said, preening. "I want to see everyone while I'm home from Wesleyan."

James agreed quickly. "Even *you* don't need to work all the time."

Lavinia mused on their motives. The children are transparent, but could Thomas still be jealous of John William's boyhood crush on me?

When they arrived, a large crowd had gathered. First Julia Ann introduced the Jones family to new physicians who had set up their practices in Thomasville, Dr. Samuel Seth Adams and Dr. David Brandon.

Lavinia murmured, "We've met Dr. Brandon." She could feel her cheeks reddening with the embarrassing memory of having a man deliver her short-lived Emma. Flustered, she turned to present him to Livy, who was poking her in the side. Livy's moonstruck face when she saw young David Brandon's blue eyes and brown hair did not surprise Lavinia, but she was appalled at her forwardness.

"Oh, Dr. Brandon," Livy gushed. "It's such a pleasure to meet a highly educated man. I believe that women should have more than a butterfly education, too. I'll be receiving a degree from Wesleyan Female College in the spring of '51."

"Really?" the young man replied. "Let's get a plate of barbeque. You can tell me about your studies."

With an exasperated sigh that neither Livy nor the young man was obeying the protocol of letting parents arrange matches, Lavinia turned toward Thomas. He was talking with Dr. Adams. It suddenly dawned on her that he was not only the circuit rider's son and but also Ann Adams father. James must have known the family had moved to town because he and Ann were standing close together. They were speechless, but they looked like cats in cream.

Lavinia fastened a smile on her face, but she was not pleased. Julie, who always seemed to know everything before she did, had surprised her when she was dressing for the party by saying, "Law, Miss 'Vinia, James oughten to marry the preacherman's granddaughter. He should find a bride with a big plan'ation."

She had laughed it off then, but now as she saw them together, she stiffened a stubborn chin. *He really shouldn't take a wife at all.*

John William stepped up smartly, bowed, and kissed her hand.

As she congratulated him on his marriage, she felt Thomas's eyes burning on her back. *It's rather fun to inspire such jealousy even though I'm a grandmother.*

Thomas put a possessive hand on her arm, glaring at the younger man.

"Ah, Thomas, old fellow," John William said. "There's someone here I want you to meet. He's touring the South opposing any secession move."

Thomas's eyebrows shot up. "Don't waste his time on me. Those fellows who had the idea to let the North secede and us keep Washington had the best solution. Most of the important people in government are southerners anyway."

Lavinia had never heard him speak so harshly, but she knew that since the Mexican War had added territory, there had been constant rancor between North and South. Even in Thomasville, men argued politics on every corner. She wondered how to save this situation.

Fortunately, a fiddle struck a lively tune. Bland-faced, John William bowed and asked her to dance. He swept her away before she could reply.

As she whirled around the circle, she saw Livy and David dancing. Ann was sitting beside James, watching as if that were as much fun.

That night as they prepared for bed, Thomas was still cross and Lavinia felt out of sorts.

"I had not realized James was seeing so much of Ann Adams," she said through clenched teeth. "I think you've been encouraging him behind my back."

"I had to. You baby him too much."

"He needs to stay at home where I — where we can look after him."

"No, he doesn't! Tommy wants to stay here and work with me, but James needs a place of his own. I've found a plantation on the east side of the county, and I'm going to buy it for him."

Lavinia dropped the hairbrush with which she was giving her usual hundred strokes and turned from the mirror. "No, Thomas, please. If he must marry, he and that girl could live here. He's not able to run a plantation by himself. Especially not so far away."

"You push the girls into marriage. Why can't you let James go?"

"He nearly died. We were so close when I exercised his arms and legs." Lavinia could not hold back the tears.

Coldly, he ignored her weeping. "We cannot make him feel like a cripple. He must be his own man — meddle with Livy. She thinks she's too good to marry a farmer."

Lavinia watched him turn away from her and get into bed. She knew it hurt him that their daughter thought herself too well informed for a man in his vocation. She sighed and climbed up on her side with her back toward him.

After a long silence, she admitted, "I was embarrassed that she so obviously set her cap for David Brandon."

"Do you think that he can make enough to support her like she's used to?" Thomas sneered. "Either a doctor gets a ham for his trouble or he's the last one to get paid."

"True. I predict they will have their feet under our table a great deal."

Suddenly they faced each other and began to laugh.

Chapter XII

Thomas stood in the backyard holding two horses. Steam rose from the swept sand on this August 23, 1851. Thomas expected to harvest the best crop he had grown in years, and he wanted Lavinia to see it.

I really need it, he thought. *Buying James's place took all my capital, and with Susan leaving for Wesleyan . . .*

"I'm sorry I kept you waiting." Lavinia came outside interrupting his thoughts. "I went back to change into my coolest riding habit."

"I guess it's a better day to sit on the porch and fan." He laughed apologetically. "I just wanted you to see the corn."

Lavinia smiled. "You know I'm always ready to stop what I'm doing to ride over the farm with you."

They walked their horses by fields of corn, already brown but standing straight and tall.

Thomas pointed. "Notice some stalks

have several ears. We'll have livestock feed and fodder for the winter."

"And meal and grits and hominy for everyone on the place," Lavinia added.

As they rode to the cotton fields, the sun blazed down upon them. Thomas dismounted and checked between the rows of tall, big-leafed plants to make certain no insects were hidden beneath the leaves. Bolls of cotton were opening to a fluffy white.

"We've only ginned a few bales," Thomas said, "but just look at this crop. We'll be picking until Christmas."

Lavinia murmured congratulations; however, she looked about uneasily. "It's stifling. I can hardly breathe," she said. "It's so still — why the birds aren't even singing."

"We'd better water the horses," said Thomas, reining toward the river.

An odd sound broke the stillness. He pricked his ears, realizing something large was moving purposefully through the woods. At that moment, clouds obscured the sun, and the day turned from bright to eerie gray. The birddogs who had come along for the run, began quarreling and nipping one another.

The thrashing in the underbrush became louder. Cows, led by Pet, emerged in front of them, blocking their way.

Thomas took a biscuit from his pocket and held it toward Pet in his outstretched palm. As she scooped it with her big lip, he patted her. "Old girl, you sense a thunderstorm, but if you'd face into it instead of trying to walk away, you wouldn't have to endure the whole brunt."

Lavinia smiled at him as the trusting cow regarded him with soulful eyes. However, as soon as the bread was gone, Pet moved south again.

Thomas scanned the skies. "Honey, this is worse than a single thundercloud. Every direction looks black. We'd better hurry back."

The moment they turned the horses' heads toward home, the nervous animals began to run unbidden.

"We must get to the children," Lavinia shouted over a suddenly gusting wind.

Rain struck horizontally, stinging Thomas's eyes. He recognized the swirling of a hurricane as he felt the rain from the northeast instead of the usual southwest. The atmosphere settled over them with a feeling as ominous as if the whole world were turning dark.

As cold water ran down the back of his neck, Thomas cast an anxious glance at

Lavinia. Her clothes were plastered to her body. Her hair escaped its pins and streamed out behind her. He agonized. *My precious wife.*

"I'm sorry I asked you to come," he shouted.

"You had no way to know," she called back through chattering teeth.

They raced under whipping trees. Only the live oaks stood unyielding, but the Spanish moss dangling from their spreading branches cavorted like drunken dancers. At last they reached Greenwood.

Lavinia slid unaided from her sidesaddle and nearly stepped on a hen gathering her babies beneath her wings as she ran toward her own brood.

Thomas shouted to the servants. "Take in everything small enough to blow in the wind."

Samuel stopped him. "Mr. Thomas, be this the end of the world?"

"No, no. We'll be all right. It's just a hurricane coming off the ocean. Gather firewood inside your cabins. Take in water. The storm could last for days."

Thomas and Augustus began closing the shutters on Greenwood. By the time they reached the last window, it took both of them to pull the heavy wooden covering against the wind. Thomas had to hold onto the big man to stand up to the gusts. He was soaked to the skin when at last he could go inside the house and bolt the door.

Home has never felt or smelled more wonderful, he thought. *Lavinia is a marvel of calmness and foresight.*

It was only four-thirty, but she knew how best to calm the children. The waffle iron was already baking on the hearth.

After supper, Thomas read Hans Christian Andersen's fairy tales. Then he tucked everyone, including Lavinia, into bed.

He prowled about rechecking windows, bracing beams across the double doors at each end of the hall, pacing, praying. He was thankful he had taken the time to build such a strong house, and even the interior walls were brick.

A sudden roar startled him. Cracking like gigantic guns sounded close. Upstairs, someone screamed.

Probably Florence, he thought. The seven-year-old was always alert, while five-year-old Mattie never heard a sound. As he started up the stairs, his candle blew out. He had never experienced a night so black.

Lavinia had picked up Florence before he fumbled his way to the girls' room. She whispered over the whimpering child's head. "How bad?"

"Mighty big or stalled. Rain torrents haven't lessened. From the sound of it, a tornado must have dipped down. We'd best take quilts and bed everyone together in the downstairs hall away from the windows."

The noise became so loud that his little ones wailed and would not be comforted. Now, Thomas could read fear in Lavinia's eyes.

"God is watching over us," he assured them. "Greenwood is strong. It will keep us safe and dry."

"I can't stop worrying about Mary Elizabeth's family," Lavinia whispered. "The Chaires Community is not much more than twenty miles from the Gulf. They are without doubt taking more force than we are."

The night seemed endless with the wondering what was happening and when it would pass. Thomas dreaded to find out what was left of his beautiful crop. *How will I care for my family and my people if I lose it?*

The day was far advanced before it was light enough to see. The family was eating breakfast when they suddenly realized that all was quiet. Wind and rain had ceased.

"Papa, shouldn't we check the livestock?" asked Tommy in a deep voice, trying to be a man. Suddenly it croaked, betraying him for a twelve-year-old.

"No, son." Thomas looked at him in surprise because the quiet boy rarely spoke. "It's still dangerous to go out. This is called the eye of the hurricane. It's a calm spot at the center of the swirling winds. I've heard it can take as much as four hours to pass. Then the other side of the storm will come." *And sometimes be more dangerous,* he added to himself.

The waiting atmosphere seemed worst of all. Thomas became so nervous that he had to let Lavinia entertain the children. Then wind and rain returned. After tormenting hours, the hurricane seemed to have moved on. Grayness and showers continued.

It's time to see the disaster, Thomas thought. *I hate to make James stay in, but I'm afraid he might fall in the wet debris.*

He considered Tommy, realizing that his concern for his crippled son had caused him not to notice that manhood was coming upon his younger brother. Thin-faced and all teeth, Tommy's whole body was struggling to break free of adolescence. Thomas tried to sound off-hand. "James, let Tommy go with me this time. He needs to sample growing up."

They went out carefully into a world littered with limbs. Tommy was wild-eyed with disbelief as they picked their way through wreckage and found outbuildings with roofs snatched off. In the quarters, downed pines trapped several of the cabins' inhabitants. Thomas gave orders to pull the trees aside with oxen before he and Tommy rode to see the crops.

The tornado had snapped off a grove of pines and laid them across the cornfield. Thomas gagged at the sight of their anticipated food ground into the dirt. Cotton plants lay in the mud. On those few standing, the locks hung in wet strings, yellow, instead of white.

"Can we save any of it, Papa?" Tommy croaked, incredulous.

"Some, but it will grade mighty low," Thomas muttered, trying to keep his son from seeing how devastated he felt.

Tommy rode ahead and stopped before a favorite live oak lying roots up. He shouted, "Papa, it's not bent or broken. It looks like a hand pulled it out of the ground whole."

Thomas felt akin to the tree as he returned to tell Lavinia their entire crop was gone.

"We'll have to take a loan to keep things going," he mumbled with his head down.

"We'll get by." She opened her arms.

Thomas clutched her close and choked out, "Yes, but, after all, it might be good for

Livy to marry a doctor."

Thomas hated borrowing money. He consoled himself that mortgaging land was better than selling it, especially since he could not get a decent price. Since the hurricane, no one in the area had money to buy anything.

He returned home from the bank in Tallahassee, feeling like a failure. He found Lavinia sitting on the front steps. Sinking down beside her, he said, "I'm worth more dead than alive."

Lavinia seemed not to hear his words. She stretched her arms over her head. "Isn't this sunshine glorious after so many dark days. And just look at all of the butterflies that have blown in."

She waved her hand toward her flattened lantana. Myriads of butter-yellow cloudless sulphurs covered the blossoms. The common Gulf fritillaries, orange and black and silver, had doubled in number.

"Look at them and take heart, my darling, because butterflies are the symbol of a new and better life."

Thomas tried to hide his desperation from his family and forge ahead as he had promised. He helped James move to a cabin on his new plantation southeast of Greenwood, nearly to the Florida line. Only then did he find out how much he had come to depend upon his oldest son.

Lavinia could not seem to stop crying after James left. He was sorry for her, but he felt he had done the right thing. It was soon proven. Living on his own place gave James the courage to propose to Ann Eliza Adams. They set their wedding date for after James could make his first crop and prepare a temporary home.

I wish Lavinia could accept Ann, Thomas thought. *The girl is quiet and reserved, but if Lavinia would try . . .* He feared James would detect that his mother was polite but not warm.

Now that James was away, Thomas respected Tommy's growing up. On February 9, 1852, Tommy turned thirteen. *Suddenly he is a beanpole,* Thomas thought. *Lavinia did the right thing waiting until he came along to give me a namesake. He looks more like me everyday, and he's quiet, calm, and most of all, dependable.*

Viewing the hurricane damage had matured Tommy overnight. Even his voice stayed in a vibrant timbre. When he did speak, people turned and listened.

"I want to stay on Greenwood and work with you, Papa," Tommy said as they rode over fields finally cleared of downed trees.

"I appreciate your attitude, son. You've become a man early, and you understand what I had to do for James. One day I'll give you land, too. But for now I need you. Not even your mother is to know what dire straits we're in. We'll borrow money for seed. We'll have to work our fingers to the bone and plant every available acre."

The whole year of 1852 streamed over Lavinia like a bad dream. She accustomed herself to being careful about money, as she had not been since she was a bride. Fall harvest produced enough corn to feed their twenty-two mules, eleven horses, and one hundred-fifty head of cattle, hogs and sheep. She knew that the cotton paid only part of their debts.

She was glad that James made a crop of his own, but misery overwhelmed her when he and Ann decided to marry on Christmas Day, his twenty-fifth birthday.

Julie was right, she thought ruefully. *It would have helped a great deal if Ann had brought a dowry into the marriage.*

She was not pleased that Ann chose to have only the immediate family for a wedding in the Adams's parlor. Lavinia watched Thomas's proud and happy face as he served as best man. Forlorn, she thought, *the mother of the groom is absolutely useless.*

When they returned to Greenwood, Lavinia went straight to bed. Not wanting the children to hear her, she muffled her weeping with a pillow. She was ashamed that she let it hurt her so much to lose James.

As months passed, she realized that her daughter-in-law had brought not only love but also patience and understanding of James's limitations. James was ecstatic when they discovered Ann was expecting a baby. Lavinia supposed she should admit Thomas had been right.

Julie, in her lofty position as head of Greenwood's household servants, spoke her mind again with a grudging admittance. "I been saying James shouldn't of married the preacher-man's granddaughter. Well, she ain't got no plan'ation, but her face sweet as ary an angel 'neath that halo of yeller hair."

Lavinia laughed and tried to make the best of the fact that she didn't see them very often since they lived on the far side of the county.

When her high-faluting college graduate,

Livy, suddenly set a wedding date with David Brandon, Lavinia wondered how she would manage with Thomas's cash flow so low. Of course, Livy wanted a wedding to equal Mary Elizabeth's, which had come at the height of their prosperity.

At least Livy won't need as elaborate a trousseau to be a doctor's wife in a village like Thomasville as Mary Elizabeth did to be a millionaire's wife in Tallahassee, she thought.

As she prepared for the wedding, Lavinia scrimped and saved, being careful not to let Livy know. *I mean she's not going to say something to hurt Thomas again!*

No one but Lavinia could tell the difference in the weddings. For one thing, Livy did not pause on the staircase for her white gown to be seen; impatient, she hurried down.

Still, in spite of everything, February 3, 1853, was a beautiful occasion. Mary Elizabeth, handsome Furman, and their curly-haired three-year-old stayed for a week. In Tallahassee, they had been calling the baby Livy, but here it caused confusion of names with her Aunt Livy. Because she was Mary Lavinia Jones Chaires, Tommy nicknamed her Livy J., and it stuck.

When the contented family returned to Florida, Lavinia felt a terrible emptiness.

Fortunately, she liked David Brandon and was glad this bride and groom would live nearby.

As predicted, Livy and David came often for meals. As a young matron, Livy had put her brown hair up in coils over her ears. She affected a comb at the crown of her head, which created a topknot that quivered when she was agitated, a too constant state. She became more pleasant when Mary Lavinia Brandon was born the next year.

Lavinia realized she was getting plump from preparing special meals everyday, but she relaxed into middle age, thinking she had survived child rearing and now life would be serene. All she wanted was peaceful days. She merely glanced at the newspapers because she hated reading of the constant squabbles and the compromises that only brought more arguments between North and South.

Why should the North be able to tell us how to spend our tax money, she wondered. *States are more aware of what their people need.*

Thomas had become disgusted with politics, and they were glad for Greenwood's remoteness even from town as the local men split into several parties.

On a stifling July day in 1854, as the family sat at dinner, Lavinia suddenly found there was no escaping. She had not been listening to Thomas and David until she sensed the rising heat in their voices. Suddenly the atmosphere at the table resembled the onset of the hurricane.

Chapter XIII

Silence descended over the dinner table. Lavinia's fan stopped. She stared at Thomas. Brows bristling, he was breathing hard. Uncharacteristically, he let his temper fly.

"Join the Know-Nothing Party?" Thomas shouted. "I should say not. I'll be part of no political party that's so secret that if you ask what they stand for all they can say is 'I know nothing.' "

Red-faced, David started to speak, but Livy sat bolt upright. Her topknot threatened to fall as she sprang to her new husband's defense. "But, Papa, David says the American Party will keep the Catholics from voting and keep foreigners out of the country."

"Foreigners? And just who do you think you are, Missy? We aren't Indians. Your great-great-grandfather came to the New World from Wales. Your Mama's people

222

were some of the first colonists from England."

Lavinia's voice was hotter than she meant for it to be when she said, "My paternal great-grandfather, Isaac Young, Sr. married a girl from Ireland, Mary Mounce. She must have been a strong woman for so many of us to have Irish tempers and red hair and freckles — What if she was Catholic?"

Tommy's voice rumbled as he spoke up. "The country was founded on freedom of religion."

But that subject is no more polite dinner-table talk than politics, Lavinia thought. She cast about for something to break the tension.

Forcing a laugh, she turned to David. "Don't be like Colonel Mitchell. He hates the British so much that . . ." She broke off. No one was listening to her.

Suddenly, ten-year-old Florence started clapping as the cook, Cherry, entered with peach shortcake.

Mattie, two years younger but still enjoying her status as the baby of the family, began banging her spoon on the table. Frank, astute at thirteen, even though he was still baby-faced, joined in creating the distraction.

Lavinia was so relieved that she did not

scold for the infraction of manners. Whipped cream melted and ran down over the warm and flaky shortbread crust. Tart-sweet peaches oozed out, capturing everyone's attention.

Conversation ceased. When the dessert was nearly gone, the silence became uncomfortable. Lavinia's voice sounded unnatural as she said, "So David, I hear you are opening a drug store in addition to your surgical practice. Tell us about it."

The tension of that evening's argument seemed to stay in the humid air. Lavinia's nerves remained on edge as the summer of 1854 brought daily storms. Thunder rolled and rain poured every afternoon; afterwards, blazing sun pulled the water back up as steam. Men's tempers rose with the July temperatures, which climbed to ninety-eight, one hundred, then one hundred three. Lavinia dreaded every gathering because people were questioning the value of staying in the Union. All of the talk was of States' Rights. The high tariff imposed at Northern insistence made the importation of farm implements from England cut profits from the exportation of cotton.

Then "Bleeding Kansas" became the subject on every tongue.

Lavinia shook her head as she read the newspaper. "The bloodshed in Kansas is worse than the Seminole Wars. I don't understand it."

"It started with the Kansas-Nebraska Act passed in the last session of Congress," Thomas explained. "It provided for the organization of those two territories, allowing people to vote whether or not to allow slavery within their borders."

"That seems reasonable."

"It should be, but Southerners are pouring across the Mississippi River to stake out claims by simply laying four logs in a square. Abolitionists organized by the Massachusetts Emigrant Aid Society are rushing after them with free-soil voters."

"That is a big change from the legal disputes that have been driving the sections apart." Lavinia nodded her understanding.

She could not worry too much about far-away Kansas. There was pressure enough here at home as Thomas and his brother Mitchell increased their campaigning for the Georgia Legislature to act on building a railroad to Savannah. Lavinia worried because Mitchell had gotten entirely too fat. Concern increased when Thomas told her his brother let himself get into such a rage about eliminating the risk of shipping through the hurricane-plagued waters of the Florida Keys that he feared Mitchell might have apoplexy.

Then Thomas fretted because heat scorched crops; only insects thrived. In the stifling heat of August, the paper reported a scourge of yellow fever had struck Savannah.

Lavinia had never been superstitious, but the epidemic seemed ominous. On hot afternoons she collapsed on the porch in a stupor only to jump up to useless work like the restless cows roving before the encroaching storm.

With sudden force, tragedy struck. When she saw a rider approaching, she clutched her heart. The black-bordered message whipped in her hand so violently that the words blurred. Mary Elizabeth had given birth to a baby boy. He lived four days and died.

While Lavinia was packing for a trip to Tallahassee, Livy's servant brought a similar note. Livy and David's eight-month-old baby girl had died.

Lavinia's mind seemed unable to comprehend that she had lost two grandchildren in a matter of days. She knew she had no time for grieving; she must be the consoler. She wrote the most comforting words she could think of to Mary Elizabeth; then she steeled herself and went into Thomasville to Livy's house.

Lavinia found her daughter strong, but David was sitting in the dark, sobbing, feeling a failure as a doctor.

I've never been so powerless to help, Lavinia thought.

Thomas came in from attending to the sad funeral details. He went straight to David. With his arm around his son-in-law's shoulders, he began talking quietly.

Lavinia slipped out of the room thinking, *What a big man Thomas is to forget their differences.* She went out on the porch and let her own tears flow.

When they were in their carriage heading home, Thomas said, "I hate to add to your worries, but we heard from Susan. She wrote grim news." He handed her a short letter from their younger daughter, who was following in Livy's footsteps by attending Wesleyan Female College.

The weather is hot, but Macon does not have an epidemic like Savannah. Our town has sent provisions to the yellow fever victims on the coast. Many families have come here by the Central of Georgia Railroad to seek refuge. Some had the seeds of the disease and are dying.

"I'm going to get her," said Thomas.

"I'll go with you."

"No. The stagecoach trip is too hard. Besides, she's probably fine, and Livy needs you." As Lavinia burrowed into the shelter of his arm, he added, "I'll hurry back."

Lavinia could hardly do her chores for watching the road. When the carriage finally returned, she ran out and snatched open the door.

Seeing Thomas alone, she half laughed. "So, Susan didn't want to leave her beloved school after all."

Then she looked in his eyes. Jerking her head around, she saw a wagon coming up the lane. It bore a small coffin.

"No!" Lavinia screamed. Her legs collapsed. "Why didn't I go?" she whimpered.

Thomas supported her with trembling arms. "It wouldn't have mattered. I was too late. Sweet Susan contracted the fever. She died before I could get there — on August twenty-second."

Friends and family came, bringing food and comforting arms. Mitchell and Eliza stayed several days. Harriet spent the week after they left. She brought books to occupy

Lavinia's mind. Mary Elizabeth could not make the trip for the funeral because she had not recovered from childbirth and the loss of her baby.

Then a friend's child died. Lavinia roused herself to go into Thomasville to comfort her.

I must gather my wits and go to Mary Elizabeth, she thought. Before she could summon strength, Furman sent a special messenger with an urgent note.

Mary Elizabeth's kidneys are failing. She is calling for you.

They rushed to Tallahassee and Mary Elizabeth's bedside. Her pretty face was already swollen, and on September 22, exactly one month after Susan's death, she slipped away.

Furman sobbed on Lavinia's shoulder. She had no strength to offer him. When at last he could speak, he asked, "Can you take little Livy home with you until I can get a hold of myself?"

Lavinia agreed, thankful to have the child. When they returned to Greenwood, Lavinia sorrowed at the vacant chairs around the dinner table. Only Tommy, Florence and Mattie were left at home. Frank, who was only thirteen and still had freckles and a baby face, had insisted upon attending the University of North Carolina, Chapel Hill.

At least he's in the South, she thought, *and we are hidden in the pines where none of the political squabbles in the nation can affect us.*

In the ensuing weeks, Lavinia felt that her heart was hollow and echoing within the empty spaces of Greenwood. Only the feel of Livy J. in her arms and the sight of her sunny smile got her through the grief of four deaths in three months time. And then Furman came to reclaim his child.

Lavinia took to her bed. Her mind too numb for coherent prayers, she claimed the promise that the Spirit helps our infirmities and makes intercession for us with groanings that cannot be uttered. She sank into a place as dark and uncertain as the hurricane's eye.

Rain fell on Thomas's bowed head as he hunched on a log at the edge of a fallow field he had burned. The light September drizzle had increased the number of doves flying in for the grain now accessible on the ground, and he had quickly shot a mess for supper. He should take them home, but he dreaded the sad house. The pain of losing daughters and grandchildren pierced his heart, but now he grieved for Lavinia as well. It was 1855; they had just endured the first anniversaries of the deaths, reliving every agonizing moment. He had work that must be done, but she remained listless. He would catch her in a flood of tears, hold her, suffer with her. But he knew he must do something more to help her clear away her totally obstructing grief.

He dropped his hand to finger the feathered ears of his latest Setter. *This one doesn't sense my feelings like Rascal did.*

As his steps dragged homeward, Thomas saw an unusual butterfly with wings of brilliant blue lying on the ground. Thinking he would take it to Lavinia, he picked up the lifeless form. The lovely creature in the palm of his hand evoked a memory of a place he had been meaning to take Lavinia.

A trip is just what we need, he thought, *but I'll keep the real reason a surprise.*

Invigorated, he hurried home. Lavinia lay in bed with a lavender-soaked cloth over her forehead.

"Honey, I want to take you down to the coast. We'll stay at a little inn and eat fish and oysters."

Lavinia barely stirred. "You're sweet, and that sounds nice, but I'm too exhausted to make that long a trip."

Thomas gazed out of the window. He did not want to give away his surprise. Then he had another inspiration. "I thought we'd stop by Tallahassee and pick up Livy J. Don't you think we need to give her a little extra love?"

Lavinia sat up. "You're right. I must forget about how bad I feel."

Thomas beamed. "I'll make the arrangements."

In two weeks, most of the harvest was gathered in, and Thomas knew Tommy could be trusted to oversee the hands for the rest of the work. Even though he was only sixteen, the workers respected the tall young man.

Florence and Mattie could hardly wait to see Livy J. The little girls chattered all the way to Tallahassee. When they took the lively six-year-old into the carriage, she talked non-stop, bobbing her mop of black curls about. She made it impossible not to smile.

In Saint Marks, Thomas bought everyone fried grouper at a waterfront café, but the youngsters barely tasted the fish in their excitement at seeing the moored ships. Suddenly a flat-bottomed steamboat, belching fire and black smoke from her tall smokestack, glided audaciously to the wharf beside the cargo ships. She was small and undistinguished looking, but Thomas noticed that the round paddle box, which covered the machinery of her side wheel, was proudly emblazoned with the name *Spray.*

Thomas could keep his surprise no longer. He pointed to the boat. "I talked to Daniel Ladd, the owner of that little steamboat, and he sometimes takes passengers down the Saint Marks River to the lighthouse. Would you all like a ride?"

"Yes!" they chorused.

Lavinia sagged against the cabin of the *Spray,* watching the girls clustered around Thomas at the rail. Florence, suddenly tall and important at eleven, had Livy J. in a tight grip. Lavinia tried to smile, knowing Thomas had planned this trip to cheer her.

The plashing of the water from the paddlewheel was pleasant, but sad thoughts overwhelmed her. Mary Elizabeth will never get to see her lovely daughter grow up. Susan will never taste the joy of having a child.

As the boat steamed down the winding black waters of the Saint Marks River, Lavinia shuddered, closed in by the dark forest that rimmed either side. She shut her eyes, but she was soon roused by a sulfur smell. The river's course had widened near the mouth, and waving brown grasses of salt marsh spread on both sides. She noticed slender goldenrod growing along the margins of the tidal marshes and in wet, sunny openings in pine flatwoods.

What an unusual number of butterflies fluttering around that goldenrod, she thought. *I wish I could see them closer.*

Suddenly a large butterfly soared, dazzling orange against the cloudless October blue. Following the flight of its strong wings, Lavinia's heart lifted.

"Mama, come up here," came Mattie's nine-year-old squeal.

Lavinia hurried to the bow to join them. The East River here joined the confluence of the Wakulla River and Saint Marks River, spreading wide into Apalachee Bay. With no barrier islands to block the view, the vast panorama of the Gulf of Mexico stretched from horizon to horizon before them. A fresh salt breeze cooled hot cheeks.

"It's magnificent!" Lavinia exclaimed. "The water is so green, so crystal clear. Thank you for bringing us to see it."

Thomas laughed. "This isn't all. Just wait."

The boat docked beside the slender white tower of the lighthouse. As they moved to the gangway, Captain Ladd told them the structure had been shaken by the latest hurricane but had stood firm. "The keeper's family survived by holding to the top rafters because the surging waves chased them ever higher up the spiraling staircase. Their house and the breakwater washed away." He pointed. "This new house was built for Ann Dudley, who succeeded her husband as keeper."

"Come," Thomas said, holding out his hand as the gangplank was lowered. "You haven't seen the surprise yet." He carried Livy J., and Lavinia held Florence and Mattie by the hand as they walked atop the dune that formed the point of land.

Enchantment lifted Lavinia's drooping shoulders as hundreds of butterflies swirled around them. In constant motion in the hot sun, fluttering over the seaside goldenrod, they ascended and descended to feed deeply from the tube-like blossoms of the waving plants. There were myriads of Gulf fritillaries, but they looked small and pale in comparison to the gleaming orange of the four-inch monarchs. She knelt to see them up close hanging by half-dozens on each stem.

"Oh, Thomas," she breathed. "I'm amazed. I've never seen anything so lovely."

She easily cupped a monarch in her hand. The girls touched the shining white dots on the wingtips around the orange body, which was traced by black lines.

"That part looks like the stained-glass windows at church," whispered Livy J.

Ann Dudley walked out from the lighthouse to speak to them. After exchanging greetings, Lavinia asked her to tell them why there were so many butterflies in this remote spot.

"These are not summer monarchs that live only a few weeks," the lighthouse keeper explained. "They are migrating monarchs that leave New England breeding sites and come through here every fall. They fill up on nectar and cluster at night in the foliage along the dikes."

"Amazing," Lavinia said. "Do they stay here all winter?"

"No. They wait for rising columns of warm air and stream up by thousands. I'm told they travel an unbelievable twelve hundred miles to reach an as yet unknown spot in Mexico. They return the following spring to the southern United States where they lay eggs only on milkweed plants."

"What is their lifespan?" asked Thomas.

"Migrating Monarchs have a natural life of six to eight months. This means the ones who go to Mexico have never been there before."

Lavinia shook her head in wonderment. "God has made many astonishing creatures," she said. "Thank you for sharing these."

Thomas followed the little girls, who could not get enough of wandering through the butterflies. Florence discovered that if she stood still, they would land on the flowers of her skirt.

Content, Lavinia gazed after them for a moment, and then she turned to drink in the grandeur of the green water stretching in all directions to the horizon. The calmness of the scene stilled the turbulence within her breast. *How great God is,* she realized, *how much larger than we can imagine! And yet he whispers the truth of the resurrection to us on butterfly wings.*

He will never forsake us, and nothing can separate us from his love. I'll see Mary Elizabeth and Susan and the babies again. I know it. If this world is so lovely, they must be in an even more beautiful place.

CHAPTER XIV

Thomas was pleased with himself that Lavinia felt so energized when they returned from Florida that she invited James and Ann for a visit. She still had moments when memories flooded and tears came, but she fared better as she busied herself with preparations. Lavinia polished the furniture, brought in flowers, and cooked enough for an army. Indeed, it sounded like a regiment when they all arrived because Livy and David and their growing brood came, too.

Lavinia placed her grandchildren around the long table, inviting them to eat with the adults and learn manners. Thomas basked in her happiness that the chairs were filled again.

James looked at his mother with tenderness as he heaped his plate. "Mama, you cooked all of my favorites."

"I tried to."

"Mama Jones," said Ann, "You must teach

me how to make this pumpkin soufflé."

Thomas smiled on each one in turn. His brows knit when he came to David; however, the young doctor was applying himself to curried rabbit with an expression of innocence. Thomas suddenly felt James looking at him.

"I hear Uncle Mitch has John Wind building him a house twice as big as ours."

Thomas laughed. "Don't most younger siblings have to outdo their big brothers? These are prosperous times, but he's really being extravagant. We handmade everything here, but Mitch is buying things like doors and windows from New York. Can you imagine the expense of shipping them by Saint Marks?"

"Eliza's plans for the grounds will be lovely," said Lavinia. "She's already planting row upon row of narcissus."

Livy interrupted. "In December and January there will be white flowers everywhere, and the place will smell like a funeral," she said, wobbling a spoon in front of her baby's groping mouth.

Everyone laughed, and the table talk remained lighthearted until the meal ended. Then David spoke aside to James.

"Come with me into the garden. I want to smoke my cigar."

Thomas started to follow until he heard his son-in-law whisper.

"I want to invite you to a free barbeque in Duncanville. The American Party is giving it, but the Democrats will have opportunity to reply."

Thomas sat back down. He remained to play with his grandchildren.

Thomas feared Lavinia's good spirits might evaporate after the company left; consequently, he proposed a visit to Oak Lawn. Thomas always relaxed and had fun with light-hearted Mitch.

They were received with the warmest of greetings. Dinner became an occasion for hilarity with old tales retold and exaggerated. As Mitch reached for a second helping of the salt-cured ham, Thomas frowned, worrying about his younger brother's increasing weight. He glanced at Eliza. She, on the other hand, remained young and slim after bearing eight children.

After everyone had eaten too much, they moved to the rocking chairs on the porch to enjoy the November sunshine and watch the children playing in the yard. Thomas's eyes rested with special warmth on Price. He tried to excuse his partiality by citing the lad's personality, but he knew it was born of pride that Thomas Price Jones was named for him — and for Eliza's family name. Price and Florence ran along rolling hoops. With no thought to her red hair streaming or to her clothes collecting dirt, she was out to beat her cousin. Mattie, on the other hand, sat cuddling a puppy. The one who surprised Thomas was Black, Mitch's oldest son. Usually as serious and steady as James Blackshear, for whom he was named, Black was almost mooning over Mattie. He seemed unable to tear his gaze from her blue eyes and pale skin, set off by coal-black hair.

I predicted she would be a beauty, Thomas thought, *but I did not expect her to become a charmer so young.*

His drowsy thoughts were interrupted by Mitch's coughing. When he finally cleared his throat, Mitch turned the conversation to a serious note.

"Did you hear I lost another shipment of cotton sailing around the Keys?"

"No! Sorry. We've got to have a railroad," Thomas replied. "Maybe we'd better get up another meeting. We really need someone to push it."

Mitchell grimaced. "Yes, like David Yulee pushed in Florida. Already his iron dragon is rumbling out from the Atlantic coast at

Fernandina. It's built halfway across the state through the swamps and pine forests, and I hear that track is being laid daily. The *Florida Railroad* is coming closer and closer to connecting the east coast with Cedar Key on the Gulf."

Eliza spoke up. "It's only right for our area to have a train. Plantations are prospering all over Thomas County. John Wind is designing mansions on all sides of us and houses in town as well. By the way, Lavinia, did you hear that your old friend John William Henry Mitchell and his wife Julia Ann have named the Johnson place Pebble Hill? It seems their daughter Jane said every time the yards were swept more rocks popped up, and it was just a pebble hill. The name stuck."

Thomas cut his eyes at Lavinia at the mention of John William. He knew his twinge of jealousy was silly, but the handsome young man always brought out that fear that she might prefer a clean-cut dandy.

Lavinia merely stretched and stood up, saying, "Isn't it time we saw what Mr. Wind is building for you?"

"Fine," said Eliza, "but the work is going so slowly that it's years from being completed. We'll do as you did and take you by the front approach."

They drove up a formal avenue of live oaks that led straight to a picket fence, which separated the naturalized grove from the landscaped grounds.

Thomas stuck his tongue in his cheek and said nothing as he noticed that the house was higher than his.

"We have six columns instead of four," boasted Mitch.

"I see you do."

"And the balcony goes all the way across," gushed Eliza. "We didn't want Oak Lawn to copy Greenwood. The handrail is different. See how that elliptical curve gives it elegance?"

Thomas winked at Lavinia. She caught her lip in her teeth and ducked her head in that grin that always made his heart jump. Their silent communication confirmed his security that they were content in who they were, and it did not matter what anyone else had or did.

They toured the unfinished interior of the house, and then Eliza said, "Come look at my garden, Lavinia. I took the idea from you to start it early. What I want to show you are some exotic plants I've acquired from Japan. Since Commodore Perry got that treaty with the Japanese last year to open their ports to America, they're exporting the most delicate trees and shrubs. And they flourish in our climate. One thing I bought is a lovely white honeysuckle vine that's climbing all over the fence."

Thomas watched Lavinia enter the garden, knowing she would be in her element. He and Mitch sat down to talk more about their need for faster access to world trade. When time came to leave, Thomas promised he would arrange a meeting about a railroad.

On a cold day the following February of 1856, the railroad issue had come to an impasse. Thomas and Mitchell Jones entered the county courtroom filled with apprehension because it was packed with angry men.

Judge Hansell shouted, "The state of Georgia is building tracks in other areas. We've been held tributary to Florida for our commerce long enough."

Mitch took the floor, and the crowd quieted while he had a fit of coughing before he could speak. "We're all agreed that the United States Constitution allows states the freedom to secede from the nation. I think now is the time for our corner to secede from Georgia."

Thomas smiled as the crowd shouted in an uproar of applause for his brother's speech. They passed a resolution, stating that unless the state Legislature acted favorably, Southwest Georgia might withdraw from the rest of the state.

In a month's time the resolution brought action. Even the men who signed it were surprised at how quickly Thomas County had captured attention with this ploy.

Mitch was gleeful when, at last, the *Atlantic and Gulf Railroad* was incorporated. "We did it! They didn't want to lose this rich land." As men gathered around to shake his hand, he protested, "No, don't congratulate me. Even a blind hog roots up an acorn sometime."

At another assembly in late May, Thomas and Mitchell bought stock in the railroad. They agreed it was wise to have some investment besides cotton.

The meeting was proceeding peacefully when the stagecoach arrived. Edward Remington burst in with news he had heard at the railhead in Albany, where he had gone to purchase goods for his mercantile.

"Civil war has erupted in Kansas," Remington shouted. The newspaper shook as he read from it. " 'On May 24, abolitionist John Brown led a self-proclaimed northern army of eight men through the darkness to the banks of Pottawatomie Creek. They marched five proslavery men from their homes and hacked them to death!' " Shocked voices interrupted, but he continued reading. " 'The massacre set the Kansas Territory aflame. Whiskey-fueled bands are burning, pillaging and killing.' " Remington looked around the group of men and added, "Hatred and side-taking is spreading across the nation as fast as that fire."

The national uproar over John Brown continued into the heat of summer, enflamed all the more by the upcoming presidential election. As Thomas sat in his office reading the *Thomasville Southern Enterprise,* he discovered just how upset people were. There were bitter letters and scathing poems. When he saw a formal challenge to a duel, he decided he should warn Lavinia about going into town.

He grimaced at the editor's caution: "Above all things we conjure our friends to make no preparations for self-defense at the polls."

Politics had never interested Thomas. He had been too busy, but now just as he was making large profits and the plantation needed his full attention, he realized he must participate more.

None of the parties suit me, he thought. He

had lost interest several years ago when Alexander Stephens, Georgia's statesman, had left the Whigs, saying they were determined to mortify the South. Stephens had remained without a party until recently. Now he had joined the Democrats. Congressman Stephens advised others to follow suit to oppose the new party forming at the North, the Republicans.

I guess I'll have to become a Democrat and vote for James Buchanan. At least he has declared Kansas as much a slave state as South Carolina and Georgia. He crumpled the newspaper and threw it away so that Lavinia would not read it. *It's better if she stays in her own little world.*

Lavinia greeted Thomas with a kiss when he came into the house wearing a worried frown. She was not as unaware of the political turmoil as he believed, but she had determined to keep Greenwood a place where he could find peace.

She smoothed his tousled mop, which had turned prematurely. Somehow the thick crown of snow-white hair made him more handsome than ever. The sight of him enflamed her passion.

"I'd like to get your opinion of my new frock," Lavinia said. "I could try it on for you now if you're going to sit and rest awhile."

Thomas sat down heavily and mumbled assent.

Lavinia hurried to change. She felt that she looked better than she ever had. This was one more effort to coax a compliment. It would thrill her if he ever said she looked pretty.

She walked into the sitting room, hoping. Thomas smiled and nodded. He said nothing, but she saw that special gleam in his eyes.

"I believe you like me best in green," she said.

As usual, he said nothing more, but at Christmastime of 1856, he confirmed his liking for green with the gift he handed her from beneath the tree. She opened a white velvet box and gasped. Diamonds and emeralds sparkled in the candlelight. She went to the mirror to try on the elaborate necklace and dangling earrings.

"This is the most exquisite thing I've ever seen!" she exclaimed. "But isn't it too extravagant?"

Thomas beamed. "We're prospering as I never dreamed. In fact, with cotton in such high demand, the whole South is producing millionaires. Now that Buchanan is elected, the country should calm down. He's stated that there is no way to prevent a state from seceding because the Constitution does not give the national government the right to make war on a state."

"Maybe with that threat removed, states will stay in the Union," Lavinia replied.

"I think so," Thomas said. "Southerners occupy most of the important positions in Washington City."

Lavinia remembered Thomas's words after James Buchanan was inaugurated on March 4, 1857. The old man was a bachelor, but his niece, Harriet Lane, presided over a sparkling society that rivaled the court in Paris of Emperor Louis Napoleon III and his spectacular Spanish wife, Empress Eugénie. In Washington the acknowledged social leaders were southerners. In the forefront of the entertaining were Georgia's own Julia Toombs and Mary Ann Cobb.

Lavinia and Harriet renewed their lagging correspondence as they eagerly passed news of elaborate dinners and masquerade balls in the capital as they once shared tidbits about Queen Victoria. Senator Robert Toombs and Secretary of the Treasury Howell Cobb might be embroiled in daily warring with northerners in the halls of

Congress, but their wives kept hostility in precarious balance with civilizing socials at night.

Lavinia decided that now was the time to revive Thomas County's cultural life. With the President Buchanan attempting to please everybody and avert the conflict that threatened the country, calm and affability seemed restored.

She wrote Harriet:

I believe I can give a house party without the fear of political arguments erupting. You and yours are the first ones I'm inviting.

The house party proved so pleasant that other families hosted picnics and barbecues and fish fries until harvest claimed everyone's attention.

Greenwood smelled of Christmas again with aromas of pine and holly, cinnamon and spice, chocolate and caramel, turkey and ham. Heart content, Lavinia smiled at her family gathered around the Christmas tree. The girls danced about, holding up silk frocks, green for Florence and blue for Mattie. Lavinia had turned her attention to Tommy as he opened a new shotgun when shrieks of laughter brought her back to her daughters.

"What in the world is this?" asked Florence. She stood over a box filled with hoops of steel graduated from small to large. "I'm too old to roll hoops."

Lavinia laughed. "Yes, ma'am. You will soon be fourteen. These are for wearing by young ladies. It's the new cage crinoline. It seems a man named Charles Fredrick Worth has opened a salon in Paris. He is becoming famous for designing wider and wider skirts for Empress Eugénie. Of course, we can't be outdone. Let's go try this on."

In the bedroom, Florence and Mattie stripped down to chemise and below-the-knee cotton drawers. They hooked the front fastenings on their new corsets, which were strengthened by steel stays.

"Breathe in," said Lavinia, laughing as she pulled the ties in back. Because Florence was a bit too plump, Lavinia tightened the waist until her daughter cried out.

Mattie waited her turn eagerly. Lavinia had known she must have the same as Florence. Considering Mattie's figure, which was budding even though she would not be twelve until the following May, she tied the strings loosely so as not to emphasize her blossoming too soon.

Next they stepped into the flexible steel hoops joined by bands of tape and pulled the cage up to tie at the waist.

"How light it is," said Florence.

"Yes," Lavinia replied. "Two petticoats over it should be enough to hold out your skirts. It's much more comfortable than the old horsehair crinoline that required six petticoats over it."

Lavinia lifted the demure silk dresses over their heads. They pranced and preened before the cheval glass.

Now for the surprise, Lavinia thought. She had been planning it ever since Florence had started attending Fletcher Institute, the new school of higher learning built on the outskirts of Thomasville. The party would honor Thomas as well because he was a member of the Board of Trustees who had established the fine, Methodist school in 1850.

"Florence, I've invited all of your classmates from Fletcher Institute to celebrate your birthday."

They threw their arms around her, but Lavinia worried because Mattie looked happier about it than Florence did.

On January 3, 1858, the Fletcher Institute students arrived. Thomas stood at the door, greeting them, the teachers, and other

Board Members who were also invited. Lavinia noticed he was beaming with pride.

Harriet arrived with her daughter Emily, who was also fourteen. Emily had remained frail after her premature birth when her father died, but she rivaled her mother's perfect features. Lavinia gazed at her and Mattie and wished that Florence had a little of the Jones beauty.

She looks like I did at that age, Lavinia thought, *but Thomas fell in love with me.*

As she stood back watching the parlor games, she realized that appearance was not Florence's only problem. She excelled at dumbo crambo, beating the boys.

Florence's attitude is far too independent. I don't know what I'm going to do with her, but it will be bad if Mattie marries first.

Thomas stood in the pecan grove, watching the assembling crowd with pleasure. This time he was giving the party. It was a perfect June day, and it looked as if half of the county had come to the barbecue welcoming Frank home, now that he had graduated from the University of North Carolina. Frank moved among the men, shaking hands and answering questions about the political climate of the Carolinas. Thomas was pleased that he spoke with the confi-

253

dence of an educated gentleman but without a touch of arrogance.

Satisfied, Thomas turned to the two pits dug in one corner of the deeply shaded grove. Drifting aromas of roasting pork drew others closer as well. The hogs had cooked all night on spits over oak coals, and now the meat was ready to chip up and be mixed with Thomas's secret barbeque sauce, a concoction of catsup, vinegar, mustard, and spices.

Tommy joined him, offering to help. "Isn't it great to have Frank home? He's hardly changed a bit. He hasn't grown an inch, and he still has that baby face, but look at all the girls chomping at the bit to flirt with him."

Thomas laughed. "I don't know what he does to charm them. He plays the field, but you'll have what you need when the right girl comes along."

"I'm not worried," Tommy said. "I'm just glad I didn't have to go." He spread his arms wide to encompass the crowd. "I have everything I want — land, family, friends. I hope I never have to leave home."

Frank excused himself from the gentlemen and moved away from the smoky barbecue pits. His freckled-faced grin took in all of the girls who milled about, the ladies who sat on golden bales of fresh straw from the recently harvested wheat, and Lavinia and Harriet who supervised long tables of vegetables, cakes and pies.

Immediately, Frank was engulfed in a circle of hoop skirts. Giggles and squeals emerged from the group, many of whom were taller than he. Laughing, teasing, recounting college tales, Frank kept them all enthralled for the rest of the afternoon.

That evening when the last of the guests had departed and the family was lounging with their feet up, Frank cleared his throat.

"Pa, maybe I shouldn't broach this so soon, but I must tell you. I want to further my education."

"We'd hoped you'd stay home," said Lavinia.

Frank jumped up and kissed her cheek. "I will for the summer." He looked back toward his father. "With all of the constitutional questions plaguing the country, I want to study law."

Thomas tensed, hoping Frank did not mean a school in the East.

"I want to enroll in Lumpkin Law School at Franklin College in Athens."

Thomas sighed heavily. "At least you'll still be in the South."

■ ■ ■ ■

National crisis cast dark shadows as 1859 began, but none of it mattered to Thomas. All he could think of was Mitch's worsening health. He feared that his younger brother had dropsy.

Thomas feigned excuses for frequent visits to Oak Lawn. He watched his brother warily because his face and neck were swelling. Knowing the inevitable, he thought he was prepared for Eliza's summons. He was not.

When Thomas and Lavinia reached Oak Lawn, congestion had Mitch coughing and struggling for breath. Thomas sat with him day and night, raising him up to give comfort as he could. On July 31, 1859, Mitch died. He was buried in Greenwood's cemetery.

With his lips pressed firmly and his chin up, Thomas had shouldered the burden of the details from Eliza. When at last he could retreat into his sanctuary, he closed the bed curtains to give privacy and cried in Lavinia's arms.

CHAPTER XV

On a crisp morning in October of 1859, Lavinia arrived in Thomasville, anticipating a pleasant day's shopping. Instead, she saw people standing in knots, talking in shrill voices. Fearing what might have happened, she stepped down from the carriage. Several women rushed over to relate a frightening story. Shopping forgotten, Lavinia jumped back in her vehicle and whipped the horses, as she never did, in her need to share the terrifying tragedy with Thomas.

Back home, she rushed into his office and blurted, "The town's talking about that awful abolitionist John Brown."

Thomas temporized. "I knew about him massacring people in Kansas . . ."

"No, now he struck Virginia. On October 16, he seized the United States Arsenal at Harpers Ferry. He planned to arm slaves for a rebellion."

"How do you know?"

"It's all over town. Besides that, I dashed in the post office to see if we'd heard from Frank. Of course, Athens had news before we did. Frank wrote even more gory details." Lavinia thrust Frank's letter at him. "Brown was captured, tried for murder and treason and hanged."

"Frank shouldn't have frightened you."

Lavinia sat down suddenly, calming a bit. "Pshaw. I'm not afraid our people will murder us in our beds. They love us and know we take good care of them. What appalls me is that Northerners hate us so much they are applauding what Brown did. They're making him a martyr."

"That is serious."

"Robert Toombs says it's time to make another war of independence. I don't want war, but I'm for secession. We should do it right away!"

Thomas laughed at her intensity.

When Thomas went through Tallahassee to sell a load of cotton, he found everyone still excited by John Brown's raid. Many had armed themselves to protect homes and land. On street corners, men shouted for secession. Suddenly, Thomas saw a man with a rocking gait walking by the hotel. Realizing it was James, he stopped his wagon and ran to catch him.

"Son, what are you doing in the middle of this uproar?"

James laughed. "Well, you knew I bought land across the state line. I decided to move onto it so I can run for the Florida Legislature. Something momentous is about to happen. Even Governor Richard Call, formally a stout defender of the Union, now agrees about withdrawal. I want to be useful."

Thomas clapped him on the shoulder. "I'm proud of you." He smiled at his son in unceasing amazement at the lengths to which James went to prevent his infirmities from keeping him from a productive life. "Come. Let's get something to eat. It will be a treat to talk to a man who can discuss things calmly."

As months passed, Thomas realized the furor was not going to die down. He had never seen men as enflamed by a presidential election as they were in 1860. With three Democrats splitting the vote and no popular majority, the question had to be determined by the Electoral College. The decision seemed to take forever. Thomas was waiting at the depot when the train came in bringing newspapers reporting the results. All around him, people reacted with shock. The winner, Republican Abraham Lincoln, was not on their ballots.

Standing back as men angrily shook their fists and shouted that the state must call a convention to decide about their sovereignty, Thomas thought, *If Mitch were here, he'd say Lincoln's election precipitated another Boston Tea Party.*

Immediately, conventions were set across the South. As Thomas approached the new Thomasville courthouse to select local delegates to attend the Georgia assembly at the capital in Milledgeville, he dreaded what was about to happen. He saw men from all of the political factions converging on the square and climbing the steep steps to the columned portico recently completed by John Wind.

The conference lasted for hours. Sweat-soaked with anxiety, Thomas sighed in relief when Samuel Spencer, A. H. Hansell, and William Ponder were elected. They would vote for secession.

Tension gripped everyone as southern states voted. South Carolina came out of the Union on December 20, 1860. As 1861 dawned, Mississippi, Florida, Alabama, Georgia, Louisiana and Texas followed suit.

Thomas read an editorial from a newspaper from Georgia's capital, the *Milledge-ville Federal Union,* to a well-pleased Lavinia. " 'We are indisputably bound up with the cotton states, which lie on all sides of us. If they prosper, we will prosper. If they are ruined, we will be ruined . . . Let us not part from them, but stand squarely by them come weal or woe.' "

"How eloquent!" Lavinia exclaimed, alive with the excitement. "I agree. The United States flourished independent of England. So shall the South excel without the North. Surely, England will side with us because they must have our cotton."

"Yes," Thomas said tersely. He realized she — like most — had no dread of Northern reprisals, but fear twisted his stomach. He now owned ten thousand acres. Most of it was planted in cotton. *What will I do with it if it comes to war?*

Lavinia continued gaily. "You haven't read Frank's latest letter from Athens. It's all about the convention forming the Confederate States of America, which met in Montgomery, Alabama. He included an article about how diamonds were even being worn for breakfast. The former leaders in Washington have simply come to the South to run our new country. Jefferson Davis was elected president, but Frank's particularly excited that Alexander Stephens has been elected Vice-President of the Confederacy."

"Why?"

"Because Stephens was an alumnus of Lumpkin Law School as well."

Thomas sighed. *I wish Frank had stayed at home with all of this unrest. At least he's in North Georgia.* He rubbed his hand over his eyes and kept his worries from Lavinia.

On an April afternoon as Thomas and Tommy were leaving for town with a wagon to bring back supplies, Lavinia ran after them, calling, "Be sure to check if the stage has come in. I'm hoping for a letter from Harriet. I haven't heard from her in ages."

Tommy grinned. "Maybe she thinks she's too good to write since the records were published showing she led the county with two hundred thirty-five bales of cotton and five thousand bushels of sweet potatoes."

Lavinia's laughter pealed. "She beat all you men and never let her pretty hair get out of place."

Thomas chuckled and threw her a kiss. He wanted to get away without Lavinia. *I wish I could shield her from the events that are shaking the world outside Greenwood.*

He slumped on the wagon seat and admitted to himself that Lavinia had surprised him. It had not upset her that trouble began from the moment of Lincoln's fall election. Florida had moved to seize its forts on both the Atlantic Ocean and the Gulf of Mexico. Pensacola, with its deep harbor, was the largest town along Florida's twelve-hundred-mile coastline. The federal forts there were claimed by quickly organized Florida troops who forced out the Union soldiers. The federals retreated into Fort Pickens on Santa Rosa Island in the bay. There, Lieutenant Adam Slemmer held out, refusing to surrender to Florida. Meanwhile, the same standoff occurred in South Carolina at Fort Sumter in Charleston harbor. All winter the situation had simmered, waiting to boil over.

Lavinia had blithely argued that, of course, states should control what was within their borders instead of some foreign power. Thomas had said little. The question was too important. The South holding its forts and keeping its seaports open was vital.

Still lost in worries, he sat up in surprise when he realized that Tommy had driven into Thomasville and stopped the wagon at McKinnon's store. The streets were strangely deserted. Panic seized him to know what was happening beyond the isolated Pine Barrens. Leaving Tommy at the general store to fill the order, he hurried to the newspaper office.

As Thomas read the *Southern Enterprise,* his hands shook. It stated that after Lincoln's March inauguration, his first presidential act was to send reinforcements to Fort Pickens and Fort Sumter. The weekly paper, dated April 3, 1861, was six days old. Thomas agonized to know what was happening now. Feeling sick with apprehension, he thought, *Lincoln realizes he's forcing a crisis.*

He threw away the newspaper before he rejoined Tommy. He found him and the storekeeper wrestling a barrel into the wagon.

A mournful sound floated down the street, and Tommy dropped the barrel on his toe, yelling, "What's that?"

The clerk snorted a laugh. "Country boy, you just heard a train whistle." He stuck his thumbs in his suspenders and boasted, "This here town's fixing to be somebody, for shore. When that train comes in, we're throwing a barbecue. The train is bringing ice from up north. Now everybody can have ice for lemonade instead of just a little piece for the saloon like comes in the boot of the stagecoach."

Thomas interrupted his spiel. "The

whistle? Where's the train now?"

"Track's finished to a couple miles out. The passenger train won't be here 'til the sixteenth, but a working locomotive is out there." He pointed. "You stay on the farm too much. Everybody's been flocking to see the 'iron horse.' "

"Can we, Papa? Can we?"

Thomas felt the old urge to tousle his son's hair because he sounded twelve, but Tommy was twenty-two and taller than he was. A smile lifted his tired face. Without Mitch to share it, the victory of getting the railroad and access to the prime market at Savannah and the Atlantic Ocean had been bittersweet; he had lost interest. Now, Tommy's excitement at seeing a train made him feel young and light-hearted, too.

"Sure son, let's go."

Lavinia peered through the lace curtains for the fifth time. *What could be keeping them?*

At last she heard the rattle of the wagon and ran out.

"I'm sorry we're so late, honey . . ."

"Mama, you should have seen it," Tommy shouted. "A big locomotive, hissing steam underneath, belching black smoke through a ballooning smokestack. Rumbling down the track, it roars like that tornado."

Mattie bounced down the steps. "Papa, how could you take Tommy and not us?"

Florence appeared quietly. "Please take us tomorrow."

Thomas laughed. "There's to be a big celebration next week. The first train of cars will arrive in Thomasville April sixteenth. Mr. Naylor, the conductor, plans to oblige the ladies by taking them out for a pleasure ride."

Lavinia placated her teen-aged daughters. "Hadn't you rather go when everyone is there and you can be all dressed up for your beaux?"

"Yes! Come on, Florrie. Let's decide what to wear."

Thomas put his arm around Lavinia's waist as they climbed the steps. His voice held as much exhilaration as Tommy's. "Just think! A train will be arriving daily from Savannah at four thirty-five a.m., and another will be leaving at twelve forty-five p.m. In just thirteen hours, our cotton can travel two hundred miles and be loaded on ships bound directly for Liverpool and the looms of Lancashire, England. Thomasville has finally become part of the rest of Georgia — and the world!"

Lavinia said nothing, but he did not notice. She felt a heaviness weighing her shoulders. She remembered how frightened she had been when she first encountered the Pine Barren's silence. *Now I fear that roaring train pressing into our paradise.*

The clanging bell set everyone's toes tapping to the rhythm, hurrying them through the streets. Swept along, Lavinia knew that most, like her, had never seen a locomotive. The whistle joined the bell, and the people surged toward the sound.

As Lavinia was pushed and shoved, she thought she had never witnessed the kind of excitement that had soared since the message came that South Carolina had fired on Fort Sumter on April 12, 1861, in an effort to reclaim their property that the Union soldiers were holding. Lincoln had pronounced the cannon fire an act of war. Immediately the United States President called for army volunteers, forcing the taking of sides.

Virginia, North Carolina, Tennessee, and Arkansas joined the lower South in secession. Now on April 16, there were ten in the Confederate States of America. It all seemed unreal to Lavinia as the usually sleepy village of Thomasville swirled around her in a celebrating frenzy.

Jostled, by the shouting mass, as they

moved toward the depot and the welcoming ceremonial, she clutched Florence's arm for support. Touching the plaid taffeta of the girl's walking dress made Lavinia cling to reality. She was glad she had insisted her seventeen-year-old daughter wear green. It set off her red hair, but her freckles stood out like copper coins even though Lavinia had spent an hour bleaching them with buttermilk. No matter. Surely today Florence would attract some young man's attention. Instead of her usual look of loneliness that pierced Lavinia's heart, animation danced in Florence's eyes.

Searching for Mattie, Lavinia glimpsed her peach blossom gown up ahead. It did not surprise her that her handsome cousin, George McRae, had taken the opportunity to put his arm around her shoulder to protect her from the crush of the crowd. Mattie carried an armful of spring flowers because she was one of the Fletcher Institute students selected to present them in the ceremony. *She really stands out from the rest,* Lavinia thought. *Half of the young bucks in the county are prancing around her, even though she's only fifteen.*

Cheers rose from the throng. Glad of her height, Lavinia stood on tiptoe to see what was happening. In a cloud of steam, the

268

train pulled into the depot. Seeming to shake the earth, it stopped with a great screeching of brakes and spewing of cinders. Lavinia thought the locomotive a monster with its pointed cowcatcher on its long snout. She pressed her hands over her ears. *It's so big and black and deafening.*

At that moment, the two-horse hack arrived from Albany. The driver blew his bugle to announce the mail had arrived. Lavinia heard it vaguely, but no one was paying attention to the old-fashioned stagecoach.

Thomas stood waiting on the platform, a head taller than the other men in the group who had played a part in bringing the railroad. She strained to catch their words as they formally greeted the conductor, engineer, and fireman. She caught a glimpse of green streamers fluttering from the tiers of a peach-colored hoop skirt. Mattie had made her way to the raised area. Making a face, Lavinia pushed her way closer. Now she could see hands reaching out from all directions to help Mattie up to the podium.

Gracefully, Mattie curtsied, showing off to perfection the elaborate criss-cross design of ribbons cascading down one side of the spreading skirt. With a well-practiced speech, she presented the flowers. The engineer secured them atop the locomotive.

Now Thomas stepped forward with his white hair shining. He introduced the conductor, Mr. T. J. Naylor, who was to speak for the railroad.

Face serious, Naylor silenced the townspeople with uplifted arms. "Friends," he shouted. "Thank you for your welcome. On this momentous occasion of the *Atlantic and Gulf* reaching its terminus in Thomasville, I bring you a stupendous souvenir." He held up a cannonball. "This is one of the first balls fired from Fort Sumter."

Cheer upon cheer precluded words. Only the sound of a brass band playing "Dixie" was louder. The people parted as the Thomasville Guards marched up the street toward the depot. Their dark blue silk flag fluttered over their heads, showing 1853, the date the militia group had been organized. Considering themselves fully prepared, they had already written Georgia's Governor Joe Brown to offer their services to the Confederacy.

Another drum roll sounded as the newly formed Ochlockonee Light Infantry stepped smartly around the corner. Their gray uniforms and Confederate flag had been quickly made in their eagerness to join the fray.

Lavinia knew she was witnessing unconquerable pride in the invincibility of the South. She, herself, had been militant, and she wondered why in the midst of all of this confidence, she was suddenly overwhelmed by sadness. Feeling weak, she left the parade and sought a bench in the shade.

I need Thomas, she thought, unable to see him since the formalities had ended. Finally she spotted him talking to Mitchell's oldest sons, Black and Price. Eliza was with them. Thomas had spent a great deal of time advising his late brother's family about business. She knew he had told them to hold back some cotton bales in the Thomasville warehouse until the train finally connected them with the city of Savannah. In addition to the ease and speed of shipment, cotton factors there were offering a better price than the ones who transacted the deals in little Saint Marks on the hurricane-riddled Gulf.

When it appeared they had finished their conversation, Lavinia motioned to Eliza. She moved through the crowd, which parted in respect of her widow's weeds. She still wore the deepest mourning even though Mitchell had been dead for two years.

As she joined Lavinia, Eliza's voice held life again. "Isn't this exciting? Our chivalrous knights are ready to defend us — just like in the pages of *Ivanhoe*."

Lavinia nodded, thinking the whole South must be reading Sir Walter Scott.

"I declare, you look depressed," said Eliza. "We'll trade with England and show New York we don't need them. This silly war will last no time. Besides, it won't touch us way down here . . ."

"Hidden in the pines," Lavinia finished for her. She forced a laugh.

"You're just hungry. Everyone's forgotten the barbecue in the excitement. Let's go in the Town House Hotel and have tea."

As they sat down in the quiet dining room, Lavinia tried to relax. Eliza folded the heavy swath of tulle veiling that covered her face back over her bonnet. Lavinia was surprised at how Eliza's hair had grayed. Her own remained dark even though, today, she felt all of her fifty-one years.

They were presented with a pot of tea and a tiered dish of open-faced sandwiches and scones. The sweets did not relieve Lavinia's melancholy, but they revived her enough to remember hearing the mail bugle. Leaving Eliza, she walked to the post office and was rewarded by three letters. She was delighted to have one from her darling granddaughter, Livy J. Maybe it would cheer her. The next envelope was her letter to Frank, returned unopened from Franklin College.

Frantic, she wondered, *Where is he?* Her hand shook as she snatched open the third, a note from Frank. Scanning words that made her feel her heart had stopped beating, she could no longer hold back tears. She struggled through the throng until she found Thomas.

"Frank's in the army. He wrote that he was afraid the war would be over and he'd miss out if he took time to come home to sign up. He joined the Oconee Cavalry because they are rushing to Virginia to guard the Confederacy's border against invasion."

Feeling faint, she sank into Thomas's arms.

CHAPTER XVI

"Mama, where are you?" called Mattie. "I got a letter from George McRae."

"In my room," Lavinia replied, quickly hiding the little box under the bed as she heard Mattie clattering up the stairs. She pressed her hand to her heart, wondering how, if it still hurt this badly to have lost infant boys, she could bear the possibility of losing a grown son. As her daughter entered, she asked in an anxious voice, "Did any of us hear from Frank?"

"No, but remember he's farther away than our local troops now that the capital of the Confederate States has been moved from Alabama to Richmond, Virginia." She pouted her full lips. "George wouldn't have to be defending Savannah if Lincoln hadn't been so nasty and blockaded our harbors."

Lavinia could think of a stronger word. She felt miffed. Now that they finally had a train to Savannah, the Union Navy had

274

blocked all Southern ports. "Thank goodness the Atlantic was open three days and your father and Eliza got to ship out one load of cotton."

How are we supposed to make a living if we can't export our crop? Lavinia wondered as she wearily took the letter Mattie offered.

Thunderbolt Battery
June 17, 1861
Dear Cousin,

Do not attribute this delay in writing to you to negligence or forgetfulness; but to the pressure of business, or, rather, hard physical labor. We have been engaged in the constitution of a battery . . . under the supervision of Captain Screven, which is the pride of his company (A) to complete and mount the guns.

Having had some military experience, I have not been disappointed in the monotonous routine of duty . . . I would rather see our company marched to Virginia than to remain at Thunderbolt inactive . . .

We have had several alarms, enough to have picket guard (among whom were Mitch Jones, Tom Few and myself.)

Florence came in and sat down on the foot of the chaise lounge, where Mattie had sprawled herself.

Mattie hugged her exuberantly. "Sister, I have a letter from Cousin George, and there's a note for you."

Lavinia read the ending aloud. " 'Ask cousin Florrie for me: What is the good word? How she enjoys life, etc?' . . . He's made a play on words 'Tell her that a "few" of our company came very near being drowned yesterday, a boat having capsized with Tom two miles from shore.' "

"Oh my goodness," exclaimed Florence. "How did they rescue him?"

Lavinia laughed. "He doesn't say, except that Tom Few is going sailing no more. We must all write to George. He sounds as if he's enjoying his first adventures away from home, but says he has the blues."

"Yes, ma'am, we will," said Florence.

Mattie's attention had wandered, and Lavinia suspected that she was plotting mischief. "Mattie?" she questioned.

"Um. Yes ma'am, I'll write. May Florence and I go visit Aunt Harriet? We haven't seen her in a long time."

"And . . . ?" Lavinia prodded for more information.

Florence spoke up. "The Ochlockonee Light Infantry and the Thomasville Guards are invited to hold a week's encampment near Duncanville. There will be preaching and patriotic activities."

"And socials and a big picnic," Mattie said, gaiety bubbling over. "May we?"

Lavinia frowned, knowing that the Guards were stable men, but the Infantry was composed of boys under twenty-one.

"We need to salute the chevaliers who are going out to defend our honor," Mattie pleaded.

"The rest of us have been honoring them by making their uniforms and flags," Lavinia said in a dismissive tone. She began brushing her hair, but the mirror showed Mattie's face puckering with tears. She relented. "All right, you may go, but I'd better go along. I'll take food for your young knights."

Lavinia was surprised that three or four hundred people had gathered to observe the encampment in Major Mash's oak grove and enjoy the July morning. She and Harriet joined women who were covering a long plank table with buttery chicken pies, terrapin stew, corn-on-the-cob, black-eyed peas swimming in brown liquor made from ham hocks, and crusty sweet potato pones. Many had brought potato salad. Instead of that Lavinia added a dish of Savannah red rice that was rich with tomatoes, sausage, and hot pepper sauce. She enjoyed being different.

A mood of high excitement buzzed on the humid air as everyone watched the unseasoned infantrymen drill. It surprised Lavinia that women who had never thought of politics applauded and gushed that the enemy would soon give up trying to force them back into the Union when they saw these stalwart soldiers, who were carrying Thomas County's ladies' colors. The Federals would soon see the Confederacy was serious about independence.

"Didn't our land pursue freedom from England in '76?" The question echoed and reechoed around the area.

Guns in the hands of the excited youths made Lavinia nervous, and she was relieved when the drill ended. Released, the soldiers stacked their weapons before their tents, which were set up at the edge of the grove. The boys double-timed toward the mouth-watering aromas of the picnic.

Lavinia was talking to Harriet when, suddenly, her guard went up. She had noticed that Mattie had spent hours with the curling iron creating long ringlets around her rosy cheeks. She had tried numerous outfits before selecting a three-tired hoop skirt with fluttering ribbons. This was not too unusual;

however, the intensity of the blue of Mattie's eyes was causing her to conceal them with her lashes as she and her friends moved through the company with plates of pound cake. Something about all of the girls' twitching dimples and sugared voices made Lavinia wonder what they were up to.

Narrowing her eyes against the noontime glare, Lavinia began to watch more closely. Florence's floating red hair and green plaid were nowhere to be seen. She scanned the crowd. *Mattie has disappeared, now.*

She watched as, one by one, the girls slipped away. The feasting soldiers did not notice.

When the smooth-faced youngsters of the Ochlockonee Light Infantry had paid their compliments to the ladies for the meal, their drummer beat out, "return to quarters." They ambled to their tents, which were set up at the edge of the grove. Suddenly, there was scuffling and shouting.

"Who stole our guns?"

Lavinia laughed and directed Harriet's attention as the boys turned to face an attack. Their own rifles pointed at them from behind pine trees and benches where hoop skirts billowed out to reveal their adversaries. Lavinia recognized Mattie's pink ribbons. The Captain ordered charge, but the giggling enemy was prepared with fixed bayonets. One lieutenant yielded his sword and enjoyed his capture.

The audience clapped and cheered as the men retreated, regrouped and attacked, trying to wrench the bayonets from the girls' hands. Disarmed of her rifle, Mattie snatched an unsuspecting boy's sword from his scabbard and dashed about brandishing it and taunting.

The drumbeat sounded, "Surround and go hand-to-hand." The soldiers jumped at the chance to get their hands on the elusive girls. In the general melee, prisoners were taken and everyone fell about laughing.

"At least no one was wounded," said Lavinia.

"Except, perhaps, by cupid," replied Harriet, nodding toward Mattie whose wrists were being held by one boy while another took advantage of the unusual opportunity to encircle her waist from behind.

In spite of the merriment, Lavinia felt her smile was forced. *Everyone treats this war as a lark,* she thought, *but I wonder, where is my little freckled-faced Frank?*

"Mama! Mama!"

A few weeks later, it was her oldest daughter's voice, ringing with agitation, which searched for Lavinia. She looked up from the couch where she was relaxing in the front hall as Livy stamped across the porch and banged in the door. Lavinia sighed. Livy was a storm cloud at the least problem, but this must be something real.

Livy flung herself into her mother's arms, sobbing.

Lavinia patted and soothed, drawing Livy to sink into the comfort of the velvet sofa. All she could understand was, "It's terrible."

Florence, as quiet as her sister was tempestuous, communicated with Lavinia with motions and slipped out to prepare a pot of tea. Livy accepted her mother's handkerchief and regained control.

"The hope for peaceful settlement of the northern aggression is over. There's been a battle!" Livy sniffed.

Mattie came in, eyes bright with excitement as she squealed, "What's happening?

"The Yankees invaded Virginia on July twenty-first. Someplace called Manassas Junction." Livy replied. "People went out from Washington City to picnic and watch the skirmish. It wasn't long before our General Beauregard sent the enemy packing across a creek called Bull Run. The foolish townsfolk scampered home like scared rabbits."

Lavinia felt faint, but Mattie danced about, watching herself in the twin mirrors. "Yea!" she shouted. "I knew our southern heroes would lick 'em quickly."

"The silly war's not over that easily," Livy said tartly. "We thought our governor wasn't concerned about using our Southwest Georgia troops, but with the Confederacy's border breached, Governor Brown has called up our units."

Mattie perched sassily on the ornately carved hall table. "You mean just as I've graduated from Fletcher's there won't be any boys in town?"

Livy pursed her lips into a sneer. "Sorry to spoil your summer." The amber comb atop her head quivered violently. "I'm to be left alone with a house full of children. David is giving up his practice and going to Manassas with the Thomas County Rangers."

Livy's tears stopped, and her voice became sarcastic. "My husband is old enough to know better than to rush off to war, but he's as bad as all of the hot-blooded boys who've made Stonewall Jackson their hero after his unyielding stand in this battle. David says doctors are needed because there were nearly two thousand wounded. Can you believe this?"

Lavinia drew in her breath at the thought of so many causalities. Relief flowed through her as Thomas entered. His comforting presence drew every eye to him.

Looking from one strained face to the other, he said, "I see you've heard about the Battle of Manassas Junction. The Thomasville Guards and Ochlockonee Light Infantry are entraining tomorrow for Brunswick to patrol Georgia's coast."

Thomas took Lavinia's hand and squeezed it. "Honey, we're to hold a prayer meeting at the Methodist Church before they go. Florence . . ." He turned as she slipped in with a tea tray, ". . . will you help give out New Testaments to the boys? Mattie, they've asked for you to sing."

Silently, they drank the steaming tea.

Thomas stood in the oppressive September heat of the street in Thomasville, rubbing the standing cords of his neck. Around him, strident voices were raised in war talk as they had been for the last six weeks. Most men boasted that the valor of southern gentleman would soon put an end to the hired Union army. They were exultant that because of the South's overwhelming victory at Manassas, Britain was poised to recognize the Confederate States of America as an independent nation. England's industry had to have cotton.

Thomas remained silent, apart from the group, but he nodded and thought, *If England and Europe come to our aid, this war could soon be over.* He breathed easier; then his elation burst. *But what these talkers aren't considering is that Lincoln is wily at waging war. He's put a chokehold on our economy.*

All through August as Thomas had picked and ginned cotton, he worried about what he was going to do with it. Everyone had guessed the Union Navy would not notice the little port of Saint Marks. They did.

Tallahassee, only twenty miles upriver from the Gulf port, feared attack from Union raiders. Even as he worried, Thomas heard more wagons rattling into town, loaded with Florida cotton. It was a bizarre sight to see it coming here instead of the other way around.

With Florida's and Georgia's crop stored in Thomasville's warehouse, it could put us in danger, he thought. *These bales are like gold bars.*

Thomas entered Judge Hansell's office to share his worries. "Sir, if the Yankees blockading Saint Marks find out we have millions of dollars' worth of cotton stored here, Thomasville could be a tempting target."

The old gentleman tugged at his grizzled beard and cleared his throat. "You are quite right, my boy," he replied to Thomas. "With all of our able-bodied men — seven hundred out of the thousand on the voting lists — gone to the battlefront and Tallahassee shipping her cotton here in case of invasion, we could be ripe for assault."

"Yes, sir. The United States gunboat *Mohawk* is chasing the Confederate steamers back into the Saint Marks River. They captured our sloop *George B. Sloat* when it tried to run the blockade. The enemy is circling like a hawk on a hen house."

Hansell banged his hand on his desk. "We must not let invaders plant their polluted feet on Thomasville's sacred soil. We should organize a reserve force of men whose age, health, and so forth keeps them from the front. I'll write Governor Brown to send muskets to equip a Thomas Reserve for local emergencies."

As he left the Judge's office, Thomas felt satisfied that the action would make the local situation safer. He headed for the post office, hoping for a letter. *I would feel better just to know where Frank is.*

On a November day in that somber year of 1861 as gray as his soul, Thomas stood by the steaming train and drew back from Lavinia's clinging arms. These wartime partings were altering the rules of etiquette against showing affection in public. He felt torn in two, with half of his heart longing to stay and protect Lavinia and his daughters and the rest of him knowing his son needed him worse. He was leaving Augustus in charge of his most trusted men posted as guards on the perimeters of Greenwood property — just in case.

"If there's hint of Yankee raiders getting past our soldiers guarding the coast and moving north through Florida, send word to Judge Hansell."

Lavinia nodded and wiped tears. "I couldn't bear for you to go onto the battlefields if Frank hadn't written that he was cold and hungry."

Thomas heaved a shuddering breath. He had known he must find his son from the minute he received Frank's letter telling that Thomas R. R. Cobb had been given his commission as colonel and had organized a legion, a regiment composed of infantry, cavalry, and artillery units that included the Athens men. Cobb's Legion was assigned to the division of General John B. Magruder at Yorktown, Virginia. Frank said that temperatures were dropping rapidly in the

Virginia Peninsula, which was created by the James and York Rivers as they flowed toward Norfolk and Hampton Roads. He needed blankets. He was also expected to provide his own meat and someone to cook it. His former body servant, Fed, had been willing, even excited about helping fight the enemy.

Suddenly, the train whistle gave them all a jolt. Thomas, Tommy, and Fed climbed aboard. Thomas looked at the young black man, expecting him to be frightened. Instead, his face gleamed with excitement. He was thrilled with the ride. *It's good he doesn't know how worried I am,* Thomas thought, *I wonder what we'll encounter and what forms of transportation it might take to complete this many-legged journey.*

I've never been this cold in my life, Thomas thought, clutching a blanket around his shoulders. The wagon he had bought for the last few miles of the trip bounced on the frozen ruts of the crude road. Tommy was shivering, but Fed kept throwing back his cover to point at icicles hanging from trees. Fed had never seen snow, and he jabbered from the moment they left Richmond and headed down the finger of land between the James and York Rivers. When they neared the old Revolutionary War village of Yorktown, they were stopped by pickets. Thomas realized the inexperienced youths could easily shoot friends and admit foes. He sighed with relief as they cleared the guards and reached the soldiers' cabins along the York River. He brushed tears from his eyes in thankfulness that the activity around Camp Marion seemed peaceful.

Tommy and Fed could hardly contain their excitement, but Thomas's only concern was Frank. He watched his boy soldier running toward him. Frank looked even smaller than he was in the tight-fitting gray uniform, so young that it made Thomas's heart ache.

Thomas opened his arms, and Frank threw himself into his father's embrace, crying out, "I'd written for you to ship the blankets to save the expense and trouble of coming — but am I glad to see you!"

Frank greeted Tommy and then noticed Fed, who was grinning broadly. "How ya doin', Fed? Maybe now I'll warm up with you to help keep a fire going. Did you bring plenty of blankets?"

"Us cold shorely did," Fed replied. "And cured hams, your ma's peach preserves, and canned tomatoes, and dried butter beans . . ."

"And fruitcake?"

"You know your mama," said Thomas, laughing. "But tell me, how are you?"

"Fine. Bored. We're eager for a fight. But they say our being here is the key to protecting Richmond from the east."

Frank turned to his brother. "How are the Thomasville girls doing? No one tells me a thing about them."

Tommy's laughing recital was interrupted as the commanding officer approached.

Frank saluted. "Sir, may I introduce my father, Thomas P. Jones. Pa, this is Colonel Thomas R. R. Cobb, who organized the Legion."

The colonel's long, serious face warmed. He smoothed back his slickly combed dark hair and spoke graciously. "May I invite my young private and his family to join me at regimental mess?"

Over the meal, Cobb talked constantly of his wife, and Thomas realized that Camp Marion must be named for her.

Cobb passed a jar of peach preserves. "See how you like them, Mr. Jones. Marion made them for me."

Thomas ate and then nodded appreciatively. "I believe those are the most superior preserves I've ever tasted."

Frank's freckles popped, and Thomas

kicked him under the table. Tommy grinned.

Cobb kept talking without noticing. "As I wrote Marion, the Athens companies give me less trouble than any in the Legion. I've never had to punish one nor has a complaint been made against any."

"I'm pleased to hear that, sir. Frank has been away from home a long time. I'm glad he remembers who he is."

The colonel nodded. "We keep hearing rumors that General George McClellan is going to land a powerful army at the tip of the Peninsula and try to seize Richmond. Our boys are itching to fight, but McClellan is moving so slow we're calling him the 'Virginia Creeper.'" Cobb laughed at his own joke and then became serious.

"Lincoln is fascinated with the invention of weapons. He's supplied McClellan with new rifled muskets that spin out a Minnie ball. The soft lead bullet does so much damage to a limb there's nothing left to do but amputate. Our plain muskets are old and few, but I have every confidence we can hold our position. My Legionnaires consider themselves unconquerable."

In the privacy of her bedroom, Lavinia clutched the letter, feeling frantic. On November twentieth, Frank had written for

Thomas not to visit, but he should have already reached the front by then. Her son dutifully wrote each family member, but because Mattie was such as constant writer, the most informative mail came addressed formally to her as Martha Tallulah; however the letters were meant to be passed around.

Now Mattie had received this letter assuming her father was home. As Lavinia read Frank's newest communication again and again, she was seized with an agony of anxiety about Thomas. *Where is he?*

The letter began routinely enough, but Lavinia's panic rose as she continued.

Camp Marion, Va., near Yorktown,
Dec. 17, 1861
Dear Martha:
I have been looking for a letter from some of you at home for several days, but none has come thus far, and as we are to leave tomorrow, I thought I would write to you tonight. We received orders tonight to leave in the morning for Young's Mills — the left wing of Cav. Battalion — consisting of our company and Capt. Lawton's . . . and don't know whether I will get a chance to write any letters down there or not. At any rate, don't expect me to, or be uneasy about me if you don't get one for some

time. I hate very much to leave our cabins to go into tents again, with not much hope of a fight either.

Gen. Magruder received information today that thirty thousand Yankees were encamped below Hampton Roads and were not allowed to leave the lines under any circumstances and were only awaiting the signal from the fleet to advance on Yorktown. They go by land and the fleet up York River. Gen. Magruder says we are in imminent danger of an attack in forty-eight hours, and, if we are not attacked in that time, we will not be until next spring. If the battle does come off it will take place before this reaches you and it will be no news to you after all. I don't put any confidence, though, in the expectations of a fight and leave here with a great deal of reluctance.

I suppose Pa will be at home by the time this letter reaches you. You can tell him I received Selkirk's letter informing me of the shipment of the boxes, but I have not received them yet. I expect, though, they will come through safe. The river boats are very much crowded with army stores at the time and boxes generally lay over until they are transported. This is the only news here at this time and it will do to talk about for several weeks to come. The Troop Artillery, which has been connected with the Legion, has just come in from Western Va. They have seen quite a hard time of it up there. They came in very good spirits, having just been paid off in Richmond.

I wrote to Ma about making me some shirts, in my last, and will tell you what I want you and Florence to do, or if you want to, tell Ma. I know she will without hesitation or reluctance . . . make me a "horse blanket" with the inside of the collar and wristbands, too, of yellow flannel, or orange colored flannel, and the binding on the top of the pockets and pleat it in the middle of the shirt, where the buttonholes will be worked, of the same material. Yellow is the distinguishing mark of the Cavalry and I want it on my shirt as well as coat and pants. She can put them in a small box and Tommy can express it to Richmond. By the way, tell Tommy that I don't want him to break, lose, or carry off my pipe I left at home. I want it taken care of until I return.

For pity's sake, try and see if you and Florence can't write to me once a week, hereafter . . .

Give my love to all the family and write

to me soon. Tell me all the news about town, and who is the preacher for next year? . . . I hope he will not get on intimate terms with you all before I get back. Let him stay in town where he belongs.

I remain

Your affectionate brother.

H. F. Jones.

Lavinia read the letter three times. No news had come of a battle, but Frank's wording indicated they would remain there throughout the winter.

As soon as we get a cold day, I must have the men kill hogs, she thought. *We must send Frank more ham and bacon.*

Then she gritted her teeth as she wondered where she would get enough salt to cure the meat. Supplies of everything had dwindled quickly after Lincoln imposed the blockade. Lavinia understood that an important seaport like Savannah would be swarmed with enemy ships, but it did seem that little Saint Marks, hidden up a swampy river, should have gone unnoticed. Unfortunately, the Federals had enough ships to patrol the whole Gulf Coast.

We can do without other things, she realized, but how will we feed ourselves without salt to preserve the beef and pork?

Music drifted up the stairs as Mattie began playing the piano and singing "Come Where My Love Lies Dreaming."

Usually Lavinia enjoyed her daughter's voice, but her fretfulness made the popular song grate on her nerves. Tossing on a shawl, she went downstairs. She tried not to look in the parlor where the Christmas tree and gifts waited. Christmas could not come until Thomas and Tommy returned.

In the garden, Lavinia focused on dead-heading the spent blossoms on the camellia bushes to busy her hands and bury her problems. She especially loved these winter-blooming natives of China and Japan. Before this terrible conflict began, she had ordered them from Berckmans's Fruitland Nurseries in Augusta, Georgia, by way of Savannah. *There are some advantages to having a train.* The thought made her mind return to Thomas. *And it will bring him back to me quicker than a stagecoach.*

She walked around her garden until she was tired enough to sleep. In the wee hours of the morning, she roused to the movement of the bed curtains.

A cold-footed Thomas slid into her warm space. "Merry Christmas," he said before she stopped him with kisses.

At long last when he had warmed and

shared news, Thomas said, "Light the lamp, and I'll show you the present Frank sent you."

Lavinia opened the small parcel and took out the Daguerreotype of Frank. His flat cavalry hat with its jaunty feather sat squarely over his little round face. She kissed it and smiled at Thomas through tears. "He's twenty, I know, but he still looks like my little boy."

A few hours later as day was breaking, Lavinia got up, knocked on the children's doors, and gaily called, "Christmas give."

Christmas dinner seemed to Thomas to be the best they had ever eaten in spite of the lack of things they could not get because of the blockade. Tommy was talking uncontrollably, and as Thomas carved the turkey, he kept shaking his head at him to stop his tales of the war zone. He must not let his mother know how bad things really were at the front.

They ended the meal with ambrosia, piled high with whipped cream to cover the lack of sugar for the cut up oranges and the substitution of pecans for the usual coconut.

As they savored the dessert, Mattie read aloud her latest letter from Frank:

"Trooper's Div." Camp Marion,
near Yorktown, Va.
Dec. 31st, 1861.
Dear Martha:

I received your letter today of date Dec. 22nd. I have written home two or three times during the last ten days, but I will answer yours immediately . . .

There is not a particle of news in camp at present. No prospect of a fight; none of peace; and I would not turn around for the difference of the two. Col. Howell Cobb of the 16th Ga., Col. Ward of the 2nd Fla., Col. Winston of the 8th Ala. Troops, and Major-Gen. Magruder all spent the night in camp a few days ago. The band serenaded them and called on Magruder for a speech . . .

The Fla. Reg. has the reputation of being the most disorderly, most disrespectful, and most roguish of any Reg. on the Peninsula. They make a clean sweep of chickens, ducks, turkeys, pigs and geese wherever they go and burn up every fence in half a mile of them.

I got a letter from cousin Black . . . today, also. He . . . says he writes to none of the girls and hardly ever inquires after them. I don't believe he is so indifferent as all that, for he generally says a good deal about them . . .

Mark says to tell Tommy not to cut him out of Miss Florida, that he (Tommy) only said she wasn't as pretty as she used to be, in order to make him think he (Tommy) wasn't flying around her while he is gone. He says tell Tommy to only wait until he returns to take an even start . . .

Write soon.

Your affectionate brother,

H. F. Jones

Mattie and Florence giggled at the last paragraph, knowing that half of the girls in the county were batting their eyelashes at Tommy as they stood looking up, up at his breath-taking height, waiting to hear the rumble of his virile voice.

Thomas remained frowning and intro-spective, knowing from Colonel Cobb's words that winter at the front would merely be a time of restless waiting. When rains had passed and mud that made it impos-sible to move equipment had dried, McClel-lan's powerful army would try to take the Confederate capital at Richmond.

Chapter XVII

Thomas drove a covered wagon into Tallahassee on a mild January day in 1862, hoping to buy supplies. He desperately needed new plows. Lavinia's list included a barrel of sugar and a barrel of flour. She had underlined coffee. She knew he would not forget salt because they must kill hogs and cure meat for the year. Only in January and February was there ever a day cold enough for the job.

It won't be any time soon, he thought, taking off his jacket. The town was abloom with the camellias Lavinia so loved. *Our balmy weather and lush growth are what have us in trouble,* he thought. Year-around planting made everything in the South geared to agriculture, dependent upon northern industry or foreign goods. Thomas was thankful that Great Britain and France had issued Proclamations of Neutrality. In theory, imports and exports could ensue.

Unfortunately, the forty-two heavily armed Union Navy vessels that patrolled all southern seaports and river terminals not only kept southern ships in but also kept foreign freighters out.

Thomas sighed as he dismounted and made his way into the general store through clusters of gray-clad soldiers who were no doubt training at Camp Leon or Camp Brokaw. He entered the general store with little hope.

The storekeeper spit tobacco juice and waved at his empty shelves. "One of them Frenchie ships slipped in during a fog afore Christmas. Since then, none of the blockade-runners have made it in or out of the bay past the *U.S.S. Mohawk*. Folks here are without bare necessities. Tell your wife that our ladies are making substitute coffee from okra seed, pumpkin seed, acorns, cotton seed, or grits."

Thomas shuddered at the thought.

With little to sell, the man wanted to talk. He boasted that the Florida Rangers were driving cattle from as deep in southern Florida as the Peace River Valley to trains in Baldwin for shipping to the Confederate troops.

"Folks are calling them the Cow Cavalry. What are you Georgia Crackers sending our soldiers?"

Before Thomas could reply that Georgia was the main state feeding the Confederacy, the clerk continued.

"Them at Cedar Key have 'em all beat for patriotism. They're catching hundred-pound sea turtles, marching them up the plank to the Florida Railroad cars, and sending 'em to Fernandina and up to Virginny."

He cackled with laughter. "Can't you imagine seeing them four-foot shells walking off at t'other end and straight into a pot of green turtle soup?"

Thomas laughed at the picture. Sobering he asked, "What am I going to do about salt? I must have some. I have to feed my people."

"Lots of fellows have gone down to the coast and set up crude seawater evaporators." He jerked a thumb in direction of the Gulf.

"Where?"

"Not sure. The United States bark, *Kingfisher,* keeps shelling them, and they have to locate in different places in the swamp."

"Thanks. I'll find one," Thomas said with more confidence than he felt. Disconsolate, he started out, but the storekeeper followed. Throwing his arm across Thomas's shoul-

301

der, the clerk leaned close. Thomas tried not to cringe at his sour breath and catch his hoarse whisper.

"I know your reputation, but a body can't tell when some Unionist might be listening. Go to Saint Marks and ask for Daniel Ladd."

Heartened, Thomas resumed his journey, heading south of Tallahassee. As the road wound through the dark primeval forest, the wheels of the covered wagon struggled, sticking in the deep sand.

This war sure is causing a lot of inconvenience, Thomas thought. *But it will be worth it when the South has independence to govern ourselves and set our own import and export tariffs.*

When he arrived at the Saint Marks waterfront, Thomas was relieved to see the *Spray* at the wharf. Daniel Ladd had grown a goatee, but he recognized the genial man at once.

"It's nice to see you, Mr. Jones. What can I do for you?"

Thomas shook his hands and smiled. "Well, I need to get cotton out and plows in, but what I'm desperate for is salt."

"Come into the cabin and have a cup of coffee," said Ladd. He laughed. "We won't talk about what it's made from."

Once inside, Ladd quickly became serious. "I don't mean to brag sir, but the *Spray* is running the blockade more consistently than anyone. She's little for a steamer, and she's fast. The *U.S.S. Mohawk* is anchored in the bay at the depths of Spanish Hole, but the *Spray* can hide in a dark inlet and then make a dash. I don't mean to brag, sir, but she can cruise open sea at twelve knots per hour." Ladd laughed. "If I throw fat-lightard pine in the boiler with a full head of steam, I can squeeze two more knots from her engine."

"Can she make it to Cuba?" Thomas knew the danger on the ocean in a flat-bottomed riverboat.

Ladd nodded and grinned. "I've added a single mast for a sail, if needed."

"You are a brave man, sir. When can I bring some cotton?"

"Right away. Just to have it in readiness. Brigadier-General Joseph Finegan stations a lookout picket at the light station. From the lighthouse, they can monitor the positioning of the Union ships so we know when there's a chance of slipping past them."

They discussed arrangements, and then Ladd told him how to find his salt factory at Newport, the largest of the five towns along the Saint Marks River.

After more miles, Thomas approached Ladd Company. Confederate troops were stationed nearby as guards. The large, well-equipped salt factory had a tall smokestack. He followed the billowing smoke to a row of brick-lined evaporators complete with iron pans. After a few negotiations, he loaded a covered wagon with bags of salt. They cost an exorbitant twelve dollars and fifty cents per bushel, but he headed home, smiling all the way at the thought of surprising Lavinia.

Lavinia hummed as she plunged her arms up to the elbows in salt. Standing over the hollowed-out log, which held the precious commodity and the freshly dressed pork, she and Cherry worked the salt into the flesh side of the meat. As she packed hams into boxes of salt, being careful no piece touched another, she laughed at the repartee of the happy folk around her.

Breath clouds puffed from each shining face, but nobody minded the icy temperature. The first two weeks in January had been sunny seventies, but this morning before the roosters crowed, the happy cry went around the quarters, "It's cold enough for hog killin'."

Thomas moved among the men who were

butchering: slitting throats, hanging hogs, scalding skins. He kept reminding everyone, "Careful not to waste a scrap. Use everything but the squeal."

The men's laughter rolled across the yard toward the women who were grinding sausage under Julie's supervision. Julie motioned for Lavinia, and she changed tasks to season the meat with sage, thyme and red peppers from her herb garden. Then the mixture was poked into the cleaned small-intestine casings.

As the day wore on, the ice, which had clung to the small branches on the north side of the trees, began falling.

"Looks like only one cold day," Thomas said, coming up behind her. "That's why I slaughtered so many. I know you're exhausted."

"I'm all right," Lavinia replied. "If we use it sparingly, we've preserved enough to feed everyone all year."

"Lock it up," he said. "They are hungry now, and they won't be thinking beyond today."

Lavinia picked out the big smokehouse key from the chains on the chatelaine, the lovely gift Thomas had presented when they moved into Greenwood. She consistently wore it fastened to her waist with its mother-of-pearl clip. These days everything must be kept locked securely. The hams would be tempting as they remained in the salt for three weeks before they could be sewn into the croaker sacks, made airtight by soaking in lime water, and hung over green oak boughs to smoke. She turned the key in the big padlock and smiled at Thomas wearily.

Around them the farm hands were taking generous supper portions of the fresh meat to their cabins, smacking their lips, and saying, "Be good eatin' tonight."

Lavinia sighed. She had already sent Florence and Mattie to the kitchen to season the tenderloin and cut the small round strips into thin slices. Tired as she was, she would cook it herself to fix it just as Thomas liked it, lightly sautéed. The browned morsels and big, fluffy biscuits were all he wanted for supper.

Later, as Thomas blew out the bedside candle, Lavinia patted him and said, "It's comforting to know everyone on Greenwood has a satisfied stomach tonight."

Thomas's smile became hard to hold as the year 1862 brought ever-worsening news to a crescendo. The North was strangling the South by cutting off food supplies. A Federal amphibian force led a devastating raid on

Cedar Key, stopping the flow of turtles. In March, the enemy seized Fernandina, ending the shipping of livestock by train. Undaunted, the Cow Cavalry began running cattle drives through Georgia. Apalachicola, Florida, where blockade-runners had been successful, was captured in March. Desperately, the small and ill-equipped Confederate Navy sank their own steamboats in the shallow channel of the Apalachicola and Chattahoochee Rivers to thwart the enemy from sailing into Georgia and Alabama. On April twenty-fourth, New Orleans fell.

We can't count on more supplies from Europe, Thomas realized. *Or even from the west. All of our gateways to the world have clanged shut.*

Even so, the South's spirits stayed high. Frank wrote that a brilliant West Point–trained general, Robert E. Lee, had taken command of all of the men fighting in units around him, naming them the Army of Northern Virginia. They were ready when, with spring, McClellan began his long-dreaded advance. Frank had wanted to taste battle, and now Cobb's Legion was in muddy trenches, winning but sustaining losses.

Busy as he was, Thomas could not concentrate on work unless he knew what was happening. Each Wednesday, he joined the crowd in town who snatched up the *Thomasville Weekly Times* while the now homemade ink was still wet. He read avidly, following the struggle for the Virginia peninsula. Unbelievably bloody battles with names like Seven Pines and Fair Oaks followed one after the other. When Frank's division had to pull back, Thomas waited a week for the next report, not knowing what had happened to his son. Finally, by repeatedly outmaneuvering the larger force, Lee drove McClellan back in the Seven Days battles ending at Malvern Hill on July 1, 1862. McClellan blew up his own supply dump and retreated.

"Lee has saved Richmond," shouted men on Thomasville's street corners. They clapped one another on their shoulders and congratulated themselves because the Confederate victories had France, as well as England, ready to recognize the Confederacy.

Thomas assured his friends that the British Navy would liberate the South's ports to get the cotton. "They've proven they need it by the risks they've taken with the blockade."

Edward Remington, the most successful

of Thomasville's merchants, agreed. "I heard a British steamer slipped out of Saint Marks last week with a load and made it into Havana, Cuba, without incident."

The next Wednesday, their spirits were dampened when they heard about the federals' retaliation for the British ship eluding them. The *Tahoma* and *Somerset* bombarded the salt works near the lighthouse. Driving out the Confederate artillery, Union soldiers burned the fort and the woodwork and wooden stairs of the lighthouse to stop the spying from the tower that enabled southerners to see the positions of the blockading fleet.

In a week's time, Confederates replaced the stairway and manned the lighthouse with spyglasses again.

Thomas reveled in the fact that the *Spray* was infuriating the enemy by escaping again and again. Around him, everyone was saying, "The *Spray* has more lives than a cat."

Lavinia hated keeping up with her children by letter. At first it had seemed sensible to send Mattie away to college in the safety of North Georgia. She had been restless with the boys gone, all thumbs when the women gathered at Fletcher Institute to sew for the soldiers. Because Frank had loved Athens,

Mattie had chosen to go there to the girls' school, Lucy Cobb Institute. Lavinia's biggest worry was about her mischief. She had made all top grades at Fletcher's — except for deportment.

Suddenly all of that changed. Just as Lavinia was agonizing that Frank was being plunged into battle in the east, Mattie's formally fun-filled correspondence reeked with anxiety about her sweetheart's danger in the west.

In April Thomasville's Dixie Boys were transferred from duty with the State Troops guarding Savannah into the regular Confederate Army because Union soldiers were advancing into the Tennessee Mountains. In a desperate two-day battle at Shiloh, seventeen hundred twenty-three southern boys were killed and eight thousand wounded. The victorious Union officer on this new western front was General U. S. Grant. Lavinia thought his initials must stand for unconscionable slaughter.

Mattie's letters, adult overnight, recognized the horror even as she extolled the perfection of Sergeant Edwin Tralona Davis. Mattie had been corresponding with a dozen boys. Lavinia was surprised that she settled on this quiet young man with his strong sense of duty.

What a terrible time for her to decide she's in love with one particular soldier, Lavinia thought as she read Mattie's letter quoting Edwin:

"We are with General Braxton Bragg, heading into Kentucky to free that state of the foul invader that has overrun it, imprisoned its citizens, and abducted their property, and mal-treated helpless women and children."

The battle line to protect southern homes now stretches a thousand miles from Virginia to Missouri, Lavinia realized. She put down the letter, sighing. *How quickly romanticism has been replaced by reality.*

A few weeks later on an August afternoon, Thomas and Tommy took a moment's rest from pulling corn to join the family on the shady porch where they were cooling themselves with lemonade.

"Can't you imagine Frank's glee at this second battle at Manassas Junction?" Thomas asked. "Just picture Stonewall Jackson's men out of ammunition and throwing rocks."

Tommy laughed. "And yet they sent the Bluecoats retreating across Bull Run again."

Livy moaned. "David will never get home if they keep repeating the same silly battle."

Thomas patted her. "This time changed things. The victory emboldened Lee to advance into enemy territory." He stood up. "Son, we'd better advance on that harvest."

As they returned to the field, Thomas worried about the small profit he was making on foodstuffs for the army now that he could no longer freely market cotton. The *Spray* had smuggled out a few bales, but the little steamboat was barely over one hundred feet long and could not carry big loads.

Thomas wiped perspiration from his eyebrows and surveyed the bountiful corn crop. The perennial anticipation of every farmer in the new chance of another year lifted the deep lines in his face. *With Lee's brilliance and Jackson's daring, we should soon win our independence. Next year I'll plant cotton and replenish my dwindling bank account.*

During September, Thomas tried to follow the news of Lee's entry into Maryland as he met McClellan at Sharpsburg Ridge along Antietam Creek. On Wednesday, September 17, 1862, the armies fought all day in cornfields. Night stopped the battle with nothing decided, but 11,000 Confederates and 12,000 Federals had fallen wounded. Five thousand lay dead.

A few weeks later, Thomas stood on the platform with the townsfolk waiting for the *Atlantic and Gulf* locomotive to pull into the depot. Conductor Naylor swung down and silently handed out copies of photographs Matthew Brady was displaying in his New York Studio. Thomas nearly retched as he viewed graphic scenes of twisted dead along the Hagerstown Pike, of swollen corpses in corn fields, and of bodies lying three deep in a sunken road someone christened Bloody Lane.

Conductor Naylor spoke to the hushed group "In Savannah, we heard that the North is horrified after seeing the face of war. The Yankees don't think forcing the South to stay in the Union is worth it. They say soldiers are not reenlisting, and people are ready to leave us alone."

"Maybe is will soon be over," passed from one heavy-hearted man to another.

On December 15, Lee liberated Fredericksburg by defeating Ambrose Burnside, who had replaced the inefficient McClellan. Frank wrote glowingly of the victory and boasted he was promoted to adjutant.

As the family garlanded Greenwood for Christmas, Thomas talked of his pride in Frank, and Lavinia invoked blessing on the civilians of Fredericksburg who had remained steadfast in support of the soldiers.

Thomas placed the candles on the tree and said, "Let's light them tonight to celebrate. With Lee's continuing victories bringing the devastation of 1862 to close, we should soon live normal lives."

Chapter **XVIII**

Two days after Christmas, Thomas's confident words rang in his memory with a hollow sound. The British schooner *Kate* tried to enter the mouth of the Saint Marks River and was captured by the *USS Roebuck;* the sloop *CS Florida* was captured as she tried to leave. This concern was quickly overshadowed by worse news.

On New Year's Day of 1863, a shock went through the world at the audacity of Abraham Lincoln. First, Lincoln claimed victory at Sharpsburg on Antietam Creek. The battle actually had no winner; it merely paused at darkness; however, Lee had thought it best to withdraw his wounded troops. Then, with this slight boost to the Union, Lincoln took the opportunity to issue the Emancipation Proclamation.

It had seemed ridiculous to Thomas, but as he and Lavinia rode over the fields, discussing what was to happen, Lincoln's strategy clarified.

Lavinia asked, "How can Lincoln 'free all the slaves in states in rebellion' when we don't even recognize his government? And he didn't include Northern states. Only the South. How can he enforce it?"

Thomas laughed harshly. "He can't. It makes no difference to us, but he's ignited his falling enlistments. He first called them to arms for the preservation of the Union. They no longer care about that so he's given them a new cause — a moral question."

He took off his hat and raked his fingers through his hair. "Encouraging the Union army isn't as important as other factors."

"What?"

"Bringing the slavery issue into the war stopped the impending foreign intervention that would have assured our winning independence. With nearly a half-million textile workers idle, England was about to come in on our side. They won't now. The wily fox has suddenly created a holy war."

Without the expected aid of England joining the Confederacy in fighting the Union, blockade running became a desperate issue. Thomas made a trip to Saint Marks the first week in January to see if the *Spray* was still slipping through.

When he reached the waterfront and went in the Blue Mullet Café for a lunch of the strong-tasting fish, he found the exploits of the little steamer on every customer's tongue.

"The *Spray* is now officially commissioned a Confederate Naval Vessel," one man said. "She's been armed with two deck cannon, fifty-one spirited crewmen, and a daring captain."

"She had already gained the reputation of the Confederacy's most effective blockade runner. Now she's a gunboat fighter," an old sailor proudly told Thomas.

Another man pulled at his beard and interrupted the confident talk. "I'm worried. Rumors are the *Spray* has so frustrated the Union Commander that he's laying plans to destroy her."

"Don't fret. She can run circles around them big Union Ships," said the first man. "The *Spray* has more lives than a cat."

"We've been saying that . . ." a fat man spat tobacco juice before he could finish. ". . . but a cat has only nine. The *Spray* has had so many narrow escapes that she's used eighteen or twenty."

Thomas tried to join in the laughter that shook the small room, but he felt frantic. *What am I going to do if I can't export cotton?*

317

Finishing his mullet, Thomas continued his journey to Newport and faced a more immediate problem. Union raiding parties had slipped ashore from the *U.S.S. Roebuck* and destroyed many of the saltworks. Ladd Company had escaped detection, but they could only sell him a few bags of salt at thirty dollars a bushel. Thomas returned home, dreading to face Lavinia.

On his next trip to Saint Marks, Thomas found the men who frequented the Blue Mullet glum. Daniel Ladd was among them. Even he looked discouraged.

Ladd tried to smile in greeting to Thomas. "The Union ships made two attempts to come up the river after the *Spray,* but the water is too shallow for their deep draft ships . . ."

Thomas tensed for what he could tell was going to be bad news.

Ladd sighed heavily. "In two raids from the *Tahoma,* the Yankees destroyed five hundred fifty-five salt kettles, ninety-five boilers, two hundred sixty-eight brick furnaces . . ." His voice broke. "Mules, wagons, cattle — and Confederate prisoners. Losses to the Confederacy are about two million dollars."

The depression in the café settled over Thomas. He returned home with only two bags of yellow salt.

"Ugh! Yellow salt doesn't preserve meat!" Lavinia exclaimed as she spit out a mouthful of spoiled beef. "Oh, Thomas, what are we to do?"

Thomas pushed back from the table. "I thought it would get us by. Yellow salt is all that's available."

"What's the difference?" she asked in dismay.

"It's just evaporated seawater produced by hastily set-up salt works. I guess it needs refining to remove some of the undesirable salts. Salt making is tricky. Only professionals like Daniel Ladd can crystallize out the table salt."

"I feel positively weak without salt," said Florence, who looked pale.

"I'm tired of tasteless food," said Mattie, pouting.

"I try to add flavor with herbs," replied Lavinia. "We don't have as much salt left as there is in the smokehouse floor."

"The smokehouse floor! A great idea," Thomas cried. "Get a shovel, Tommy."

Forgetting to take a shawl against the February chill, Lavinia followed them to the windowless log house. It smelled of smoke from green oak boughs, but all that was left

319

of well-preserved meat was one lone spicy-greasy smelling ham hanging from the joist. She sighed, realizing how sparingly she must use it.

Tommy dug up the dirt floor and put it in an iron kettle with a hole in the bottom. Slowly, Lavinia poured water through the dirt. They waited while the now salty water dripped into thin pans, which the girls placed in the sun for evaporation.

For days, they hovered over their treasure. Then they ate salted food, relishing every bite. Even Lavinia took no thought that it had come from dirt.

Wind rattled windows as Lavinia sat by the fire knitting socks for Frank and his tent mates.

Thomas came into the parlor and read her a report about pitched fighting with armed Union ships that had gone up the mouth of the Ochlockonee River to capture the loaded sloop *CS Onward.*

"Not *our* river?" she shrieked.

"Yes, honey, but wait. Listen. 'March, 1863. Captain George W. Scott and the Fifth Florida Cavalry filled the trees along the riverbank and sent the Yankees packing with a howitzer.' "

Lavinia exhaled a deep breath and then

caught it sharply as she glanced out of the window and saw someone approaching.

Thomas peered out. "It's one of sister Harriet's most trusted servants." Apprehensively, he rushed to the door to receive the note the man had brought. With a shaking voice, he read:

Mother is gravely ill. Can you come?
James Joseph Blackshear, Jr.

Frightened, Lavinia hurried her family in preparations for the trip, but when they reached Cedar Grove, Harriet was slipping away. Choking back her tears, Lavinia held her hand and recited the twenty-third Psalm.

Her sons sealed her coffin immediately, fearing an epidemic. They thought the smallpox brought to Duncanville by a returning soldier had caused her death. On that same day, March 13, 1863, they buried Harriet Jones Blackshear in the plantation cemetery beside her beloved husband, James Joseph Blackshear.

Lavinia cried all of the way home.

Thomas patted her, musing, "It's hard to believe she's gone. She was still beautiful at forty-five."

"Yes." Lavinia dabbed her eyes. "I was closer to her than my own sisters."

321

"That made me happy — but you resented her at first. Why?"

Lavinia's grief made her blurt her secret. "Because she was a perfect beauty. I-I was afraid you'd compare us and see — how ugly I am."

Thomas's mouth fell open in shock. He grasped her arm so hard she flinched. "Don't you ever let me hear you say that again!"

As spring turned into summer, a sense of waiting hung over Greenwood. Thomas, accustomed to meeting life aggressively, could hardly restrain himself. He felt helpless as the war intensified. His mind kept returning to General Lee, who had been heartened by his brilliant victory at Chancellorsville. Frank had been there; but now they had no word from him as the Army of Northern Virginia advanced into Pennsylvania.

At the same time, Edwin wrote Mattie from the western front. She shared his letter:

We're stationed at the riverport of Vicksburg, Mississippi. It is like the Rock of Gibraltar. With our batteries set on high bluffs, we can keep the Yankees from going down the Mississippi — if we can only keep supplied with subsistence.

No further word came from east or west. As July's heat shriveled the corn, Thomas could stand it no longer. Mattie saw him preparing to go into town and begged to go along.

Their horses moved slowly because the humidity made breathing difficult. They rode without conversation. Thomas glanced at Mattie. Listless, she showed she was as sick with apprehension as he.

The scene at the depot frightened them further. People gathered around the train, leaning close, talking in hushed voices. Thomas dreaded to hear Conductor Naylor.

Again and again Naylor repeated the sad news. "Lee's forces met stinging defeat on July first, second, and third at a place called Gettysburg."

Thomas's face burned. He fanned with his straw hat. Searching the wounded lists, he did not register the scream.

Someone touched his arm and said, "It's Mattie. She's fainted."

He turned and saw her crumpled on the ground. Mrs. Hansell was bending over her, waving smelling salts.

As Thomas cradled her in his arms, Mattie fluttered her lashes and cried hysterically, "The Yankees have taken Edwin prisoner!"

Judge Hansell explained in a hushed aside. "General Grant laid siege to Vicksburg. He couldn't take the stronghold any other way, so he starved them out. The last seven weeks, when we thought they were doing well, they survived by living in caves, eating mules and rats. So many were dying of disease and starvation, they had to surrender July fourth, ironically, the same day as Lee's defeat at Gettysburg. The Confederacy is broken in two."

Mattie sat up. "Oh, Papa. Edwin is in a prison camp, and all of them are barbaric." She gulped a sob. "In our Camp Sumter at Andersonville, Yankee prisoners are starving because the Confederacy has no food. I hear the North is retaliating by refusing to feed southern prisoners even though they have plenty."

Thomas's brows went up in surprise that his flighty daughter knew these terrible facts. He started to say that prison could not be worse than Vicksburg under siege, but he thought better of it as Mattie's tears flowed.

She can't ride horseback three miles home,

he thought. *I'll hire a hack and take her to Livy's.*

When Livy opened the door, her usual superior, overeducated air vanished, and the efficient doctor's wife in her took charge. As she ushered Mattie toward a bedroom, she was already loosening the flushed girl's hot clothing.

"Tell Mama not to worry," Livy said over her shoulder. "I'll give her enough laudanum to make her sleep for three days."

A month later, Lavinia looked up to see Mattie floating down the staircase. Fully dressed for a change, she smiled and waved the letter Florence had brought from town.

"Good News?" Lavinia asked unnecessarily.

"Oh, yes! Edwin says the Fifty-Seventh Regiment, which includes our Dixie Boys, has been paroled! The Yankees told them not to return to fighting, but as soon as they are properly exchanged, they will return to duty — guess where?"

"Well . . . ?"

"Savannah! A train ride away!"

Mattie hugged her and danced out on the porch, where she read the letter over and over.

Her renewed liveliness echoed through

Greenwood for the next few weeks. Clattering up and down the stairs, styling her hair, remodeling a dress, she sang at the top of her lungs.

"Old Abe Lincoln keeps kicking up a fuss,
I think he'd better stop it, for he'll only make it worse;
We'll have our independence, I'll tell you the reason why,
Jeff Davis will make them sing — Root hog or die!"

As days passed into the last of September with no word from her beau, Mattie's agony of waiting had the whole family on edge. They were gathered around the table finishing their noon meal when barking dogs announced a stranger's approach. Mattie scattered her fork and napkin on the floor as she ran for the porch. The family sat in silence.

Finally, Florence half-rose, saying, "Maybe I'd better check on Mattie."

"No!" Lavinia intervened.

At last Mattie returned arm-in-arm with Edwin Davis. Their flushed faces showed evidence of a tearful reunion.

Lavinia tried to hide her shock at his

splotched skin, emaciated frame and thinning hair. Her heart ached for him and the others who had endured the starvation seige at Vicksburg. She feared he would never overcome the effects. *But Mattie thinks he's still the handsomest man in the world,* Lavinia realized. *She looks as if she could eat him with a spoon.*

While Thomas and Tommy pumped his hand in welcome, Lavinia piled a plate high, heaping on extra mashed potatoes.

Edwin wanted to hear news of home, and he replied with brevity to their questions about living underground at Vicksburg. Then he grinned, "There was one good thing though. When the Dixie Boys were captured, we were forced to stack our rifles and lay our company flag upon the row. We felt we could stand it all except surrendering our flag. In the night, I slipped out — it was moonless — and grabbed our flag. I slithered back without the picket seeing me."

"Oh, Edwin, you could have been shot for that!" Mattie gasped.

He chuckled. "It was worth the chance. Anyway, Robert Harris and I used a locust thorn needle to sew our banner into the folds of Lieutenant Colonel G. S. Guyton's saddle blanket. Somehow his horse had survived without being shot — or eaten. Guyton rode right out of Vicksburg with the flag under his saddle." He threw his arms wide. "And he didn't even know it!"

They all laughed and Mattie cooed about his courage.

When Edwin declared he could not eat another bite, Mattie said, "I'll bet you could still graze the scuppernong arbor."

Lavinia followed discreetly, taking her sewing to a corner of the porch where she could maintain a presence as the happy couple ducked beneath the vines hanging from the head-high structure. Her wily daughter had maneuvered Edwin out of sight. The big bronze grapes hung in pungent clusters, but Lavinia knew eating scuppernongs was not on their minds. Where Livy J. was ethereal, Mattie was earthy, and Lavinia worried.

I hope they don't want to get married while he is on furlough. She'd have a total collapse if he didn't come back.

When they came out into the sunlight, their foolish expressions gave ample evidence they had been kissing. Still holding hands, they held a whispered conference. Then Edwin went toward the back into Thomas's office. Mattie fidgeted about the yard, breaking off twigs.

Lavinia held her breath when they approached her a few minutes later with faces aglow. She pretended to be absorbed in stitching the uniform in her lap.

"Papa gave permission," Mattie said. "He wasn't pleased at first because Edwin isn't Methodist, but when he explained that he's a good Baptist — even Sunday School Superintendent and head of mission work — Papa relented. We're engaged to be married just as soon as the South wins the war."

Lavinia kissed them both, but her relief was short-lived. Before Lavinia had time to welcome Edwin to the family, a spotted horse, loping up the driveway, again set the dogs barking. This time it was a messenger from Oak Lawn. As he swung down from his saddle, Lavinia's hand flew to her throat. He wore a black armband.

"Edwin, get Thomas," Lavinia said in a whisper. She recognized her sister-in-law's handwriting and glimpsed the name of Eliza and Mitchell's oldest son. Then she snapped the black-bordered note shut until Thomas joined them. Florence followed him. She put her arm around Lavinia's waist and clung tightly.

Thomas's voice was gruff. "Black has been killed in a battle some place in North Georgia called Chickamauga."

Florence grabbed a handful of her own red hair and pulled. "Not fun-loving cousin Black," she whimpered.

Mattie sagged against Edwin. "Killed? At a battle inside Georgia?"

Thomas readied the carriage while Lavinia gathered food and flowers to take to the bereaved household.

When they reached Oak Lawn, a pale Eliza handed Thomas the chaplain's letter, which stated that James Blackshear Jones had been killed on September 20, 1863, at Chickamauga Creek, Georgia. The Federals had lost sixteen thousand while nearly eighteen thousand southern boys had given their lives in the two-day battle.

Thomas grieved with Eliza for her first-born son, her mainstay. *I'm glad Mitch doesn't have to bear this,* he thought.

As the afternoon shadows lengthened, Thomas read the chaplain's words again. He tried to comprehend that the Confederates had lost Chattanooga, had escaped through the rocky crags of Tennessee's mountains, and had tried to make this stand in north Georgia.

It's unthinkable that our state's border has been violated.

■ ■ ■ ■

A week later, every inch of Greenwood glowed in the sunlight of the brilliant October morning. Florence had arranged chrysanthemums and asters for the hall while Lavinia, who thought October roses had the most pungent fragrance of all year, used them on the dining room table. Mattie kept stopping mid-task to play the piano and start the others singing in echoes throughout the house.

Lavinia felt bathed in happiness. Suddenly her smile stiffened at the nagging voice of guilt. All around Thomas County, tears were falling. Her nephew William Young had returned, but his right arm was amputated. Oak Lawn was draped in mourning as Eliza awaited the arrival of her second son, Price, who was bringing Black's body. Lavinia gripped the chair.

I must not think of that now, and it's useless to fret because I have no sugar to make a caramel cake. No one will care that I'm wearing made-over clothes. All that matters is Frank's furlough. Today he's coming home!

She smoothed her skirt to settle the new trim she had cut from another dress to hide worn places. Deciding it looked fine, she went out to the porch to wait.

She was joined by James and Ann who had come the night before from their home near the Florida line. Their three children played in the yard with Livy and David's growing brood. Livy was determined to equal the eleven her mother had borne.

Julie had commanded that all the household servants look their best in clothes freshly boiled, starched, and ironed. They stood about in front of the porch. When the farm bell rang at noon, the field hands came in singing and joined the crowd.

At last, the carriage appeared. Frank ran up the steps and swung Lavinia in a hug. "Perfect, Mama. How I love home!"

Frank's siblings surrounded him, but first he had to shake hands with Augustus, Samuel, and some of the other men; then he hugged Julie.

Cherry ran up, flapping her apron, and grabbed him in her fleshy arms. "It be good to cook for my boy again," she cried.

Finally, with great ceremony, the family ushered Frank to the dining table. In the general hubbub, no one paid attention to her good meal, but Lavinia was satisfied.

Frank ate ravenously. "These turnip greens and corn dodgers are better than cake," he said as he lifted a cornmeal dumpling in his spoon in salute before he consumed it to accompanying laughter.

"We do have dessert," Lavinia said, "fresh pears baked with honey from the beehives by the watermelon patch. And coffee." Lavinia held her breath as Frank sipped what she had concocted from toasted okra seeds and chicory root.

A grin spread across his now-weathered face. "Delicious, Ma. Food at your table doesn't simply stave off hunger. It makes a body feel comforted, warmed, loved."

With tears in her eyes, Lavinia kissed him. His brothers and sisters sat back, drinking the strange brew and urging Frank to talk.

He turned to Thomas. "Pa, I wish you could have met General Robert E. Lee and General Stonewall Jackson when you were there. They're fine Christian men, and we frequently saw them kneeling in prayer with their troops."

Thomas nodded. "I know it was agonizing when Jackson was accidentally killed by his own men at Chancellorsville."

"Yes, sir. To think that gallant Stonewall is now sleeping in the soil he has so nobly defended. It cost many of our bravest and best men for that great victory. The successes there and at Fredericksburg are what made Jeff Davis send Lee to invade Maryland and Pennsylvania."

James said, "You've been involved in all of the important battles. I envy you."

Frank gave a harsh laugh. "Don't envy Gettysburg. I don't think Lee would have been defeated if he hadn't lost Stonewall. I must admit I didn't actually fight there. After Jackson's death, Cobb's Legion of Cavalry was put under General J. E. B. Stuart."

He turned toward his fellow redhead. "Florrie, you'd be taken with him. He's a showman in a scarlet-lined cape, plumed hat, and shiny jackboots. He put 10,000 of us cavalrymen through a gaudy review before Lee. Then he led us through the bloodiest — sorry, Mama — the hardest fight of the war. We were late getting to Gettysburg. Got there in time to retreat."

Frank leaned back, stretched, and patted his stomach. "Y'all have got me stuffed. Let's ride over the place to shake this food down. I want to see how everything has grown."

Mattie kissed his cheek. "We ladies have to go to Thomasville this afternoon for one of Mrs. Fisher's 'packings.' Mama is the Second Directress of the Soldiers' Aid Society."

Frank's eyes glinted, and his whole face

twitched with smiles. "Will the girls be there? I'll help."

As the family left the room, laughing and joking, Lavinia slipped under Thomas's sheltering arm.

"Did you notice Tommy?" she whispered.

"No — come to think of it — he hardly said a word."

"Exactly. I watched him. You're going to have to talk him out of joining."

"I'll try to let him know how much he's needed here."

The depot was already thronged with ladies when the Jones family arrived. Mrs. Fisher, who had replaced her husband as the Chief Engineer and Conductor of the train, stood on the platform beside the boxcar to direct the packing.

Her tongue is going like a flutter mill, Lavinia thought. *She's enjoying her glory. When all the men went off to war, I wasn't surprised seeing the young ladies taking their places clerking in stores and such, but I never thought I'd see a woman doing a big dirty job like this!*

Everyone in the county had given something to the Soldier's Aid Society for the packing. Lavinia busied herself checking her director's list of provisions being loaded:

packages of lint for bandages, home-knit socks, bed comforts, towels, mattress linens, shoes, four packages mazina, blankets, frying pans, caps for privates, officer's caps, kersey pants. On and on her inventory went, and her heart warmed at the generosity of her neighbors.

Lavinia chewed her pencil and watched Florence and Mattie at the other end of the car stowing foodstuffs of every kind that could be shipped to Virginia in good condition — and some that could not.

She laughed when she saw Frank. His "helping" was in the form of teasing several young ladies.

By the time they had loaded an estimated ten thousand pounds of provisions, the locomotive had taken on wood and water and was hissing steam. Mrs. Fisher climbed into the cab with a wide grin and promised the crowd that she would take the shipment through to Atlanta.

Lavinia was too tired to join the cheering, and she turned toward her carriage. She grasped a post for support when she saw Tommy. Serious-faced, he was talking to Ella Capers. The petite brunette was pressing a lace handkerchief to her mouth.

Frank's short furlough seemed to have

vanished in a vapor. On Monday morning, silence suffused Greenwood. It was time for the fun-loving boy to return to the front. When he came down the staircase, everyone was gathered in the hall. Lavinia stood before the mirror, fussing with her hat, trying to hide the tears.

"Take off your bonnet, Ma. You, too, sisters. I don't want to tell you good-bye in the noisy, dirty depot. I want you sitting on the porch, serene and beautiful." Frank choked. He took his mother in his arms and buried his face against her shoulder before he could continue.

"It's a hard fate for one who loves home as much as I, to have to go, but my thoughts will become resigned to a military necessity when I get into camp and meet old friends."

Lavinia let Frank lead her to the porch. In the side yard there was a loud wailing and shouts of "Help me Jesus" as Fed's family took leave of him. The lanky black would hear of no one but him going back to the front with Frank.

Lavinia listened to them, thinking, *I wonder if they don't have a better way by letting out grief.*

"Pa, let's take the carriage into town." Frank laughed. "I get enough of horseback." He fastened the shiny brass buttons on his

337

coat. "Ma, thanks for making my new uniform."

Frank kissed his sisters and clapped on
his plumed hat. Then he was gone.

Thomas had suspected that Frank wanted
to use the carriage so they could talk. As
soon as they emerged from the sheltering
arms of the live oaks, he became serious.

"Pa, the Federals have a replacement for
every man who falls. We don't. Our boys
are marching across battlefields toward
advancing bayonets with their names and
addresses pinned to their backs. They offer
their lives as sacrifice to keep the enemy
from invading homes such as ours. It's
hopeless against such odds, but we *won't*
give up."

Tommy rose up from his corner of the carriage seat. He threw back his shoulders.
Red-faced, he blurted. "I'm joining, too.
Papa, I can't let my little brother do my
fighting."

"No!" Frank shouted. "I didn't mean that.
I was just warning Pa I might not make it
back — growing corn and beef is important,
too. They're calling Georgia the Bread
Basket of the Confederacy."

Thomas clinched his teeth on his pipe
stem. Despite his objections, Tommy had

started drilling with T.S. Paine's Cavalry. After all, he was a man of twenty-four, and Thomas had worried that this was coming. The company would be part of the Twentieth Georgia Battalion, which would be fighting in Virginia near Frank. Thomas knew it was useless, but he made a last effort to dissuade him.

"Son, some of us have to stay behind as a lifeline to support the troops."

Frank slapped Tommy's knee. "I heard the girls teasing all the boys still at home. Don't let that bother you. Did Ella . . . ?"

"Ella's fine," Tommy snapped. "It's not because of what you just said. The day of the packing I told her I'm joining. She's promised to wait for me."

Thomas rubbed his aching temple. *So. It's decided. I wish I could go myself. I'm strong and fit if I am sixty-one.*

Even as his heart beat faster at the thought of serving in the army, Thomas realized that with Frank and Tommy and David at the battlefront, he was the only one to protect Lavinia and the girls.

One of these days, the Yankees are going to realize how much Thomas County is supplying the Confederacy and how easily they can land infantry at Saint Marks and attack us from the Gulf.

Chapter XIX

Thomas threw another log in the bedroom fireplace, hopped across the cold floor, and leaped beneath the quilts. Lavinia snuggled into the circle of his arm as she prepared to read Frank's latest letter aloud. Frank had sent Fed home to bring back food and supplies, and the lad had told Thomas how desperately they needed provisions. Now, as he listened to Lavinia read about Fed's return to Frank, Thomas wished he knew the real situation; however, it soon became apparent that this letter was for the amusement of the ladies.

Hd. Qrs. Cobb Legion Cavalry
January 25, 1864.
Dear Martha:
Your letter was received to-day and before I finished reading it Fed stepped in General Young's tent and made himself perfectly at home. I received Flor-

ence's letter about a week ago and have been intending to answer it; but thus far I have not had time unless I had done it late at night. No particular business has prevented me, either, but you know we have very few opportunities of enjoying ourselves and I have been making the best of my time.

Since writing last I have had the pleasure of attending several dances in Fredericksburg. We are making preparations to give a Military Ball there to-morrow week. We have two Brass Bands and a String Band to make music for us, and we anticipate a good time generally. The ladies of Fredericksburg think that there are no soldiers like Young's Brigade and we return the compliment by telling them they had entirely enlisted out affections in their behalf. The dances heretofore have been entirely without expense to either party. Invitations are generally given by the young lady of the house of her willingness to have a dance at her house, and at the appointed time the young men will go after the young ladies and begin the dance at 6 or 7 o'clock. Our dances will continue probably until 4 or 5 o'clock in the morning and the young lady of the house is never expected to offer any refreshments of any kind and consequently, they are of no expense and go by the name of "Starvation-Parties". After the dance is over every gentleman takes his lady-love and escorts her home and thus they end with an understanding where the next will be.

I could tell some very amusing scenes and incidents connected with these dances; but as so much complaint was made at home about my being "crazy" on the subject of women, I have been very mum on the subject since I returned and have never mentioned one's name or said anything about them in any way. Suffice to say I have had a charming time also, and have divided my attentions between a dark eyed brunette and one, the peach bloom tint of whose cheeks would rival the delicate coloring of the Greek Masters. Well, I have had time to ask Fed a few questions this evening and he says he told Miss Turnbull he couldn't give her a positive answer as to whether I would have her or not. He told Few that Miss Hattie Winn sent her love to him. Some French gentleman, by way of illustrating his efficiency in slight of hand performance, relieved him of two pair of my socks and all my handkerchiefs before he arrived here. The balance of the things he delivered all right, and the letter also, which was sewed up in the back part of his breeches or coat, I don't know which, He told me at General Young's Hdqrs. He had a letter for me, as soon as he came up in the presence of some 15 or 20 officers and of course, I being anxious to see it, told him to give it to me. But he pulled out his knife and began to unbutton and shuck off and I soon found out that he had it in some remote corner and so told him never mind — that I could wait until I came home to read it. When I got here he had performed the operation with his knife and produced the letter without any preliminary arrangements. I have not had time to ask him many questions, yet, but will get him, Caesar, and Few together and hear the whole tale. I do hope my box will eventually come, for I am craving for it, as Sergt. Harris (Sgt.-Major) had received one from home, which is just about out; but he has another on the way, which I hope will soon be here. I suppose you have received my letter before this in regard to Col. King's coming and hope you will not let him go away disappointed. His expectations were very high in every particular. Tell Ma that he will enjoy the peach brandy that's coming. Tell Pa I will endeavor to buy him some McClellan Saddles, tho' every one has to be accounted for to the government twice a month now and they can't be bought for anything under a hundred dollars. I expect Cap. Julian will call to see you before long. If he does, entertain him very nicely.

Remember me to Miss Bud and tell her all sorts of nice things for the gloves. My friends are trying very hard to turn it into a joke however, and seem to think some young lady has given me the mitten instead of her hand.

Love to all the family and believe me
Your affectionate brother
H. F. Jones.

Lavinia laughed. "It's good he can find fun and relaxation so close to the battle-front. Can you imagine the courage it must take for those young ladies to put on smiles in such danger and privations as they are suffering?"

"Southern women are unequaled in strength and charm," Thomas said, blowing out the candle and pulling her against him. "I guess that's what keeps me loving you more each day, even though we're old marrieds."

Lavinia agreed. "I can hardly believe this coming September we'll celebrate our thirty-eighth anniversary."

Thomas pressed his lips against her hair and said nothing. His heart pounded at the thought of what might happen before then. Silently he prayed for strength to protect her from the invaders. So far he had kept the news from her that the attack he had long feared had come. His mind could scarcely comprehend that six thousand Union soldiers had landed on the east coast and seized Jacksonville.

Lavinia awakened at daybreak to the sound of horses. She ran to the bedroom window and recognized the crested coach-and-four from Verdura that had belonged to Mary Elizabeth.

Flinging on a flannel wrapper, she stumbled down the stairs two steps ahead of Thomas.

The liveried coachman opened the door and their granddaughter Livy J. stepped down from her mother's carriage. Fifteen, the beautiful young woman normally moved with a serenity that seemed to spread sunshine. Now winter wind whipped black hair around a face smudged from scrubbing tears. She looked like a frightened five-year-old. Shrieking, she threw herself into Thomas's open arms.

"Grandpa-pa! We had word that Yankees occupied Jacksonville. Now they're slashing their way through the swamps singing, 'We're bound for Tallahassee in the morning.' " She gasped for breath. "Our local soldiers from Camp Leon and Camp Brokaw are guarding the Gulf approach. They don't know the enemy is coming from the Atlantic."

Lavinia suppressed a scream, but Thomas replied quietly.

"Where's Furman?"

"Pa-pa joined the army. He sent me to you."

They hurried her into the house where the awakening household started fires and breakfast.

Florence came into the dining room and squealed, "Livy J!" Ever thoughtful, she warmed an Afghan by the fire and wrapped the shivering girl, holding her close.

Over eggs and steaming grits, Livy J. explained the situation in Florida. "The Bluecoats are marching across the state confiscating cotton, lumber, and turpentine. Rumor is that they plan to seize the whole state of Florida and establish their government."

As Livy J. was filled with warming food, she talked intelligently with her grandfather. Lavinia merely watched, unable to accept this unthinkable news.

At that moment, Mattie dragged sleepily into the room. "Livy J.?" she shouted. "What's happening? Why didn't someone wake me?"

Florence laughed. "You'll sleep through Judgment Day."

February's cold gripped them without its usual respite as they waited with no news of what was happening in Florida. Finally on the last day of the month, Florence came in from Thomasville, uncharacteristically banging the front door as she entered the hall with a shout.

"The Confederates won!"

Lavinia's hand flew to her heart. For one brief moment, she dared hope that the war was over. As Thomas entered, she reached out, and their fingers entwined and held as they waited to hear Florence read the newspaper she had brought.

" 'On February 20, 1864, as Union troops

stationed in Jacksonville, Florida, continued their march westward to capture the capital at Tallahassee, they were met near the town of Olustee by Florida's General Joseph Finnegan and five thousand Confederate troops.' " Florence looked up.

"It goes on to list Florida battalions and units of Georgia infantry and cavalry who stopped the Yankees at Olustee," she said, passing the paper to Thomas.

Thomas continued the article. " 'Fighting a larger force of six thousand Federals, our men were victorious in defense of their homes and firesides.' "

Thomas shook the paper in triumph and read in a loud voice. "After a three-hour battle, the Union force retreated into Jacksonville — and the southerners captured their military arms and supplies."

"Verdura is saved!" said Livy J. Suddenly her pent-up tears fell, and she buried her face in Lavinia's lap.

Thomas knelt before them and enwrapped them both in his arms. "It's all right, dear, the scare is over, but we want you to stay for a long visit while you're here."

Lavinia studied his face. She sensed there was more he was not saying. She drew a questioning breath, and then decided she would prefer not to know.

■ ■ ■ ■

Lavinia set a pleasant pattern for their days to make them forget the war, and indeed, Livy J.'s presence wafted their imaginations into the cosmopolitan atmosphere of Tallahassee. One March afternoon she amused them by telling anecdotes and sharing some lovely Paris gowns that Furman had managed to buy from a French ship that ran the blockade.

"When the war is over . . ." said Livy J. wistfully, ". . . Pa-pa wants to present me to Tallahassee society in a formal debut. These frocks are from 'Chez Worth'. Would you like to try them on?"

With delighted cries of acceptance, the girls pounced, but the dresses were too tight for curvaceous Mattie and too elaborate for plain-faced Florence. Lavinia thought that Charles Frederick Worth's use of wide hoops, elegant fabrics and magnificent trims was just right for Livy J.'s classic looks. It pleased her that Mary Elizabeth's daughter had blossomed into a belle with a charm heightened by a French flair from Furman.

In the midst of their fashion show, Julie announced callers.

Lavinia went downstairs immediately.

"Eliza — and Price — how delightful to see you!" she said, entering the parlor with arms outstretched.

Price jumped to his feet, clicking the heels of his boots as he bowed formally over Lavinia's hand. "Good afternoon, Aunt Lavinia. I hope you are well."

She blinked. "You're home on furlough?" She thought young Price looked dashing in his cavalry uniform with his saber swinging at his side and his gold sash adding a jaunty note. Still, his face was bland, uncertain; his blue eyes were guileless. As she started to say more, Price's features came alive with expression, and his eyes softened into rapture.

Lavinia turned, realizing the girls had come in behind her. Livy J. was still wearing an evening gown. Rich sapphire velvet framed her bared shoulders and spread over a wide hoop that made her waist look as if a pair of hands could span it. Her lashes fanned back as she met Price's gaze and held it.

Mattie giggled, and she and Florence moved around Livy J. as Julie rolled in the mahogany teacart.

Lavinia could hardly pour tea as her gaze kept straying to the couple who might as well have been alone in the room. It surprised her that Price was utterly captivated. They had been congenial playmates as children when the families visited, but now it was as if they were meeting for the first time.

As they accepted the cups of herb tea, Price talked, exhibiting an extra share of his father Mitchell's charm. Indeed a straying black lock fell over his forehead as he bent to whisper something in Livy J.'s ear.

Lit by his attention, Livy J. sparkled like a crystal chandelier.

Lavinia drew in a frightened breath. *Oh dear,* she thought, *should I intervene?* She sighed. *Could I?*

Livy J. had difficulty gaining her ear. "Grandma-ma," she repeated. In a flutter of lovely French, the dazzled girl asked that she and Price be excused to the garden.

Lavinia could not help but watch out the window as the couple strolled through the romance of spring's delicate blossoms. Lavinia well knew the headiness of wisteria. The vine's clinging arms embraced everything in swaying purple swags that wafted intense perfume. Beneath the canopy, Livy J. and Price walked in step as if they were dancing.

As the couple moved in unison, already one, Lavinia turned to Eliza in dismay.

"What do you think? They aren't *first* cousins?"

"Only kissing cousins," said Eliza. "I think we'd have beautiful grandchildren."

Mattie burst out laughing, but Lavinia soberly squeezed Eliza's hand. "We all need youth's optimism that life goes on."

Livy J.'s glow remained even after Price returned to duty. She and the others wrote letters each day after dinner while Lavinia took her afternoon nap.

The replies they received were infrequent and, except for Frank's newsworthy epistles, brief. Tommy, especially, had as little to say in his letters as he did in person. Every letter merely asked about home and crops and begged them to look after Ella Capers. For Tommy's sake and to keep up their spirits as war news worsened, Lavinia asked Ella to a spend-the-day. When Lavinia welcomed her into the hall, Ella's tiny frame was engulfed by the tall Jones girls.

I doubt she has the stamina to be a farmer's wife, Lavinia thought. *And being a Methodist preacher's daughter, she must be quite reserved.*

To Lavinia's surprise, Ella immediately displayed a vivacity that was a startling contrast to Tommy's personality. The moment she met their Tallahassee guest, Ella's eyes snapped with initiative.

"Livy J., you give me a marvelous idea to raise money for the soldiers' fund," Ella said. "How would y'all like to organize a series of tableaux? I'm certain everyone will pay fifty cents to see Livy J. dressed in a beautiful costume and posed as a great painting."

They looked at her with their mouths gaping as she turned to Mattie. "You could sing between times while we change the living pictures."

"Oh what fun!" Mattie clapped her hands.

Florence remained in the background, but Ella wrinkled her nose and grinned at her. "You'd be great at comic recitation."

"I could do that funny elocution about the bad girl acting up and her mother telling her mistress, Miss Fanny, about it."

Imitating the daughter, Florence jumped up and down, grabbing her legs against an imaginary whipping. "Yes'm, Mama. Yes'm, Mama. I'm going back to church every Sunday," she screeched in a high-pitched voice. She danced from more blows of an almost visible flapping strap. "Yes'm, Mama, I'm going read my Bible from lid to lid."

Waiting for Ella's giggling to die down, Florence delivered the anticipated climax in the lower voice of the mother. "I tell you, Miss Fanny, I can make more Christians out of sinners with my old trunk strap than a preacher can in forty lebben years."

Applause and foot stamping followed Florence's performance.

Mattie said, "Some of the girls in our Sunday School class might even do a skit."

Lavinia spoke up. "Would Rev. Capers allow a tableau?

Ella's laughter pealed. "He will if I convince him it will be artistic and raise money for a good cause."

"Then I'll get Thomas to ask Judge Hansell to let you have it in the courthouse so you can seat a crowd," Lavinia replied.

The excited girls began work in earnest. On the following Tuesday, the first performance raised one hundred forty-five dollars. Spurred by success, they continued the tableaux for several weeks. Then the local children put on a tableau, and ladies in nearby towns took up the idea.

After an exhausting month, Lavinia conceded that tiny Ella was a powerhouse.

With the entertainment over, it was Mattie's confidence in her sweetheart's invincibility that rekindled Lavinia's hope.

"Edwin's Dixie Boys are on the way to

the Tennessee border to stop those Blue-coats who are trying to sneak through Georgia's mountains."

Even as she tried to keep some of Mattie's courage, Lavinia worried over reports of hard fighting for every inch of home soil. *Are they losing ground?* She wondered. *Will the invaders trod our own dear state?*

Then a letter came from Frank that had a different tone from the ones he had written about the amusements between skirmishes. She cried when she read it.

Headquarters Cobb Legion Cav.,
Camp Marion, Va.,
April 4th, 1864
Dear Martha:
The ennui of camp and the drowsy feelings of a drowsy day were somewhat dispelled by the reception of yours and Florence's letters, which were sent by Col. Piles. I did not see him myself, as he went to Orange C.H. The letters were sent to me by one of our men with whom he traveled from Augusta. To add to the already contracted feeling of unpleasantness of the camp, the weather seems to do its worst to make Old Winter take its departure with as little comfort to the soldiers as possible. Last

Friday was ushered into existence with a full coating of snow. The trees bowed their suppliant limbs in humble acknowledgement to its power and quaked and quailed beneath their weight like dying men writhing under the tortures of a long and lingering disease. With all these inconveniences to a soldier, we were thankful that we had the great and glorious privilege of enjoying our frugal meal of bread and quarter pound of bacon, unmolested, both by the elements and the enemy.

By the by, speaking of bread and bacon brings to mind the late act of Congress, allowing officers rations. It seems like all fools, or at least the greatest portion of them in our country, are the most fortunate in the gifts of people. The last Congress was reviled by the papers long before it displayed its ignorance, and I sustained; but I fully agree with all of them. If it can be accused of having any wisdom, it certainly has a poor way of showing it. They have passed an ACT allowing officers to draw one ration the same in quantity and quality that is issued to the men — and deprive them of the privilege of buying. The ration of meat is one quarter (1/4) pound of bacon, and with that we are expected to feed ourselves, our servant, and entertain various aides and inspectors, who are frequently sent to our camps on duty of various kinds. I am ashamed to invite an officer to dine with me now. As a general thing, we eat meat once a day, and, but for the syrup, my Sergeant Major brought from home with him, I don't know what would become of us. Nearly all of the men have made arrangements to have meat sent from home for them, not depending on the Government for a supply. Some of the men have already sent their servants home after the meat, and others were contemplating the same thing; but the arrangement of the express company has facilitated this means by bringing all boxes free of charge, besides giving them preference to all other freight.

I wrote Dick Harris last week, telling him to go home before he left for Va. We had fish today for dinner, and discussed its merits with great respect for our craven appetites.

It is impossible as of yet to form an opinion of the coming campaign. Grant, who has been assigned to the command of the Army of the Potomac, has displayed much energy and skill in reorganizing it. It is thought that he will be ready to move in the course of from four to five weeks. On the other hand, it is supposed that Gen. Lee will be in readiness to turn his face northward at the same time, and, by sending Longstreet up the Valley, will force Grant to fall back in order to cover his flank and rear. Gen. Stuart has already said he would again penetrate Pennsylvania, and if Gen. Lee goes into it again this summer, I think it very probable with his last year's experience before him, he will go fully prepared to maintain himself in every emergency. Gen. Stuart has certainly strained every nerve to increase his cavalry, and has succeeded so far, in the organization of two Brigades (Butler's and Young's) from the Coast, with the addition of other old Regiments. He will enter the field with a bright prospect of adding new laurels to his brow, with a column of at least ten thousand sabers, and as many strong arms to wield them.

It may be a source of gratification and pride to some to know they are safe from the chances of death by occupying a field of inactive operation, but the feeling is quite different from that which animates this army.

Lulled into a state of repose by the chilling blasts of winter, the return of spring greets them with ready hands, and willing hearts, to meet the foe on the oft' contested fields of Victory. Actuated by a feeling of romance and adventure, prompted by the spirit of chivalry and cheered on by the bright smiles of fair women, they await the coming contest with stout arms and brave hearts and, though the curtain of death may fall about them, they willingly offer themselves a sacrifice on the Country's altar, already consecrated by the blood of the fathers and brothers. From the Valley of the Rappahannock to the crest of the Blue Ridge where it lifts its frowning head above the heights of Gettysburg!

My hand is improving from its sprain, and I am now able to use it.

It is thought the young ladies of Fredericksburg will soon invite us to a dance and I hope I will not be so unfortunate as to fall then. However, I don't expect to get on a trunk to dance. Do tell me all you can find out about the lamentations of those interested in the Millen's

Battalion. Tom Young of Bullock is in the 7th Ga. Cav. I will see him. Cousin Mac told me Cousin Jimmie had gone to Thomas. Tell her he is well. I understand the Reynolds, from Burke, are down there on a visit. If they are anywhere within reach of you, be certain to call on them.

Ask Ma what she thinks of my buying a uniform, and paying for it in syrup? I think it can be done in Richmond at the present prices of provisions.

Give my love to all. Tell Ma I have been expecting a letter from her. Hope to hear from you soon.

Your affectionate "Bud,"

H. F. Jones

Thomas poised the scythe over the golden grain that glistened in the May sunshine. He was surprised to see Mattie riding toward the wheat field. She slid down from her horse and hugged him, sweat and all. "Papa, I wanted to see what you thought about Edwin's letter. I don't want to show it to Mama."

Thomas raised his eyebrows in surprise at his unpredictable daughter. He read the letter aloud. " 'At last the advance upon Atlanta is stymied by the perpendicular knobs of Kennesaw Mountain. Even the hundred thousand men under General William Tecumseh Sherman can't take that impregnable fortress.' "

He lowered the letter. "That sounds like good news."

"Read on."

" 'But the Federals have enough men to flank. They're going around, threatening Atlanta and Macon. Our spies tell us Sherman ordered General Stoneman to cut the *Macon and Western Railroad,* but he means to make a name for himself by releasing the thirty thousand prisoners at Camp Sumter in Andersonville.' "

"Do you think they'd turn them loose on unprotected women and children?" Mattie asked. "That's why I didn't want Mama to see this."

"Sumter County is about a hundred miles away. There's no reason for them to find us here," Thomas said soothingly.

"Yes, there is. Edwin's at Andersonville now as a guard, and he says the stockade was built for half the number of prisoners they've been sent. There's no food for them or the guards, or even the people in Sumter County."

"We are blessed with food." Thomas put his arm around her. "I don't like keeping things from your mother, but perhaps you were right to do so."

When Mattie received her next letter from Frank, she also showed it to Thomas, privately.

Headquarters, Young's Cavalry,
Brigade, near Ashland, Ga.
June 1, 1864
Dear Martha:
  Your last letter was received and read yesterday on the battlefield. Your first was received ten or fifteen days ago, but, like this, under circumstances very inconvenient to be answered. I have only received three letters since the campaign opened and, to save me, I have not had time to write — only at the dark, dim hour of the night, when, soul and body both exhausted, the soldiers lay in silent groups, with their bridles in their hands, have I had time to write. The coming of tomorrow had always found us in the saddle and from then 'til the setting of the sun, we are in the saddle, or engaging the enemy. One night, after a hard day's march from the enemy's rear, I wrote a short letter to Ma but not mentioning anything in your letter, I presume

it has not reached you.

It is useless for me to attempt any description of Grant's campaign. All has been minutely stated by newspaper correspondents that has taken place and, I dare say, a good deal more than ever took place. It is positively true that I know very little about the campaign as a whole. Our operations have been confined to our branch of the service and the Infantry has been as separate and distinct from us as distance can make us. For instance, our lines are twenty-five miles long; the Infantry is on our right and we (the Cavalry), on the left, and our Brigade is on the extreme left of everything. We have no communication with the infantry, and hence our inability to keep posted with their movements.

I saw Wofford's Brigade some time since and learned that Pliny Sheffield lost his right arm close to the shoulder. Douglas was painfully wounded through the shoulder, but was doing well when last heard from. Ben Rogers came out safe and several others of my friends I have heard from. I have been unable to hear from Jim Blackshear. His brigade suffered terribly, I understand, in the Wilderness Battles.

I came very near getting furlough some time since. On our retreat our Regiment was fighting dismounted and, while engaged, a ball struck me on the left foot, but was too far spent to hurt me. After falling back behind the banks of the North Anna another ball struck me on the right leg, just below the knee; but like it's predecessor, it was too far spent to hurt a great deal. I was almost sorry it didn't come a little harder and get me a furlough. On the whole I have been very fortunate and can only thank a merciful Providence for intervening in my behalf. Cleve, poor fellow, was painfully wounded in his neck while going in dismounted. He is esteemed very gallant by his comrades in arms. For the last three days we have been fighting the 6th Army Corps, under Gen. Wright (since Sedgwick was killed) near Hanover Court House. Our force was too small to even contend with their sharpshooters, and they drove us before them as chaff before the wind. Our Regiment lost several wounded and several prisoners.

Gen. W. H. F. Lee (nicknamed "Rooney") came up and relieved us just before sundown, and he, too, was driven from the field. Rooney Lee is the son of

Gen. Robert E. Lee, and first cousin to Fitz Lee. Gen. Hampton has been placed in command of the Cav. Corps since Stuart's death. Gen. Young has been detached to the command of Gordon's Brigade of North Carolinians, and Col. Wright is now in command of Young's Brigade.

Poor Millen! I regret his death. He was killed last Saturday in his first fight. They say his command went into the fight beautifully; but, being inexperienced and eager, Millen was killed before he was engaged twenty minutes. Major Thompson was wounded and a good many of the men killed and wounded. I have not been able to see any of them and don't know any of the unfortunate ones.

The mysterious letter you spoke of I know nothing of. I presume it belongs to Mr. Shine's Negro. My "Birdie" is in Richmond — being a refugee at present. She was there when the enemy took possession of Fredericksburg. She is well however. When I take the foolish notion of getting a "Birdie" you will be advised of the event. Where is Florence? Tell her I hope she will be prevailed upon by a brotherly feeling to write me occasionally.

Give my love to all the family and remember me to my friends. Tell Pa to plant all the cane he can, and kill a thousand hogs next winter, if he can. Write soon to-
  Your affectionate brother
  H. F. Jones

Thomas handed the letter back to Mattie, sadly realizing that his baby had been forced to grow up.

"You should be having a party for your eighteenth birthday next week with half the young men of the county asking for your hand — and here you are shielding your mother from the encroaching horrors."

"I only want Edwin," Mattie said. "If he can just come back to me . . ." She could hold back her tears no longer.

Thomas held out his arms, and Mattie cried on his shoulder. When she regained control, he said, "Since Frank said he wrote Lavinia, too, don't show her this." He drew a shuddering breath. "We won't be able to protect her much longer. There's a crisis looming from every direction."

CHAPTER XX

Thunder crashed. The storm raging above Greenwood was as violent as Lavinia's emotions. She paced the hall, wishing she could go outside to work out this frenetic energy. Wringing her hands, she tried to control herself. She dropped to the couch and fondled the yellow silk scarf.

She reread part of the letter that had accompanied it:

That golden-hearted, loveable gentleman, gallant Frank Jones of Thomas County, who was then Adjutant, took me, as I had a good mount, with him on an uncomfortable reconnoitering ride and we came near being shot by Yankee sharpshooters. Poor dear Comrade! He received his death wound later that same day who, after eating the last sorry meal with some of us, he laughingly said: "Eat, drink, and be merry, for tomorrow you may die."

As he stormed the works, leading the men, a piece of shell tore away his side, exposing the lungs and heart. Still he lived nearly two days in that condition. I held his hand when he died. After the last faint smile, which I shall never forget, the nobility of his soul shined out as a glittering gem among the purest, guiltless, knightliest gentleman, whose wealth and blood were spent and poured out, a willing libation on the altar of Southern Liberty.

James Gadsden Holmes
2nd Of Charleston, S.C.

How kind of this young man to write these words, Lavinia thought. He had enclosed Frank's neckerchief, which he had used to staunch the wound. She touched the bloodstains, shivered.

She reread the formal letter from R. E. Cooper, Chaplain of Cobb's Legion, informing them of Frank's death on June 13, 1864, during the Battle of Trevilian Station. Her head pounded. She needed the relief of tears, but she was too stunned to cry. *I want the comfort of Thomas's arms holding me tight. Even if he is working on necessary accounts, I must interrupt him.*

She opened his office door quietly.

Thomas was not at his desk. He sat by the window, staring, mesmerized by the raindrops sliding down the wavery glass. A sob caught in her throat. He turned. A single tear hung on his ashen face.

Lavinia rushed to him, clutching his head to her bosom. Kissing, stroking Thomas's hair, she gently rocked. From the moment she left her childhood home, Thomas had taken care of her. Now she held him, trying to impart her strength.

He sobbed against her, moaning, "I wish I could have died in Frank's place."

When Thomas's emotions were spent, he said, "I must get this work done."

"Show me how, and I'll help."

Lavinia stood waiting. She felt herself trembling, but even as she did, she drew herself to her full height, knowing, knowing, *This has broken him as nothing else could. The time has come when I must be the strong one.*

At last the rain stopped. Lavinia walked to the cemetery weeping, then sobbing, and once out of earshot of the house, screaming out her grief. She sat for a long time in the place where she must bury her child. It would be weeks before Tommy and Fed would arrive with Frank's body. Lavinia grimaced as she thought of what her old granny always said, "If you have a bad task, just be like a mule: back your ears and do it."

With Thomas so devastated, details were up to her. She planned a carved monument depicting the belt and saber of a cavalryman and telling of his death in battle. It would remain for posterity to read. Remembering Chaplain Cooper's comforting letter about Frank's daily devotions and prayers, she wrote the epitaph: "Blessed are they who live and die like him. Loved with such love and with such sorrow mourned."

Activity sustained her until the funeral; then listless hours consumed her. She seemed unable to function, until a letter came from Frank's friend Charles Hansell. Lavinia read and reread one paragraph:

. . . "Sims had recovered his breath by this time and we all went on together. We got back to where I spied some of the 20th and joined them. I found several of our Company and Capt. Paine in a few minutes came up with Frank Jones, Adjutant of the Cobb Legion, and we sat on our horses and laughed over the many ridiculous things that happened that morning . . . Frank Jones told us how our wagon of medical stores had been captured and the Yanks rolled out a barrel of whiskey that was in it and shot holes in the barrel and were filling their canteens when our men came upon them and captured them, and then proceeded to fill up their canteens from the barrel . . . We spent some time here in pleasant conversation, the last we were ever to have with Adjutant Frank Jones, as he was killed the next day, or rather so badly wounded that he died on Monday.

Smiling, Lavinia imagined the scene. She heard her son's laughter at the silly incident. The image of Frank's merry spirit calmly performing his heroic duty gave him back to her. Now the vise around her heart opened. As she breathed deeply, she imagined being in the cloud of monarch butterflies on the brink of the sea. They, too, had been preparing for a journey, but God was in control, and one day they, and he, would return.

Lavinia felt nauseated in the July heat, weak from lack of salt in her food, but she stood beside Thomas as the train screeched into the depot with worn axles squealing like hog killing time. Townspeople were seeing off the remaining men of the county who were waiting to board in answer to Governor Joe Brown's order. As of July 9, 1864, Brown summoned all men between the ages of fifty-five and sixty and the sixteen- to seventeen-year-old boys to the defense of Atlanta.

Lavinia reached for Thomas's hand. They were needing that touch often these days. *I'm glad Thomas is sixty-two,* she thought. *I couldn't bear the thought of him going.*

She waved her handkerchief as the mismatched soldiers — young, old, fat, skinny — boarded with a jaunty air. The locomotive pulled out. Defiant rebel yells echoed from the train until it was out of earshot. Townsfolk returned silently through deserted streets.

As the Jones family climbed into their carriage, Mattie's plump cheeks were quivering. Edwin had sent word that his Fifty-Seventh Georgia Regiment was leaving guard duty at Andersonville Prison to fight for Atlanta. Thomas's face worked with emotion. Lavinia closed her eyes so she would not be looking at either one of them if they could not hold back tears. She was too numb to cry. She had begun to realize how much Thomas had been sheltering her from the gravity of their impending doom.

Raising his big hand to her lips, she prayed for strength to help him.

Waiting. Waiting. Atlanta held the gateway into North Georgia. Not only was the railroad hub vital to serve the state, but also to serve and connect the whole Confederacy.

Lavinia knew the truth now: with all the strength Georgians and Tennesseans could muster, General W. T. Sherman's forces outnumbered them two to one.

By late August, refugees began arriving by train from Savannah. Stagecoaches and wagons brought them from Albany. Elegantly dressed ladies, saving portraits and heirloom beds and rosewood rockers, herded their crying children and worse: their aged parents confused into incoherency. Thomasville's hotels overflowed. People opened their homes, treating refugees like family instead of strangers.

Denying her own heartache, Lavinia rushed to aid these displaced people, paying calls and inviting families for meals. Thomas, who still drifted in a haze, made weak jokes that he hoped the Lord would keep sending quail to them as He had to the children of Israel in the wilderness. She was glad for him to have the diversion of guests surrounding the big table. Unfortunately, the proper, polite conversation always turned to wondering what was happening in the battle for Atlanta.

In September Atlanta fell. Yankees moved into the ruins.

Livy J. tearfully sought Lavinia when a messenger brought a note from Florida. "Grandma-ma, my Chaires relatives say for me to stay here. The enemy has landed on the Gulf coast, and they're moving across the panhandle to raid Marianna. Governor Milton has called for the arming of every male. Listen to what my cousin wrote:

" 'With all able-bodied men at the front, the Cradle and Grave Company has gone out to meet the invaders. Boys thirteen and tottering gentleman as old as seventy-six armed with flintlocks and ancient shotguns are all we have between us and the enemy. You must remain in Georgia where you are safe.' "

Lavinia opened her arms. "Of course, you'll stay. We must send for Eliza. She should not be alone at Oak Lawn with the enemy so near."

Livy J.'s body relaxed against her, and her tears turned to a smile. Lavinia knew that since she and Price had declared their intentions to be married, she was probably glad of the chance to get acquainted with her future mother-in-law.

After Eliza arrived, Lavinia tried to give her visit the air of a house party. They were all sipping soothing tea brewed from her garden with chamomile, roses, hibiscus blooms, and mint leaves when the good news came. Even though the Cradle and Grave Company had been badly wounded by the enemy's new Enfield rifles, they had fought so fervently for home territory that the invaders retreated to Pensacola.

"I declare, Eliza," Lavinia said, "I feel like bits of glass in that kaleidoscope we bought to entertain James when he was bedridden. No sooner does life pattern into bright days until it shakes again, and all is dark."

Darkness fell with the unreality of nightmare. Thomas now needed Lavinia's strength to withstand the agony, and he told her the news at its worst. Everyone had expected the Federals in North Georgia to rejoin their main army in Tennessee. Instead, on November 16, 1864, Union General W. T. Sherman left Atlanta a burning inferno, and unheard of in the annals of war, broke communication with his superiors and struck out into enemy territory. Rumors raced that Sherman's Bummers were blazing through the heart of the state in two columns, each thirty thousand strong. This war had begun politely with Napoleonic rules; now Sherman was making war on women and children and the land itself.

Lavinia refused to believe the tales she was hearing of the rapine of the land until they received a letter from Thomas's cousin, Mrs. William B. Jones.

Birdsville Plantation
Burke County Georgia
November 25, 1864
Dear Cousins,

Hide your valuables and food. The Yankees came through here burning, pillaging, and destroying everything they did not steal. They set fire to Birdsville and told me to get out. I refused, telling them I had just borne twins who had died. They still tried to make me leave. I said my husband's ancestor, Francis Jones, had built the house in 1762, and I'd rather die than see it burn. They dug up the fresh graves, expecting to find my silver. When they saw the twins, they put out the house fire and moved on.

Oh, Lavinia, they left the little bodies lying out on top of the ground!

No one in our area has anything to eat except sweet potatoes, which had not been dug for harvest when the rapscallions came through. At least I have a roof. Many of my neighbors have nothing but Sherman's calling cards: naked chimneys.

With Love from your cousin

Birdie Jones

Lavinia sobbed at the thought of the babies' tiny forms left unburied. "Can't we send her some food?"

"I don't know how we'd get through the sixty mile swath Sherman is said to be cutting," Thomas replied sadly.

"Let's saddle the horses and ride to our secret place for awhile," she pleaded.

Cold wind buffeted them as they rode to the hammock, which they had left hidden by impenetrable vines. As they waded the creek and ducked under the encircling creepers, they looked at each other and exchanged silent thoughts.

Thomas smiled wistfully. "There will never be another dog like Rascal," he said, as they emerged into the clear center sheltered from the wind. "If it had not been for him bringing you here that day during the Seminole War, my family would have been wiped out, and my life would have ceased."

They slid down from their horses and into each other's arms. Holding tight, they prayed until they found peace. Sitting on a log in quiet communion, they gathered strength for the coming ordeal.

At last Thomas grinned. "I don't think they'll find Greenwood. You've always fussed because we were 'hidden in the pines.' "

Lavinia tried to share his humor. "Probably not. But we should store some barrels of foodstuffs . . ." She looked around. "Inside the branches of the magnolia would be good. That old tree served us well before."

"Yes. But I can't think where we can hide your special silver service. It seems the first place they look is the cemeteries."

Mattie cried out in ecstasy when her sweetheart surprised her by appearing at Greenwood on November twenty-eighth. Edwin told her that his Fifty-Seventh Georgia Regiment had marched the sixty miles from the railhead at Albany to catch the train in Thomasville and rush to the defense of Savannah. Lavinia could not help but intrude on their moment. She had to have real news because the rumors were flying.

"We don't have enough men to stop Sherman's march," Edwin told her. "He's crippling the state by ripping up the *Central of Georgia Railroad.* They're heating the rails over burning crossties and then twisting them around pine trees so we can't repair the line. We're moving across below their path to reinforce Savannah's Fort McAllister."

Mattie flung her arms around him, but Lavinia did not reprimand her. This boy would be her son-in-law — if he lived. She agreed with her daughter's cry, "Don't let them burn beautiful Savannah!"

A week later, Mattie, Livy J. and Florence galloped into the yard from a trip to Thomasville. They slid from their horses, all talking at once. They clattered up the steps to the porch where Thomas and Lavinia sat warming in a spot of the December sun.

Thomas stood up, spreading his hands in a gentling motion. "Calm down, girls. I can't understand with everyone babbling. "

The younger two looked to Florence, who explained. "The train pulled into town bringing four hundred prisoners from Camp Sumter at Andersonville."

"Why?" Thomas asked, fearing this new threat to his family.

"Colonel Henry Forno is the officer in charge. He said they thought Sherman would turn the prisoners loose when he left Atlanta so they moved them to Savannah." Florence gulped air. "Now that the Yankees are besieging Savannah, they brought them here."

"More are coming," Mattie added.

"Oh, Grandma-ma, they look like skeletons," wailed Livy J.

"Mrs. T. S. Hopkins sent little H. W. with a tray of coffee and biscuits. They said it was the best food they ever tasted," Mattie said.

Lavinia came alert. "You girls got that close to prisoners? Stay away. They have to be desperate men."

"Yes," Thomas agreed. "You three will *not* leave the yard while they're here. Guarding so many will be almost impossible . . ."

"Oh, I almost forgot," Florence exclaimed. "Judge Hansell said for you to bring all of the labor you can spare to build a stockade."

"Mama, can't we send food, too?" pleaded Mattie. "The guards were passing out only three crackers to each man from the supply wagon. The prisoners are so hungry — so dirty, please?"

"Me feed Yankees?" Lavinia's voice rose hysterically. "After they killed my little Frank?" She buried her face in her hands.

Mattie put an arm around her mother's shoulders and spoke softly. "Think about Edwin. I hope some Christian Yankee fed him when he was a prisoner after Vicksburg."

Bonfires around a five-acre square on the northwest outskirts of Thomasville led Thomas to the encampment. Other plantation owners had already arrived with their crews. They had begun digging a ditch eight-feet deep and twelve-feet wide to enclose the five acres. A cannon guarded the entrance. There was no way to provide shelter for so many. Thomas felt sorry for the men who could only huddle under trees as cold rain came in a sudden downpour. He was not surprised that a few prisoners had slipped away in the darkness, and the sheriff was after them with bloodhounds.

A train whistle echoed through the December night. Soon another twelve hundred prisoners marched toward the stockade.

How can we feed so many? Thomas wondered. He had known Lavinia would come through with food — she even added freshly made soap and towels — but all of the plantations in the area had their supplies taxed because of refugees.

At that moment he heard someone calling for Dr. Brandon. Thomas turned in surprise to see his son-in-law, who had been invalided out of the army because of lingering illness.

"David! You shouldn't be out in this night air."

"I'm needed," David replied. "Many of these prisoners have typhoid fever or smallpox. Dr. Hopkins had been trying to cope as prison doctor at Andersonville with little help and no medicine. Here, we're blessed with doctors who are fleeing Sherman, but we need a hospital."

"I'll talk to the Board of Stewards about using the Methodist Church," Thomas said.

"We'll need Fletcher Institute, too. When they all arrive, they will number five thousand."

"Great Jehoshaphat!"

Lavinia smelled smoke. Rushing into the yard, she spotted a black cloud coming from the direction of the cemetery. Running to the belltower, she clanged the farm bell. The girls responded first.

"Livy J., keep pulling the rope. Mattie, bring women and children with buckets.

Florence, send me what men we have."

She pressed her hands to her temples. Thomas and the ablest field hands were still in town after three days. She took a deep breath. *It's up to me.*

By the time she ran to Miss Elizabeth's old house, now their guesthouse, it was beyond saving. Fire blazed across brown grass toward the barn. Her people converged, and she set women and children to a bucket brigade. The men broke pine boughs, using them to beat out the flames. Yellow tongues of fire escaped them, popping up in other patches of dead grass, licking their way toward Greenwood.

"Leave the barn," Lavinia ordered. "Save the house."

Lavinia and the other women grabbed green pine. She beat and beat and beat until her arm felt as if it would drop off. Even the strongest ones were gasping for breath. Smoke seared her nostrils. Just as Lavinia thought they had won, the wind freshened, turned. Flames spurted towards the quarters.

Lavinia's hair had fallen from its pins, and she pushed it out of her eyes. *What am I to do?* Cold wind pierced her perspiration-wet bodice. Beside her, Mattie, soot smudged and wind blown, looked exhausted. Suddenly Lavinia saw a low spot still wet from the rain three nights ago.

"Head the fire that way," she shouted, hoarse now. "Grab your buckets. Add water to the puddles. Fast. Your homes will be gone."

With a surge of their last strength, they worked until there was nothing but the smell of scorched earth. Trembling with tiredness, Lavinia started toward a home that had never looked so beautiful.

"Miss 'Vinia!"

Startled at the urgency in Augustus's voice, she whirled. The grizzled old giant held two men bound by ropes.

"Us found those what done sot the fire," he said, including Samuel.

Blue rags hung on big-boned frames of men whose deep-socketed eyes glared at her with contempt.

Overwrought, Lavinia screamed, "You insolent wretches! How could you do this to people who have fed you and tended your sick?"

The dark haired one, whose shoulder patch proclaimed Sixteenth Illinois Cavalry, sneered at Lavinia. "You malcontents don't deserve these mansions you haven't sweated for."

"You Yankees!" She spat the word. "You

don't deserve to live. You killed my fine upstanding son worth ten of you."

Around her, the servants stood wide-eyed, wondering if she would kill the escaped prisoners herself.

Augustus coughed. "Ben, he been feeding them. He hid them in the barn when the sheriff and his bloodhounds first started searching the swamp. Now he's sorry."

The boy twisted his hat. "I was skeered, Miss 'Vinia. I ain't never seed Yankees afore."

"Me either, Ben," Lavinia said, calming down. "I hope these are the last. They aren't your friends. Don't you see they were set on burning your homes, too?" She faced her two most-trusted old men. "Samuel, you and Augustus get the buckboard and return the prisoners to the stockade."

The Union sergeant laughed to his fellow. "At least Lieutenant Cherry got away."

Lavinia cleared her smoke-inflamed throat. "And Augustus, tell Mr. Thomas to set Sheriff Pitt after the other man."

Lavinia still felt tired the next week, and she was not pleased to have a visit from her son-in-law, Dr. Brandon. Her head ached, and she looked at him dumbly, not comprehending his words.

"Sherman's army passed us by. The prisoners have been ordered back to Andersonville."

"Good! I've been afraid to let the girls out of the house." She shuddered at the memory of how the men who set the fire had leered at them.

"Yes, ma'am. Disease has left many of them in the Methodist cemetery." David smoothed his neat beard, hesitating. "I have a typhoid patient who is too weak to send back. He might recover with good nursing . . . there's no one better than — I've brought him to you."

"To me? Have you lost your mind? The Yankees killed my child — burned my house and barns. You can't expect . . ."

David's deep-set blue eyes bored into her. "I understand all that, but you're the best nurse I know. He must have constant sponging to cool the fever and liquid diet for his inflamed intestines. His name is E. W. Clark. He's from Paris, Maine. He's your enemy, but he's a human being."

Lavinia clenched and unclenched her fists. "I can't risk my family getting typhoid."

"We don't know what causes it, but we're pretty sure it isn't spread by breath or touch. It's epidemic in filthy, overcrowded prisons, but if you keep him isolated — I must get back to the hospital."

"No, David. I can't." She ran after him.

On the porch, a lifeless form lay on a stretcher. She tried to turn away, but a bony hand clutched her skirt.

"Water," Clark whispered.

A few days later, December 20, 1864, Savannah was evacuated. Refugees fleeing to Thomasville related that the mayor had gone out to meet Sherman, surrendering rather than letting the invaders burn the lovely squares of Georgia's founding city.

Lavinia fluctuated from joy that the old homes were saved to anger that Sherman had presented Savannah to President Lincoln as a Christmas present.

She could not get her mind on her accounts as she sat at her mahogany secretary, and it took long moments for her to realize Julie was standing beside her.

"Miss 'Vinia, the hands want to know if it's true what they heard."

"What, Julie?"

"That the Yankees won't let nobody through the blockade, and they done shot Santa Claus."

Lavinia's mouth worked, but no sound came. She took Julie in her arms, and they sobbed together.

Chapter XXI

The carriage hit a bump, knocking Lavinia's bonnet awry. Now her clothes were as rumpled and out of sorts as she felt. She adjusted the long swath of her heavy mourning veil and checked to see if the girls' black armbands were in place. Events had swept them along, and then Christmas brought memories of Frank rushing into the empty corners of her soul. She could fairly see the baby sleeping under the kitchen table, worn out from finding the perfect Christmas tree. She could hear the young boy calling "Christmas give."

Now this new thing to tax my emotions.

"It doesn't seem proper that I should be making a New Year's Day call," she whined. "Not when I've only been in mourning a few months."

"Mama, with it turning 1865, and the war news worsening, the whole South is in mourning," Florence reminded her. "A third of Thomasville's young men won't be coming home." Her voice softened to a whisper. "So many of the ones I've been writing . . ."

"You've got to do this for Tommy's sake," Mattie said.

Lavinia sighed. My whole world is crumbling. How can people expect so much of me? I feel so angry. It was those northern seamen who traded rum for slaves, and now they want to tell us how to live with them instead of tending to their own workers in unhealthy factories.

When the carriage stopped, she got down stiffly and then drew herself to her full height, chin up. Shaking off the girls' helping hands, she climbed the steps to the Methodist parsonage.

She greeted Reverend and Mrs. Capers formally. Then she glanced around the dark little parlor and saw the object of her visit alone in a corner.

"Ella," she said, going straight to her business. "Tommy wrote that you two were planning a wedding when he gets a furlough."

"Yes, ma'am. He's due a short leave this spring, and . . ."

Lavinia frowned and shook her head. She felt that her emotions could not cope with a

389

supposedly happy event in the midst of this sadness. "Are you sure you want to marry in the midst of war?" Her tone was stern, discouraging. "Do you want to be left a bride?"

"If that's what Tommy wants." Ella seemed smaller than usual as she replied in halting words that were barely audible. "I know we'd just have our wedding night, but he hopes . . ." Ella blushed and could not continue.

What Tommy wants. For a long moment, Lavinia could not breathe. She studied the courageous girl. Sighing, she pushed her own needs aside.

"Your wedding must be a beautiful memory even though we're in mourning for Frank. Properly, it should be a quiet family affair, but — would you like to have it at Greenwood?" Lavinia's voice brightened, and she finished in a rush. "Then when he goes back he can envision the picture of you coming down the staircase."

Ella threw her arms around Lavinia. "Yes. Yes!"

Lavinia relaxed. James's wife was reserved, but she saw that this loving girl was going to keep her young.

"I know it's wrong of me," Ella said, hesitating, ". . . and impossible in such hard times, but I wish Tommy's image of me could be in a wedding dress."

"Of course, you should have one," said Mattie, joining them.

"There's no cloth to be bought." Ella tried to hide a tear.

"Not bought, but traded," Florence supplied. "I read in the newspaper that Mrs. Hopkins wants to swap a bolt of white taffeta for a bag of salt. Mama . . ."

"Um. Your father is planning another visit to the Gulf for salt. Badly as we need it, I will spare a bag."

"A proper bride must have lace," Livy J. said with her contagious smile. "One of the things my Aunt Sarah Jane left me when she died was a bolt of delicate French Alencon. It can be your something old and something borrowed for your veil."

"Oh, no, I couldn't." Ella's happy tears rolled unashamed down her cheeks. "You must save it for when Price . . ."

"You and I are going to marry Jones cousins. Sharing the veil will bond us to sisterhood." Livy J. bent to kiss Ella. "Of course, you must use my lovely lace."

Mrs. Capers had left her other callers to be entertained by the preacher. Choking with emotion, she said, "None of the stores have buttons. It will take time, but I could cover Chinaberry seeds with taffeta."

Mattie swung Ella around in a dance. "Now all you need is something blue. It's been such a bore with no social life. What fun we'll have all pitching in to make you a wedding gown!"

Thunderclouds as dark as Thomas's mood threatened to drench him as he set off in the Greenwood wagon, but he did not care. The hack that carried mail and packages between Thomasville and Tallahassee pulled up behind him, but he waved it on. *I'm in no hurry,* he thought. He had to get away from home.

I don't know how Lavinia stands all the confusion when she's grieving for Frank as much as I am. She has no time for me.

Lavinia had to give the prisoner, Clark, constant care. She had pulled him through the typhoid crisis, but he remained bedridden. On top of that, she had a house full of chattering women working on a silly wedding dress.

How could Lavinia give away a bag of precious salt when Tommy might not even make it home? Thomas wondered.

The women kept adding more stitching and tucking and trimming as if it assured Tommy would live if they just kept working and believing.

I believed Frank would come home, and he didn't. I feel so useless. My son gave his life for me to be safe to grow feed and search for salt. I've done nothing. I'm old. I'm useless.

Thomas shook his head in despair and almost lost his hat to the March wind. He had fretted his way into Tallahassee.

A milling crowd, large even for a Saturday, startled him to attention. Thomas spotted Judge Du Pont and hurried to overtake him.

"Excuse me, sir. What's happening?"

"Ah, Jones, haven't you heard? A courier from the lighthouse reported a Federal fleet converging on them with eleven steamers and three sail vessels. Apalachee Bay is so large, especially because the East River and Wakulla River empty there, too, that they tried to sail right up the Saint Marks River and reach Tallahassee. Of course, they soon ran aground. Not only is the water too shallow for a deep-draft, ocean-going ship, but also they reckoned without the oyster shoals. Their propellers were completely fouled. They can't bring their fleet, but they've disembarked a force of fifteen hundred men who are heading this way."

Wild-eyed, Thomas stared at the heavy man who lurched along on small sore feet. Du Pont wheezed before he could continue.

"All we have is a few soldiers at the lighthouse post and the gunboat, *Spray*..." the Judge panted, "... between us and devastation."

"Man, have we no army?"

"The only seasoned soldiers we have on the scene are with Lieutenant-Colonel George C. Scott. He has been patrolling the coast with the Fifth Florida Battalion. They are in possession of a cannon, but they have few men."

Thomas slapped his forehead. "What about the troops that have been stationed at Tallahassee?"

"They are still giving chase to the Blue-coats retreating from Olustee." Judge Du Pont wiped his face with his handkerchief. "Spies must have told the Federals there's nothing to stop a major assault on Tallahassee."

Lightheaded, Thomas thought. *And only open road between here and Greenwood.*

The two old friends sank to a bench and watched as gray-bearded men hobbled toward the railroad. Some walked with canes and had servants to carry their guns. Young boys followed.

"Brigadier General William Miller is commander of the Military District of Florida by personal order of President Jefferson Da-

394

vis. He will coordinate our efforts with the few militia and reserves available. Our defense force is this motley group you see before us. We need you."

"I'll send a message to my wife that I'm delayed on business — and another to alert Judge Hansell. Then I'll join you."

By Sunday evening, Thomas's stomach churned from the waiting as the pitiable army assembled by the railroad tracks. Smooth-cheeked militia, clad in homespun butternut uniforms, arrived from the battle at Marianna. These lads became the veterans as pimply-faced cadets wearing caps from West Florida Seminary boarded. Some of the boys were rejected for service because they were too young and did not have notes from their mothers.

At last the long train chugged off, pulled by three engines that could scarcely haul it. If the rag-tag army was to confront the enemy who was following the river northward toward Tallahassee, they must first reach the river themselves.

Thomas thought about the mystical Saint Marks. Somewhere beneath them, it was rushing through limestone caverns. It burst forth at an unexpected spot, a clear, flowing spring. Farther south, it dipped underground again beneath a firm bar of sand wide enough for vehicles to cross. Waters emerged again, now a black, swamp-like river that snaked its way to the sea. Only at the strange phenomenon known as Natural Bridge could the enemy cross. Here they must make a last stand.

Thomas dozed only to awaken with a jolt when the train stopped in the midst of dark piney woods. Relieved, he saw a horseman who wore a cavalry uniform like Frank's with gold collar and cuffs on Confederate gray.

Thomas leaned out to hear what the soldier told Colonel Daniels, who was in charge of the train.

"Colonel Scott has met the Bluecoats and had to fall back twice," the scout reported. "They're marching up the road on the east side of the river. Scott has burned two bridges, and he's dismantling the one at Newport. He's delaying the enemy all he can until you rendezvous at Natural Bridge."

Daniels glanced back at the feeble group in his command and sighed. "We must hold them off there, or all is lost."

The train chugged on into the night. Then it stopped at the point where they must continue on foot to reach Natural Bridge. Thomas, who never went more than a few steps without a horse, dreaded walking through the woods almost as much as he did the coming battle. Short of breath, he marched behind the militia. A stretch of road became smooth, and the exhausted boys seemed to be marching along asleep. Suddenly one fellow stumbled and five or six went down like tenpins. Colonel Daniels reined his horse and encouraged them; it was not much further.

When they arrived at Natural Bridge, it was four o'clock on Monday morning of March 6, 1865. Colonel Scott deployed the troops in a curved line in front of the bridge crossing with two cannon guarding the center of the pass and two more on each side. Then the men hunkered down to wait.

Thomas watched the play of starlight on the dark water and wondered if the northerners, used to strongly moving streams, had ever seen such a river as this. Even now with spring rains, the flow of the Saint Marks was imperceptible to the naked eye. Cypress knees protruded from waters made black with tannic acid. Beneath the dark depths, alligators teemed.

Just as Thomas and those around him began to doze, a single gun fired some half-mile away. Then all was silent. Tense muscles tried to relax. Then a scattering volley of musketry rained on the bridge. A Minnie ball whizzed over Thomas's head, singing a plaintive tune of a well-spent ball.

Fifty or a hundred guns flashed in the dark, accompanied by a wild Confederate yell. Surprised, the Federals shouted out new commands. The artillery pieces guarding the bridge belched forth grape canister in rapid succession in long sheets of angry looking flame, illuminating the darkness.

Thomas thought the chatter of the small arms and the roar of the cannon enough to paralyze. The acrid stench of the black powder burned his nose. A piece of shrapnel hit close by his foot, making dirt fly. When the battle lulled, he put it in his pocket for a souvenir.

Across the river, the Bluecoats fell back with a rattle of canteens and cartridge boxes. After sounds of their wild retreat, silence emanated from the front.

Daylight broke. Beside Thomas, a man named Grubbs lay dead, shot through the heart. Others, wounded, were taken out, and the unseasoned troops settled back, hoping against hope that the enemy was gone.

Thomas fell into exhausted sleep. A single shot awakened him. As his eyes flew open, he saw a blue jay falling before him.

A sound, half snort, half chuckle, came from the one who had taken Grubbs's place. Thomas blinked at the smooth-faced boy in his teens.

"Why'd you kill that harmless bird, son?"

"They admonished us meleesh to keep a sharp lookout and shoot anything that looked blue. That jay pitched on a limb, and I obeyed orders by shooting him."

Thomas laughed in spite of himself.

Arrogance gone, the boy looked sheepish. "Joshua Hoyet Frier, II, at your service, sir. I guess I was trying to keep awake. We've been days without sleep."

"Thomas Jones, Joshua. You caught me napping."

Suddenly, both came awake as blue appeared in front of them again. The battle erupted in earnest. Hours passed. Four times the enemy made efforts to pass over the narrow defile formed by the sinking and rising of the river. Each time cannon exploded about nature's bridge.

Thomas realized he was gritting his teeth as Minie balls whistled and shrieked, cutting bushes, clipping off trees at various heights, stripping trunks as if by lightning. Federal soldiers were lying beneath them near the water's edge.

Suddenly Thomas saw a long black snout

ease up from the water and grasp a blue leg. Slowly the body moved into the mysterious depths of the river.

Thomas shuddered. I hope the poor devil was already dead.

Shortly before sunset, Joshua punched Thomas and said, "Listen."

Beneath the general racket, Thomas detected the rumbling of wagons and caissons, the neighing of horses. Activity indicated the Federals were retreating. Colonel Scott and forty of his cavalry pursued, harassing them. In their haste to return to their gunboats, the Yankees left a large number of their dead and many of their wounded.

The victors at Natural Bridge sent up a rebel yell starting low in the throat, rising higher and higher, echoing, reechoing through the piney woods. General Miller stood smiling until the sound stopped. Then he addressed the troops.

"From boys of fourteen to men of seventy, from humble woodsmen to highest civil dignitaries, your bravery needs no comment. While all behaved handsomely and are worthy of highest praise, I must select one of many brave officers for special notice. Lieutenant-Colonel Scott evinced great power of command, bravery, and vigilance."

As the weary soldiers rode the train home-ward, a group of little girls flagged it down and boarded. They placed wild-olive wreaths on the caps of the teenage cadets from West Florida Seminary, singing to the tune of Dixie:

The young cadets were the first to go
To meet and drive away the foe
Look away!

By the time Thomas had rested at the hotel in Tallahassee, Leon County's citizens were going out to picnic and hunt for souvenirs on Natural Bridge.

As he started for home, Thomas thought, *I have no salt. But what a tale I have to tell!* He knew now that he would not break down at Tommy's wedding and disgrace himself by crying. He no longer felt useless.

Thomas stood back, watching in amaze-ment at how quickly Lavinia assembled the wedding when Tommy arrived. Food ap-peared on the table. Roses filled the house in such profusion that Thomas feared that the pale, thin groom would be overcome by the heavy perfume. For suspended moments as Ella descended the staircase in a white gown with a veil of lace, it seemed they were in another time of peace and love.

Reverend Capers began the ceremony. "Today, Palm Sunday, April 9, 1865, I take pleasure in uniting my daughter, Ella Guild Capers and Thomas William Jones."

Thomas heard no more. After all of the preparations, it was over in minutes and the couple slipped away for their one-night honeymoon.

The next day, Tommy left his courageously smiling bride on the porch of Greenwood with Lavinia's arm supporting her. He had asked Thomas to take him to the train.

"Papa, I'm counting on you to look after my wife," he said. "I hope I've left her with a child to carry on our name. You need to understand — I doubt I'll come back."

"Son, surely —" Thomas broke off, shocked. "We repulsed the enemy attacks here."

"With equal numbers and well-fed men. All we have is valor. The Cow Cavalry hasn't been able to penetrate enemy lines to take meat to Lee's army since the first of the year. Sherman destroyed the food Georgia was supplying. Now he's burning his way through South Carolina to join Grant in attacking Lee. They have men, munitions — their food and ours — while Lee's men are actually starving and barefooted in the snow."

Thomas dropped his head in his hands. "Then there's no hope. Maybe you shouldn't go back."

Tommy embraced him. "Honor compels me."

The following Sunday Thomas and his newly enlarged family attended the Easter worship service. The singing of "Christ the Lord is Risen Today" was suddenly interrupted as the stationmaster strode up the aisle. Communications had been slow since the Federal occupation of Savannah, and the congregation gave him full attention as he held up a message and tried to read.

His voice failed. He was visibly trying to control himself. Suddenly he intoned, "General Robert E. Lee surrendered the Army of Northern Virginia to General U. S. Grant at Appomattox Court House, Virginia, on April 9. 1865."

Silence filled the sanctuary. Then came sniffling followed by open, loud weeping by men as well as women and children.

Thomas looked across the aisle to the women's side, searching for comfort from Lavinia. Beside her in the midst of everyone's tears, Ella's face had a radiant smile.

When they filed into the churchyard, Ella hugged him, exulting, "Papa Jones, the surrender was the same day as our wedding. Tommy didn't have time to get back to the battlefield. He's got to be alive. He'll be coming home after all!"

Thomas felt physically sick as shock followed shock. Abraham Lincoln had died April fifteenth, assassinated by John Wilkes Booth.

Mattie heard from Edwin, who was with General Joseph Johnston in North Carolina. Johnston had surrendered his army to Sherman. Confederate armies in Mississippi and Alabama had no other choice. The last holdout was General Kirby Smith in Texas.

There was no word from Price. Livy J. paced Greenwood's halls like a pale and silent ghost.

The war was over. The terrors began. Drunken mobs roamed the South, unleashing vengeance for one man's act in killing Lincoln. Thomas prayed Tommy would soon be home to help him protect their women.

Thomas County had been spared a battle or a burning, although it had spent its lifeblood. Now the little town was to feel the full brunt as the conquerors lost no time in grinding the South under their heels. Jackboots of the Federal Army of Occupation marched into Thomasville on May 9, 1865. One thousand of the posted troops were black.

A week later Thomas wondered how much more he could stand as he heard a heavy knocking on the barred doors of Greenwood just as the clock struck midnight.

Chapter XXII

As the pounding became persistent, Thomas peered through the sidelights of Greenwood's front door, trying to tell who was knocking at this unearthly hour. The night was too black to see. He slid back the bolts and held his candle high, expecting their Bluecoat captors.

Seeing a Confederate gray uniform shocked him. The tall man wore the stars of a Brigadier General. Thomas staggered back and swung wide the door.

"I'm John Crawford Vaughn, sir, late in service to President Jefferson Davis. May I come in?"

"Quickly, quickly. We're under martial law. The oppressors are shooting anyone out after dark. How did you get here, man?"

The General laughed a deep rumble. He swept off his hat and bowed. "My apologies, ma'am."

Startled, Thomas looked around. He had

not realized Lavinia was standing on the stairs. Florence was peering from the top. He motioned that it was safe for them to come down and introduced them.

"Good evening, General Vaughn," said Lavinia, as graciously as if he had arrived for afternoon tea. "We want to hear of President Davis, but first we must fix you something to eat."

Over waffles, eggs, and makeshift coffee, John Vaughn related his recent experiences.

"I was escorting President Davis as he headed south from Richmond. We were trying to reach Florida because Tallahassee is the only Confederate capital that the enemy did not capture. From there Davis planned to join our troops in Texas. Unfortunately, by the time we reached southern Georgia, we had pursuers. General Breckinridge peeled off with five brigades of cavalry, hoping to divert them. We were left with only a handful of men to guard the presidential family. On May 10, we were camped in a stand of pines just north of Irwinville, Georgia."

"That's some sixty miles from here," Thomas supplied.

"We were awakened in the middle of the night by Federal Cavalry shooting from both directions. Mrs. Davis saw a form advancing on the President with a bead at point-blank range. She threw her arms around his neck, and that stopped his chance of getting away."

Vaughn helped himself to another waffle, and beamed at Florence as she poured more coffee before he continued. "The saddest thing was that the Federals took custody of his wife and four children as well as the cabinet members who were still with them. The soldiers were so intent on tearing through their things and stealing their money, they didn't care about the few of us in the escort who slipped away."

"Those poor children," said Florence, wiping her eyes.

"There was nothing I could do, little lady," Vaughn said to Florence. "We were sadly outnumbered."

Thomas scowled, concerned for his vulnerable daughter. He didn't like the worshipful way Florence was gazing at the conceited man in his flashy gold-braided uniform.

Vaughn turned full attention upon Florence as he told in detail how he'd escaped to Savannah and there caught the *Atlantic and Gulf Railroad*. "Not knowing where I was going, I simply rode the train to the end of the line in an effort to get away."

Thomas studied him as he talked. There were streaks of gray in his brown beard. *He's fully twenty years older than Florence. He could just be nerve-wracked, but I'm afraid his eyes are shifty.*

"How did you find us?" Lavinia asked.

"When the train stopped, I noticed blue uniforms and jackboots, so I got off on the dark side. There was a riot going on in town. I heard women hollering and pigs squealing. That kept the troops busy, and I slipped around dark corners until I found the Methodist Church — I'm a staunch Methodist myself — and Rev. Capers told me you were a big-hearted man . . ." Vaughn laughed again. "And large enough that perhaps you could fit me in a suit of less conspicuous clothes before I try to go farther."

"Oh, you must hide here until you rest up," Florence gushed. Eyes shining and cheeks flushed, she dared to place a staying hand on his arm.

Thus trapped, Thomas showed the General to a guest room.

The next morning, Lavinia looked down from her bedroom window as a detail of Union soldiers rode into the yard, trampling her flowerbeds. She ran down the stairs, following Thomas. He opened the door.

A young officer swaggered up the steps with his four-foot scabbard dragging, scaring the porch as he crossed. He wore a short blue jacket, resplendent with brass buttons and, tucked into knee-high boots, light blue trousers with a yellow stripe down the leg. Full of his own authority, he spoke brusquely with no respect for Thomas.

"I am Lieutenant Scott, commander of the troops posted here. There's a report charging you with harboring . . ."

Lavinia suspected he knew about the General, but she spoke up quickly before Thomas could reply. "Yes, we have a prisoner here. I'll take you to him." Quickly, she guided the intruder to Mr. Clark's bedside.

Clark tried to rise up and salute, but he was too weak. "E. W. Clark of Paris, Maine, sir," he said.

"You may take him, of course," said Lavinia, with a shrug. "But you must care for him. Be sure you give him liquids every hour and a soft diet."

Deflated, the lieutenant stared openmouthed, not knowing what to say.

Lavinia held her breath in the long moment of silence. She hoped the General was well hidden. Even in Thomas's clothes,

Vaughn was an eye-catching man with an unmistakable military bearing. *If they take him prisoner, poor, lovesick Florence will be inconsolable.*

Thomas cleared his throat. "Union prisoners from Andersonville were here for two weeks," he explained. "Mr. Clark was too sick to travel when they were returned to the stockade. As you see, my wife has grown rather attached to her patient." Thomas tried to laugh.

Clark said, "Miss Florence has written my parents that I'm here. They plan to come for me."

"Well, uh . . ." Lieutenant Scott stammered. His accent sounded less clipped and harsh as he said, "Mrs. Jones, you are a kind nurse." He looked her in the eye.

Lavinia met his gaze unflinchingly even though her heart was pounding. *Is he fooled? If he's not, will he be kind?*

"We won't trouble your house further," the lieutenant said and turned to go.

"Tommy!"

"Tommy!"

"Tommy's home!"

Thomas heard the joyful cries echoing through Greenwood. As he started to get up from his desk, his tears flooded, embar-

411

rassing him. He had never admired sensitive men. Unable to join the homecoming, he bowed his head on his desk in thankful prayers.

Tommy found him there. They embraced and sat quietly for a while.

At last Thomas said, "I plan to deed you the rest of Aucilla Plantation. You know I gave part of it to Livy for her dowry when she married David."

Tommy nodded in agreement.

"I expect Greenwood to go to Lavinia."

"Of course, Papa, but not for a long time."

"I'm a tired sixty-three."

"Tired, yes, but now the younger generation is coming home to help."

Thomas sighed. "We're under martial law. They've told our labor force they can't work without pay. We can't raise the money to pay them until they work and make the crop. It's a hopeless situation for everyone."

Tommy shook his head. "When I got off the train, I saw crowds of the townsfolk's servants roaming the streets."

"Most of our Greenwood people stayed. Only Ben and a couple of his cronies left — for which I'm glad — but I don't know how we will feed the rest if we can't work them."

"What about our cotton that we stored in the depot warehouse during the blockade?"

Thomas brightened. "They're keeping it under guard. The price has gone sky high, and when they let us sell it, we can begin again."

The door burst open, and hoop skirts filled the small office as the girls rushed in, grabbing them both by the hands.

"Come on," said Ella, fairly dancing. "Let's celebrate."

When they had eaten and were sitting around the table, Tommy said, "What we all need is some fun."

"Yes," the girls chorused.

"We've been like prisoners in our own home," said Mattie. "They say it's too dangerous for us to go into town even to church."

Florence chimed in brightly. "We couldn't even have ridden our horses around here if the General hadn't escorted us." She had finally grasped her mother's teachings about being fresh and well groomed, and she lifted a radiant face to the beefy man beside her. He had been surprisingly quiet during the reunion.

Thomas sank back in his chair, morose again. *Vaughn might have been an aid to Jefferson Davis, but I've got to find some way to get rid of him.* As he pondered, the happy chatter filling the room spilled over him.

Lavinia admonished Mattie, "You know why we haven't been letting you go into town. Even the guards might accost you."

"They'll be safe with me," Tommy answered her. "On the way home, several who used to be in the Young Men's Debating Club planned a picnic at Rocky Ford on the Ocklockonee for July twenty-seventh."

Mattie moaned. "That's such a romantic spot with the music of the water playing over the mossy shoals. I wish Edwin were back."

"The newlyweds may go, of course," said Lavinia, "but Livy J. and Mattie and Florence couldn't attend unless chaperones . . ."

"We thought of that," Tommy said. "We'll ask Sister Livy and some of her respectable married friends to go along."

"I'll be happy to lend my protection," said General Vaughn.

"Mama, I must speak with you at once," said Livy Brandon, pursing her lips. "In private."

Lavinia eyed her oldest daughter. Something must have happened at the outing because Livy's topknot of auburn hair was quivering. Lavinia decided her bedroom was the best place for a confrontation.

"How was the picnic?" she asked in a false

tone as she led the way upstairs.

"A grand occasion," Livy replied. "A hundred and fifty or two hundred young people went. Everyone brought a fine array of food, and Tommy and James Dixon netted a quantity of fish to fry."

Livy closed the bedroom door and stood with her back against it. "Did you know that General Vaughn is married?"

Lavinia dropped to a chair. "Oh, my goodness gracious!" Stunned, she stared at Livy. "Did he make advances to Florence."

"No. He was a perfect gentleman. And believe me after I heard it, I watched him like a cat on a rat. So did Mary Stegall."

"How did you find out?"

"Some of the returning soldiers served with the Army of Tennessee. That's where Vaughn is from. He's married, sure enough. He has children!"

"My poor Florence. She is besotted with him. She's so sweet, but there have been no young men left here to gallant her."

"What are we to do?"

"Go. Bring her here. We'll try to break it gently." Lavinia blew her nose. "Then your father must confront the scoundrel and order him to leave our home."

"Yes, Mr. Jones, I do have a wife — and

children — back home in Tennessee."

Thomas felt his face reddening. He could not control his temper. Glad he had taken the man out into the grove, he shouted, "Then by all that's holy, why haven't you gone to them?"

Vaughn remained calm. "I'm afraid of being arrested. I've served importantly throughout the war. I was in Charleston when the first shot was fired. I was there when the Confederacy's last ember died as Jefferson Davis was captured."

Thomas was too angry to risk asking if Vaughn did all he could to save the President. He said nothing.

"Did you know, sir, that Davis is confined in a dungeon at Fortress Monroe? A light is kept burning at all times and guards march back and forth so he can get no sleep. Vice-president Alexander Stephens is incarcerated below the water line at Fort Warren in Boston Harbor. Even Postmaster General Reagan is imprisoned there because he was traveling with Davis."

Thomas's voice was harsh. "I'm aware the conquerors are punishing and humiliating us all, but that gives you no excuse for leading on my innocent, spinster daughter. You did not tell her you had a wife."

"No . . . But I've made no advances. I've

taken all three young ladies riding. The others are so young, but Miss Florence and I have enjoyed stimulating conversations." He blustered, "I, of all people, respect the flower of southern womanhood. The northern army was supplied by factories. We had none, but our women kept us fed, clothed, and armed."

Thomas thought of how Lavinia had made bandages from cherished sheets and financed a gunboat with some of her silverware, but he would not be swayed by this tactic.

"Be that as it may, General, I must rescind the hospitality of my house!"

"Grandma-ma!" Livy J. knelt beside Lavinia's rocking chair and laid her head on her knees.

Lavinia stroked her lustrous hair and braced herself for what was coming next.

"I've received two letters. One is from a nurse who is attending Price. He was wounded at Haws Mill, Virginia. The kind lady insists that he's recovering, but it will be a long while before he can travel back to Georgia. The other note was from Pa-pa. He wrote that he's back home. He contracted lingering dysentery in the army, and he's quite ill. He's asking for me."

"Then, of course, you must go. Oh, how we will miss you!"

"I hate to leave with Florence about to wash everyone away with her tears, now that the General is gone."

"You'll take the sunshine from the house, but you're needed. Your grandfather will escort you. I'll give you my heaviest mourning veil to conceal your lovely face from the Occupation Army. Even so, be careful. We're accustomed to smiling and speaking to everyone we meet, but you must not smile at a Yankee."

"We'll plan the trip after we eat," said Thomas, as he, Lavinia, Livy J., and a listless Florence sat down at the dinner table. He wanted a peaceful meal first.

Mattie interrupted their first bite as she stormed in with Edwin in tow.

"Papa, Edwin refuses to marry me!"

Edwin blanched. "No, sir. It's-it's not a breach of promise," he stammered. "Help me make her understand. I have no money . . ."

"We can live on my dowry." Mattie pouted her lips.

"I must get my farming established first and have some means to take care of her," Edwin said. "Forgive me, sir, but I've taken the forced oath to support and defend the Constitution of the United States, the union of states, and the new emancipation law. I had to do it in order to start in business."

Thomas rubbed the creases in his forehead. He did not intend to sign the hated oath himself. He wished Edwin had not, but he bit his tongue for Mattie's sake.

He spoke to his baby daughter more sternly than he ever had before. "You must allow Edwin what manhood he can muster with our captors holding us on such a tight rein."

A few weeks later, Lavinia was watching for Thomas who had gone to the warehouses in town in hopes of shipping his stored cotton to Savannah. *If at last we can sell our cotton, we can eat better and buy seed for winter crops,* she thought.

When Thomas rode into the yard and dismounted, his knees buckled. Lavinia ran to support him and help him into the house. He sank onto the hall couch.

"Mattie," she called. "Bring water. Florence, fetch smelling salts."

When his color returned slightly, Thomas mumbled so low, she could hardly understand.

"The soldiers are emptying the warehouse

and loading our cotton bales on the train."

Lavinia held her breath, wondering. "I — don't understand."

"They've confiscated our cotton! They claim it belonged to the Confederacy. First they liberated our labor force and gave us no compensation. Now they've stolen all our assets. I don't believe they want us to live."

Chapter XXIII

"I never imagined I'd invite Yankees to stay in my house," Lavinia said, talking to the broom and giving it a vicious shake.

She finished sweeping the porch steps and sank down on the top one with her head against a column. The October sunshine warmed and relaxed her and she sighed, thankful to be quiet and alone now that fast-talking Mr. and Mrs. Clark had returned to Maine.

Then she felt remorseful. *They looked so pitiful when they saw the condition of their son — what else could I do but ask them to stay here?*

It was a shame that the Clarks had been so long in coming. Many of the railroads across the South had been destroyed, and the trip was a tedious changing of modes of transportation. The young soldier had lived only a week after his parents arrived. He was buried in Greenwood Cemetery on

October 4, 1865. The family had held a council, and all agreed; because he had lived at Greenwood so many months, it was the thing to do.

Not next to Frank, of course. Nobody could have expected that of me.

Weariness from the ordeal and the changes life was bringing made Lavinia feel overwhelmed. She snorted in displeasure when she saw a rider approaching on horseback. *Not one more thing,* she thought as she started to run into the house and bolt the door. Chagrined, she recognized her own daughter. *Livy's all aquiver! What now?*

As Livy neared, Lavinia called out, "Where's your carriage?"

"My carriage?" Livy exploded. "I still have the shabby old thing, but I can't drag it around Thomasville myself. Somebody stole my mare mule, one of the matched pair of iron grays that pulled the carriage."

Livy flopped down on the steps. "With us under this martial law, thieving is terrible in town. Even my eggs are gone if I don't run out to the henhouse the minute I hear a cackle."

Lavinia laughed in spite of herself, but her agitated daughter did not slow her tongue.

"Burglars took goods from both the Harrell's and the Hardwick's stores last night and money from John Stark's Confectionary. Trouble is, thieves know the military authorities have incarcerated our Marshall Pitts, accusing him of arresting drunken colored troops and hanging them by their thumbs."

"Did he?"

"Of course, but that's a usual punishment. One they understand."

Livy looked around to make sure no one else could hear. She lowered her voice. "There's worse. Did you know that scoundrel Vaughn is still in town?"

"No!" Lavinia's hand flew to her heart. She sickened with worry over Florence.

Livy's voice showed her agitation. "I thought he'd left town until the newspaper named him a hero." She handed Lavinia the *Southern Enterprise.*

Lavinia scanned the article, which told of an incendiary fire originating in a cotton warehouse. ' "High winds spread flames to several stores. For some time the fire threatened to prove the greatest conflagration in the annals of Thomasville, but owing to the indefatigable efforts of citizens, the blaze was checked before it reached Broad Street. Thanks are especially due to General Vaughn . . .' "

As Lavinia's voice trailed away, Livy

added, "I found out he's living at Mrs. C. W. Eaton's Boarding Home."

Lavinia sat dumbly for long moments, and then she said, "Why doesn't he go home to his wife? The gall of the man to stay around after Thomas confronted . . ." She jumped guiltily as a footstep sounded behind them.

Mattie bounced out the door. "The *Enterprise*! Let me see."

She reached, but Livy snatched at the page Lavinia had been reading. Mattie was quicker. She saw the article.

"Don't tell Florence," Lavinia cautioned.

Mattie tossed her long curls. "She knows. He sent her a note."

Lavinia and Livy stared at her in consternation, but Mattie read on, chattering blithely. "Oh, look at this. Since the mean old Union let ships into our ports again, the stores have goodies. Let's go shopping."

Livy shook her head until the coils of hair over her ears threatened to escape the pins. "You don't know how dangerous Thomasville's streets are with these Occupation Troops everywhere. It's worse since we have no mayor."

"I thought the Union army appointed A. P. Wright," said Mattie.

Livy laughed harshly. "He's been indicted on a cotton scandal. When the army confiscated the cotton in the depot warehouse — you know some was Papa's — Mayor Wright spirited several bales away and sold them in England as his own."

Mattie pouted. "What difference does that make? I want . . ."

"It means with no honest law there are twelve illegal distillers in town and saloons in nearly every store. The One-Hundred-Third United States Colored Troops had never fought in battle. They know nothing of discipline. All they do is drink and have knife fights."

Mattie frowned at her big sister. "If we went early in the morning — just listen to the things we haven't had since the war started. 'Coffee, almonds, Brazil nuts, coconuts, raisins, yeast, soda, oysters in cans, lobsters in cans. Candy! And salt, Mama, salt.' "

Lavinia roused from her distress over Florence and that man Vaughn. "I don't want salt from the Yankees," she declared. "I'd rather eat it off the smokehouse floor!"

The front door banged as Florence exploded onto the porch. "You and Papa can't keep us prisoners here forever!" she screeched. "I know you trust old Augustus and you set his son, Gus, Jr. to following every time we go horseback riding through the fields."

"We're not keeping you prisoners!" Lavinia's voice rose. "Your father is protecting . . ."

"Why couldn't Gus, Jr. escort us to town," Mattie put in above the others.

At that moment, Thomas walked around the corner of the porch. "Silence! I never thought I'd hear my young ladies shrieking like fishwives."

Riled, Florence flung out, "I know you're trying to keep me from going into town because of John. I only want to see him . . . talk to him . . . try to understand," she ended in a whimper.

Thomas's voice was low and even. "I think a daughter of mine is too intelligent to run away to a married man. Gus is keeping watch over both of you."

"Of course, he's protecting the pretty one!" Florence snapped, always quick to emphasize her plainness and Mattie's beauty.

Thomas ignored her words and continued quietly. "If Gus took you to town, his life might be endangered . . . It's your mother I really worry about guarding. They might — assault — her in order to shame me. You must understand the situation we're in. The North is humiliating all of us for what one man — John Wilkes Booth — did in shooting Lincoln. We are an occupied nation so they can strip us of all dignity and the self-rule we fought for. The so-called Reconstruction is a farce. Nothing in the burned out, bombed out South is being rebuilt. They mean to keep us down. They resented our wealth, and now they're grinding us into abject poverty."

Thomas's voice broke, and he dropped to the steps with his head between his knees.

Lavinia waved her daughters away as she embraced her husband, murmuring soothingly, "The girls really did not understand the gravity of the situation. We've been through trials and tribulations before. We'll all stick together, and God will give us strength to bear it."

Livy Brandon put her arm around Florence's hunched shoulders and disappeared with her into the depths of the garden, but Mattie came back and knelt before Thomas, kissing his big, rough hands.

"I'm sorry I said anything, Papa. Poor Florrie is just hurting. I don't need any town food to eat. Why, I might get too fat before I get to use my wedding gown."

Arms encircling, all three laughed through their tears.

■ ■ ■ ■

A few days later, Mattie joined Lavinia as she walked along the avenue of live oaks that welcomed visitors to Greenwood.

"I love these trees," mused Lavinia. "Especially the way they reach out their branches to entwine with each other across the road."

"I want to hold out my arms to others, too, Mama," said Mattie. "I understand what Papa said about not pushing Edwin to get married, but I see how you bolster him, and I know Edwin needs me that way, too. My dowry land would certainly add to his diversified farming. He's tying to adapt to modern ways by planting those new Le Conte pears, and he's bought some Brahma cattle. But more than land, my comforting . . ."

"Marriage must be built on a foundation of God's love," Lavinia replied quietly, "and then you must exhibit that same kind of love where you forget self and seek the highest good of your partner. Can you do that?"

"Yes."

"You've grown into a fine, perceptive woman. I think you can. I'll pray with you, and maybe we'll find a way. Carpetbag government can't stay this bad forever."

■ ■ ■ ■

Reconstruction remained unbearable throughout fall and Christmas; however, on a Sunday morning in January 1866, the family rode into Thomasville at last. With the New Year and a capable former Confederate officer elected mayor, the town was somewhat less a tinderbox. Respectable people could walk down the streets.

Lavinia entered the Methodist Church with joy in her heart that she could attend worship services again. The little frame building reverberated as voices lilted, "O for a thousand tongues to sing my great Redeemer's praise . . ."

Lavinia's heart warmed with the words, and she was beaming as Reverend Capers greeted the congregation.

"Welcome all. It is especially delightful to have the ladies with us again. We extend the right hand of Christian fellowship to our Baptist visitor Colonel Peter McGlashan, who made the ladies presence possible. Sir, we offer prayers of thanksgiving that you are now Mayor McGlashan and that you ran on a plank to get rid of liquor and to arrest drunks from our streets."

The congregation had an expectant air,

but the pastor held up his hands for silence. "We must also express admiration for the organization of our fire department — now you folks may give him a standing vote of appreciation."

McGlashan made a modest bow.

Lavinia smiled and nodded at him. She knew that the Fire Company secretly circumvented restrictions against southerners organizing. It provided a group of townspeople who could maintain law and order.

Thinking to catch Thomas's eye and share the moment with him, she looked across the aisle to the men's pews. Her hand flew to her mouth to stifle an exclamation. In the midst of this pleasure of being able to get out of their house and worship again, Thomas sat preoccupied with his face etched in deep lines of worry.

Just as Reverend Capers began his sermon, Lavinia felt Florence jerk erect and catch her breath. Florence's face flamed. Lavinia peeped behind her.

Striding in confidently as if he were not late, General Vaughn acknowledged everyone on both sides of the aisle. He had the effrontery to sit down beside Thomas.

Lavinia's prayers fled from her angry thoughts. *Why doesn't that man go home to his wife where he belongs?*

■ ■ ■ ■

Thomas was thankful for Peter McGlashan. He thought the young man one of the most capable he had ever known. He had joined the Ochlockonee Light infantry as Orderly Sergeant and had risen to commanding Colonel of the Fiftieth Georgia Infantry, about to be commissioned Brigadier General at war's end. As Mayor, McGlashan did a remarkable job of using his fire department to bring about order in Thomasville. The city regained sound financial shape because he had the Town Marshal collect taxes.

On April 16, 1866, the black troops left. Conditions were better; however, twelve soldiers remained to remind them they were under the Occupation Army's martial law. Carpetbaggers stood on every corner of town, filling innocent ears with promises of forty acres and a mule, promises that never materialized. Unfortunately, just hearing the spiel made men refuse to work.

Thomas wondered how he could make a crop, but with faithful Augustus and Samuel he got some cotton planted. Then summer rains came and stayed, soaking everything, creating puddles, ponds, and swamps.

Malaria swept the county.

On a hot August afternoon as Thomas sat in his office with his accounts before him, he thought, *As bad as things are, at least that accursed Vaughn has gone back to Tennessee.* He had heard — with a great deal of satisfaction — that the great general had been indicted for fraud by the War Department.

A knock sounded on his office door, and he jumped, a bit guilty for his enmity. James, who had come with his family to spend a few days, poked his head in.

"Am I interrupting?"

"Yes, and in the nick of time. Let's go hunting."

The dogs darted through the plumes of drying fall grasses, eager for the hunt. Thomas still felt tense as he and James followed on horseback, admiring Rascal's offspring. The young Setters carried their sire's traits of domed head and Belton blue ticking in flowing white hair; more importantly they had inherited Rascal's hunting skill.

As the leader quietly froze in position to alert the men there was a covey of quail ahead, Thomas relaxed his shoulders. There were birds aplenty. It was a relief. *I never imagined I'd have to worry about putting meat on the table.*

James's family had increased. Thomas looked at his son's paralyzed leg and remembered how James had doubted a woman would ever love him. Instead, he had found love twice. When Ann died young, he married Margaret Holzendorf. They had four children added to the three he had with his first wife. Supper would be short if they did not get a big mess of quail.

The covey flew up on whirring wings. Both men made their shots count. They continued the hunt until they had bagged enough. Then they sought the cool of a live oak hammock and the refreshment of a spring.

James sprawled out to rest. "I hate to be the bearer of bad tidings, but you'll want to know that Aunt Eliza put up a notice to rent out the farm Uncle Mitch left her on Lake Miccosukee."

"I have worse news," Thomas replied. "Livy's husband David is having to sell all of his property in town. He will probably find buyers because many people who came here as refugees have nothing to return to since Sherman burned everything across the heart of Georgia."

"David Brandon shouldn't be that hard up. Can't he still practice medicine?" asked

James in surprise.

"Don't you remember that he was discharged from the army because of debilitating illness? It continues to worsen. He's too weak to perform surgery. To tell you the truth, he had to do so many amputations as army surgeon that I don't think he can stomach blood anymore. He has a few medical patients, but they pay him with food."

"My problems seem light," James said. "Did I tell you I lost my seat on the Florida Legislature?"

"I shouldn't be surprised since none of us who aided the Confederacy are allowed to vote."

"Who'd have ever thought our lawmakers would be carpetbaggers, scalawags, and freedmen? I'm almost glad Governor Milton shot himself before the Occupation Troops marched into Tallahassee. At least he doesn't have to see how bad the so-called Reconstruction really is."

"I read that he predicted 'the Union's bonds would prove to be a loathsome embrace,'" Thomas said. "He was right. I can almost agree with him that death would be preferable to reunion."

"Hey, enough gloomy talk," said James, pushing on his cane to help him stand.

"Let's go home. Nothing can cheer a fellow like Mama's sweet smile — plus her cat-head biscuits and thickening gravy."

As the grandchildren gathered around the supper table, Thomas tried to be pleasant. After a good meal, he sat down to read the *Enterprise,* and his melancholy returned. The newspaper printed current tax returns.

"Listen to this, James. 'Because of loses sustained by the war, Thomas County's taxes have fallen off by six million dollars.' "

Depression settled over Thomas like a shroud as he stood at the graveside of his old friend Augustus. Julie held up the floral wreaths and Samuel announced, unnecessarily, that Lavinia had made them. The couple led the way with the flowers aloft, and everyone marched around the open grave.

Augustus's wife and children began a loud wailing. Tears ran down the cheeks of his own wife and daughters, and Thomas reached a reassuring hand to Mattie. When the funeral ended, he let Lavinia follow the family to speak with them, but he lingered at the grave.

A day in his father's barnyard stood out clearly in his mind. Thomas had been a scrawny ten-year-old admiring brawny

Augustus's muscles. The man had asked the boy to carve his initial on his mule bridle. Somehow that "A" Thomas carved had created a lasting bond between them. Thomas scrubbed a tear with the sudden realization that his father had sent Augustus to the Pine Barren wilderness to look after him.

His people have such big hearts so full of love and loyalty, Thomas thought as he looked at all of the weeping souls walking away. They were no longer legally his responsibility; nevertheless, his heart ached that he had no way to feed them. Innocent of the world, they took no thought of planning for the morrow. They thought freedom meant they did not have to work at all. *It's a crying shame people who did not understand thrust independence upon them without preparing them. They have never lived in such lack.*

Thomas feared that Augustus's burial was a heart-rending symbol of the end of an era when people, black and white, helped each other through love.

Chapter XXIV

In the midst of her cluttered bedroom at Greenwood, Mattie lifted her wedding gown from her cedar hope chest and smiled so radiantly that Lavinia felt as if the whole world brightened. Her baby daughter's long-awaited day, May 2, 1867, had finally come.

Hope for a better tomorrow is always in the hearts of the young, Lavinia thought as she and Florence helped to dress the bride.

Florence's face was so sad by contrast that Lavinia wanted to take her in her arms; however, since John Vaughn's departure, Florence remained stiffly aloof from her parents. With downcast eyes, she was arranging a crown of white roses to go in the bride's hair. Lavinia could almost feel her thoughts that at twenty-three, life had figuratively remanded her to a backroom with a spinning wheel.

Mattie had not been able to rush Edwin

with offers of helping him, but he had laughingly yielded when she said she must set the date two weeks before her twenty-first birthday to escape the dreaded term: spinster.

Lavinia picked up the cloud of Alencon lace that belonged to her granddaughter, Livy J., who had insisted they continue the bonding tradition of the borrowed veil.

As she and Florence lifted the sheer wisp over Mattie's long black curls, Lavinia realized how empty the house was going to be without her clattering about singing at the top of her voice. No tear must mar the happiness of this day, and she excused herself quickly to go downstairs to greet guests.

Stepping down into the garden, Lavinia blinked at the intense greenness. No other month rivaled the lushness of May. A sweet, pungent scent made her look up. The magnolia trees Thomas had planted to welcome her to the wilderness towered overhead. Today, amid their glossy green leaves, creamy blossoms as big as dinner plates permeated the air with the fragrance of romance.

Lavinia was pleased to see that her dear sister-in-law, Eliza, who had come early, was already placing food on tables set amid circular beds of purple and pink poppies and larkspurs. Behind Eliza, her son Price, who was making a slow recovery from his war wounds, seemed to be questioning her. Price still had one arm in a sling. With the other, he swung on a crutch as he stumbled around his mother, getting in the way.

Lavinia could never stop herself from staring into Price's eyes. They were such a clear guileless blue. *What beautiful great-grandchildren he and Livy J. will give me some day.* She chatted with him, trying to calm the young man's impatience as he waited for the arrival of the Chaires' carriage.

Much later, an elegant brougham pulled up, but the man who stepped out and turned to give his hand to his daughter, Livy J., hardly looked like the once dashing Furman Chaires. It was obvious that Furman would never overcome his war wounds. Long white hair and beard almost obscured his ashen face. He leaned heavily on a cane.

Lavinia hurried to meet them. She tried to welcome her son-in-law and carry on conversation without mentioning his condition or his new carriage. No planter in Thomas County could afford to buy anything new, but it was obvious that Benjamin Chaires' son had followed his father's lead by spreading his investments beyond farm-

439

ing and into banking and railroads.

Price hobbled up to Livy J., and for once his glib tongue deserted him. He was speechless at her stunning appearance. Livy J. was the only woman at the festivities not wearing a pre-war bell-shaped hoop skirt. Her frock had a flattened front with fullness drawn back into swags that draped into a train. Her coiffure followed the same new style. Swept back and up, it coiled high before it fell into long curls down the back of her neck.

Lavinia thought she had never looked more adorable. Price undoubtedly agreed because he spirited her away as soon as possible. Lavinia smiled after them fondly, thinking, *How glad I am that Livy J.'s inheritance will keep them from being entirely dependent upon Price's land and planting cotton.*

Hearing a commotion, Lavinia turned and saw Edwin's old unit, the Dixie Boys, arriving in full regalia. Wearing Confederate uniforms was forbidden by the Bluecoats. She hoped they caused no trouble. The Dixie Boys were perennially hungry since their starvation at the siege of Vicksburg. They could demolish all of the food in sight. Lavinia hurried to greet them and put them in their places for the ceremony.

As she guided the exuberant young men into the central hall, she was relieved to see Tommy. He winked at her. Straight and proud, he stood in the doorway with his son held in the crook of his elbow and his other arm protectively draped around Ella who was glowing with the unmistakable air of an expectant mother. Lavinia knew she could depend on Tommy to contain the Dixie Boys as the guests assembled.

Music began, and the group intake of breath made Lavinia look to the top of the staircase. Mattie descended on her father's arm with amazing decorum. Thomas met Lavinia's eyes, and she could read his thoughts of remembering Mattie in her cradle and how he had predicted she would be the family beauty. Lavinia's pride went deeper. Mattie had reached a turning point. Once she had constantly busied herself about being pretty. Then as her heart grew with the love of such a devout man as Edwin Davis, Mattie's thoughts became selfless, and she had become a lovely young woman who was beautiful within.

At the foot of the stairs, Edwin looked distinguished in his captain's uniform of Confederate gray.

The moment Reverend Capers pronounced Martha Tallulah Jones and Captain

Edwin Tralona Davis man and wife, the Dixie Boys snapped into two lines. At the command, "Arch sabers," they raised their blades, touching points. Merriment unleashed, Mattie and Edwin ran under the arch and out into the garden.

At the cake table, Edwin unsheathed his saber. Together they cut into the towering confection and fed each other.

Lavinia was proud of her handiwork. She had managed most of the food from her home-grown products, but she had swallowed her pride and gone to the store to purchase almonds, citron, candied orange, and nutmeg to make the traditional spicy wedding cake.

Florence stood behind the table, placing souvenir pieces in tiny boxes for guests to take home before the ravenous Dixie Boys devoured the crumbs. Lavinia winced when she noticed Florence hide a box for herself. Even though that scoundrel Vaughn had evidently returned to his wife, Florence would no doubt put the cake under her pillow and try to dream of a future husband. Lavinia looked around at her guests who had come from throughout the area. She missed faces. *How many young soldiers did not survive!* She feared Florence's lucky cake was a false hope.

Lavinia mingled, greeting groups from branches of the family she had not seen in a great while, chatting with Edwin Davis's clan to forge new bonds. For a little while, everyone could forget that times were hard. Weddings meant renewal.

In the cool of the evening, Lavinia sought a secluded bench where she could simply savor. Her life had come full circle now. Her family was raised, and all had turned out well. She let her mind drift over Mattie from her cradle. At two, she was so pretty, even strangers wanted to touch her hair. By six, she was singing, always singing. Lavinia thought of the others playing together. Florence, always running with red hair streaming. Beautiful red hair. Soft little Susan, wanting only to be snuggled. Mary Elizabeth playing school, taking care of everyone. Lavinia could see James lying on the ground clinging to a puppy as he battled "the pestilence that walketh in darkness." Dear James — refusing to give up. Funny little Frank, always falling and skinning his knees.

How many times did I pick him up and nibble his nose, pretending to eat his freckles? Lavinia chuckled to herself.

Even her resident tattletale and storm cloud, Livy, had made the most of her Wesleyan College degree.

She felt a hand on her shoulder, and a quiet voice asked, "Are you asleep?"

"Of course, not." She opened one eye. For a moment she thought it was Thomas, but it was not his snow-white hair. The hair was black. She cleared her throat and amended, "Tommy."

Her tall son smiled fondly. "We're going home. I don't want Ella to get too tired. But we'll come again soon."

"Please, do. Darling Ella is my mainstay."

Her eyes followed Tommy he walked away. Somehow she had waited to make Thomas's namesake the one who bore his father's image. Was he born a man? He undoubtedly became one the day of the hurricane. I can be certain that Tommy will not only carry forth Thomas's name but he will also live with the same integrity.

Shadows were lengthening, and she went to join Thomas in bidding guests good-bye. She was surprised at how many men had gathered around him, obviously wanting to shake his hand. One after the other thanked him for what he had done for the community from the first bridge, the Methodist Church, *Fletcher Institute, Atlantic and Gulf Railroad,* and now the *Cotton Planters Bank,* on which they were placing their hopes for the future.

■ ■ ■ ■

Alone at last in the quiet of their bedroom, a satisfied Lavinia took down her hair and brushed it into one long plait.

"I was thinking this afternoon that our life is complete now that we've settled our baby girl in marriage," Lavinia said, smiling. "We've done a good job. They've all turned out well."

"Yes, they have," Thomas replied as he stretched wearily on the bed. "But have you forgotten your grandchildren?"

"You're thinking of Livy J.? The Chaires will want her wedding in Tallahassee, and she wouldn't give up having the event in the grandeur of the ancestral home at Verdura."

As Thomas raised up to blow out the lamp, a quiet knock sounded.

"Grandma-ma? Are you asleep?"

"Come in," said Thomas, flashing a knowing smile at Lavinia.

Livy J. entered, looking as fresh and sparkling as if it has been midday instead of midnight. "I don't mean to disturb you, but Pa-pa wants to return home first thing in the morning, and I wanted to share my news. Price insists his wounds are clean of gangrene. He took no Minie balls. He will soon be well and strong. He's going to buy the part of Aucilla Plantation you gave Livy as a dowry when she married David, so we won't have to wait on his inheritance. We're ready to start building a house and making plans for our marriage!"

Pain flashed over Thomas's face that Livy and David had reached the necessity of selling her dowry land, but he held up his arms and received Livy J.'s happy kiss. "How could I not be pleased that you are marrying the man dear brother Mitch saw fit to name after me?"

When they were alone again, he chuckled and said, "So your life is over."

Lavinia caught her lower lip between her teeth and grinned. "I didn't say over, I said complete."

Thomas blew out the lamp, and they moved closer, laughing.

Lavinia awoke with a plan. She rose early because she wanted to copy some of her favorite recipes for Livy J. before she and her father returned home to Tallahassee.

During breakfast she suggested, "Thomas, why don't you take Furman for a ride over the farm. I need a little time to give Livy J. some special cooking lessons."

Happily, she led her granddaughter outside to the kitchen house. When they were alone, Lavinia said, "I want to teach you the secret of my caramel cake."

They made the yellow batter and placed it in the oven built into the brick wall. Next Lavinia checked the fire in big iron stove. "Be sure it has burned down and is not too hot." She poured white sugar into an iron skillet. Livy J. picked up the stirring spoon.

"Wait. Wait. Don't stir too soon or it will make lumps. Be certain the sugar is turning to syrup before you stir."

While they watched for the sugar to brown, Lavinia told the story of her first attempt to cook for Thomas and how the sugar had turned to rocks. They laughed in warm togetherness as Lavinia added milk, warning that it must be full of cream.

"I would like to be as good a cook as you, Grandma-ma," said Livy J. as they spread the rich icing on the cake. "More than that I want to be a good mother and have a home like yours."

Lavinia took advantage of their coziness. "Darling, it's not just my caramel cake I hope you will carry on. You and Price will be as happy and as much in love as we have been if you base your marriage on God's love. Raise your children by the Bible."

Livy J. smiled assent. Her eyes misted.

"I'm glad you have all of your mother's beautiful things to start housekeeping."

"Yes, Pa-pa would not let her silver service or even her linens go for the war effort."

"Remember, even if times are hard, you can live with graciousness. Beautiful manners always put everyone at ease. Keep your home serene and filled with good food and your husband will always rather be there than anyplace else. I've been proving that for forty-one years."

There was so much more she wanted to say, but Thomas and Furman would be returning. As they licked the spoons, laughing at everything now, she realized it was enough. She had been spreading her values throughout the years.

Livy J. hugged her. "May I ask you something? When the time comes, could we have our wedding here?"

Lavinia's jaw dropped. "But Verdura is so grand."

"Greenwood has quiet elegance. It is here I have memories."

Chapter XXV

The funeral of Furman Chaires, on August 15, 1867, was not unexpected; nonetheless, Thomas's heart wrenched as his family rallied around Livy J. to give her strength. The Chaires Community was large, consisting as it did of Benjamin Chaires two brothers' families as well as those of his own descendants. Thomas thought that the whole of Tallahassee must have attended as well to pay tribute to this fallen son of a dynasty.

The moment they returned from Tallahassee, Thomas hurried to inspect his crops. He sat under a tree beside his cotton field with his head in his hands. This year's yield was the worst he had ever seen.

I've never had a field like this where you can't see the cotton for the weeds.

Thomas tried to console himself that he was not the only plantation owner with trouble. Rains had been incessant again this summer. Half of the crew was too sick to work because the Occupation Troops had started epidemics of smallpox and cholera.

Thomasville was solvent again with people able to pay taxes, but the Thomas County government had become desperate and printed money, which only plunged it deeper into debt. To compensate, the lawmakers, still carpetbaggers, scalawags, and freedmen, kept increasing taxes.

Our uneducated commissioners don't have sense enough to know farmers can never pay their debts if taxes keep going up.

Thomas saw that everything was changing, but he set his chin, knowing that he could not.

He thought about the plan for a railroad to Albany that some of the men were bribing the freedmen to vote for. It would connect Thomasville to the hub of Atlanta and from there north.

What use could I make of it? I don't believe any of my fruits and vegetables will ship. Cotton is my only available money crop, but can I sell it for enough this year to break even?

The worst blow of all was that England no longer had to have the South's product. After Lincoln's Emancipation Proclamation, England had given up trying to run the blockade and turned to Egypt and India for cotton.

Ruin is upon us.

Thomas sank to his knees in the mud. He prayed aloud, "Dear Lord, what can I do? How can I go on?"

Somehow they survived the next year and a half until a bright winter day in 1869. Lavinia scanned the skies. *February is changeable as any woman ever dared to be,* she thought. Daffodils were blooming like sunshine reflecting on the scarlet quince. Wheat fields were green. However, unpredictable temperatures could suddenly plummet and bring some of the year's worst weather.

She should not have worried. The usual week of false spring ushered in seventy-degree temperatures to bless Livy J.'s choice for a wedding day. Life had a way of smiling upon her as if to make up for the fact that her mother had died when she was only a child.

The doors of Greenwood were open wide on February 2, 1869, as Lavinia and Thomas greeted guests, many of whom had come from Florida. All who entered commented on the beautiful grounds resplendent with the pink blossoms of Camellia Japonicas and the sweet fragrance of

Daphne Odora.

Lavinia sank into her chair as the music began, feeling all of her fifty-nine years from the exertion of preparing for yet another wedding. However, tiredness was forgotten when Livy J. appeared on Thomas's arm at the top of the stairs.

Willowy, elegant, she paused just as Mary Elizabeth had done. The Alencon veil floated around her, ethereal as it had been on no other. Lovingly, Livy J. squeezed her grandfather's arm and smiled at him. In her other hand, she held her mother's prayer book with a white camellia resting upon it.

As she moved downward, the seed pearls embroidered onto her dress caught the candlelight, and the train, which was formed by sweeping fullness back and leaving the skirt slim in front, flowed gracefully behind her.

Tears filled Lavinia's eyes for the first time at any of the weddings as Livy J., the most exquisite of any of the brides, gave her hand to the now robust young man awaiting her. The preacher intoned, "I now pronounce Mary Lavinia Jones Chaires and Thomas Price Jones, husband and wife."

Lavinia was flooded with emotion. Of all their descendants, she knew this pair, their granddaughter and Mitchell Jones's son, was best equipped to build on the foundation of their heritage to meet the challenge of the new era. This third generation had captured the vision she and Thomas had conceived when they first saw Greenwood. They would perpetuate the legacy.

Treacherous February, Thomas thought. The first three weeks of the month had been warm. Now the afternoon sky was as dark as evening. Icy rain had fallen all day.

Thomas tugged on his boots and put on his warmest hat and coat as he called to Lavinia, "I'm going out to check the cows."

"Must you," she said, hurrying to the door. "You'll catch your death of cold. The rain shows no sign of letting up."

"All the more reason. We'll have to get them to sheltered woods and feed them extra hay. Several have just dropped calves."

Hurriedly, he left her, but he shuddered as he went out the door. He knew the herd was in the farthest pasture.

As Thomas and a now grizzled Samuel rode along on horseback with a young hand named Dan driving the hay wagon, Thomas called, "Here cows, here cows. Come on, cows."

His deep voice carried, and soon a rustling sounded. Cattle appeared from all directions. Trustfully, they followed as Thomas led them to a better place. While the men pitchforked hay to the gathered herd, Thomas counted.

"Daisy's missing. We'd better look, Samuel. I noticed yesterday that she was about ready to freshen."

Searching, calling, they rode all the way to the river. The shallow Ochlockonee had swollen from recent rains and was a rushing torrent overflowing its banks.

Daisy stood in the center on the sandbar. Only a sliver of it was left. Bone-white sand stood out starkly against the black waters. Stranded on the ever-decreasing spot of land, Daisy lowed plaintively.

"Here Daisy. Here girl. You can swim it," Thomas called. Sleet obscured his vision, but then he saw the tiny red and white body behind her. She'd had her calf, and she would die rather than leave it.

Unhesitant, Thomas plunged his horse into the swirling waters. The stallion fought the current, but he reached the sandbar without mishap. Thomas fed Daisy the biscuits he always carried in his pocket.

"Easy girl, easy. I'll take your baby, but you've got to swim."

As Thomas bent to lift the newborn in his arms, his hat fell into the foaming waves and swept away. Sleet penetrated his hair, making it feel like a helmet of ice.

He secured the calf before him on the horse and convinced Daisy to swim. They struggled to shore.

Thomas's throat burned as he called to Samuel, "This little fellow's in bad shape. Let's take these two to the barn."

Night was falling as Lavinia peered out the window and saw him at last. She had coffee and soup simmering on the back of the stove. Thomas's nightshirt and robe waited nearby, warming.

As soon as he came in, she rubbed him down, watching him anxiously. Even after he had consumed the hot liquid, his voice rasped. *I don't like the sound of that,* she thought.

"To bed with you," Lavinia said when Thomas had eaten. "I'll join you as quickly as I can."

By the time she could snuggle against his cold body, Thomas was shaking with a chill. Throughout the night, she listened in fear to his deep rumbling coughs.

The next morning Lavinia put hot mustard plasters on Thomas's chest. She fed him chicken soup and lemonade, but when she sponged his forehead, it was so hot that she whispered to Julie, "Send someone for Dr. Brandon."

In spite of all David could do, Thomas worsened, rattling with pneumonia. For two days he lay, not knowing his own daughters as they nursed him. It had happened so quickly, so unexpectedly that they moved about silently, unable to talk.

Once Thomas roused as Lavinia bent over him. "I'm not going to make it, am I? I wish we could go together."

Heart breaking, Lavinia could only hold him and weep.

The next day, Thomas improved. He sat up in bed and knew everyone who came in to see him. With his head higher, his breathing rattled only occasionally.

Night fell. When they were alone, he pressed her hand to his parched lips and whispered, "Remember, we are more than conquerors. Nothing can separate us from the love of Christ — or each other. He has a place prepared for us."

"Hush now. You're better. Rest. Sleep." Feeling hopeful, Lavinia lay down beside him. She kissed him and said, "I love you."

She dozed and roused, wondering what had awakened her. It was a long time before she realized he had stopped breathing.

She raised up. Too stunned to cry, she kissed his face again and again. For an hour, she lay quietly, unwilling to let him go. Then, as dawn broke, she knew she must tell the children.

Red streaked the morning sky. It was February 24, 1869.

A sea of black umbrellas floated in the cemetery. In spite of the inclement weather, everyone wanted to shake Lavinia's hand and talk about the things Thomas had accomplished to build a strong foundation for the whole community: the church, the bridge, the school, the railroad, the bank.

Lavinia could only nod and try to smile thinking, *I knew from the beginning he would be a man of great worth.*

She had held up, leading the children through the rigors of losing their father, but suddenly her knees gave way. Tommy put his strong arm around her and led her to the carriage. She started to step up, but seeing that Samuel and Julie were the last to leave the cemetery, she paused.

Samuel bared his graying head in the streaming rain. "Don't you worry none, honey. Me and Julie'll look after you."

Lavinia moved through a haze of unreality

as she and the children struggled through their grief, trying to deal with the business affairs that had to be settled.

As days passed, she felt her strength ebbing away, and she could not seem to stop crying.

I thought I had been through the sorrow and anger of death. This is different. I don't feel angry. Only that it's impossible Thomas is not beside me. After forty-eight years of taking every breath with him, I can't breathe.

Chapter XXVI

Panic hit Lavinia next. As she sat in Thomas's office going over the records and accounts, she felt real fright, wondering how she was to live. Even after she cut every expense she could, there was not enough for daily needs. She decided to sell the cattle. She could not care for them. Beef would bring ready cash from the hotels in town.

At least the hungry Union soldiers are good for something, she thought.

Throughout the spring, Lavinia went about the farm, attempting to run things as Thomas had done. She had little success under these impossible new conditions. She tried to hold her head up and keep a smile for everyone, but it was difficult because tears would surprise her at odd moments when a mockingbird sang or a butterfly drifted by.

The loneliness of nighttime seemed unbearable, and she wished she could join Thomas. After six months of not sleeping, she picked out a pup from the latest litter. She chose a female who looked like Rascal, named her Molly, and put her in the big empty bed. The pup made things a little easier. Sensitive to Lavinia's sorrowful moods, Molly almost seemed to put arms around her at the worst moments.

Lavinia felt that only the dog knew how hard the first year was for her. The children had their own grief to deal with. Gradually, Lavinia realized that she was not as alone as she had felt. Samuel and Julie kept her in constant care, but others of her people were watching as well. Someone seemed to pop up if she were about to fall in a hole, and heads nodded down a line to each other when she came in safely from a ride. She knew that she was still loved, but the ache would never be filled that she no longer had anyone to cherish her.

Somehow she made it until the next spring. On a crisp morning in March of 1870, Lavinia walked into Florence's room and found her sewing. Before she could stop herself, she spoke harshly, "Florence! What on earth are you doing making a dress out of calico?"

Florence looked sheepish, but she set her chin as stubbornly as Thomas ever had and said, "*I'm* not too good to wear calico."

Lavinia shook the gaudy print. "It's demeaning for you to dress in that cheap cotton cloth meant for — poor people."

"Well, aren't we now in the poverty group?" Florence clamped her teeth, and her freckles popped.

Lavinia felt her face getting hot. She turned and stalked out of the house. Two redheads' tempers did not mix. As she climbed in the buggy to ride over Greenwood, Molly jumped onto the seat beside her.

"I thought I'd done rather well keeping us in necessities this past year," Lavinia told Molly. She stroked the dog's silky ears, and her tension eased.

Lavinia put her attention to checking fields, making sure land preparation had begun. Then she drove through the woodland, enjoying the snowy drifts of dogwood. Suddenly she knew she had gone too far. She heard the sound of the Ochlockonee. Tears came in an unexpected rush. She had thought she was getting better control.

I'm glad I sold that parcel of land along the river, she thought. *It will always be a sad reminder.*

It had brought a good price, and she had
invested some of the money in a fertile field
being sold at the courthouse door for a pit-
tance. She was pleased with herself that she
had remembered March was the time to
burn the pine forest to get rid of hardwoods
and open up the canopy to allow sunlight
to grow food and cover-plants for quail.

*Thomas would be proud I remembered what
he taught me.*

When she returned to the house, she had
calmed down, but Florence was packing a
carpetbag.

"I'm going to spend tonight with Mattie.
Edwin is out of town on business for the
Fair Association," she said abruptly.

Lavinia could tell she was lying. She
fastened her gaze, hoping to face Florence
down, but it was she who relented. She
merely nodded.

"Molly will look after me." Lavinia knew
she would spend a restless night because
many houses were still being burglarized,
but with Molly on guard, no one could approach her bed.

The next morning soon after breakfast,
Lavinia was surprised to see Livy already
making the trip out from Thomasville. She
could tell from her pinched face that some-

thing displeased her volatile daughter.

"Mama! I'm shocked that you let Florence attend the Calico Hop at the hotel," Livy said without a proper greeting. "It was simply scandalous!"

Lavinia sighed. "I knew she was up to something, but I never thought she'd do anything so shameful."

"She did. I don't know how she got involved with the northern visitors at the hotel, but it seems the ladies made calico dresses — worse — they made matching cravats of the same figured material. At the door they placed the cravats in a bag. The gentlemen drew, put on the ties, and found the wearer of a matching print to be their partner."

Lavinia stood up so suddenly that her chair kept rocking. "You mean she danced with a stranger?"

Livy's top comb bobbed so hard that her whole hair arrangement threatened to tumble. "For all we know — an enemy soldier."

Lavinia sat down hard, fanning herself.

When Florence returned, Lavinia had a lecture prepared about the devil's kind of dancing and men to whom she had not been properly introduced. She opened her mouth to deliver the scolding, and then she saw Florence's eyes. They sparkled as they had not since John Vaughn left.

Because Lavinia's arms ached with the emptiness of having no one to hold her, the angry words died on her lips. *Poor Florence. She's had such a little taste of life.*

Not seeing the emotions playing on her mother's face, Florence burst out, "Oh, Mama, it was such fun." Florence did a waltz turn around the room. "I danced and danced. The hotel is so luxurious. Town people have plenty of money . . ." Her voice trailed as she looked at Lavinia, who stood shaking her head.

Suddenly Florence was contrite. "I'm sorry I deceived you, but I get so lonely. Papa sent away the only man I ever loved."

Even as Lavinia's heart broke for Florence, she was thankful for the love she had shared with Thomas. *I know I must not focus on the fact that I've lost him, but on the wonderful blessing that I had him.*

Yet, paradoxically, Lavinia knew she could no longer dwell in the past. She must stiffen her spine and fight for the future. Dressing in her Sunday best, she told Julie's grandson to drive her into Thomasville. She visited several merchants before she found one who satisfied her needs.

David Brandon accompanied Lavinia as she returned to Greenwood and called her people together.

Lavinia stood before them, trying to exude more confidence than she felt. "Folks, it's been a long time since any of us had meat to eat or a lot of other things. You know the stores no longer take Confederate money. We've got to start farming in a new way."

A murmuring went over the crowd, but she raised her hands and continued. "Dr. Brandon is helping me set up one-mule and four-mule patches. You may choose one by the number of workers in your family and how hard you are willing to work for yourself."

Lavinia looked at their blank faces, wondering how to make them understand. "The plan is called sharecropping, and the way it goes is this. I've found a storekeeper who will let me borrow seed and plows and even your brogans in the spring. You will plant your patches and pick your cotton. In the fall when it sells, one third of the money will go to pay the merchant, one third to me as landowner, and the rest will be yours."

The men shuffled about with head scratchings and asides. She turned from the confusion in their eyes and walked away so they would not see her cry.

They are used to Thomas setting them to one task they do well. This new management is too complicated for any of us. But we have no choice. I must try to make them understand.

Feeling a great weariness, Lavinia faced the men again and explained the system in simple language, over and over. Gradually they lined up before David.

From then on throughout spring and summer, Lavinia was up at dawn. All day she drove her buggy with Molly on the seat beside her as she went from plot to plot, instructing and encouraging. It grieved her that she could no longer afford to give them medical care or even clothing, but she tried to impart wisdom and spiritual teaching as she went.

As she inspected pitiful patches instead of beautiful fields of cotton, she thought that Thomas could never have relinquished this much control over the land. Neither could he have abided getting this deeply in debt, but these were the consequences of the war that she must live with.

She stopped the buggy and spoke as if he were with her. "Thomas," she said quietly, "I know you don't believe in credit, but with no money, I can't pay wages. There's nothing to do but borrow in the spring with the cotton crop as pledge and hope it makes enough to pay the debts in the fall."

When autumn came, cotton prices had declined. There was not enough profit to satisfy the crop lien, and more money had to be borrowed. Lavinia realized that a tragic cycle had begun. At least the system gave them all a daily living, however meager.

One afternoon as Lavinia sat a Thomas's desk with her head bowed on her arms, hot tears ran the ink, smearing her accounts. A hand patted her shoulder. She scrubbed her eyes and looked up at Julie.

"I know we ain't rich no more," Julie said softly. "But what with blackberries and wild turnips, everybody's belly pretty full. Miss 'Vinia, when you come here, you was so scrawny and scared, I thought you'd never amount to nothing. Here you are old and you should be taking ease, but you've looked after the whole plan'nation. You do take the prize at the cakewalk."

The October sky was so brilliantly blue that Lavinia had to be in her garden. With a basket swinging on her arm, she hummed a tune as she cut flowers to take into the house. A sound made her jerk around. Holding a pink rose as if it were a weapon, she stood speechless.

John Vaughn barged down the path, knocking petals off the bushes. Hand extended, he said, "Good afternoon, Mrs. Jones. I hope I didn't startle you."

The wattles of her cheeks shook, and she ignored his hand. She had never expected to see the man again.

Vaughn continued glibly, "I see Miss Florence didn't tell you I was coming."

"No. I certainly did not know y'all were corresponding."

His eyes, an oddly light shade of blue, rolled with confusion, but he recovered quickly. "Then she hasn't told you that my wife, Nancy Ann, died in 1868, two years ago?"

"No."

"May we sit down?"

Grudgingly, Lavinia led him to a cast-iron bench shaded by hollies. She said nothing, determined to make this difficult.

He cleared his throat. "I know you consider me an outsider; nevertheless, I've been accepted in Thomasville because of my distinguished military career . . ."

He waited for a reply. She gave none. Plunging on, he finished in a schoolboy rush, "I'm asking for Miss Florence's hand in marriage."

Lavinia got up, walked a few paces away, and turned her back on the great general. She wrestled, weighing all sides. *Thomas had such great distaste for the man,* she thought, *but my own loneliness makes me understand Florence's longing.*

She half-turned. "She is only twenty-six. You sir, are . . ."

"Forty-six. But you know she loves me. We are of the same faith. I'm a staunch Methodist."

Softened, Lavinia envisioned Florence's desolate face. "Yes. I give my permission."

Florence appeared from behind the hollies and hugged her tearfully. "John wants us to be married in late November."

"A southern lady should have a longer engagement."

Vaughn spoke up quickly. "I expect to be elected State Senator by then. Miss Florence would enjoy the social season at Nashville."

Filled with foreboding, Lavinia kissed Florence and held out her hand to her prospective son-in-law.

When Florence's wedding day arrived, November 29, 1870, Lavinia greeted guests by holding onto the doorjamb. She felt the loss of Thomas's presence so deeply she could hardly stand.

Tommy's strong arm escorted Florence down the circling stairs. With his thick black hair, he looked so much like his father that Lavinia had to duck her head and wipe tears. She had feared Florence merely wanted her chance at this moment, but when she lifted her face to see her daughter, her heart lightened.

Florence is not the prettiest bride to grace John Wind's staircase, Lavinia thought. *She looks too much like me. But decidedly, she's wearing the biggest smile.*

Lavinia had to admit that the General, in full military regalia, looked distinguished.

Immediately after the reception, he swept Florence away to Tennessee.

Greenwood rattled with loneliness. Without Florence, supper alone was eaten because she knew she must, and the hours until bedtime seemed endless. Even though Lavinia had deliberately stopped going into Thomasville, she decided that she needed to spend a few days in Mattie and Edwin's happy home. She smiled at the thought of their two little girls, Martha and Marion. Nothing could chase away depression like cuddling babies.

One afternoon during her visit, Mattie

proposed going to the Young House Hotel for high tea. Lavinia knew her daughter would expect her to pay. She checked the money in her reticule twice. She had been forced to sell a strip of land along the Quitman road to pay for Florence's wedding, but she had enough to give them this treat.

As they strolled down the street on a warm December day, Lavinia muttered under her breath when they met patrolling Union soldiers. Her anger became amazement when she and Mattie turned onto Broad Street. Crowds of affluent-looking strangers examined the Christmas displays in the shop windows.

Lavinia gaped. Her plantation friends all still wore spreading skirts of rusty black. She stared at a red-haired woman. She had on bottle green! Her skirt was so tight she could hardly walk. All of its fabric was pulled in a pouf behind her already ample backside.

"The new fashion is called a bustle," Mattie whispered.

Lavinia shook her head. Most of these women were either tall or heavyset. No eighteen-inch waists coveted by southern women in this group.

A voluptuous figure strode by them. She

wore a high-billed bonnet and an extremely protruding bustle.

"Why, she's positively goose-shaped," said Lavinia. Then she realized she had spoken in the manner of the elderly, imagining the creature could not hear the moment her back was turned. She blushed. *Livy would be mortified.*

Mattie laughed merrily. "It's fun to have you, Mama."

Lavinia gave her hand a squeeze. "But where did these obviously wealthy people come from? They look Swedish or German."

"Different places up north. By steamship to Savannah and across by railroad or down from Atlanta via Albany on that new track."

"Why?"

"Unfortunately, after the Yankee soldiers saw Thomasville, we weren't hidden anymore. Even some of those who were here as prisoners have come back. But it's mostly the doings of our new mayor, Dr. Hopkins."

Lavinia looked at her in confusion, and Mattie giggled. "Let's go in and order our tea. Then I'll explain."

Over cucumber sandwiches and dainty cakes, Mattie related the events since Lavinia's self-enforced exile from town.

"You know that most all of the millionaires

in the United States were in the South before — what Edwin calls 'the war to stem northern arrogance.' "

Lavinia laughed. "Yes, and of course, our boys really thought the Confederacy would win since we were only outnumbered four to one."

Mattie nodded and took a sip of tea. "You remember that Mayor T. S. Hopkins, was a doctor at Andersonville Prison. After the war, he was ordered to Washington to testify at the trial of Commandant Henry Wirz. Hopkins explained that the Confederates had no food or medicine to give the prisoners, and Wirz did the best he could. The Yankees hanged Wirz anyway."

Lavinia grimaced, and Mattie hurried on with the story. "Doctor Hopkins noticed on his trip that while the South is in utter devastation, the North had sustained no damage. They profited by the war, and their industry is booming. Wiley old Hopkins figured we needed some of that money. He looked around and saw that we're healthy here without the malaria they have in Florida. We have a low incidence of consumption. He decided it's because our pine trees put out oxygen."

"So?"

"So when he was elected mayor, he wrote

letters to northern Medical Associations, touting Thomasville as a winter home for invalids — especially those with consumption. People have poured in for lengthy visits."

Mattie looked around and whispered behind her fan. "Mama, these folks aren't like the sleazy carpetbaggers who came to bilk us of all we've got. These people are wealthy northern industrialists — millionaires ready to pay for their pleasure. Talk around town is that one Yankee is worth two bales of cotton and twice as easy to pick."

"Well, I do declare," Lavinia, exclaimed, forgetting her tea.

Nine months later, Livy brought Lavinia a letter, which she had obviously read.

"I'm so ashamed," Livy said, sniffing into her handkerchief. "I admit it. I've always tattled on Florence."

Lavinia sighed wearily. Any encounter with Livy was always emotional. She read the letter from Tennessee with news that Hattie Brandon Vaughn had been born September 6, 1871.

"I guess she understood you had her best interest at heart," Lavinia said.

"But to name her first baby after me. I wouldn't have thought she'd even remember my name is Harriet Lavinia."

"You were named for your father's sister, Harriet Blackshear. I loved her dearly, but now I know I should have spent more time with her after she was widowed. You don't realize how lonely one gets without a spouse until you experience it."

Livy put her arm around her mother. "You miss Florence, I know."

Lavinia nodded. "It's especially bad eating alone."

"You should move into town."

"I want to stay in my home as long as I can . . . Poor Florence. I just hope Vaughn is taking care of her."

Lavinia received monthly letters from Florence, detailing the baby's progress. She wrote with never a complaint; consequently, Lavinia sickened with shock when she answered a knock on Greenwood's door to find Florence standing there. Disheveled and forlorn, Florence held one-year-old Hattie on her hip. Lavinia reached for the child, shrieking for Julie. Florence appeared to be expecting another baby at any moment.

Julie laid Florence on the couch, removing the shoes from her swollen feet and calling her granddaughter to bring cool water and warm food.

Lavinia paced the hall, trying to quiet Hattie's cries. She realized she could do a better job if she were not entertaining such evil thought about the baby's father.

When at last they were settled and fed, she saw that Florence's condition was not immediate. She let her explain that her husband and his former brother-in-law were being prosecuted by the War Department for fraud.

"Is he guilty of dishonesty?" Lavinia asked.

"How can I know? It's the United States Government that has arrested him, a Confederate. Besides that problem, his oldest daughter, Lucile, is about to marry a Union soldier."

"Humph. There couldn't be much to Lucile."

"Tennessee no longer seemed the place for me," Florence said faintly.

"Never you mind," Lavinia said as she rocked Hattie. "I'm thankful you're here so I can look after you."

John Crawford Vaughn, Jr. was born September 18. 1872.

Florence received no reply from her husband when she sent the news of his son. At last, Lucile wrote that he had come down with brain fever after five days of trial. If Florence ever knew the outcome of the case, she did not share it with her family.

A year later, Lavinia was once again surprised to find John Vaughn on her doorstep. Florence rushed to throw her arms around him, but her eyes no longer sparkled.

Vaughn moved his family to Florence's dowry land in Brooks County and went into business in Thomasville. Lavinia was glad that he was respected because of his Confederate service, as he had predicted; however, she could never forget Thomas's opinion and her own questioning. Just before Christmas of 1874, she found out that Florence had mortgaged her plantation.

Lavinia pushed her feelings aside, and her heart broke for Florence when she became a widow after only five years. John Crawford Vaughn died on September 10, 1875, at age fifty-one.

"I know how Papa felt," Florence said, weeping, "but, please, may I bury him on Greenwood?"

Crowds of men appeared at the cemetery dressed in their forbidden Confederate gray. They conducted a full military funeral.

Lavinia stood beside the tall obelisk that

marked Thomas's grave, seeking solace. She watched warily, fearing reprisals from the Bluecoats for the large uniformed gathering. None came. As the bugler sent taps echoing through the woodland, she thought it the saddest sound she had ever heard.

Lavinia sat at Thomas's desk on a sultry afternoon in late August of 1876, going over her books. She faced debts at the bank and the commissary and, inevitably, ad valorem taxes were due. She desperately needed cash.

She had not ginned a single bale of cotton. In both '74 and '75, Edwin had set the record of bringing the first bale into Thomasville by the eighth of August. This year he had not done any better than she. Rain had delayed picking. Worse, many of the workers had left their families and gone to the North.

Four years ago, the price had been eighteen and three-quarters cents per pound. Now it was down to ten and one quarter. *If I get every scrap, will it be enough to pay my bills?*

I hate the Yankees, she thought, running her fingers through her hair. *I feel so bad seeing these freed families with nothing to eat — but what can I do?*

It was taking every ounce of her ingenuity to provide for her own household now that Florence and her babies had come back home to stay.

Feeling defeated, she went out on the porch to cool. She slumped in a rocker and fanned. Suddenly she sat up straight, gritted her teeth, and stuck out her chin. "I will not give up. I will *not* give up. I may have to feed my family nothing but black-eyed peas — but I'll do it off a china plate!"

Chapter XXVII

Lavinia's chin was still clenched with anger and determination when Florence came out on the porch. Not noticing her mother's pursed mouth, Florence burst out with her plan without first softening the blow.

"Mama, there's only one thing we can do to pay our debts and make our living . . . Take in northern boarders at Greenwood."

Lavinia exploded. "Don't be ridiculous!" "I'll never allow *those people* in my house."

"You had the Clarks," Florence retorted.

"That was different. How can you expect me to open my home to Yankees who killed my son and burned my barns and conquered my country and continue to humiliate my family with Occupation Troops?"

Breathless from her outburst, Lavinia gulped the thick August air and coughed.

"What's this about Occupation Troops?" a male voice broke in.

They turned, startled by the sudden appearance of James. Lavinia was appalled at how bad he looked. He was only forty-eight, but both his hair and his skin looked gray, and he seemed to be having great pain as he maneuvered his crippled leg up the steps.

"Mama," he said, "you look about to have apoplexy. Calm down." James fanned her vigorously.

Lavinia reached out to him, not questioning why he was here. She only knew she needed him. Much as she tried never to show favoritism, he had always held a special place in her heart. "Help me talk some sense into Florence."

Florence bristled. "There's nothing acceptable for a widow lady to do except teach or run a boarding house. We should take advantage of all these winter visitors who spend money like water. They pay the Mitchell House Hotel eleven dollars for a suite. A regular room is four dollars a day."

Eleven dollars? She must be mistaken, Lavinia thought. Even four dollars was sky high over local wages for a day. She tried to slow her breathing and think about how badly she needed that money, but her temper got the best of her.

"The Mitchell House ought to be big enough to take care of all of the intruders. Why that monstrosity covers a whole block with three stories of that ostentatious New York architecture!"

James laughed. "Even so, it's not big enough. More hotels are being built, but while they're under construction, it's the time to grasp the opportunity to make some of the money."

"Why should all of these people come to our remote spot?" Lavinia puzzled.

Florence leaned forward. "Northern newspapers — even some foreign ones — are touting Thomasville as a winter resort." She scooted her chair closer and pleaded. "Mama, we have a hidden jewel. When I traveled across Georgia and Tennessee with John, all I saw were ruins! Houses burned to naked chimneys and fields reverted to jungle growth. People up there won't speak to northerners."

"Humph. I don't blame them."

James wiped his hand across his mouth to hide his smile and took up Florence's explanation. "Here John Wind's classic architecture survived the war. People like to see it and experience the glories of the Old South — and our subtropical winters."

Florence fought tears. "I have two fatherless children to raise. I'll do the work. You just plan menus and act as a gracious hostess as you've always done."

James said, "I'm hoping for better times soon. The reason I'm here today is that I'm traveling around, urging men to take the hated citizenship oath so that they can vote again. We must get the government back in the hands of honest men. Corruption and scandals aren't just local. They infect the highest officers of President Grant's administration. This November, southerners *must* elect a President who will end Carpetbag rule."

James rose to go. He kissed her cheek and pleaded, "Tolerate boarders 'til then."

Lavinia threw up her hands. "All right, but I feel like the Philistines are upon me."

Mr. and Mrs. Gould of New York arrived on a November afternoon in 1876, two weeks after the Hayes-Tilden election, which was still undecided.

Lavinia knew they were there, but she kept them waiting in the entrance hall as she finished her toilette with deliberate slowness. She took her emerald and diamond necklace from the secret compartment in her dresser and held it against her cheek, remembering Thomas's joy in giving her the precious gems. Why had she tried to elicit words of praise from him? She needed none.

His eyes had told her all she desired to know.

She pinned a lace housecap on her graying hair in the manner of Queen Victoria. *I look as fat and formidable as the old queen, herself,* she thought, as she gazed in the mirror.

The dreaded time had come. She drew herself erect and made her grand entrance down the staircase making sure the lamplight glittered on her jewels and her new black taffeta. She intended that her looks and demeanor impart that she was still as good as they and did not need their money.

Slowly, she reached the bottom step and held out her hand in greeting. Her stiff lips refused to smile.

Mrs. Gould exclaimed over the blue skies and blossoming sasanqua camellias, and Lavinia's tension lessened slightly.

Lavinia directed Julie's grandson to help Mrs. Gould's indentured Irish maid carry steamer trunks, bandboxes, and carpetbags upstairs while she ushered the guests into the parlor for tea.

As Lavinia poured from her silver tea service, which she had risked taking out of hiding, she struggled to decipher the fast-talking Gould's conversation. She could not put her finger on exactly what it was about their accent that grated on her nerves.

When the Irish maid announced her room ready, Mrs. Gould went up to rest from the train trip. Mr. Gould stalked about, inspecting the premises.

That evening, Lavinia had fallen asleep in the parlor with Molly snoring beside her when the couple descended in full evening dress. Florence had been warned that they dined at eight.

Lavinia took her place at the head of the table, determined to display southern hospitality; however, Mrs. Gould picked up a piece of her lovely old silverware and turned it in the candlelight.

"This is Colonial fiddle-thread pattern," she said in a tone that indicated her hostess did not have sense enough to know this.

Lavinia felt as if steam must be escaping her ears.

Mr. Gould talked loudly, waving his arms about. He did not seem appreciative of the exquisitely presented, six-course meal until the fowl course was served. He took a second quail.

At that moment, Molly woke up and wandered into the dining room to her accustomed spot beside Lavinia's chair.

Mrs. Gould shrieked, "Do you let that animal in here?"

Lavinia laughed shrilly. "Molly's lineage is higher than mine or yours. She's descended from royal Spanish game preserves."

The woman's pale face showed two red spots, but Lavinia continued airily with great detail about the English Setter's breeding and hunting prowess for Bobwhite quail.

Mr. Gould's interest quickened. "This meat I'm eating? It's the whitest, tenderest poultry I've ever tasted. Is this dog responsible?"

"Not Molly, but her fellows. Do you shoot, sir?"

"I'm a crack shot. I'd enjoy a shoot, but I don't ride."

"I can have my grandsons fit up a wagon for you. They will handle the dogs."

Lavinia directed the rest of her conversation to him until the interminable meal ended.

The next day, Livy's sons James and Frank Brandon hitched a wagon with a matched pair of brown mules. Molly rode on the seat with Mr. Gould, as if she were overseeing the hunting dogs that ran ahead of the horsemen.

That evening when they returned, Mr. Gould boasted, "I bagged one hundred-forty quail!"

"One Hundred and Forty!" Lavinia squeaked. She almost lost control. He had killed so many more than they could eat that she wished she could stuff them down his fat throat.

Later as she was walking out her anger, Lavinia passed the kitchen and overheard James Brandon speaking.

"How did Aunt Florrie get Grandma to take in these people with her intense hatred for all Yankeedom?"

"Don't know," replied Frank, who was as freckled-faced and mischievous as his name-sake. "I wouldn't be surprised to see her boil over and pour forth the vials of her wrath on the heads of her amazed 'paying guests.' "

Lavinia grimaced. As she started on by the kitchen, she heard her grandson James agree. "I'd advise them to keep quiet in her presence on the subject of the late war or politics."

Politics soon became the subject on every tongue. The furor gave Lavinia hours alone to control her temper because Mr. and Mrs. Gould rode into Thomasville daily to check the news. At first it appeared Democrat Samuel J. Tilden had defeated Republican Rutherford B. Hayes; then returns came in from Louisiana, South Carolina, and Florida. Two sets. One by the Carpetbag governments and the other from governments set up by ex-Confederates.

Lavinia refused to give Mr. Gould opportunity to voice his sentiments, but she knew if Hayes received the electoral votes from those three states, he would be President.

All winter controversy raged while the votes were recounted. Lavinia received news from James:

> Tallahassee is center stage of national attention as votes are tallied. It is a military camp. Two generals and some five hundred troops are here. Yankee Governor Sterns knows that he is defeated, and he's called in the army to deter people from insisting on an honest count.

In January, Congress appointed a federal commission to recount the electoral votes. Lavinia watched for results as closely as her difficult houseguests. Carpetbag rule hung in the balance.

In February, the uncertainty nearly resulted in war. Democrats threatened to take the government by force. President Grant called out troops.

No news reached Thomasville. At last they learned that Grant had held a secret swearing in on March third. Hayes had been confirmed at four o'clock in the morning of March 2, 1877, upon his promise to remove the remainder of the federal troops from the South and end Reconstruction.

Lavinia never understood the secret deals. Few did. She suspected Mr. Gould could tell her, but she would not ask. What mattered was that the unlawful times were over. For eleven years they had endured horrors. They were free to go about their lives at last.

Lavinia could hardly wait to congratulate James, but the victory had not come soon enough for him to enjoy it. Three months later, May 16, 1877, James Young Jones died.

Lavinia's mourning was tempered with pride in all James had accomplished during his fifty years. *Infantile paralysis could not stop him,* she thought. *He found love and honor and achievement. His body was disabled, but his spirit soared.*

Lavinia felt she could not stomach another winter with boarders, but she had to admit their rent paid the taxes and other debts.

Finally she and Florence agreed that, for the 1878 season, Florence would stay at Greenwood and cope with Yankees, while she moved to Thomasville to Mrs. John Pittman's Boarding House. It was a much cheaper establishment than Greenwood Plantation, and she would have money left; however, staying there was not much help for her temper. She still had to eat with *those people.*

While she was living in town, David Brandon took to his bed, giving up the long battle with the illness he had contracted while serving in army hospitals. After his funeral, Lavinia stayed with Livy for a few weeks to help her through her grief. Lavinia soon decided she was getting too old to survive in a house full of half-grown children.

I must get back to the peace of my own home.

Florence, stalwart as always, found another solution. "You've settled enough debts to enjoy Greenwood again," she said. "On the other hand, if I'm to raise my children, I must start a business. The opportunity is in Thomasville. All kinds of entertainments are being provided for the millionaires who are coming for the pleasures the town has concocted. I've decided to sell my dowry land and buy a lot on Madison Street. I'll build a modern boarding house to take in lots of guests."

Lavinia dropped her head in her hands. "Papa promised himself when we first started out that he would set up each of our children. Now you and Livy have had to sell."

Florence stroked her mother's bowed head. "It's because of Papa's forethought that we have security from his legacy of land to raise our families."

On April 14, 1879, Edwin Davis died suddenly at age thirty-six. Lavinia rushed to a devastated Mattie.

"How could this happen?" Mattie wailed. "He was so happy and so busy being president of the South Georgia Fair Association. He was such a fine man, noble, generous, helping anyone in need." Sobbing, Mattie buried her face in Lavinia's arms.

"He was a very large hunk of the salt of the earth," Lavinia said.

Tommy and Ella came to support Mattie through the funeral. As Lavinia listened to the tremendous crowd at the Baptist Church giving paeans of praise for his generosity, she realized Edwin had left a legacy. Sighing, she knew it was not in money for his wife.

After the burial in Greenwood cemetery, Lavinia hurried through the woods to her house where the neighbors had prepared food for the mourners. Her thoughts kept pounding.

Now I have three widowed daughters — hoards of grandchildren. I must get a hold on myself and look after them.

Lavinia made up her mind that she must keep Greenwood and make it a sanctuary so that her family could continue gathering. Many times she did without things she needed in order to feed them, but they never knew. She felt her efforts were rewarded because they remained so close knit that they continued to name the next generations after their brothers and sisters.

Lavinia discovered the cure for loneliness was to do for others who were even lonelier. Thomas had bought her a fine carriage at the height of his prosperity, and now it was safe enough for her to use it again. She drove all over the county visiting the many widows left by the war.

Lavinia helped to reorganize their old Soldiers' Aid Society into the Ladies' Memorial Association as their sister groups were doing all over the South. These associations agreed upon April twenty-sixth of each year as Confederate Memorial Day when flowers were to be placed on each fallen soldier's grave. Lavinia's group moved the bodies of the Union prisoners who had died in Thomasville from makeshift graves into a cemetery. Lavinia's garden provided so many blossoms that the graves of their former enemies were decorated as well as those of their fallen heroes. Out of their want, the ladies struggled for several years to raise enough money to commission a twenty-foot Confederate monument of Italian marble.

As time passed, Lavinia realized she was coming home from these efforts more and more exhausted. On such a day in 1887, overcome with weariness, she sat in the garden swing. Around her, shrubs needed pruning. She had reached the age where she could no longer attend to them. She felt especially lonely today. Molly had joined the long line of English Setters in the dog cemetery. Lavinia had picked a new puppy with so much of the bluish-black ticking that she decided to call him Belton Blue.

Blue sat dozing in the swing with her. Suddenly, he came alert and stood up. A middle-aged man in hunting clothes parted the shrubbery and started toward them.

Lavinia squinted at the scrawny man approaching. *Oh, that's Mayor Hopkins's boy. What on earth could he be doing here?*

CHAPTER XXVIII

"Morning Miss Lou-venia," H. W. Hopkins drawled without removing the pipe that hung below his handlebar moustache. A shotgun was slung casually over one arm while the other held a turkey, head down, iridescent feathers spreading.

"I bagged this here turkey, but it might of been on Greenwood land. Anyhow, I thought you'd like it for dinner."

Lavinia scowled. No one could mistake Greenwood land. Virgin pines, wide apart, straight, towering high, could not be confused with others where timber had been cut and replanted.

It might have been shot on my property, but I've a mind to refuse it.

H.W. held the bird higher. "He's big enough to feed your whole family."

"Thank you," she said stiffly. "How are your folks?"

"Middlin'. Middlin'. May I set a spell?"

He was a local judge and realtor and his deliberate lapse into southerness set her teeth on edge. *He's up to something.* She waited, and at last he came out with it.

"I thought you'd like to know that Thomas Blackshear sold Cedar Grove. I handled it for him through Hopkins Real Estate Agency." He lost his drawl. "A New York Physician, Dr. John Metcalfe, bought it and renamed it Susina. He's the first northerner to buy a plantation specifically for hunting."

Lavinia fought tears. *Harriet's son sold her beloved home. How could he?* She fished her handkerchief out of her sleeve.

"I didn't mean to upset you — just to let you know many of your neighbors are letting me handle transactions for them. That way they don't have to deal with the Yankees."

While you get rich off of Southerners' misery, Lavinia thought with anger stopping tears.

H.W. fiddled with his pipe. Then he blurted "A lady of your yea— uh — ancestry should have all the comforts Thomasville offers: electric lights and telephones such as are only found in great cities, entertainments from nationally known celebrities — the great March King, John Philip Sousa is scheduled to play at the Thomasville Opera House when it opens next year . . . I could

496

get you top dollar."

"I intend for Greenwood to endure as Thomas planned," Lavinia replied tartly. "I've held it together this long."

"You've done well. You still have thirteen hundred ten acres. A great buy."

Lavinia arose with as much dignity as her aching knees allowed her. "Greenwood is not for sale." She threw up her chin. "Give the turkey to someone who needs it."

Head high, she walked away from him, trying not to look at Greenwood's peeling paint.

The news must have reached Thomasville before H.W. even got there, Lavinia thought sardonically as her family descended upon her.

"Selling would be best," said Livy. "I worry about you out here all alone."

Lavinia hugged Blue. "I'm not alone. I want to stay in my home as long as I can. I gather strength when I can walk out and pick violets."

She saw her daughters exchange glances at that.

"Mama," Mattie said softly. "I didn't have Edwin as long as you had Papa, but you taught me how to give love that seeks the highest good of the other, and we had a blessed home. I'm lonely, grieving. Come live with me."

Mattie's daughters, Martha and Marion, were suddenly blossoming into belles almost as beautiful as their mother, but they clapped their hands like children. "Bring Blue," they chorused.

"We're too big to sit in your lap any longer," added Marion, "but we'd like you to read *Tom Sawyer* — with all the voices — until we say stop."

Lavinia opened her arms to them, unable to speak.

Florence loosened her hair from the knot she had affected and shook it back. "If you make this step, I might be brave enough to move to Savannah, if you'd write me a letter of entrée to our Young relations."

"Savannah?" Livy, ever the big sister, looked ready to argue.

"Yes. There I could raise John's children with the respect due a Confederate General's family."

Lavinia felt contrite for the way she felt about her son-in-law. After all, it was the United States Government who had accused him. "Of course, I'll write letters, Florence. You must go now, if you think best. As for me, even if I were ready to leave my home, I can't bear to think of the enemy who changed all our lives taking over Greenwood."

On February 3, 1889, a day filled with the warmth and sunshine that always seemed to follow Livy J., she and Price appeared for a surprise visit. They had come alone without their six children.

"I brought something for you to see," Livy J. said, handing Lavinia a hand-painted menu. "Price took me to dinner and to spend last night at the Piney Woods Hotel for our twentieth anniversary."

"My, my, it seems only yesterday when your grandfather so proudly gave you away. Then . . ." *Thomas . . . so soon after. Have I really been alone for twenty years?*

"Read this," said Livy J. quickly. "I know you don't like the bright yellow outside of the Piney Woods Hotel, but the dining room is elegant. Potted palms sit about to ensure privacy. An Italian orchestra is playing." Her fingers rippled imaginary music.

"It's very romantic," agreed Price, smiling at his wife. He seemed as captivated by Livy J. as he had been that first day in the garden. "We want to take you there for your next birthday."

Lavinia beamed at the handsome pair. Her throat too full to speak, she read the menu:

Lynn Haven Oysters
Clear Green Turtle au Madere ~ Cream
of Chicken Princess
Olives ~ Celery
Fresh Lobster Pâté a la Cardinal
Broiled Kennebee Salmon, Sauce Diplo-
mate
Cucumbers ~ Parisian Potatoes
Fried Chicken a la Maryland
Diamond Back Terrapin en Caisse, Club
Style
Queen Fritters, Vanilla Flavored
Roast Ribs of New York Beef
Tame Duck Stuffed ~ Apple Sauce
Roman Punch

"It sounds mouthwatering. I'll hold you
to my birthday party."

All too soon Livy J. and Price were gone,
and February became cold and wet again.
Samuel died and Julie moved into Greenwood. On a day when the unpredictable
month was showing her worst temper and
the two of them could not keep a fire hot
enough to keep warm, H. W. Hopkins reappeared.

This time he started seriously. "Miss
Lavinia, *Harper's* magazine has stated, 'Thomasville, Georgia, is the best winter resort

on three continents.' The people who own America like it here so much they are becoming permanent. Buying property, building big houses they call 'cottages.' "

Lavinia sat frozen in silence.

After an uncomfortable interlude, H.W. asked, "May I stoke up the fire?"

When a roaring blaze warmed the room, he pulled a stool before her. "Mr. Selah R. Van Duzer, a manufacturer from New York City, has fallen in love with Greenwood. He made a tremendous offer you can't refuse.

"How does he know what it looks like?" Lavinia snapped.

"Uh . . ." H.W. fiddled with his pipe. "I took the liberty of bringing him out while you were at church."

Lavinia felt her face redden and her heart skip several beats. She was so angry that she wanted to throw the man out. Clenching her fists, she breathed snatches of prayers.

H.W. spoke quickly, "He wants to turn Greenwood into a shooting preserve. He won't plant cotton."

"No cotton? My people . . . ?"

"They'll be hired to handle the dogs and the hunting wagons. They'd plant only bird-feed."

"Then he'll perpetuate the quail?"

"Yes."

"The pines? The wildflowers?"

"Preserve them."

The time has come, Lavinia realized. She had longed for Greenwood to stay in the family, but none of them could afford the property taxes and upkeep. Lavinia fixed a firm gaze upon the realtor. "You must make him put it in the deed that my people can stay here and be given work."

He nodded agreement. They sat in silence for a long while.

In a voice that sounded far away, she added, "Stipulate that my family will have perpetual access to the Greenwood Cemetery." Then she closed her eyes.

H.W. had sense enough to leave other details until later. Quietly, he let himself out.

It was mid-April of 1889 before Lavinia was packed. She made sure no one saw her add the box of Francis Remer's clothes from under the bed. When she did this, she realized that she must make a last visit to the cemetery.

Cutting two baskets of roses to scatter over the graves, she went alone. As she laid a pink rose on the tiny grave of Francis Remer, she recalled how his loss had caused a dark night in her soul when she turned from God. But her faith had come back stronger, strong enough to face life undaunted. She had never again wavered.

Beside the infant lay Miss Elizabeth, who had become the dearest of mothers-in-law when she had opened her heart. Next was Frank, whose impressive marker related how the fun-loving boy had become a hero in his country's service. One by one she communed with them all. She stood long at Thomas's grave, covering it with tear-wet roses, whispering, "Soon, soon I'll be with you again."

Lavinia returned to the house to find the wagons loaded with her belongings. The family was ready to leave. She issued curt instructions to Julie's grandson.

"Stack fat lightwood in my carriage and set it on fire. I may have to let *those people* sleep in my house, but I'll be strung up to an oak tree before they'll ride in my vehicle."

"Mama!" Florence said, shocked. "Papa never said ugly words in his life."

"Thomas never dealt with Yankees." Her anger deflated. "I'm glad he didn't live to have to."

Against arguments, Lavinia sent the family ahead, including Julie who was moving to Mattie's house with her. She must have a

503

little more time here, and she wanted to say good-bye to Greenwood alone.

Lavinia walked beneath the pines, knowing this was the last time until she would be brought back to rest beside Thomas. Ferns glistened in the sunlight. Stems of Snowy Orchid beckoned her closer to see the delicate blossoms, breaking her heart. *How can I leave here?*

A yellow swallowtail lit before her. In the butterfly's fluttering wings, she could envision the day with Thomas and the children amid a cloud of migrating monarchs. Peace flooded her. Now she felt ready for her journey as she remembered the brilliant butterflies soaring over the sea on the breath of God.

"Bobwhite." The call floated on the soft April breeze. Across the way, the mate answered, "Bob-bob white!"

Lavinia could almost see Thomas, young, strong, smiling as he had been the day they had first ridden among these trees.

She climbed into the buggy with Blue beside her. Slowly she drove down the allée of live oaks, Thomas's precious gift to her as a bride. Still growing, with a thousand more years of evergreen life, they stretched twisting branches across the road and met like lovers shawled in gray lace of Spanish moss.

I've tried to fulfill our dreams, Lavinia thought, *but I'm old and gnarled now.* Suddenly her courage failed, and it seemed she could not go. She stopped the horse and let her tears flow.

A rattle made her look up. A wagon loaded with painters passed, headed toward Greenwood.

With Van Duzer's money to repair it, Greenwood will endure! She smiled, as a stone seemed to lift off her chest.

She took the check from her reticule and looked at it again. Suddenly she realized what an immense blessing this was. *Twenty-five thousand dollars! A fortune.* She caught her lip between her teeth and grinned. *One Yankee really is worth two bales of cotton and twice as easy to pick.*

"Blue, this is enough money for my daughters and me to live comfortably for the rest of our lives."

She recalled that she would be seventy-nine in a few weeks.

"I think I'll take the whole family to the Piney Woods Hotel. I'll eat Savannah shrimp for my birthday."

Lavinia clucked to the horse to move forward. As the buggy rolled from the glooms of the live oaks through the towering pines, a shaft of sunlight filtered from on high, lighting her face.

Lavinia looked up and smiled. "Thomas, you might say this isn't the right meaning . . ." She held the check aloft. "But you'll have to admit — we are more than conquerors after all."

AFTERWORD

Lavinia Young Jones lived at ease for two years until, on February 13, 1891, at eighty-one, she went to be with her beloved Thomas. She was buried in Greenwood cemetery in a coffin covered with ferns and violets.

Although I have written this as fiction, it is the true story of the Jones and related families carving a wilderness into a civilization of charm and culture that remains today. The book is as carefully researched and as accurate as I could make it. The family was so prominent that their papers are preserved at the University of Georgia down to minute details such as Mattie's report card. After Tommy returned from the army, the local paper carried an account of his picnic and "netting fish." Frank's letters are as he wrote them. When Lavinia was forced to take in boarders, the newspaper stated that Mr. and Mrs. Gould of New York spent the winter at Greenwood. This might well have been Jay Gould, who was an infamous railroad magnate and stock manipulator, because Mr. And Mrs. C. Vanderbilt and Mrs. B. F. Goodrich signed the Mitchell House Hotel register on the same day. Thomasville's entertainments ranged from John Philip Sousa to Annie Oakley.

I have used poetic license only twice to involve the reader. The Seminole attack on Greenwood is a composite of neighborhood occurrences. I do not know if Thomas was at the Battle of Natural Bridge, but the event is historically accurate.

Van Duzer sold Greenwood in 1899 to Oliver Hazard Payne, treasurer of Standard Oil. He willed it to Payne Whitney who honeymooned there with Helen Hay, daughter of the Secretary of State under McKinley and Theodore Roosevelt. It next passed to John Hay (Jock) Whitney and his wife Betty Cushing Whitney, who entertained President Dwight D. Eisenhower for quail hunting. Jacqueline Kennedy was hidden at Greenwood after the assassination of President John F. Kennedy.

Greenwood endures, a lovely gem. Today a nature conservancy, Greentree Foundation, preserves the virgin pines and endangered wildflowers.

Harriet and James Blackshear's Cedar Grove was sold and renamed Susina. It has continued through the years as a private home.

James Blackshear's sister, Elizabeth Coalson Wyche, lived in one of the oldest houses (1799–1830). Ultimately, it was purchased by Howard Melville Hanna of Columbus, Ohio, one of four siblings who bought adjoining plantations. It was they who entertained President William McKinley. Today the original building is absorbed into the main house on Coalson's Plantation, an upscale vacation resort.

Thomas Jones's sister, Elizabeth Neely Winn's home, Pleasant Hill, is beautifully restored as Winnstead Plantation. It is the residence of an artist who occasionally opens it for charity events.

Mitchell Jones's Oak Lawn burned, but Eliza's narcissus still bloom each winter.

Pebble Hill, the home of John William Henry Mitchell, was purchased by Howard Melville Hanna for his daughter Kate Hanna Ireland. Today it is open to the public as a museum.

Verdura, the Chaires mansion, burned in 1885; however, the three-story columns stand in the woods, ghostly reminders of past glory.

Perhaps the reader can understand the significance of the Thomasville-Tallahassee area better if the rest of Georgia is considered. In 1864, Union General W. T. Sherman burned and destroyed a swath sixty miles wide and three hundred miles long from Atlanta to Savannah. Georgia did not recover from this until 1949, according to Medora Field Perkerson in *White Columns in Georgia*. In 1864, Georgia's taxable assets record was $1,612,592,806. Not until January 1, 1950 did the figure finally climb back to $1,487,321,566.

Thomasville continued as a premier resort until the discovery that mosquitoes carry malaria and the subsequent building of railroads opened Florida in the Twentieth Century. Thomasville's grand hotels are gone; however, seventy plantations on 300,000 acres between Tallahassee and Thomasville remain in use by the rich and famous. Winter inhabitants have been generous. Kate Ireland is especially remembered, as is John F. Archbold, who endowed Archbold Memorial Hospital to honor his father. Highways pass a breath away from unseen antebellum mansions, but no one ever knows what millionaires, presidents, or kings, are in residence, hidden beneath the pines.

CARAMEL CAKE

Handed down through generations of the Pace Family

Cake
3 Cups plain flour
2 teaspoons baking powder
1/2 teaspoon salt
1 Cup butter (2 sticks)
2 Cups sugar
4 eggs
1 teaspoon vanilla
1 Cup sweet milk

Sift dry ingredients together twice and set aside. Cream butter, add sugar gradually, add eggs one at a time beating well after each addition. Add dry ingredients by blending one cup of flour mixture alternating with 1/2 cup milk. End with flour. Add vanilla. Grease and flour (or use Baker's Joy) two long pans or three round ones.

Bake at 350 degrees for about 25 minutes. Test with toothpick. Remove from oven as soon as toothpick is clean because cake will be more moist if it is not overcooked.

Filling
3 1/2 Cups sugar
2 tablespoons white Karo syrup
1 Cup sweet milk
1/2 Cup sugar
1/2 cup (1 stick) butter
1 teaspoon vanilla

Combine in saucepan the 3 1/2 Cups sugar, Karo syrup, and milk. Bring to boil. At the same time, brown the 1/2 Cup sugar in an iron skillet. Do not stir until most of the sugar is melted or it will cause hard rocks. When nearly melted, stir and remove when light brown. When mixture in saucepan reaches a rolling boil, remove from heat and slowly add the browned sugar syrup, stirring all of the time. Return the mixture to low heat and cook until soft ball stage (232 degrees F. on candy thermometer.) Remove from heat. Add butter. Cool to 150 degrees F. Add vanilla. Beat with electric beater until filling begins to lose its gloss and becomes thick enough to spread. If it becomes too hard while spreading, add a little <u>hot</u> water.

This filling takes practice to make. It is usually handed down by an older person instructing a young cook step by step. At church "dinners on the grounds," it causes sneaking to get a piece ahead of the crowd coming through the line. And down here in the Deep South, we don't say *kar-mul*. We call it *care-a-mel*.

ACKNOWLEDGMENTS

Appreciation goes first to C. Tom Hill, Curator of the Thomas County Historical Society Museum. He took me to Greenwood, igniting my instant love affair with the place and its people. Hill generously shared his amazing fund of knowledge, his time, and the contents of the museum. The staff, especially Ann Harrison and Cynthia Nickerson, was extremely helpful as I spent endless hours researching lectures, displays, photographs, books, and papers.

Thanks goes to Kathy Mills, director of the Thomasville Genealogical, History and Fine Arts Library, Inc. for research material, especially copies of their publication *Origins,* which contain the letters of Henry Francis Jones to Martha Jones (1861–1864).

The extensive Thomas Jones family papers, collected by Elizabeth F. Hopkins, are in the Hargrett Rare Book and Manuscript

Library, University of Georgia Libraries in Athens, Georgia. The Henry Francis Jones letters are used by their permission.

Although I delved into many books, I would especially like to credit the works of William Warren Rogers and Clifford Paisley.

The Florida State Library and the Florida Archives, both at Tallahassee, yielded information about the prominent Chaires family and local Seminole attacks.

Cathy David Rieger of Roddenbery Memorial Library, Cairo, Georgia, and Carol Peak of Lee County Library, Leesburg, Georgia provided many books.

At Greenwood, thanks goes to Todd Ingstrom and Leon Neel of Greentree Foundation for allowing me to roam the house and grounds and cemetery. Plantation manager, Gary Palmer, whose father had the position before him, grew up on Greenwood and began working there as a boy. As he introduced me to the wonders of the woodlands, he conveyed his love of the land, trees, and wildflowers and made me understand what Thomas and Lavinia Jones felt.

Melhana Grand Plantation Resort provided me with ambiance during a lovely anniversary weekend with my husband, and they generously supplied historic records.

Thanks go to: John and Lois Hand for

knowledge of John Wind's architecture and
for family information on his ancestor,
Mitchell Jones; Daniel Sanford for facts on
Peter McGlashan and Reconstruction in
Thomasville; Andy Edel for articles on the
Spray and the Battle of Natural Bridge;
Robin Will of the Saint Marks Wildlife
Refuge, where monarchs may be experi-
enced each October on their way to over
winter with tens of millions of monarchs in
the Sierra Madre Mountains west of Mexico
City; Charles Larry Gordon for insight into
General John C. Vaughn; Dr. George Bag-
ley for information on the origin and char-
acter of English Setters; Annette Harrell,
who said I must write about the plantation's
beginnings; J. N. Cook; Carolyn and Jack
Nicholson; Patsy Musgrove; Sarah Cook;
Marvlyn Story; Betty Ann Clay; Mona
Nelson; JoAnn Chadwick; Jessica Cook;
Lynne and John Cook; Samantha McFar-
land; John Hyde; John Wilson; and Casey
Dixon. A special thanks goes to Lila Karpf
who encouraged me and guided me all the
way.

BIBLIOGRAPHY

PRIMARY SOURCES
MANUSCRIPT COLLECTIONS

Hargrett Rare Book and Manuscript Library. University of Georgia Libraries. Athens, Georgia.

Jones, Thomas, family papers.
Henry Francis Jones letters (1861–1864)

Published Sources

Henry Francis Jones to Martha Jones, 20 November 1861. 17 December 1861. 31 December 1861. *Origins,* Thomasville Genealogical, History and Fine Arts Library, XII.IV. (December 2002.), 26–29.

Henry Francis Jones to Martha Jones, 9 May 1862. 25 January 1864. *Origins,* Thomasville Genealogical, History and Fine

Arts Library, XIII.I. (March 2003.), 23–26.

Henry Francis Jones to Martha Jones, 4 April 1864. 1 June 1864. *Origins,* Thomasville Genealogical, History and Fine Arts Library, XIII.II. (June 2003.), 17–20.

Chaplain James Gadsden Holmes to Mrs. Thomas Jones, 12 June 1864. *Origins,* Thomasville Genealogical, History and Fine Arts Library, XIII.III. (September 2003.), 17–18.

Charles Paine Hansell, June 11, 1864. *Origins,* Thomasville Genealogical, History and Fine Arts Library, XIII.III. (September 2003.), 19.

SECONDARY SOURCES
BOOKS

Blackshear, Sr. Perry Lynnfield. *Blacksheariana.* Atlanta. 1954.

Cothran, James R. *Gardens and Historic Plants of the Antebellum South.* Columbia, South Carolina: South Carolina Press. 2003.

Dasher, Wayne and Judy. *In the Shadow of the Pines:* Thomas County, Georgia, Newspapers. Vol. 2. 2001.

Dasher, Wayne and Judy. *In the Shadow of the Pines:* Thomas County, Georgia,

Newspapers. Vol. 10. 2003.

Dean, Blanche E., Amy Mason, and Joab L. Thomas. *Wildflowers of Alabama and Adjoining States.* Alabama: U. of Alabama P., 1973.

Duncan, Wilbur H. and Leonard E. Foote. *Wildflowers of the Southeastern United States.* Athens: U. Of. Georgia P., 1975.

Ellis, Mary Louise and William Warren. Favored Land, Tallahassee: a History of Tallahassee and Leon County. The Donning Company: Norfolk, Va. 1988

Foote, Shelby. *The Civil War: A Narrative, Red River to Appomattox.* Vintage Books: New York. 1974.

Gleason, David King. *Antebellum Homes of Georgia.* Louisiana State University Press: Baton Rouge, LA. 1987.

Hodges, James E. ed. *A Comprehensive Study of a Portion of the Red Hills Region of Georgia.* Thomasville, Georgia: Thomas College Press. 1st ed. 1994.

Hollingsworth, Ed. *The History of Screven County, Georgia.* Dallas, Texas: 1989.

Johnson, Jean Hagan. *Feast of Pleasure: From the Kitchen and Memories of Pebble Hill Plantation.* Tallahassee: 1987.

LaCavera, Tommie Phillips. *Anna Mitchell Davenport Raines.* Atlanta. 1994.

MacIntyre, W. Irwin. *History of Thomas County Georgia.* Thomasville: Thomas County, 1923.

Mason, James S. *Oh, Susina!* Ed. Robert Lucas. Thomasville: Craigmiles & Associates, Inc., 1995.

Miller, Edgar G., Jr. *The Standard Book of American Antique Furniture.* N.Y.: Greystone Pr., 1937.

Paisley, Clifton. *The Red Hills of Florida: 1528–1865.* Tuscaloosa. 1989.

Paisley, Clifton. *From Cotton to Quail: An Agricultural Chronicle of Leon County, Florida, 1860–1967.* Tallahassee: University Press of Florida State, 1981

Perkerson, Medora Field. *White Columns in Georgia.* Bonanza Books: New York. 1956.

Rainwater, Hattie C. *Garden History of Georgia.* Ed. Loraine M. Cooney. Atlanta: 1933.

Rogers, William Warren. *Antebellum Thomas County: 1825–1861.* Tallahassee: Florida St. U. P., 1963.

Rogers, William Warren. *Thomas County: 1865–1900.* Tallahassee: Florida St. U. P., 1973.

Rogers, William Warren. *Thomas County During the Civil War.* Tallahassee: Florida St. U. P., 1964.

Smith, Wm. Hovey. *Guide to Homes and Plantations of the Thomasville Region.* Sandersville: Budget Publications, 1984.

Sheppard, Peggy. *Andersonville Georgia USA.* Leslie, GA: Sheppard Publications. 1973.

Stegeman, John F. *These Men She Gave: Civil War Diary of Athens, Georgia.* Athens: University of Georgia Press. 1964.

Stewart, Charles W. *Official Records of the Union and Confederate Navies in the War of The Rebellion.* Washington: Government Printing Office. 1903.

Taylor, Walter Kingsley. *The Guide to Florida Wildflowers.* Dallas: Taylor Pub. Co., 1992.

ARTICLES

Bass-Frazier, D. A. "Ersatz in the South During the War and Reconstruction." UDC Magazine, LXVII (November 2004), 16–17.

Castile, Nora Faye and Linda Rosenblatt. "Florida Sentinel: The Confederate Monument at Olustee." UDC Magazine. LXIX. January 2006. 24.

Gray, Mays Leroy. "The Little Ship That Could: The Steamboat *Spray.*" Wakulla Area Digest. June 1998.

Harrell, Annette C. "Confederate Prison

Site: Thomasville, Georgia." UDC Magazine, LXI (February 1998), 12–14.

Howard, Frank. "Some Civil War Action." Wakulla Area Digest. October 1993.

Laurie, Murray. "Yulee Railroad Days 2004." *Alachua Alive*. Summer 2004. pp 11–13.

McMullen Tindle. "The Cow Cavalry in the Peace River Valley." UDC Magazine, LXVIII (January 2005), 40.

Miller, William, Brigadier General, C.S.A. *The Battle of Natural Bridge*. Florida Historical Quarterly.

Paisley, Clifton. "How to Escape the Yankees: Major Scott's Letter to His Wife at Tallahassee, March 1864." Florida Historical Quarterly. 1971.

UNPUBLISHED WORKS

Frier, Joshua Hoyet, II. "Reminisces of the War Between the States by a Boy in the Far South at Home and in the Ranks of the Confederate Military."

Gordon, Charles Larry. "General John C. Vaughn."

Hentz, Dr. "Diary of Doctor Hentz: Marianna and Quincy Fla., May 3–31, 1863." Jacksonville, Fl,: Historical Records Survey, 1937.

Melhana Grand Plantation. "Historic

Records."
Rogers, William Warren. "A History of Greenwood Plantation."
Sanford, Dan. "Peter McGlashan."
Stephens, Virginia and Carolyn Crew. "Turner Family Civil War Information."
Taylor, Thomas W. "The Saint Marks Lighthouse."

ABOUT THE AUTHOR

Jacquelyn Cook, the nationally acclaimed author of historical and inspirational fiction, has a strong dedication to research, vivid drama and biographical accuracy. With sales of nearly 500,000 copies, her books chronicle the lives of real people and places. *The Greenwood Legacy* is the third novel in her trilogy about fascinating Civil War families and the legendary estates they created.

X5